CAPTIVE OF DESIRE

"What do you want from me?" she hissed. "Why did you take me captive?"

A long brown finger reached out and lifted her already proud chin. He looked deeply into her eyes and repeated softly, "What do I want?" He leaned closer. "Why, *Chummuss*, I want you."

Mesmerized by his glance, Haina went still. His lips touched hers gently, then he surged against her and his arms pulled her closer. She raised her hands to push him away, but her futile efforts went unnoticed against his strong body. His lips were tasting, exploring, then consuming hers and she grasped the heavy fur of the bearskin across his chest. Her fingers kneaded the fur and then she was scraping her nails across his bare chest. He groaned and pulled her closer. "Aah, *Chummuss*. You taste so sweet."

Other *Leisure Books* by Theresa Scott:

SAVAGE BETRAYAL
BRIDE OF DESIRE

SAVAGE REVENGE

THERESA SCOTT

LEISURE BOOKS NEW YORK CITY

For Rob, Alysson and Gervaise
whose love and support helped make
this book possible.

With special thanks to Mr. John Thomas
of the Makah Museum, Neah Bay,
Washington, for his kind help.

A LEISURE BOOK®

October 1991

Published by

Dorchester Publishing Co., Inc.
276 Fifth Avenue
New York, NY 10001

SAVAGE REVENGE Copyright ©MCMLXXXIX by Theresa Scott

All rights reserved. No part of this book may be reproduced or transmitted in any form or by any electronic or mechanical means, including photocopying, recording or by any information storage and retrieval system, without the written permission of the Publisher, except where permitted by law.

The name "Leisure Books" and the stylized "L" with design are trademarks of Dorchester Publishing Co., Inc.

Printed in the United States of America.

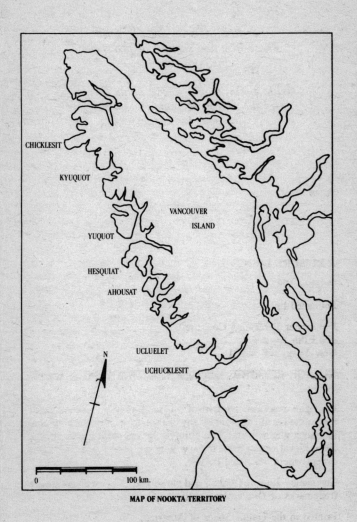

MAP OF NOOKTA TERRITORY

Prologue

Spring, 1794
The sea, off Chicklesit Village, West Coast of
Vancouver Island

The howling wind and beating rain lashed against
the two men who clung to the mizzenmast ropes of the
wildly pitching ship. The men's feet barely touched the
deck as the vessel heaved. Each wave tossed the ship.
The storm in all its awful fury whipped and screamed
around them. Their bleeding fingers clutched the ropes
in death's grip and two pairs of haunted eyes stabbed
frantically through the black night.

"Eleanor! Eleanor!" shrieked Mitchell into the
wind. He would have thrown himself from the deck
and into the violently raging sea had not Daniel, a
heftier man, made a grab for him.

"Let me go! Let me go to her, Dan'l!" He beat
viciously at Daniel's encircling arm, struggling to free
himself.

Clinging tightly to the rigging with one arm, the
other wrapped around the enraged, distraught man,
Daniel used all of his considerable strength to keep

1

Mitchell from flinging himself into the churning water. The ship shuddered beneath them.

"Dan'l! Let me go! I can save her!" Desperate, Mitchell lunged again, and Daniel almost lost his hold on the rigging.

"You fool," he cried into Mitchell's ear. "If I let you go, you'll drown too! She's gone! Gone, you hear? You cannot save her!"

Mitchell struggled frenziedly, throwing himself again and again at Daniel's restraining arm. Finally, exhausted, he collapsed onto the heaving deck. "She's gone." Hoarse sobs wracked his limp body. "Gone." His guttural keenings were thrown back in his face by the shrieking wind. A great black nothingness surrounded them. "My wife is gone." The distraught man rocked back and forth on his knees. "She's gone. My love, my love! Eleanor! Gone!"

Daniel winced, sharing Mitchell's agony. But he couldn't give in to grief. Not yet. He dragged the sobbing man across the deck and into the ship's hold. He threw the wretched Mitchell onto a bunk. Then and only then did he allow himself to grieve. He sank to the floor and covered his face with his bleeding hands. Sorrowful groans choked out of his throat.

Eleanor, his beloved sister, was dead. She was dead, leaving only the heartrending cries of her husband and her brother behind.

The morning sun broke onto the isolated gravel beach, glowing with a warmth that denied the power of yesterday's storm. It touched the body of a woman lying half-in, half-out of the water. She groaned and tried to sit up. Holding her stomach, she groaned again. A bedraggled mess, her red hair wet and stringy, she shivered uncontrollably as the weak rays of the sun touched her icy body. The most noticeable thing about her was her large protruding stomach. She was very

2

pregnant.

She struggled to her feet, but her knees buckled under her and she sank to the beach. She lay very still on the wet stones. From behind a tree, two Indian men watched her.

When the woman showed no signs of movement, the two crept from their hiding place. Her eyes widened in terror at their approach and she gave a feeble groan. They leaned closer when they saw the flutter of her eyelashes. "She lives."

"We must fetch the midwife," said the older man, taking pity on the bedraggled creature. "The woman's labor is upon her even now."

It was true. Her whole body tensed and the woman moaned, clutching at her stomach. The men carefully lifted the poor woman between them and staggered up the beach with their burden. They plopped her onto the softer sand and leaned her back against a log. The younger man raced down the trail to the village to get the midwife.

Much later, a middle-aged Indian woman left the beach carrying a naked, squalling, white infant. His little fists trembled and his lusty cries announced his arrival to the village.

The older Indian man who had found the pregnant white woman asked, "How is the mother?"

"She is dead, Tyee," answered the midwife. "She lost too much blood. Too exhausted."

The chief nodded and reached out to touch a tiny fist waving in the air. The baby grasped his finger and held on with a tight grip. The older man smiled for the first time. "He will be very strong. He has been through much, this little one." He watched the baby intently. "Take him to my third wife."

"Yes, Tyee," murmured the woman. "It shall be as you say." The woman bowed and walked over to the largest longhouse. A crowd of curious onlookers

3

trailed behind, but no one stopped her. The older tyee followed slowly.

The midwife entered, carrying her precious burden carefully, and went to the chief's corner where a young woman sat slumped before the fire. Day after day the young woman could be found staring, unseeing, into the flames, a look of profound sorrow upon her face. This had been her place since the terrible day she had lost her baby. Too tiny when born, her boy child had not lived out the first month of his life.

"Look, my lady," said the midwife. "Look what your husband bids me bring to you."

The beautiful young woman lifted tired eyes. Despair and grief had etched grooves around her lovely mouth and lines across her high forehead.

"For you," murmured the older woman, holding the baby out to her. "A gift from the sea."

The noblewoman stared uncomprehendingly at the baby. Her eyes went to her husband and then back to the baby. Disbelief flitted across her countenance, then a slow, dawning, hopeful smile spread across her face like the sun peeping out after a ferocious storm.

With a glad cry she reached for the baby. She hugged the child to her tightly. Tears of joy dripped down her cheeks as she held the little one. "My baby, my baby," she murmured over and over. Her husband watched her with hopeful eyes. The woman gazed at the baby and put her lips to his little shell ear. "So beautiful, so sweet," she whispered. "My beautiful baby, you've come back. The strength of my love brought you back to me!"

She tore off the cedar robe the midwife had wrapped him in. She gazed down at his tiny twitching body. "So perfect," she murmured soothingly. She felt each little limb and examined each tiny toe and finger. "My baby, oh, my baby." She hugged the child to her breast.

4

The baby settled down to a snuffling cry and the woman beamed at the tiny face. Behind her, her chiefly husband slowly let out his breath and relaxed. Now his favorite wife could stop mourning the baby they had lost. Now happiness could once more visit their longhouse.

Chapter 1

Spring, 1818
The sea, off the coast of Ahousat Village

"Keep fishing. Act as if you do not see them," ordered Haina with a frown.

"Yes, mistress," answered Scarface, glancing nervously over his shoulder at the approaching war canoe.

The occupants, several dark-haired young men, paddled strongly toward Haina's small dugout canoe. They were still too far away for her to discern who they were, but none of the men were smiling or waving. She had had no word of raiders in this area lately, so it was doubtful they were enemies, she thought apprehensively. They were coming from the direction of her village, they must have been guests of her father last night, she reasoned. She watched the canoe plough steadily through the waves.

Her eyes darted to the nearest point of land, a small island. There really was no escape should the men prove unfriendly. Very well, the best thing to do was remember she was the daughter of Fighting Wolf, a great Ahousat war chief, and be prepared to battle if a fight was what they wanted. She straightened her shoulders.

Her smaller dugout canoe bobbed gently on the waves as a new day was born on the west coast. Though Haina was too far offshore to see her village, had she been so inclined she could have easily sighted the huge blue-gray mountains that towered behind, the rounded humps hiding the rising sun. Only pink and orange streaks announced its presence to the mortals below.

Haina and her slave, Scarface, had paddled farther out to sea than she had intended. The only sign of land, the small tree-covered island, was surrounded by sharp rocks jutting out of the gray-green water. Golden brown kelp bulbs with their long flowing tails bobbed on the surface. Haina knew the wily salmon liked to hide under the kelp beds but the jagged rocks kept her from paddling too close to the island.

The Ahousat noblewoman and her slave continued to hand their fishing lines over the side of the dugout while her mind worked feverishly. Rhythmically lifting the line, Haina would pull it up as high as her arm would reach, then let the line drop back to the bottom, the V-shaped hook inviting an unsuspecting fish. All the while, she planned what she should do if the swiftly approaching men intended harm.

Ordinarily, fishing was one of Haina's favorite activities. She loved to dangle her fingers in the dark green liquid, to peer down into the sea's opaque depths in the hopes of seeing a passing fish or even a shark. Sometimes she just liked to lean back and stare at the gray canopy of sky, while a slave paddled the tiny craft through the waves.

Haina loved to listen to the sea noises: the gentle snap under the canoe as it rocked on the waves, the swirling and sucking of her paddle as she lifted it out of the water, the occasional squeak of wood on wood in

7

the canoe, the scream of an impatient sea gull demanding fish for breakfast. And the smells! No aroma was as cool, as fresh, as wonderful as the salty tang of the sea air. Nothing cleared her nose and lungs like that sharp, free scent.

Her love for the sea had drawn a yawning Haina out to her canoe early this morning while the rest of her village slept on, the inhabitants satiated after the grand feast her father, Fighting Wolf, had given the night before. Haina had paddled out to the fishing grounds with only one slave, so certain had she been she would be safe from any slave-hunting raiders straying into Ahousat waters.

And now this. Anxious, she glanced toward the war canoe that was steadily advancing closer and closer. Haina could now see several grim-visaged men sitting in the large craft with its gruesome black and white markings.

"What do they want with us?" muttered Scarface, throwing another surreptitious glance over his shoulder.

"Nothing, I am certain," came the reply. It would not do to let her slave see how worried she was about the approaching men. "I will soon send them on their way." Haina hauled up her fishing line and noted vaguely that her bait was gone. Little wonder she had caught no fish.

She turned to face the intruders squarely. It would not do to show them any fear, she reasoned. Remembering her proud heritage, she wrapped her noble status around herself as though it were a cedar cloak and straightened her spine.

Surprised, she saw that one of the men had hair the color of dried summer grass. What manner of Indian is this? she wondered. As the unknown canoe came closer, Haina saw that the man had a dark stubble of beard on his face. He's not clean-cheeked like a man

8

should be, she marveled. Every man she knew plucked his beard hairs. How strange he looks, she thought.

But no sign of her thoughts showed on her beautiful, set face. She waited until the men in the war canoe pulled alongside her much smaller craft. Hands reached out and grasped the gunwales of her canoe and effectively locked the bouncing crafts together.

Haina felt her anger rise at such brazen disregard of her status. These men had no right to touch her canoe!

Dressed in ordinary brown cedar kutsacks denoting their commoner status, all eight young men were staring at Haina. That they were commoners caused her fears to recede. Commoners would not dare harm a noblewoman, she thought.

"I presume you have a reason for daring to interfere with my fishing?" she inquired frigidly of the stubble-cheeked man sitting in the bow.

Dark blond hair fell to his broad shoulders. A twisted cedar rope headband encircled his forehead. He had a wide, tanned chest. His curling blond chest hair was half-hidden by a bearskin robe tied at one shoulder.

Why, he's like a bear himself with all that blond fur on him, she thought. She stared at his hairy arms, too.

And his eyes! Eyes the color of the summer sea were set in a handsome, ruggedly carved face. Those green eyes sent a shiver of warmth through Haina when she gazed into their crystalline depths. Haina stared. She had never seen eyes of such an entrancing color.

Cool now, those eyes ranged assessingly over Haina's delicate features. Then, apparently liking what he saw, the stranger had the audacity to give her a lazy grin.

Haina, irritated at his slow persual, and distracted by his strangeness, dragged her thoughts back to what she had said. When only silence was forthcoming, she said in a louder voice, "Take your hands off my

9

dugout."

To her dismay, she heard soft chuckles from the men in the war canoe. The leader still wore that same infuriating smile. Haina could feel her notorious temper starting to rise again. Heart beating rapidly with fear and excitement, she picked up her pointed canoe paddle and looked down at the strong, brown knuckles still holding her boat captive. Blond hairs sprouted on the back of his tanned hand. Even his hands were hairy!

Then she remembered. Her parents had spoken of white men, *mumutly*, on the west coast. This man, then, must be one of the *mumutly*. But what was he doing with Indians?

"Leave my canoe alone," she managed. "I am a noblewoman. I will not be threatened by you commoners!"

The men chuckled at her words. Insolent, she thought. They are very insolent.

Before the grinning leader could anticipate her actions, she brought the paddle down sharply with a rap across those same knuckles. His grunt of pain both scared and gratified her. They would not find *her* an easy target for their commoner games! "Now, I will advise you once again," she stated evenly. "Take your hands off my canoe."

The mood of the men suddenly sobered. One of them, a rangy man with lean, corded muscles, and clenched fists, rose abruptly but the leader signalled him back down and muttered something in an undertone. The man obeyed reluctantly but shot Haina an ugly stare.

Surprised by his hostility, Haina quivered inside. Something was very wrong. These strangers were not behaving with the deference that was her natural due as a chief's daughter. She could see they were mere commoners. Why then, were they so upset when she struck the white man? Of course, she would never strike another noble. To do so was death.

She decided to defuse the situation. After all, there were eight of them, all strong young men. She had only Scarface for protection, and he was getting old. "Where are you commoners from?" They were not from her village, she knew. She did not recognize their faces. Besides, *her* people knew to behave properly around a noblewoman.

After another assessing look, the white man answered. "Kyuquot," he said in the soft drawl of that region. His deep voice sent shivers down Haina's spine. She swung her gaze to his, only to find his entrancing eyes regarding her intently in return.

"Oh," she managed. "Then you must have attended the feast my father gave last night." The stranger had the impertinence to continue staring at her, so Haina decided to put him in his place. "My father, Fighting Wolf, is known throughout our land as a great war chief," she said distinctly. "Perhaps you commoners have heard his name?"

Her sarcasm was ignored. The man merely nodded in response.

Haina did not care for the way the conversation, what little there was of it, was going. "Well," she said brightly, "Thank you so much for attending my father's feast. I know he would wish you a safe return on your voyage homeward. It is a long journey back to Kyuquot and I am sure you are most anxious to begin."

Instead of politely releasing her canoe as she had hoped, the men kept their grip on it. She listened as they conferred in undertones. An uneasy feeling stole over her.

Suddenly the white man, who appeared to be the leader, reached over and removed the paddle from her grasp. Her jaw dropped at his audacity—a mere commoner daring to touch a noblewoman—and she let

11

the paddle go without a fight.

When he reached for *her* and grabbed her upper arms, she froze in shock for an instant. What had happened to her determination to fight? she wondered. His hands felt warm on her bare arms, and small goosebumps rose on her skin. His grip was strong. She had no hope of overpowering him.

Her slave, however, was not so helpless. With a cry, Scarface lunged from where he was squatting in the canoe; the point of his paddle aimed at the blond leader's head. The canoes wobbled dangerously. A harsh warning rang out. The leader dropped his hold on Haina and raised his arms to ward off the blow.

He need not have bothered. A fellow warrior struck the slave on the back of the head with a war axe and the slave toppled over, half falling out of the boat. His head dangled in the cold sea water for the space of several frantic heartbeats. Sick with horror, Haina tried to pull Scarface back into the dugout, but he was too heavy. Even the fear-induced strength that coursed through her was not enough for her to lift him.

"Push the body back onboard," the blond man ordered his men. "As for you," he said, turning to Haina, "you are coming with us."

"No, I am not!" she shrieked, pure fury at Scarface's brutal murder overwhelming her fear. "I am not going anywhere with you killers!" She lashed out viciously with her fists while trying vainly to keep her balance in the rocking dugout. Several of the men watched warily.

"Guard yourself, Chance, she fights like a wild-cat!" warned one of the men. But the dark blond-haired leader already had his strong arms wrapped around Haina and was dragging her into the war canoe. Screaming and kicking, canoes rocking perilously, Haina managed to land a strong blow to his chin. He grunted and held her tighter. "Little cougar," he muttered.

Subdued at last, panting heavily, breasts heaving, she was pushed down to the floor of the war canoe. Several smelly cedar mats, encrusted with dried salt and fish guts, were tossed over her. Then something that felt like a foot was planted squarely on her back. "If you value your life, little cougar," came the soft Kyuquot drawl, "you will lie very, very still."

Realizing the desperation of her position, Haina went weak all over. Exhausted and frightened, she lay limply in the putrid darkness of the mats. Every breath she took made her want to retch from the awful smell. Fear and anger twisted her stomach.

She noticed the canoe was rocking less, and she heard muffled sounds of the men talking amongst themselves. A little later, she felt the canoe grind against gravel, as though they were on a beach.

The next thing she knew she was waking from a dreamless sleep. She must have fainted, she decided.

The smooth, rolling movement of the canoe beneath her told her the men in the war canoe were making fast paddling time. Haina guessed her captors were anxious to return to Kyuquot.

She wondered how long she would be forced to lie under the stinking mats before anyone would remember her existence.

"Let her up," ordered Chance. In the bow of the canoe, one of his warriors pulled the cedar coverings off the woman they'd kidnapped. She looked to be asleep. "Wake her."

At the warrior's prodding, the young woman opened her eyes. She sat up slowly and blinked at the strange faces.

Chance smiled. "Welcome, my lady."

"Kyuquot snakes!" she spat.

Amused, Chance surveyed her. Several strands of

13

her long black hair had come loose from its cedar tie. The strands blew gently across her face and she brushed them aside. Her skin was very light, unlike the usual dark tan of Kyuquot women. Judging from her arms and the little he could see of her legs, she appeared small boned and slender, but it was difficult to tell as she was wearing the bulky, yellow cedar kutsack of the nobility.

Large, fiery black eyes defiantly returned his slow appraisal. She had a straight nose with delicately flaring nostrils set above full, sculptured lips. Those same lips were tightened now in anger. Altogether a delightful captive, Chance decided lazily. This trip may prove more exciting than he had first thought.

Her words cut into his speculations. "My father will kill you Kyuquots! He will catch you and chop you into tiny pieces and set your heads on pikes!"

Chance stifled a grin at her fierce words, so at odds with her proper appearance. He heard his warriors chuckling behind him.

The laughter only served to infuriate the young woman. "Laugh now, cowards!" she warned. "When my father comes for me, it will be I who will laugh! I will laugh at your pleadings to spare your miserable hides! Then I will throw your cowards' hearts to the sharks!"

"Bloodthirsty little cougar," commented Chance casually.

"Even sharks would gag on your foul Kyuquot remains," she snapped. "Before this day is out, Kyuquot dog, I will see your head cut from your neck and your life's blood dripping into the sea!"

One of the warriors, Chance's cousin, Mudshark, shuddered melodramatically as though in great fear. Clearly his men were enjoying the entertainment, noted Chance.

"You will cut off my head?" inquired Chance,

baiting her further.

"My father will find me and *he* will cut off your head," she corrected curtly.

"Very difficult," pointed out Chance kindly. "Your father has no way of knowing where we are."

The woman stuck her firm chin out. "He will find the body of my slave. He will find my canoe. He will know something happened to me."

"Indeed?" Chance paused. Better to let her know the truth so she could accept that she would not be rescued. "Your slave *and* your canoe lie at the bottom of the sea," he explained coolly.

For a moment disbelief flitted across her features. Then stubbornness closed in once more. "You lie, Kyuquot worm!"

Chance felt, rather than saw, Mudshark with his knife drawn, ready to lunge for the girl. The leader's strong arm shot out and prevented his cousin from seeking satisfaction with his knife. "Leave it be," he ordered.

"She called you a liar, Chance," came Mudshark's hoarse reply.

"She does not know what she's saying," remarked Chance calmly. He turned to the girl. "No more insults." He grinned his lazy grin. "My men do not take kindly to insults."

The woman stared at the two warily, then shrugged casually as though being threatened by armed warriors was a commonplace occurrence. Chance had to admire her bravery. Most women he knew would have been sobbing and begging to be returned home by now, not caustically scolding their captors.

"They are very protective," the woman acknowledged. "And over you, a mere commoner."

Mudshark looked like he wanted to lunge for her again. She must have recognized this for she hastily returned to the previous topic.

"It will not matter how protective they are of you. My father will still bring many men to kill you, white man." She sneered as she said this, obviously satisfied she spoke the truth.

"Such confidence," goaded Chance. Her constant mention of her father in such glowing terms was beginning to grate on him. Her slur about his white heritage further irritated him. "And how will your father find where you are? We Kyuquots are no fools. While you were cowering under the mats—"

"I was forced under those hideous, stinking mats!" she cried. At her angry glare, Chance almost burst out laughing.

"While you were cowering," he could not resist repeating, "we were filling your old dugout canoe with heavy rocks. We towed it, along with the slave's body, far out to sea and cut the line." He shrugged expressively. "It's gone. Sunk to the bottom. Even your mighty father will not be able to find it—or any evidence of you." He smiled smugly.

The woman did not look quite so confident now, he noted. But she gamely stuck her chin in the air and hissed, "Murderers!"

"You mean the man with you?" Chance shrugged. "He was only a slave."

"He may have been only a slave," she cried, aghast, "but he risked his life for me!"

"And lost it. If he had not tried such a stupid trick he would still be alive. We had no quarrel with him."

"Quarrel? Do you have a quarrel with me?" she asked quickly. The woman had picked up on his unfortunate choice of words. He must remember not to underestimate her.

Chance's eyes narrowed as he debated answering her question. He decided against it. She did not need to know everything yet. She would find out soon enough exactly what kind of quarrel he had with her family. He did not stop to analyze the faint feeling of guilt that swept over him at her question. The fact that she was an innocent party to his quarrel with her father should not matter. He and his warriors had resolved to capture one of Fighting Wolf's children and she had been chosen. It was as simple as that.

His glare appeared to silence the woman and for a long while the only sound was a soft liquid swish as paddles dipped rhythmically in the sea. The Kyuquots were making good time and Chance was pleased.

That night they pulled their canoe ashore and camped on the lee side of an island. Normally, when only warriors were with him, Chance would have kept paddling through the night. But in a concession to their captive, he decided to rest.

Confident the Ahousats had no suspicions of where their war chief's precious daughter was, the Kyuquots risked a campfire.

Chance came over and sat down next to the captive while she was nibbling daintily on a piece of fish. "I see we are eating my father's smoked salmon," she observed acidly to her host.

Relieved to see her spirits had revived, but not stopping to think why it should matter, Chance answered with a grin. "It was very kind of him to provide us with all the salmon we'd need for the trip back to Kyuquot."

The woman almost choked on the flaky morsels in her mouth. She swallowed some water from a nearby vessel and cleared her throat. "What did you do, steal it?" she asked contemptuously.

"You wound me, my lady," he answered. "Your father gave it to us. We were honored guests."

To her sniff of disbelief, he added, "We were visitors from afar. How was he to know we had come to steal his daughter?"

"How, indeed?" Getting no response, she asked,

"Why did you steal me?"

"I saw you and I was so smitten by your great beauty that I determined to have you."

She glanced at him from beneath her long lashes as she considered his statement. Chance continued to calmly munch his salmon.

She repeated her question. "Why did you steal me?"

Chance attempted a change of subject. "What is your name?" he asked brightly.

"Haina," she answered immediately. Chagrined, she clapped her hand over her mouth, but it was too late.

"Haina. Hmmm, Haina," he rolled the name around on his tongue. "Meaning Quartz Crystal. Very pretty. Like you. And spiritual quartz crystals are very valuable. Only the bravest men dare pluck them from the dark caves where they hide," he mused. "Well, I dared."

He watched the blush rise to her pale cheeks. So she was not as impervious to him as she pretended, he thought.

"What is your name?" she inquired stiffly.

"Chance Gift from the Sea," he answered. "But I prefer 'Chance'."

"So, Chance Gift from the Sea," she said pointedly, "if you will not tell me why you stole me, will you at least tell me what you plan to do with me? Until, that is," she added sweetly, "my father catches up with you."

He grinned his slow grin, and answered obligingly. "Hold you for ransom."

"Ransom?"

"Mmmhm. I am taking you back to Kyuquot. I will hold you there until your father comes up with enough wealth and slaves to release you."

Haina nodded absently. Relief swept over her. She

18

had feared being forced into slavery. It occasionally happened that the enemies of a chief would steal his wives and children and press them into slavery, thereby destroying the chief's name and his family in one blow.

Being ransomed was far better, thought Haina. Now her father would learn where she was and he would ransom her promptly. Her father and her mother, Sarita, loved her very much. Haina was their youngest, and, she thought, their favorite daughter, and she had no doubt they'd pay whatever was asked. Not like some families who were too shamed by a kidnapping to ransom the victim. Such families left their relative to fate and never mentioned the unfortunate one again. This way the terrible blot on their family name of being kin to a slave was avoided. Or so it was thought.

Relaxed now, Haina yawned. It had been a long, eventful day, and she was tired. "I wish to retire for the evening," she stated dismissively to Chance. She did not miss the amused gleam in his eye and braced herself for his retort, but he merely bowed and wished her a good night.

Though it was spring, the evenings were cold and she shivered in the dark. She gave a start when one of the men approached, but she gratefully accepted the cedar blanket he handed her. She was glad of the warmth on this cool night. Settling herself near the fire, she soon fell asleep.

Haina awoke the next morning to unfamiliar sounds. She sat up and looked around. The shock of seeing strangers rolling up their blankets and throwing on their kutsacks quickly faded as events of the day before flooded over her.

Today would be her first day as a hostage. She knew she would need every bit of her courage to merely get through it. She yawned and stretched before rolling up the cedar blanket. Everywhere she looked, the land

and sea were shrouded in fog. Eerie silence reigned. She got to her feet just as Chance approached. "Get into the canoe," he ordered. "We're leaving immediately."

Surprised at his curtness, she nevertheless obeyed. She sensed that now was not the time to challenge him.

The men pushed the canoe off the gravel beach and paddled swiftly away from their overnight camp. As the beach and cedar trees receded, Haina heard her stomach growl.

Along with another one of his slow grins, Chance offered her a piece of fish. She wanted to refuse but she was too hungry. Haina took the fish and turned away from him to watch the deep green water slip past the pointed canoe paddles.

As the men paddled, Haina ate and stared out into the heavy mist. She wondered how the Kyuquots knew in which direction to travel. She, herself, strained to see the coastline. After awhile, she noticed that her captors were careful to keep within occasional sight of it, but also far enough away to avoid the sharp rocks that edged the coast. Such rocks could easily punch holes in a wooden canoe.

With her stomach full, Haina's usual grittiness returned and she decided she would try once more to make these strangers see the folly of kidnapping her.

"Kyuquots" she began in a firm voice, "I will give you one more chance to escape my father's ferocious wrath." Several pairs of eyes swivelled in her direction, and she was satisfied she had their attention. She ignored the smirks on their faces and continued, "I know you do not wish to be fed to the sharks. I know you do not wish your heads to be posted on spikes in my village. Therefore, Kyuquots, listen to me. You *must* turn this canoe around. Now!" Her voice shook with sincerity. "Turn around before it is too late. Return me to my village, Oh Kyuquots! Only in this way can you save yourselves and prevent further bloodshed."

She waited breathlessly for their response, but the men kept paddling, some of them chuckling as they looked away to sea, others laughing openly. Trying for patience, she added, "Return me now! I promise that my father, the great Ahousat war chief, Fighting Wolf, will treat you mercifully and spare your lives."

After a long silence, broken only by the occasional snicker, Chance spoke up, "It appears none of my men want to accept your Ahousat mercy." He was grinning his slow grin and for a moment Haina wanted to reach over and claw that complacent smile off his handsome face.

Instead, she smiled tightly and said, "It is still not too late, Chance. I am sure you could convince your men that it is the wisest course, and they would gladly follow you back to Ahousat."

"I am sure, too."

She tried again. "Chance, you have several fine men with you," her hand swept in an arc indicating her other captors. "But my father will kill every one of them when he catches up with you. Do you want that?" At his silence, she lifted a brow and said, "His reputation for ferocity is well deserved. It is better not to test him. Please, please listen to me and stop this—this foolishness. Please take me back."

"If he is as ruthless as you say—and I believe he is—then your tearful pleadings will not stop him from killing us, will they?"

Irritated that he had used her own argument against her, Haina's eyes flashed as she bit out, "I want to return to Ahousat. Take me back. Now!"

"I cannot do that."

"You mean you will not!"

"Whatever," he shrugged nonchalantly.

"Kyuquot dog," she hissed.

"And I thought you were suddenly so concerned about our precious Kyuquot lives."

21

Haina suddenly shifted her beautiful eyes to gaze with rapt interest into the fog. Her concern was for herself and not his men, and he knew it. She steeled herself to meet his knowing look and caught the amused gleam in his eyes. "I told you last night," he was saying. "We are going to hold you for ransom. There is no danger to you in that. We will not harm you. I thought you had accepted that."

"Why should I?" she spat. "I do not know you. You could be lying! You could have plans to kill me right here and now. You've already murdered once. Why should I trust the word of a kidnapper and murderer?"

"Why, indeed?" he said bemusedly, his eyes running over her face. She looked so vulnerable, her beautiful brown eyes glaring intently back at him. She was fighting for her life and for a moment he regretted ever starting this plan of revenge. At that thought, he felt disloyal. No, his brother deserved to be avenged. Coolly Chance observed, "But then, you have no choice."

In truth, he was right, and she knew it.

"Do you fear your father will not ransom you?" Chance asked softly. Fighting Wolf could well afford to ransom this daughter, and he loved her well, Chance had heard. Perhaps the girl thought her father would leave her to languish as a hostage, fearing to sully his family name. Chance felt a sudden need to reassure her as best he could.

Unaccountably angry at the pity she heard in his voice, Haina lashed out. "My father will ransom me. Have no fear of that, Kyuquot! He and my mother will pay anything you ask." Her chin lifted proudly as she faced him.

Ah, she was beautiful. Well worth ransoming. "Then we will ask for much more."

"My father is not stingy," Haina replied. "He

would pay many slaves for me."

Chance coughed to hide his chuckle at her words. "You will cost your father even more if you continue to boast that he's a spendthrift."

"Spendthrift? He is not a spendthrift!" defended Haina angrily. "He is merely generous." She sniffed haughtily. "Something you Kyuquots would never understand."

For a moment Chance pretended to look suitably chastened. Then he teased, "Would he pay as much for one of your five brothers? Or perhaps your older sister?"

Haina gasped, then quickly snapped her mouth shut. Eyes narrowed, she muttered, "So. You know I have brothers and a sister."

"Commonplace knowledge," he shrugged. "Easily learned at your father's feast. We have been waiting for a chance to steal one of you." A shiver ran through Haina as she realized this man had been stalking her and her family like a beast of prey.

"One of us?" she echoed.

He nodded. "Any member of Fighting Wolf's illustrious family would do. As it was, we chose you." He smiled, showing strong white teeth.

She decided there were times when she did not like his smile. Like now.

"We thought you would give us the least amount of trouble." Several derisive guffaws broke out among the listening men. One glance from Chance, however, and the men fell silent. Nothing could be heard but the creaking of wood on wood, and the musical sucking of the sea on the paddles.

At Haina's still questioning look, Chance explained, "We brought some rum to the feast your father gave. We were hoping to get your people so drunk that we could easily carry you away."

Haina shook her head. "My father detests rum.

He hates what it does to our people."

"So we learned," stated Chance. He laughed. "When we saw him pouring our expensive gift into the bay, we quickly changed our plans. We could not approach you outright, you were too well guarded. So we decided to wait until morning."

"When you saw me leave to go fishing," concluded Haina in exasperation. If only she'd stayed close to home, where it was safe. Many times her father had chastised her for going fishing, urging her instead to leave that chore to the slaves and the commoners. It was only when her mother, knowing how Haina loved the sport, had added her pleas to those of her daughter's that the stern Fighting Wolf had reluctantly allowed Haina to fish. How she wished he had never indulged her. . . .

Chance read the regret on her face. "You made it easy for us," he admitted.

And now here she was, a captive. Haina shook off her despondency. She would not make it easy for these Kyuquots from now on.

"Will you return me to my father?"

"No."

She swallowed her disappointment. "Then I am telling you now: do not look to me for mercy when my father finds you." More guffaws.

Haina haughtily turned her back on the men and ignored them. The large canoe sped through the waves.

Haina wondered if her parents knew she was missing. She hoped they were not worried. . . .

Chapter 2

It was evening. Slave women were preparing the evening meal. Fighting Wolf, the Ahousat war chief, walked into the main living area of his longhouse.

He was a tall man, strong and straight with a head of thick graying hair that belied his youthful stance. His stomach was as flat as in his younger days and he carried not a spare ounce of fat. Fighting Wolf's eyes, bright and piercing, roamed the room searching for Sarita, his wife of many years.

She saw him and waved him over with a spoon she'd been dipping in a pot. As he walked towards her, he thought of their years together. Laugh lines fanning from Sarita's eyes and creasing her cheeks told their own story, as did the white threads in her seal-brown hair. She had lived a long life of love and happiness with him and he was glad.

Golden brown eyes, gentle and loving, looked up into his. He looked tired, she thought. She must make sure he got more rest. Dipping the spoon once again into the pot, she brought up several large chunks of venison. She piled the meat into a wodden bowl and set it aside to cool. Warm food was best for his digestion, not the hot, steaming food the white man favored so much.

Fighting Wolf squatted down on a nearby cedar mat and motioned for Sarita to do the same. For a long moment, they sat quietly, content to just enjoy each other's company.

Around them the bustle continued. Small children were hanging onto their mothers' cedar kutsacks, pulling at them for attention, while the busy mothers prepared the meal. Men sat quietly in groups, talking politics or discussing the day's catch of fish.

All about Fighting Wolf's longhouse were signs that his people thrived. Drying herbs and fish beyond counting hung from the rafters overhead. Large carved cedar chests and baskets piled high with personal possessions marked off the individual living areas. Many people came and went, the hum of their voices a backdrop for all that took place within his home.

The family dog ambled over and thrust his nose into Fighting Wolf's hand. Fighting Wolf scratched behind the dog's pointed white ears. "No food this time, Stinky," the war chief said. The dog ambled away.

Yes, life was good, thought Fighting Wolf with satisfaction.

He turned to the woman who had shared his life through the good years and the lean, and something of his thoughts must have shown in his eyes. She reached up to touch his face, her eyes full of love.

"Did you catch many fish today, my husband?" She smoothed a lock of his shoulder-length hair behind one ear as she waited patiently for his reply.

"A few," he grunted. "I had to get away from the village and paddle out to sea. I was weary of all the feasting and entertaining last night."

Sarita nodded. The Nootka way of life carried

many social obligations, as she knew all too well. "Last night's feast was a big one," she acknowledged. "Even I was surprised at how many people came. I had to borrow from our winter supplies for enough fish to feed them all. And there were many guests I did not recognize."

"Probably because they came from so far away. There were several chiefs from Uchucklesit and Nitinaht to the south. And I invited chiefs from as far north as Chicklesit and Kyuquot."

"A goodly distance," murmured Sarita. "And what did you and these chiefs from up and down the coast discuss? Every time I spotted you, you were speaking with someone."

He sighed. "The *mumutly*, white man, grows more numerous. Each season that passes brings more of them. They want our sea otter, they want our fish. They build little wooden houses on our land. Useless little houses where only two people can live. Houses that you cannot take down and move, like we can, to where the fish are. They bring guns that kill our men. They bring rum that makes our people crazy. I thought that if we, who all speak the same language, were to band together, to form an alliance, we could keep these interlopers in one area." He shook his head. "It is not good to let them run free on our coast."

"And were the chiefs interested in what you had to say?"

Fighting Wolf sighed heavily. "No, they cannot see any danger from the white men. There are not enough *mumutly* to be dangerous, the chiefs say. The chiefs were discussing the *mumutly*, but all the while their underlings were plotting behind each other's backs. The Nitinaht want to raid the Uchucklesit. The Uchucklesit want to kill the Ohiat. Raiding and warring on each other is all they can think about! That," he said sadly, "is our real problem. We raid each other instead of the white man."

Sarita was silent. There was so little she could say to comfort him. She reached out and took one of his hands in hers. She looked at it, felt its warmth, knew the blood coursed through the strong veins standing out against the brown skin. She turned his hand over, the pink palm was calloused, the blunt fingertips worn. Working hands. Hands that held the fate of his people. Beloved hands. She brought them to her lips. "It is sad the chiefs cannot see the truth of your words. Do not be hard on yourself. You did what you could. Later they will realize your wisdom."

"I fear it will be too late by then."

Fighting Wolf and Sarita sat in silence for a long while. "I wish I knew who brought that damn rum," growled Fighting Wolf finally. "Whoever it was should have known better. I will not allow that poison around my people."

Sarita giggled and for a moment he was reminded of the girl she once was. "Well, whoever it was, I am sure they were gnashing their teeth when you poured their precious rum into the bay."

"Damned stuff probably killed off all the fish," he muttered. Their conversation was interrupted by the approach of a tall young man, his eyes exactly like Fighting Wolf's. "My son," acknowledged the older man. "Please join us."

The young man, so much like his father, thought Sarita proudly, nodded politely. "*Umiksu*, mother, *Nuwiksu*, father," he greeted. "I am looking for Haina. Have you seen her?"

With a start, Sarita realized she had not seen her youngest daughter all day. Fighting Wolf looked to her to answer. "No, no, I have not." Sarita shrugged thoughtfully. "Haina should be here soon for the evening meal."

"I will wait, then," answered Sea Wolf. The small

28

family ate their meal together, Sarita and Fighting Wolf plying Sea Wolf with questions about his four brothers who had also moved away from home to start their now burgeoning families.

The talk continued, Sarita and Fighting Wolf telling him news of their recent visit to his older sister who had married a nobleman from the Uchucklesit tribe. "Those three children keep her busy," chuckled Fighting Wolf. "For awhile there," he reminisced, "we thought we would have another war on our hands. Luckily, the Uchucklesit was an honorable man and married your sister despite the Ohiats' treacherous offer." They laughed together, the whole incident having been resolved several years previously.

Sarita watched, amused. Fighting Wolf had not been quite so complacent then. His anger had been terrible to behold, she remembered. Their beautiful oldest daughter, Fire-on-the-Beach-Woman, had been betrothed to a nobleman of the warlike Uchucklesits since she was but a child. Then Fighting Wolf had learned that the Ohiats, a nearby ambitious tribe, had offered the same nobleman the highborn daughter of their own Ohiat chief if the Uchucklesits would go to war against Fighting Wolf. At first, guessed Fighting Wolf, the Uchucklesit nobleman had been tempted by the offer, until he set eyes upon the beautiful Fire-on-the-Beach-Woman. Then he quickly rejected the Ohiats' despicable offer and married his lovely betrothed. Yes, Sarita sighed, the two tribes had come close to war that time.

"Now there is only Haina to marry," she said aloud. "I hate to see her go. She is my baby."

"Baby!" snorted Fighting Wolf. "That 'baby' is a grown woman who is more troublesome than all five sons you have given me!"

"Fighting Wolf," chided Sarita. "That is not true. She is merely adventuresome; curious, yes, but certainly not troublesome."

He snorted his contradiction. "What about the time she took a small canoe out alone, and paddled to the village of her friend, the one who lives far to the south of us? It took two days to find her."

"Haina thought she knew the way," defended Sarita stoutly.

"Yes. Except that she was heading north," jibed Fighting Wolf.

Sea Wolf, proud of his sister, could not resist adding, "And then there was the time she hid in the bush and watched those visiting shamans do their mysterious rituals at the hidden cove. You were furious about that, *Nuwiksu.*"

"You would be too, if you had to potlatch ten angry men." Fighting Wolf shook his head, remembering the lavish feast and gifts of blankets he gave the ten. "I had to assure them my little daughter was merely curious, and not intent on learning their secrets so she could cast spells on them." He chuckled. "I almost had them convinced until she came out dancing and imitating the chants of old Gas-in-the-Guts."

Sarita laughed heartily, remembering how that noble chief—his real name was Faces-the-Sea—had puffed up with fury and his face had screwed up tight with anger when he'd watched Haina do her mimicking dance. The laughter of the watching crowd had not improved his mood, either.

Fighting Wolf added, "That little dance cost me one very expensive otter skin for appeasement." He shook his head. "And you say she is not troublesome."

"But she is not," insisted Sarita, her eyes wide. "She is brave, curious, intelligent. . . ."

"You do not have to watch the young men following her around with their tongues hanging out," scowled her husband. "You do not have to wrangle and bargain with suitors from as far away as Nitinaht."

"Nitinaht? What suitor is this? You never told me!" exclaimed his wife.

"That is what I mean," he answered. "If I told you of every marriage proposal we received for that girl we would do nothing from morning 'til night but discuss her prospective husbands."

"But, but—"

"She *is* getting older," pointed out Sea Wolf kindly. "It is time for her to marry."

"What do you know?" snapped her mother. "She is younger than you were when *you* married."

"It is different for men," expounded Sea Wolf. "Women are expected to get married at an earlier age. Haina," he announced, "is no longer young."

"She is the same age I was when I married," shot back Sarita.

"That is my point," said Sea Wolf smugly.

Sarita tightened her lips to hold back her laughter. Her son was so sure of himself. She had never been so confident when she was young. Had she?

"Enough of this," she said at last. "Haina should have been here by now."

"Unless she is on another escapade," inserted Fighting Wolf wryly.

"Fighting Wolf, she should have been here by now. Where can she be?"

"I will look around for her," offered Sea Wolf. "She might be dining with friends in another longhouse." His parents nodded as the young man rose to look for his sister. "Come on, Stinky." The dog shot up from his warm place near the fire pit. He trotted after Sea Wolf.

Haina had a special place in Sea Wolf's heart. As the youngest of four brothers, Sea Wolf had often turned to playing with his active little sister when his brothers were too busy. She had been his best friend until about the age of eight when his father and mother had quietly discouraged him from spending time with her. Boys were expected to learn to be men, and girls learned household tasks, explained his parents kindly.

Sarita had almost finished with the cleanup when her son returned. "I could not find her," he announced. His dark eyes were worried.

"She must be somewhere," answered Sarita. "Haina has done this before—gone off and forgotten to tell us where she was going."

"I will look through the village," said Fighting Wolf grimly. "When I find her, she will be sorry she left without telling us. She'll be kept in the longhouse for two days. Mayhaps the next time she will think before she goes off!"

But later, no clue of Haina's whereabouts had been turned up. Sarita sank to her haunches in concern. Where was her baby?

"At first light, we will search the bay," stated Fighting Wolf gravely. "Someone reported seeing her and a slave paddling out in a dugout early this morning." He hit a fist against his open palm. "Damn! Why could she not stay at home like other girls? Why does she always have to be out exploring and getting into trouble?"

"I am sure she will be safe," soothed Sarita, her voice trembling. Fighting Wolf glanced at her and saw she was trying hard to be brave. He opened his arms to her and she fled into his offered comfort. They stood together, holding each other tightly, hoping that morning would indeed bring their daughter back to them.

The next evening a quiet Fighting Wolf returned to his wide-eyed wife. His gaze slid away from hers. She patted his hand reassuringly. "She will return," Sarita whispered.

"And when she does, she won't leave the longhouse for a week!"

"She's done this before." Sarita repeated the

32

comforting litany. Fighting Wolf nodded in agreement.

Several days passed. Fighting Wolf combed the beaches, but there was no sign of Haina, her canoe or her slave. It was as if they had never existed.

Fighting Wolf no longer made threats about keeping Haina confined to the longhouse. He knew now that if he found his daughter, he would hug her to him for a long, long time.

He had dark circles under his eyes from worry and lack of sleep. Sarita too, went about looking haggard and despairing over her daughter's disappearance. Stinky, the dog, spent his days wandering through the quarters, whining whenever he stopped to sniff at Haina's bed.

Something had happened to Haina. She had never been gone this long before.

Fears that Fighting Wolf had tried to keep down pressed to the front of his mind. He could not, would not, accept that Haina might be dead. But it was unlikely she had simply gotten lost. She, and the slave with her, knew these local waters too well. She had fished them for years. No, it had to be a grudge, an act of revenge that had taken her.

And he had unwittingly aided this terrible disappearance by hosting that feast. He knew it. Someone at the feast had taken his precious daughter. But who?

Fighting Wolf knew he had many enemies, from a long life as a war chief on the coast. Methodically he reviewed the men who might want to hurt him. The Uchucklesits? Had his son-in-law made an alliance against him after all? Possibly. The Uchucklesit nobleman now had Fire-on-the-Beach-Woman and knew she could not leave her three children. It would be very easy for him to ally himself with the Ohiats now, admitted Fighting Wolf.

The Ohiats? Though a small tribe, they had conspired against him before. But surely they would not dare challenge him by stealing, or, here Fighting Wolf swallowed, by killing his daughter. He would wipe out their tribe, vowed Fighting Wolf. If he should find one shred of evidence against them he would destroy every Ohiat man, woman and child. His blood pounded fiercely in his veins at the thought. Then slowly his rage passed. No, the Ohiats were crafty, but they were not foolish. They would not cross him. He hoped.

The Nitinahts? They'd shown an interest in Haina by asking for her hand. Perhaps one of their chiefs had decided to steal Haina rather than marry her. But Fighting Wolf had related to them in his grandmother's generation. Surely they would remember and honor that blood relationship.

Then who was left? The Chicklesits? Too far away. He knew those chiefs only under ceremonial circumstances. He had never fought against them or raided their villages.

The Hesquiats? Sarita's people would never lift a hand against him. Fighting Wolf knew this and dismissed the notion.

The Kyuquots? No, they had been allies of the Ahousats for years. Not staunch allies like the Hesquiats, but allies, nevertheless. Old Throw Away Wealth, the Kyuquot chief, probably still bore a grudge for losing Sarita as a wife, but surely he'd gotten over that. . . .

Who then? Who? The question tortured his brain until Fighting Wolf felt numb. Haina was not dead. He knew it, knew it as his very blood was part of him. She was his youngest child, his dearest. . . .

No, she could not be dead. A great sigh shook his body.

He thought of Sarita and how she was taking this. Ah, Sarita, his beloved . . . She was getting too old for such terrible pain. How to help her? He heard her sobs at night, though he knew she tried to muffle them in her fur blanket. To prolong her grief by holding out the faint hope that Haina was alive would be too cruel. No, he could not do that to the woman he'd loved for so long. Better to let her think that Haina had died. Let her grieve and then get on with living. That would be the kindest. And the village people, too, needed to know that some conclusion had been reached. That Haina either was, or was not alive.

Day after day, search parties returned empty-handed and weary. No bodies had been found. Travelers questioned about Haina's whereabouts had sadly answered that they had not seen her. It was as if a sea monster had swallowed her up, said the more superstitious of the village people. At last Fighting Wolf and Sarita could no longer deny the truth. Their daughter was gone. Dead.

They announced a feast to be held in Haina's memory. Because there was no body, the first part of the ceremony, the burial, was dispensed with.

At the feast, Sarita sat huddled in a ball, her women around her, and watched Fighting Wolf slowly distributing gifts to the village chiefs. His thick gray hair was cut to just below his ears as a sign of mourning. Her own gray streaked hair was now shoulder-length, hacked off with a knife in her grief, then singed with a hot coal.

She heard his voice break as he murmured, *"Laktskwai,"* with each gift. Yes, he was heartbroken with the loss of their daughter. They both were.

Desperately, she clenched her hands into tight fists, the nails digging into her palms, as she fought back the tears. Her head fell forward, her hair swung over to cover her face momentarily, giving her a respite from the many brown eyes watching her, sympathy in every gaze.

For Sarita wanted to hide, hide from those eyes

35

that believed her daughter was dead. Hide from Fighting Wolf who, too, had given up. But Sarita had not given up. A mother's heart would know, she told herself over and over. She knew her youngest daughter so well, had loved her so much, surely she would know in her heart if Haina was dead.

Her dreams, when she finally managed to fall asleep, told her Haina was still alive. Alive and far away from her. Surely those dreams did not lie. No, Haina was not dead. She could not be. Sarita felt it down to her very bones. But she could not tell anyone. Could not tell Fighting Wolf, that haggard man who had aged before her very eyes, of her hopes. To give him false hope would be unutterably cruel. This she could not do to her beloved mate, the father of her children, the love of her life. And so she kept silent and wore the outside marks of mourning. But in her heart, she hoped. And kept the little flame of hope alive.

Sarita could choke down nothing at the ceremonial feast. At last it was over and she and Fighting Wolf walked to their quarters to mourn in privacy.

Sarita and Fighting Wolf would stay in seclusion for two moons before finally venturing forth and taking up their lives again. During that time, the people would respect the taboo against mentioning Haina's name. Later, when her death was accepted, they would speak of her again.

And Fighting Wolf watched and waited, waited for his suspicions to bear fruit. He hoped the burial ceremony would cause the kidnappers to get careless. That they would think her family truly had given up and thought Haina dead. For a careless kidnapper would make mistakes, mistakes that would lead an angry and avenging Fighting Wolf to burst through their very doors.

Chapter 3

Halfway through the third day, it occurred to Haina that Chance was in no hurry to return to Kyuquot. Whereas on the first two days he and his men had paddled speedily homeward, today they were paddling slowly and had even stopped at a deserted beach to eat their midday meal.

Lighting a fire to cook the fish they had caught that morning, the Kyuquots were obviously unconcerned that they might be followed. Haina ground her teeth together at the thought that they felt so safe. They should be shaking in fear of what her people would do when they caught up with them. Nothing the Kyoquots had done up to that point had proven so clearly to Haina that she was indeed on her own. She could expect no help from her father and his men.

Haina's gaze wandered over Chance's broad back as he bent over the fire. His tanned flesh was half hidden by the bear skin robe tied at the shoulder. Around his waist was a twisted belt of cedar from which dangled a lethal-looking knife. The other men were dressed in plain, serviceable, cedar kutsacks and they were also armed. But none of them had the presence of their leader. She shivered. Just looking into those eyes the color of a stormy sea was enough to make her forget everything she knew to be right. She sighed. She should not be feeling such things about the man who had kidnapped her, and who, furthermore, was a mere commoner. Haina tried to hold on to that contemptuous thought. Still, he was an attractive man. . . . His different coloring, rather than putting her off, intrigued her.

Chance saw Haina sitting quietly and he wondered what she was thinking. He watched uneasily as Mudshark walked over to the girl and offered her some fish. This was the second time that Chance had seen Mudshark offering food to the captive. Chance did not like it. Two days ago his cousin had been willing to stab the girl to defend Chance's name. Now here he was, gazing into her large, beautiful eyes and offering her salmon cheeks, the choicest part of the fish.

And Mudshark was not the only one. Beachdog, another of Chance's warriors, had offered the woman the use of his cedar blanket on the previous evening. Several of the men—and Haina—overheard Beachdog joke that he would just as soon join her under it. Unsmiling, Haina had immediately cast the blanket haughtily at Beachdog's feet. Beachdog took his blanket back and Chance had loaned Haina his bear robe for the night. She accepted it with well-bred grace, he remembered. And now Beachdog was approaching Haina holding out a handful of berries.

Chance had seen enough. He sauntered over. "Looking for a new mistress, Beachdog?"

Beachdog turned to see who was addressing him. He grinned at Chance. "Perhaps."

Haina glanced casually at Chance. Standing there, feet planted firmly apart, strong arms crossed against his wide chest, the fur of his black bear robe ruffling in the wind, he was prince of all he surveyed. That conceited man, she thought. She smiled beguilingly at Mudshark, hoping to exclude Chance from the conversation. Chance caught her smile and his own lips twitched.

Chance turned to Mudshark and asked casually, "I wonder if our lovely hostage would be interested in what happened to Beachdog's last mistress?"

Taking the bait, Mudshark grinned, realizing the weapon his cousin had just handed him. Now he knew how to extinguish his rival's hopes for the beautiful woman.

Interested in spite of herself, Haina watched Beachdog squirm uncomfortably under her wide-eyed gaze.

Mudshark launched into his tale with relish. Still grinning, he began, "One night Beachdog told his wife he was going to pray and bathe in the sea. Then he was going to hunt many sea otters." Haina nodded in understanding; there were similar hunting rituals in her own village.

"Instead of bathing, however, he sneaked back into the village to spend the night with his lovely mistress, Kingfisher, whose husband was away on a sealing expedition. Her husband is a high-ranking chief," explained Mudshark, warming to his story. "Early in the morning Beachdog heard a warning rap on the longhouse wall. The seal hunters were back. He managed to crawl out an escape hatch in the back of the longhouse. Seeing that no one was watching, Beachdog raced for the woods."

"It was unfortunate," remarked Chance drily, "that his wife saw him."

Beachdog merely grinned, a mixture of pride and embarrassment on his handsome face.

"Beachdog's wife did indeed see him," acknowl-

39

edged Mudshark. "That she did. She tore after Kingfisher. And you should have seen poor Kingfisher when the wife finally caught up with her." He shook his head at the memory. "Pitiful. The wife was tearing at Kingfisher's hair, kicking at Kingfisher's legs and punching at Kingfisher's head. Most of her blows missed," explained Mudshark. To further enlighten his listeners, he leaped about, striking invisible blows at an invisible adversary and pulling invisible hair.

"She was yelling and screaming insults." Here Mudshark hopped around in little circles, imitating the angry wife, while he cried out in a high-pitched voice, "So *you* are a sea otter! You are the sea otter my worthless husband was after!" Then he shrieked, "I was awake all night, doing my own ritual to help my husband, just like a good wife should!"

Haina could not help but choke back a laugh as she imagined the poor woman awake and praying all night so that her husband could catch the elusive sea otter. Everyone knew how important the wife's help in the ritual was. Without it her husband would come home emptyhanded.

"And all the time he was sleeping with you! *You* are no sea otter. You look like a skinny, scrawny Kingfisher to me! My husband hunts kingfishers! Aaaaiieee!" Mudshark's voice rose to a sing-song on the last words as he skipped around a few more times.

Haina was too busy laughing at his antics to do more than hold her stomach. When she had almost recovered from laughing she managed to gasp, "I know you will find another mistress, Beachdog. But it will not be me!" And she went off into another burst of laughter.

Chance relaxed and uncrossed his arms, satisfied that Haina had understood the message he had been trying to convey. Beachdog was not the man for her to get involved with, though Chance never stopped to ask himself why he should care.

Beachdog, not realizing he had lost all hope of winning the new woman, the most beautiful he had ever seen, merely grinned and answered, "Do not be so sure, Ahousat flower. Many women speak of my prowess." He puffed up his thin chest proudly. Haina did not have it in her heart to do anything else but smile at his remarks. He seemed harmless enough, unless one were married to him!

Mudshark, certain of having vanquished his rival, seized his chance to preen before Haina's lovely eyes. "She prefers a man, Beachdog. Not a little duck-chested thing like you," he said, his voice as deep as he could make it. Seeing Haina's eyes swing to him, he announced, "Why would she want you when she could have *me*? I am the second son of a Kyuquot chief and my family is a very old and noble one. I have many fishing territories and slaves. And," he added slyly, "I have no wife."

"Why do you tell her that?" asked Beachdog contemptuously. "You would not make an Ahousat hostage your wife."

Haina looked at him sharply, surprised at his astute comment. Then she swung her dark eyes back to Mudshark. The truth of his rival's words showed in the dull red flush darkening his tan. So, she thought, Mudshark too, wants a woman to keep him warm at nights, but not to marry. What game was this they played? Why were they fighting over her? She turned questioning eyes on Chance, but he merely returned her gaze and shrugged, though she thought his eyes narrowed. Why? she wondered.

Has the woman no idea of her attractions? asked Chance of himself. He was unaware that Haina's family had always lectured her on her noble status and highborn heritage. That she was beautiful was not emphasized because the other members of her family

41

accepted their superior physical beauty as their natural due. Consequently, Haina was proud of her family name but not vain. Indeed, she was almost unaware of the outstanding beauty of her face and form.

"Mayhaps not as a wife, but I would take good care of her," Mudshark was boasting, though the effect was somewhat lost by the whine in his voice, thought Haina. "I do not need to marry a woman to love her." He looked to his cousin for help in his suit. "I am much sought after by our young Kyuquot maidens." Relief flashed across his features as Chance nodded his head in agreement. "Any woman would be glad of my devotion. I would give her many fine gifts," he added, watching Haina out of the corner of his eye. Seeing no change in her impassive expression, he increased the rewards. "Any woman who stays with me would have much food and even slaves to wait upon her. She would do no work."

"Pah," snorted Beachdog. "Any woman who stayed with you would have to put up with your miserable ways. You do not even say a decent word to your mother before the sun has passed its zenith."

Angry now, Mudshark answered, "By which time *you* may have rolled out of bed, you lazy braggart."

"Enough," said Chance.

Beachdog and Mudshark paid him no need. "Braggart, am I?" snarled Beachdog. "I do not pretend to lure a woman with lies of marriage!"

"Now who's lying?" shouted Mudshark, reaching for a handful of his rival's hair. Fully enraged now, the two men squared off, each grasping great handfuls of the other's hair. Pushing and pulling each other, they moved about in a circle like a giant wounded crab.

Chance tried to step between them, wondering how something so amusing had gotten so quickly out of hand, when he received a sharp blow to his head and was shoved to one side.

Haina stood, horror-stricken, watching the fight erupt before her very eyes.

By now the two men were fighting in earnest, delivering smashing body blows to each other. Mudshark had the advantage of a bigger and stronger build, but Beachdog was surprisingly agile and wiry for his size. Heavy breathing, punctuated by snorts and grunts, were the only sounds on the quiet morning air.

Chance shook his head several times, trying to recover from dizziness.

Several of the other warriors came running over—not to intervene, noticed Haina, but to watch and urge on the fighters. The two combatants were rolling around on the hard gravel, trying to get a death grip on each other's throats, she supposed, when Chance finally yelled at the watching men. Reluctantly, they moved to break up the fight and pulled the two furious men apart.

Still lunging at each other, Mudshark and Beachdog had to content themselves with shouting insulting names.

"Enough!" bellowed Chance, his even tone forgotten as he grabbed the two combatants, each by a handful of hair. "There will be no more of this fighting," he roared. He gave each shaggy black head a sharp yank and pushed them away. "That is enough!"

He turned to Haina, "And as for you . . .!"

"Me?" she asked incredulously. "What did I do?"

"You are the cause of this!" he snarled.

"Me? Why, I—"

"You will stay away from my men. Leave them alone, do you hear me?"

Haina swallowed once, and nodded. The man was beyond reasoning. She could see that. She, Haina, as the cause of this fight? Ridiculous!

"Get moving," he ordered the two. "Fighting like starving dogs over a tasty morsel! Kyuquot warriors

43

should behave like men, not dogs!"

His words touched the prickly pride of the two combatants and they looked sheepishly at each other. Beachdog wiped his bloody nose, leaving a long red streak across one cheek. Mudshark touched the side of his scalp tenderly. A large clump of hair came away in his hand.

"You have caused enough trouble today. Get to the canoe." Chance did not trust himself to say any more, he was so angry with the two of them. "And as for you," he rounded on Haina, "what am I going to do with you? I cannot have my men fighting over you."

As he gazed at her some of the anger went out of him. "I think, little cougar," he said thoughtfully, "that you are going to be nothing but trouble." He nodded, as if to himself. "Yes, I am beginning to suspect we would have done better to steal all five of your brothers." And with that cryptic comment, he strode after his men.

Haina watched the men walk away, the big man with the dark blond hair and the two lesser built men with black hair. Men fighting over her, she thought angrily. She did not ask for men to fight. Especially now that she knew what they had in mind. She did not want to be courted by any of these Kyuquot dogs, she thought disparagingly. She only wanted to be ransomed and sent home. Haina determined to keep that thought uppermost in her mind.

"Time to pack up," ordered Chance. The men began bundling their meager possessions and loading them into the war canoe. Haina had nothing to pack, so she walked slowly down to the water's edge and dipped her greasy fingers in the water. She was surprised to see her hands were shaking. The fight had scared her more than she realized. Rubbing sand and gravel over her trembling fingers, she managed to wash away most of the grease. The men were still not ready to leave, so she waded out into the cool water, uncaring that her sea otter anklets were getting soaked.

One of the men reached into the canoe and grabbed a shovel-like cedar scoop used to bail out the canoe. He filled the bailer with water and ran over to pour it over the fire. The hissing steam of the coals signalled that the fire was out. The Kyuquots climbed aboard their war canoe, their hostage reluctantly following.

Haina had a long time in which to contemplate the events of the morning. At last, she resolved to stay away from Beachdog and Mudshark. As far from them as she could. Let them fight over someone else!

And as for their conceited leader, she would stay away from him, too—very far away from Chance Gift from the Sea. That he dare blame *her* because his bullies fought rankled immensely.

By the evening of the fourth day, Haina had spent most of the time alone. None of the other warriors bothered her, although she had caught Beachdog and Mudshark watching her when they thought she did not notice. Her only contact with the Kyuquots was with Chance. He gave her fish and loaned her his robe for the cool evenings, but other than that, he, too, kept a polite distance. His beahvior annoyed her, but she refused to dwell on why his aloofness should provoke her so.

As for Chance, he found himself intrigued by his hostage. Her fiery mettle appealed to him. He noticed that she kept her distance from the other men, and was pleased by that. When she would return his robe to him in the mornings, it was all he could do to keep from burying his nose in it, to smell her warm sleepy scent. He found himself watching her more and more often, only dragging his eyes away when he noticed his own men observing him. He decided he would be glad when they reached Kyuquot, yet perversely, he felt no inclination to hurry.

Haina began to think she would never reach Kyuquot. The weather was clear, ideal for traveling, yet her captors poked along, stopping on this beach or that to pick berries. They pulled into this cove or that for a swim and to drink fresh water from a hidden stream. They dawdled over a fishing bank to catch a few cod for the evening meal.

She should be rejoicing, Haina thought, nervously fingering her blue glass bead necklace. The slow pace made it likely pursuers would catch up with her. But as each day passed and no canoes appeared on the horizon behind her, she at last accepted that she must rely on her own wits.

As to what awaited her at Kyuquot, Haina assumed that the Kyuquots would send a messenger with their ransom demands to engage her father in talks. She would be forced to wait, locked up in some strange, dark longhouse, listening to the incessant dripping of oil from seal bladders in the rafters above. She sighed at the thought. Hopefully it wouldn't be too boring. Perhaps she could persuade one of the Kyuquot women to let her do some weaving. Haina prided herself on her basketry and had received numerous compliments on her work.

Then, once her father arrived with the necessary slaves in payment for her release, she'd be free! She clenched her fists. It was all so unnecessary—and so humiliating.

It was the last evening of their voyage. Tomorrow they would arrive in Kyuquot. Haina had overheard the men talking and had gleaned as much from their conversation.

The night was still. The Kyuquots' campfire threw an aura of flickering orange light into the vast darkness. The burning wood popped and cracked sporadically.

46

Behind Haina rose the deeper, darker shadows of high wooded mountains. The sea stretched out from the beach where she stood. A pale yellow disc of moon hung in the sky and white stars glistened against a backdrop of soft black. Somewhere in the trees, frogs croaked, singing their enchanting songs to all that listened. Crickets harmonized with them.

It is so lovely here, thought Haina, moving a little away from the campfire. The night is so clear, the moon so beautiful. She looked out over the water and saw silvery light dancing on the placid liquid. It is good to be alive.

Her meandering thoughts drew her feet onward along the beach until she came to rest beside an old weathered log. She sat down in the sand, leaned against the log and wrapped her arms around her legs to keep out the slight chill.

Escape flashed briefly through her mind, only to be dismissed. She knew the Kyuquots watched her closely, and, even if she could elude their eyes, where would she go? Not into the forest where ghosts might walk at night. She shuddered at the thought. Also, it was cold at night. She had no fire, and only the clothes on her back for warmth. She was not worried about food. She could eat berries and roots, perhaps catch a fish to sustain her. But if she did run and hide, quaking until dawn in hopes that a passing canoe would see her, what then? This part of the coast was seldom traveled. She might spend days, nay, moons, waiting for someone to rescue her. No, she sighed regretfully, this was not the time for escape.

Gazing up at the heavens, she wondered where her family was tonight and if they thought about her. She missed them all so much—and Stinky, too. Did he wonder where his mistress had gone? The same moon looks down on us all, she thought. The same stars wink in the same vast sky. She brushed a tear from her eye

47

and was startled from her reverie by a deep voice.

"Tears, little cougar?"

Whirling, she faced the intruder. It was Chance. She relaxed. "Where did you come from? I did not hear you."

"It is a nice night for a walk," he answered. He could not explain even to himself why he had followed her.

"The beach is large," she answered stiffly. "I am sure you can find somewhere else for your walk."

He ignored her words and settled onto the sand beside her. A contented sigh slipped from him as he leaned back on the old log.

The warm smell of him drifted past her. How well she knew his fragrance. She had breathed it in her dreams every night that she had lain in his bear skin robe. Her eyelashes fluttered at the thought and she looked out at the gentle waves kissing the shore with little bubbling noises. Somehow the night did not seem so lonely now that he was here. His large presence was reassuring, she admitted in an unguarded moment.

They sat together in silence, each caught up in their own musings.

Haina slid a glance at him. His arm muscles, developed from extensive paddling, bulged against the black of his robe. A cool ocean breeze blew his long hair back from his face, and exposed his strong neck. She could see the rough texture of his skin where he had plucked his beard hairs.

He swallowed as she watched and for a moment he looked vulnerable. Her eyes ranged slowly over his face, drinking him in, and came to rest on his nose, hawk-like in profile. It countered the illusion of vulnerability she had thought she had seen on his features. She must go carefully with this man, she sensed. Such a man might be unguarded with his friends but he would be implacable with his enemies.

Now where had that thought come from?

Haina glanced at his profile again. Aah, but he was so good to look at.

Chance stared out to sea asking himself again why he had come. But now, sitting next to her, relaxed, he knew. It was because he could no longer stay away. Her voice, her scent, her body, everything about her drew him.

He wanted to know her, to learn more about this Ahousat woman he had captured. She seemed so different from the other women he had known. She was brave, enticing, intelligent and, like the cougar that he named her, there was something untamed, wild, about her. And, like a cougar, she would not let him get too close, he suspected. But, he encouraged himself, even cougars sought a mate.

The thought of such a challenge thrilled him. To pit his wits against a woman, to get past her claws, intrigued him.

He would get to know her, he decided impulsively, then her mystery would be laid to rest. And what about your brother's revenge? asked a small voice in his mind. Will you betray him for your little cougar? Never! he answered fervently.

Their silence went on until, curious, Haina asked, "What do you want, Chance?"

He picked up a smooth oval rock and threw it into the water, the action somehow fitting with the tranquility of the night.

He glanced at her. Ahh, she was beautiful. He had to admit to himself that each day she grew lovelier to him. Each morning when he awoke there was a new spring in his step because he would be seeing her. How long this feeling had been upon him he did not know, but it seemed that he had lived with it forever. Yet he had only known her a few short days.

How to say what was in his mind and in his heart?

Or would he only be laying himself open to her wildcat claws?

"Haina," he breathed, reaching for her. She tensed slightly but did not push him away. Encouraged, he pulled her closer to him until they were locked together against the log.

What is happening? she thought wildly. I shouldn't let this—Kyuquot hold me. But she could not summon enough indignation to push him away. It felt so good nestled there in his arms. So fitting.

She could hear his heart beating and feel the soft fur of his bear robe tickling her face. Ahh, to be held for just a short moment, she thought.

But he had more on his mind than holding. "Haina," he murmured again. Then his lips were lightly touching her face, roving gently over her features like a dainty butterfly, she thought. The butterfly perched on her nose, then brushed across her cheeks and made its way slowly to the corner of her mouth. When it reached her mouth it turned into a ravenous, devouring creature.

She pushed against him but he would not let her go. His mouth was hot and heavy on hers, and his tongue was pushing against her clenched teeth. She broke free. "Please!"

Chance looked at her as if bewildered at what had come over him. "Haina, I did not mean—" he began.

"Stop!" she cried.

But he could not. He reached for her again, and she leaned away from him, all to no avail. He easily dragged her closer and locked her in his strong arms as his lips ravaged hers again. Again and again his lips plundered hers, taking all the sweetness that he could.

Haina, gasping with excitement, thought she would faint with desire. Somehow her arms wound their way around his neck and she held on against the overwhelming tide of his embrace. She returned his hot kisses with her own demanding ones. Tentatively she let his insistent tongue into the soft interior of her mouth. Shivers ran down her backbone at his probing. Then he pulled away. She pulled him back. She wanted more. Much more. Where had these wonderful feelings come from? She felt herself drowning in sensation and wondered if she should not just give up her struggle now.

She felt the warm pressure of his hand, even through the cedar kutsack, as he sought her breast. No man had touched her there before and fear returned. This was her kidnapper! What was she doing lying in his embrace? She clawed at his back, trying to pull him away.

Suddenly a loud cry split the night. Chance's head shot up and he listened intently. More cries. Intense anger at the interruption coursed through his already heated blood. Roughly, not realizing his own strength due to frustration, he threw Haina from him. "Damn! What is it now?"

Jumping up, he started for the campfire. He looked back at the surprised woman that he had cast back against the sandy beach. She was curled up in a ball, watching him. Cursing under his breath, he strode back to her and seized her by the arm.

Hauled to her feet, she found herself being carried along, stumbling over rocks and pieces of wood in the dark night. She cried out and he slowed his pace.

Arriving back at the campfire, he shoved her to one side of the encircled warriors. "What goes on here?" Chance demanded. The anger in his normally mild voice surprised his men and they turned to look at him.

Chance's gaze came to rest in the midst of the men. There stood Mudshark and Beachdog, grappling with each other. Each grasped great handfuls of the other's hair as they pulled and pushed their adversary, straining to bring him to his knees.

"Cease! At once!" Chance roared and his outright display of anger visibly shocked his men. The two fighters guiltily dropped their hands and froze in their shuffling steps. Sheepishly they turned to face their wrathful leader. "Leave off this fighting!"

The watching warriors murmured their disappointment. Chance ignored them. "What is the fight about this time?" At Mudshark's hesitant look, the answer flashed to Chance. "Over her?" He jerked his chin in Haina's direction.

The two nodded slowly, not daring to meet his eyes.

"Damnation!" They were still after her. Those pups dared think they had any prospects with her. His anger soared anew. "You still stay away from each other. And her!" Chance's voice became deadly. "Neither of you shall have her. She is mine!"

Chapter 4

Silence reigned. The Kyuquots turned as one man to stare at their outraged leader. Haina, too, was watching him, her mouth open. Chance met the stares with jutted jaw. Firelight from the campfire flickered over his determined features, leaving the others in shadows. "Get to your beds," he ordered after a moment. The others slowly moved away. The two fighters slunk quietly into the gloom, intent on keeping out of their leader's presence for a while.

Chance turned to Haina who managed to snap her mouth shut. "You, too," he said softly. "Get some rest."

"What did you mean," she asked belligerently, "by stating that I am yours?"

"Just that," he answered. "I am in no mood for more fighting. I suggest you do as you are told."

Haina did not know what to answer. This man was so different from the man who a short time ago had been kissing her passionately. With one last sharp glance at his stern visage, she departed for the far side of the fire. Earlier she had spotted some tall salal bushes curving over the beach sand. A few logs lay between the bushes and the fire. She would rest behind the logs for the night, she decided uneasily. Better to stay out of the men's sight.

"Haina," her name, softly called, drew her around. "You need this." Chance had taken off his bearskin robe and was offering it to her as he did every night.

Eyes averted, she reached for the robe. Her fingers grazed his and she snatched the robe away as if burned by his touch. "Thank you," she murmured and fled.

He stood contemplatively, watching her disappear. Well, he mused, he had done it now. He had stated before all his men that she was his. Now he must decide what to do with her. All his noble plans for avenging his brother were in jeopardy because of his impulsiveness.

Shaking his head slowly, Chance walked to the war canoe. It had been pulled safely out of reach of the tide, and he rummaged through it looking for a cedar blanket. Then he, too, sought a comfortable place to bed down for the night. He needed a place to rest his body and ponder this new development.

Haina awoke the next morning before the rest of the war party. Again thoughts of escape flitted through her brain only to stop when she heard someone else moving around. She lifted her head and peeked over a log.

Mudshark was lighting a new fire on the ashes of last night's blaze. Better not to approach him while there was only the two of them awake, she decided. She resolved to shun both Mudshark and Beachdog. Another foolish fight between them was not to be borne.

As Haina lay there, thoughts of last night swirled around her and she remembered Chance's powerful statement of possession. 'She was his.' She shivered

54

involuntarily in the snug bearskin. When would he claim her? How could she fight him off if he was determined to have her? His size alone ensured it would be an easy matter for him to take her by force. Fear swept through her. For the first time in her life she was without the loving protection of her mighty family. She was at the mercy of a man who had proclaimed her publicly as his property and who, she knew instinctively, would brook no interference in that claim. And what was worse, she had reason to believe he was pursuing some kind of revenge against her or her family. If he regarded her as an enemy, as she did him, she had no doubt that he would treat her brutally if pushed. She shivered again. If only her father could find her in time!

Despair tried to claim her, but she fought it bravely. No, she must not give into her fears—or into him, the Kyuquot sea slug. She had her wits to rely on, after all. She would survive and return to her beloved home and family.

While Haina was reassuring herself, Chance was busy with his own thoughts. Today they would arrive in his half-brother's village of Kyuquot. Before leaving Kyuquot, Chance had not told his chiefly half-brother of his plans for the raid on the Ahousats. He had wanted to surprise Throws Away Wealth. For a moment, Chance almost dreaded telling his older half-brother that he had stolen the daughter of Throws Away Wealth's greatest enemy. Then Chance's natural confidence reasserted itself. He had struck at the enemy for his family's sake, after all. Throws Away Wealth should be jubilant at this triumph over his sworn enemy, the arrogant Fighting Wolf.

Chance had grown up listening to Throws Away Wealth's bitter tales of how he had been promised the beautiful Sarita as his bride, only to have her snatched from him at the last moment by the detestable Fighting

Wolf. When Throws Away Wealth was talking, at feasts and special occasions, he seemed to dwell almost obsessively on the incident.

Sometimes Chance wondered if that was why Throws Away Wealth seemed cruel to his wives and family. Perhaps Throws Away Wealth had been so disappointed in love that he had never recovered.

Chance, himself, merely shrugged off his half-brother's words, recognizing the pain that was their source, for Throws Away Wealth had been kind to him. He had kept Chance with him when their father had died.

The two shared the same father, but Throws Away Wealth was a grown man of thirty summers when Chance was born.

Chance had heard the strange story of his birth. A white woman had crawled from the sea, given birth to him, then died. His Indian mother, Ocean Wave, had been in mourning for a baby she had recently lost. Nothing could bring her out of her sadness. Chance's Indian father, a Kyuquot chieftain, was much older than his beautiful third wife, but he loved her to distraction. The birth of the white baby on the beach near his wife's home village had been a miracle. Wanting her happiness above all else, he had given her the baby. Ocean Wave had been a true mother to Chance. The people of both his mother's and his father's villages accepted him completely as Nootka Indian. Chance himself thought of his birth as merely a curious event, nothing else. As far as he was concerned, he was Indian.

Oh, it was true that sometimes, especially as he had grown to manhood, he had wondered about the white woman who'd given him birth. Who was she? Where had she come from? Who were her people? And his white father—who was he? What had he been like? So many questions and no answers. After awhile

Chance had ceased to speculate much about his white parents and now it was a topic he seldom thought of. He accepted the Nootka Indian heritage as his own, now.

Chance had lived in his mother's village, Chicklesit, for the first years of his life, then his family had moved back to Kyuquot. They had lived there happily until Chance's and Throws Away Wealth's stern but loving father had died when Chance was twelve. Chance's mother had followed him a scant two years later, a victim of pneumonia.

Only Throws Away Wealth, of all the half-brothers and sisters, had shown any interest in the young orphan boy. Throws Away Wealth had insisted that Chance live in his longhouse, though once the boy was there some might judge the chief's actions as neglectful. Chance had grown to manhood having the run of the village. Nevertheless, Chance was grateful his brother had taken him in and could forgive his brother many things.

Done with his musings, Chance rolled out of his cedar blanket and stood up, naked and shivering in the misty morning air. The fire was a pile of hot embers. Mudshark squatted nearby, pushing a fish into the ashes to cook. Breakfast would soon be ready.

Chance stretched and yawned, then ambled to the water's edge. Without missing a step he waded into the cool water and ducked, coming up sputtering. He swam around for a time until, finished with his morning ablutions, he walked back to the fire and studiously ignored the beautiful dark brown eyes that followed his every move.

Reaching slowly for a short woven cedar wrapper, he wound it leisurely around his waist and secured it before wandering over to visit with Mudshark. He had yet to glance at the hostage, but he felt her eyes on him and smiled to himself. Let her be curious about his body, he thought. Soon she would know him—intimately. The little hostage was sweet and he would soon taste her. All to further his family's revenge, of course. He grinned to himself. The thought of Haina's lithe young body wrapped around his in the throes of passion was very pleasing.

Chance glanced at the familiar landmarks around him. Now that he was nearing his home territory, he could relax and enjoy the well-known islands and bays that welcomed him. Yes, he thought with satisfaction, it would be good to see his brother's face when he learned of their beautiful new hostage.

Chance Gift from the Sea sat in the longhouse of his brother, Chief Throws Away Wealth. The house, the largest in Kyuquot village, was five war canoes in length, and just over one war canoe in width. The roof on the house was the highest in the village, higher than the height of a man standing on his brother's shoulders. For the other houses in the village a tall man could merely reach up and touch the ceiling. The roof of Throws Away Wealth's home was gabled and covered in overlapping cedar planks. Large rocks placed on top of the roof kept the planks from blowing off in the furious winter storms. Long split cedar boards ran the length of the side of the house and were lashed between pairs of vertical small poles spaced at intervals along the side. A wide arched doorway into the house was centered on one end. Small escape hatches ran along the back side of the house. These would be used for flight should enemies raid the village.

It was dusk and the house was lit by hearth flames and a scattering of lamps here and there. Women prepared the evening meal while naked children darted about chasing each other, dashing out of reach of the older brothers and sisters doggedly tending them.

Throws Away Wealth's quarters were in the highest ranking section of the house. Seal bladders full of oil hung from the rafters as did row after row of smoked fish, supplies that had kept his family's stomach full through the long wet winter. Cedar boxes, piled haphazardly about the living quarters, marked off his family space from that of neighbors. Cedar garments, trade clothes and various household items spilled out of the boxes to add color and a certain lazy air to his home. Throws Away Wealth's two wives and their female slaves scurried back and forth serving the chief and his brother.

"What news, younger brother?" asked Throws Away Wealth, forcing the words around a huge mouthful of salmon.

"Good news, Tyee, my chief," came the confident answer. Chance took a swallow of water and several bites of fish. He wanted to prolong the telling and to heighten his brother's suspense.

"Well?" demanded Throws Away Wealth impatiently. "Are you going to sit there drinking and eating or are you going to tell me your news? And if you are going to drink," he added acidly, "drink rum, a man's drink, not weak water fit only for children still at their mother's knee."

Chance merely laughed at the goading words and waved the half-full bottle away. "None for me, brother." Too often Chance had seen the effects of rum on others' words and actions. Let them drink the foul stuff and play the fool but Chance Gift from the Sea did not court such behavior for his own.

Throws Away Wealth sighed and filled his cup once again. Tossing it back in one gulp, he leaned forward and wiped his mouth with the back of one brown hand. "So? What is it you have to tell me? My men report that you brought a woman back with you. Does she have something to do with your news?" he asked slyly, eyeing his younger brother out of narrowed eyes and reaching for the bottle.

"Aah, Brother," said Chance in an admiring tone. "There is little that escapes you."

"Little of what goes on in this village escapes me," corrected his brother in a surly voice. "It is what you have been doing recently that escapes me."

Chance chuckled goodnaturedly. He had lived too long near the man to be put off by his brother's angry tone. He risked another swallow of water, all the while keeping his green gaze on the smaller man. "Who is your greatest enemy?" he asked at length. "Who, more than anyone else, would you like to see brought low?"

"Fighting Wolf," snapped Throws Away Wealth. "What I would not give to see that worm ground into the dirt and his worthless body flung into the sea!"

"Just so, Tyee. Just so."

"Come. You speak in riddles," answered the chief irritably. "Tell me why you ask such a question."

Chance sensed his brother's small store of patience had reached its limit. Savoring the moment, he said, "I have captured Fighting Wolf's youngest daughter."

Throws Away Wealth appeared momentarily stunned. Speechless, his mouth opening and closing like a gasping fish, he stared at his brother. Finally he croaked, "You—you have his daughter? Here? Why?"

"Dare you guess why?" laughed Chance. "Yes, I have his daughter. Haina is her name." In a triumphant voice he announced, "I am holding her for ransom."

Ashen beneath his brown tan, Throws Away Wealth mopped his sweating brow and muttered, "Ransom? I do not understand. . . ."

"Oh, come now, Brother. It is clear to me, and I would think, to anyone who knows you." Chance took another swallow of water. He was enjoying his brother's rare fit of discomfiture. "How many years have I listened to you bemoan the loss of Sarita, your promised bride-to-be?"

When Throws Away Wealth merely stared at him

as if stricken, Chance continued. "I cut my milk teeth on stories of Fighting Wolf's treachery in stealing your bride. Everyone in this longhouse has heard the story, again and again, of how he wrested the woman you loved away from you. Now I have stolen his daughter. I have done this to right the terrible wrong to you and our proud Kyuquot name!" Chance took a last swallow of water, enjoying the feel of the cool liquid sliding down his throat. Yes, it was correct and noble to avenge the family pride.

Throws Away Wealth appeared to be regaining some of his normal color, at least the ashen pallor was slowly receding. He waved to a wife for another bottle of rum. She hastened over with it, then scurried away.

"So you took it upon yourself to right the terrible wrong done to me so many years ago," he muttered, as if seeking clarification.

"Just so." Chance reached for a handful of herring eggs from a mounded platter before him. Biting into the crunchy eggs, he savored their delicate flavor before adding, "Fighting Wolf has no idea who has taken his daughter. And he will not know—until I send my man with the ransom message. Then it will be too late for him to do anything."

Throws Away Wealth nodded. "He should be very willing to pay ransom for his daughter. The old fool dotes like a woman on his worthless offspring. Many times at feasts and potlatches I have watched him with his cubs. And," he stroked his chin thoughtfully, "he has always favored and protected the youngest one." Throws Away Wealth laughed maliciously. Then as if to himself he muttered, "At last, a chance to bring that foul man low. How many years have I waited for such an opportunity!" He rubbed his hands together gleefully. "We will ask a high price," he assured his younger brother. "A very high price." He laughed again.

Chance glowed at the use of the term 'we'. For as

long as he could remember, he had admired his brother, but seldom was his admiration returned or even acknowledged. Now, at last, his older brother could no longer ignore him or his actions!

Throws Away Wealth was talking. "I will not let her go cheaply." He paused in thought.

Chance's doubts about what to do with the woman were gone. He had done the right thing to capture her and bring her here as an instrument of his brother's revenge, he reassured himself. As for taking her as he wanted, he could still do that and then, when he had satiated his desire for her, he could ransom her. Yes, it was a good plan.

But the Ahousat woman *is* attractive, persisted a small voice in his mind. Supposing he did not want to give her up? Chance immediately squelched that thought. There were other attractive, *Kyuquot* women available. He had momentarily lost his head over the Ahousat hostage, but it would not happen again.

"You must not keep her here," Throws Away Wealth was warning him now. "You endanger all our Kyuquot people should Fighting Wolf refuse to pay the ransom and try to rescue her instead."

Chance looked at his brother in surprise. "Not keep her here? But I shall. Fighting Wolf has no idea where she is, I tell you."

Throws Away Wealth shook his head firmly. "No, as your tyee, your chief, I forbid such action. You must take her elsewhere." He looked speculatively at Chance for a moment. "Take her," he said at last, "to Chicklesit, your mother's ancestral village."

"Chicklesit is an old village, and isolated," protested Chance. "It is too quiet. Nothing ever happens there. If my young men are too far away from the main village, they may desert me."

He reached for his cup of water and missed the hopeful look that lightened Throws Away Wealth's lined face.

"Do not argue with me on this matter, younger brother," stated Throws Away Wealth sternly. "I do not wish to bring Fighting Wolf's wrath down on the heads of my people."

Reluctantly Chance nodded. "It will be as you say, Tyee," he conceded. "When may I return? I refuse to rot away for long in that lonely little village."

Throws Away Wealth smiled happily at Chance's acquiescence. The puppy was becoming too popular. Time to get him away from the warriors and influential commoners, a following he was building in the village. Right under my very nose, thought Throws Away Wealth. Does he think I cannot see through his plans? I know once he has enough followers he will overthrow me.

But no, little brother, you shall not do that to me. I, who took you in when my father died. He doted on you. You, who are not even a son of his own loins. Your white blood sickens me. But I had to keep you away from Ocean Wave's family and their loyal allies. They might seek to rally around you, the only male heir. If they gave you their support you would seize my chieftainship. I know you. I know of the danger you are to me. I saw it long ago.

Throws Away Wealth suddenly chuckled to himself. Letting Chance cool his heels at Chicklesit was an inspired move, the chief congratulated himself. That village is too run-down to ever rise as a threat to me or my village of Kyuquot.

Aloud he said, "I will send a message when you may return. It will not be a long wait," he promised slyly. "But, do not bring the woman to this village until I send for her. I mean these words, my brother."

"As you wish, Tyee," said Chance stiffly and rose. Bowing politely, he took his leave of the chief and strode out the door and into the night.

"Get Dog Shadow," ordered Throws Away Wealth curtly as soon as he had finished his meal. His timid first wife hurried to obey.

Soon, a husky slave was slipping through the longhouse to his master's call and ignoring the fearful glances directed his way.

"Meet me later tonight at the hidden cove. We have much to discuss," the tyee informed the slave. Nodding once, Dog Shadow, aptly named, glided silently away.

The chief's timid wife watched him go and muttered to herself. She wondered who her husband was plotting against now, for plot he did whenever he called for *that* one.

Chapter 5

Haina sat, ramrod straight, in the canoe. Anger coursed through her as she told herself how insulting it was that she, an Ahousat noblewoman, should be sitting in a canoe, waiting on that impudent Kyuquot commoner to return from whatever foolishness he was doing in that longhouse she had seen him duck into. Did he not know it was cold? That she was freezing in the chill night air?

It grated that she should wait upon his convenience. But what else could she do? Every time she started to rise from the canoe one of the warriors waved her back into place. The one time she had refused to obey the casual gesture, a heavy hand on her shoulder had quickly plopped her back onto the canoe bottom. Now she was hungry and tired and forced to sit in this stinking old war canoe.

When one of the men handed her a thin, worn cedar cloak, her first thought was to fling it in his face. Back home such a garment was only fit for a slave. But the night air was too cold so she reluctantly accepted it and wrapped it tightly around her shoulders. Soon she felt warmer and she was able to concentrate on her hunger pangs. Blast that man! When would he return?

Just then she caught a glimpse of Chance exiting the doorway. The light from within the longhouse outlined his large physique for a moment when he lifted the skin over the door. She heard voices from within the longhouse, children calling, adults conversing in a low hum, then the noise and the light were blotted out by the skin falling back into place.

He strode down the beach to the waiting woman. He stood staring at her thoughtfully, hands on his hips. "Time to go," he said.

"Why?" she asked, her voice dripping sarcasm. "I was so enjoying my stay in your lovely village."

A smile curved his lip. "Good. I was concerned you might be bored or even afraid. I see I need not have worried."

Haina bit her lip in exasperation. "Where are we going?" she asked. She barely trusted herself to speak to the man. One word would lead to a torrent, she knew.

"To your temporary quarters," he answered. "You may stay with the slaves."

Her loud gasp reached his ears and he laughed. "I was joking, Ahousat woman. We stay at my tyee's house and he has seen fit to put you near the slaves' quarters. I am sure you will not object to his hospitality." When she glared at him, he merely stared back, but his eyes were laughing at her.

Haina ground her teeth together in frustration and anger. "It would not surprise me to learn that *you* always stayed with the slaves," she responded disdainfully. That she, the daughter of a powerful chief, should stay with the slaves. How insulting!

Chance's answering chuckle irritated Haina into silence.

She was led, blinking, into the light of a long-house. Still fuming, she followed Chance down the narrow path that ran the length of the longhouse. On either side of them, families went about their evening chores, ignoring the intruders. Her anger fading, Haina's bright eyes darted about in curiosity as she walked the path. In one corner there appeared to be the wealthier families, she decided, judging from the yellow, fur-trimmed cedar kutsacks the adults wore.

As she followed Chance down the concourse, it became evident that they were passing the commoners' quarters. Fishing implements hung from the rafters attesting to the men's most frequent occupation. Just ahead, however, Haina noticed the people were wearing rags and looked thinner than the other inhabitants. Her heart sank. The slaves. Chance had not been joking about placing her with the slaves. Mercifully he stopped short of entering the slaves' quarters and she bumped into him, her head still swivelling to take in all the sights and sounds and smells.

"You will stay here," he stated. "Since you have not eaten," he nodded to a young matron, "this woman will see that you are fed." Then he strode back the way he had come.

Mortified at his rudeness, Haina clenched her small fists at her side and held her head high. The young matron approached and smiled shyly. "Welcome to my humble home," she murmured.

"Thank you," responded Haina with dignity. Just because Kyuquot commoner *men* showed little courtesy was no reason to forget her own manners. At least the woman before her appeared polite.

"Please sit, and I will fetch a drink to refresh you," the woman was saying. Haina sank gratefully to the floor and looked about her. The woman's home was neat and clean, unlike some of the other apartments she had passed. Two small children played on the fur-covered planks that did double duty as beds at night and benches during the day. An old woman dozed peacefully on a cedar mat nearby. Other mats were spread over the swept dirt floor and a cheerful fire burned in the firepit. Blue smoke drifted lazily upwards to the smoke hole opened in the roof. A small stack of wood lay beside the fire and delicious smells wafted from the iron pot set to one side of the flames.

The young woman brought the drink and Haina sipped the cool water gratefully. She watched as her hostess ladled out some of the steaming broth from the iron pot and walked carefully over to her guest. Accepting the bowl politely, Haina stared aghast at the contents. Fish soup. Surely these Kyuquots had better manners than to offer a guest mere fish soup. Suddenly she remembered that she was not an honored guest, but only the captive of a commoner. Humiliation made her want to hurl the contents of the bowl on the floor and she glanced angrily at the woman before her. Something of Haina's thoughts must have shown on her face, for her hostess bowed shamefacedly and said, "Please forgive my humble offering. I am but a widow . . . ."

Then Haina understood. As a widow, the woman would not always have fresh meat or fish available and would have to rely on the generosity of her chief to distribute meat when it was plentiful.

The woman pushed a small bowl of smoked clams in front of Haina who had by now lost her appetite for eating the woman's food. Would Haina, a healthy guest, be taking clams out of two little children's mouths?

Sensing her guest's discomfiture, the woman hurried away and returned with another small bowl full of orange herring roe. "Eat, please," she urged.

Haina looked askance at the woman. "How—?" The eggs of herring were considered a rare delicacy and Haina wondered how this impoverished woman could afford such a lavish food.

"These were distributed this afternoon," explained the woman. "Our family received more than we need."

"Your chief is very generous," commented Haina.

"Not our chief," corrected her hostess, "but our chief's brother. He is the one who ordered that all the people were to have a share in the herring roe harvest. Our tyee's brother is very popular with the people." Suddenly aware she should not be discussing Kyuqout politics with an outsider, the woman clapped her hand over her mouth. "Forgive me. I have said too much." And she hurried off to feed her children.

Haina chewed thoughtfully on the crunchy herring roe as she watched the woman's hasty departure. Why should Haina care if the Kyuquot chief's brother was popular with the people? Of course, back home a chief would not want such talk to get around his village. If people heard another leader openly preferred, they might get ideas about replacing their chief. No man wanted to be deposed and have his power taken from him by anyone, let alone a brother. As if she should care! These Kyuquots were so strange.

Now back home . . . she let her thoughts drift as she savored her taste of the first roe of the season. Soon the herring would be spawning in southern inlets, near Ahousat, and the women and slaves would be setting out hemlock branches which the eggs would adhere to. She sighed. Would she be back in time for the herring catch? Her village always made a festive occasion of drying the roe on racks in the wind and sun.

Satiated at last, she staggered wearily to her feet and thanked her hostess for the delicious meal. The woman nodded and asked, "Do you wish to retire, mistress?"

"Please."

"This way." She led her guest to the foot of one of

the wide beds. Several worn furs covered the hard cedar planks and never had bed looked so inviting to the exhausted Haina. "Thank you," she murmured, and threw herself across the furs. She barely noticed her hostess covering her with a cedar blanket before she was sound asleep.

Haina awoke later into the night, when all was quiet. Something had awakened her. She lay blinking in the darkness, trying to get her bearings. Sitting up slowly, she had half-arisen when the hairs on the nape of her neck stood on end. Someone was watching her.

She glanced at the fire, but only embers burned there, throwing little light. Then a shadow moved, and for a moment Haina sat stunned. Gasping, she locked eyes with a woman who, in the poor light, uncannily resembled herself. The woman was dressed in rags that failed to hide her small, thin form, also like Haina's. Moving gracefully, the stranger walked over to Haina and bent over her, staring deeply into the noblewoman's eyes.

Haina refused to shrink from the gaze, which appeared no more than curious. Haina was about to speak when the woman heard a sound and turned her face to one side. A large, purplish scar covered half of one smooth cheek. Haina involuntarily gasped.

The woman turned back to her. "I had to see for myself," she murmured. Then she glided out of the weak light and away into the darkness.

What—or who—was that? wondered Haina. Strangely, she felt no alarm, only the same curiosity she had seen mirrored in the other woman's eyes. Snuggling into the furs, Haina soon fell asleep.

It was far into the next morning, when she and her captors were paddling for a village Chance had called Chicklesit, that Haina recalled her nocturnal visitor and wondered, in the clear light of day, if she had but dreamed the whole incident.

Chapter 6

A day and a half later, after an uneventful trip, the war canoe with its ten men and one woman hostage grated up on a gravelly, rock-strewn beach. Lined up in front of them were five small, gray, dilapidated longhouses. Barking dogs greeted the new arrivals and several unsmiling children stood watching silently from the water's edge.

"Chicklesit," muttered Chance in explanation. His men sat staring at the forlorn village and several shifted uneasily. Mudshark cleared his throat. "How long did you say we were to wait here?" he asked.

"I did not say," answered Chance matter-of-factly. "My brother will let us know when we can return to Kyuquot."

"Let us hope it is soon," one of the men murmured fervently.

Haina's thoughts echoed the murmur. She had visited many of the small villages near Ahousat, but this one looked so—so impoverished, she thought. Split, drying salmon on racks above the hightide line failed to belie the sad, depressed air of the village. Now that she looked closely, even the dogs appeared thin and malnourished. The children still stood staring intently, no smiles of welcome or curiosity on their drawn faces.

Despite the spring weather, a chill wind blew at the visitors. As if to discourage us from venturing farther into the village, thought Haina.

"Now what?" asked one of Chance's men.

"Now we go up to the main house," said Chance, but the hearty tone he strived for was swallowed in the silence. He started slowly forward, his men reluctantly falling into line behind him. Shrugging, Haina followed the last man and the small party wound its way up the beach to the largest of the longhouses.

An old woman stepped forth from the door to greet them. Her eyes were narrowed against the sun at their backs. "What do you want?" Her friendliness reflected the hospitality of the place, thought Haina sourly. Both were absent.

"Is that any way to greet a man returning to his own village?" asked Chance, undaunted, a grin curving his lips. The old woman shuffled slowly forward and peered up at him. "Chance Gift from the Sea! Is it you?"

He laughed, showing those beautiful straight white teeth and for a moment Haina forgot the dismal surroundings. How handsome he was! How the sun shone when he smiled!

She watched hungrily as Chance swooped the old woman up in his arms and whirled her around until her bones creaked and she pushed at his arms, insisting he put her down. Even his men were astonished at such a playful display from their leader.

At last he released the woman and she tottered a few steps away from him, trying to salvage her dignity in front of so many strangers. "Welcome," she croaked at last.

"Thank you, Aunt," replied Chance respectfully.

'Aunt'! This old woman was his aunt. Haina wondered again at the poverty of the village, then shrugged inwardly. What should she expect for a commoner but some such humble beginnings. It was not as if he were a great chief with an illustrious heritage. No, he would never be more than a commoner. The village he had taken her to showed that. She felt sad at the thought. If only he was not so attractive . . . Perhaps if he limped, or had bad breath, or was constantly tripping over his feet, but no, she found him so attractive in every way. Enough! she scolded herself. Now was not the time to moon over one's captor.

"This way, men." And the Kyuquots all filed into the darkened longhouse. Haina looked around and saw the usual fishing implements and baskets on the surrounding walls. No different from home, she thought. And yet there was a difference. There was a touch of poverty here. The fishing hooks looked dull, the metal ones rusty. The basketry was unravelling in parts and everything looked well-used to the point of falling apart. She saw Chance shake his head and wondered if he saw the sorry state of everything, too.

Chance's first homecoming in many years saddened him. His memories of Chicklesit, a boy's memories, he realized now, were of swimming in the warm summer sea, and chasing his playmates or hunting for crabs and clams. Small expeditions to hunt for deer in the forest, came back to him, too. There was nothing in his store of memories about the decrepit buildings, the obvious poverty of the people. He sighed. Boys could not be expected to notice such things. But now, as an adult, he certainly saw the decay around him. He should not have stayed away so long. These were his people, his mother's people. He had a certain responsibility to them and to himself to see that they fared better than they obviously had. He had definitely stayed away too long. The nagging thought crossed his mind that Throws Away Wealth, too, had done little or nothing to help the village of his boyhood. Why had he never wondered before how his mother's people were faring, he asked himself. He had been so caught up in his father's people.

He covertly studied his aunt. Salal Woman had grown so old in the time he had been away. Too long, too long. Her once smooth skin was now finely wrinkled and her once bulky figure was skin and bone. He remembered being dandled on her knee when but a babe. She had been a second mother to him, his mother's sister. She had followed his family to Kyuquot and lived with them until Ocean Wave had died. Then Salal Woman had sorrowfully returned to Chicklesit. Chance had stayed on in Kyuquot with his friends and brother and given no thought to his aunt or the small village where he had spent the beginning of his life and several summers thereafter. He sighed unhappily. So many years of neglect—his neglect. He shook his head again.

Chance and his retinue sat down and the old woman clapped her hands together. Two bedraggled slaves answered her call and set forth cracked wooden cups of water for the visitors. The slaves hastened away and returned bearing platters of smoked salmon. At least the people had food, thought Haina.

After the meal, during which Haina partook of only a little—she suspected the woman had only a meager supply of fish as no second helpings were offered—the men got up at Chance's muttered order and filed quietly out into the waning light. Haina was shown a small palette in a corner and she gratefully sat down to watch the few inhabitants go about their activities.

She was not surprised when Chance returned later, carrying several large cod and two salmon. Smiling inwardly, she watched as he presented them to the old woman. Commoner he might be, but he certainly was noble in his own way and took care of his own, Haina thought approvingly.

The old woman fussed first over the fish and then over her nephew and then over the fish again. Her gestures told Haina the pathetic state of affairs in the village. Oh, how she hoped she would never see the day when a few fish would cause *her* to flutter about so.

After their hostess had calmed down, the men settled in for the night. Haina turned over on her palette with her face to the wall, preparing to go to sleep. But it was not to be.

"Haina," came a deep whisper. She stiffened. Perhaps if she pretended to be asleep . . .

"Haina, I know you are awake. Sit up," came the now arrogant command. She lay still a moment longer, hoping to bluff him, hoping he would believe she was asleep.

His low chuckle reached her straining ears. "I know you are awake, *Chummuss*, but I will let you play your little game—for tonight. Pleasant dreams."

His gentle touch on her shoulder for a moment was as soft as swan's down. Then he was gone, leaving a musing Haina to stare at the gray cedar plank wall. *Chummuss*, indeed. She was not his 'sweet', no, nor anyone's!

Haina awoke to the sounds of hammering and banging. And, wonder of wonders, someone was walking on the roof right over her head! She leaped from her bed and pulled her kutsack over her head. There was one advantage the traditional cedar kutsacks had over the dresses made of trader's cloth: the kutsacks, while bulky, were always presentable for the next day, no matter what they had been put through. Unlike me, thought Haina with a groan. She felt as if she had lain awake all night, though she knew she had fallen asleep shortly after Chance had left her last night. . . . Chance, where was he?

The hammering and banging interrupted her thoughts and she hurried out of the longhouse to see what, or who, was making all the noise.

Chance was perched on top of the gabled roof of the longhouse. One of his men stationed below would pass a large boulder to him and he would walk across the roof and place it heavily on one of the many roof planks. Spring storms would not rip the planks from their settings now, not with big boulders to keep the boards in place.

Haina turned towards the banging sound. She watched as Mudshark and two others busily hammered several new planks over a wide gap on the windward side of the longhouse. Surely the inhabitants would be happy to escape the severe drafts that must have resulted from such a gap, she thought.

Haina ate her breakfast to the accompaniment of pounding. Her hostess, the aunt, darted about between her guest and door, then back again, all the while muttering, "Oh, those young men! What are they doing to my house?"

Haina wanted to answer that they were obviously fixing it, but good manners forbade her from being rude to a hostess, no matter how fluttery she might be.

Haina finished her smoked fish and oil and delicately wiped the back of her hand across her lips. "Is there anywhere I might bathe?" she asked politely.

The aunt stopped wringing her hands for a moment and thought. "We always go to the cove over on the next beach," she replied, jabbing her finger in the air. Haina thanked her and borrowed a proffered cedar blanket to dry herself off later.

Haina had missed her daily baths and felt filthy. Now that she was in this village, she intended to have a bath every day, just like at home. She did not know if commoners bathed frequently, but she and her family had always prized personal cleanliness and captivity was certainly no reason to stop good habits.

A heavy mist covered most of the beach and sand. Undaunted, Haina sauntered down to the beach, knowing the fog would lift and the warm sun would beat down on her at about the time of the midday meal. She was walking across the beach in the direction the aunt had pointed when a loud shout hailed her. Turning, her thick, loose black hair blew in her face for a moment before she pushed it aside to see Chance striding towards her.

"Where do you think you are going?" he demanded.

She held up the cedar towel and said sweetly, "For my daily bath. Surely you commoners have heard of such a thing?" and she turned on her heel and walked away.

She did not see Chance's lips twitching in mirth, nor see the amusement in his eyes. She heard only his answer. "Very well, *Chummuss*. I will come with you."

She stopped in her tracks. "I think not," she said in her best chief's-daughter's manner. "I prefer to go alone." This time she saw the sparkle in his eyes. Irritated at being found amusing by the annoying man, she stamped her foot and said, "You stay here. Your men need you to continue the repairs on the longhouse."

"My men can get along fine without me for a short while."

"So can I."

He laughed outright and repeated, "I am coming with you."

"No." She turned to walk away.

"Stubborn woman. What if you meet a bear in the woods on the way to the cove?"

"I will yell at him and scare him away. Anyway," she tossed over her shoulder, "he would certainly be better company than you!"

Chance grimaced, then baited, "What if wicked slavers paddle by and see a tantalizing young woman bathing unprotected?"

She swallowed and answered, "You are the only wicked slaver that I know of."

Silence greeted this retort and she peeked over her shoulder at Chance. He had the grace to look embarrassed. And so he should, she thought. Maybe he would be embarrassed enough to leave her alone and let her go for her bath in peace.

He continued to walk along behind her, then caught up and walked beside her. Uncomfortable silence reigned. The soft sand of the beach cushioned their feet, and usually Haina relished the feel of the trickling sand between her toes. But not today.

The silence between them thickened unbearably by the time they reached the treeline. Haina's dark eyes searched for the beginning of the trail that would lead through the forest to the cove on the other side. She found it, and struck out along the trail, pretending she was alone. The constant padding of Chance's bare feet on the trail behind her somewhat ruined her fantasy.

They walked up a small rise and through the thick undergrowth of rain forest. Thick salal bushes grew everywhere. Cedar and fir trees towered high above their heads. Haina noted the profusion of small, bright pink flowers on the scattered salmonberry bushes. There would be a good crop of berries this season.

Haina gasped as she reached the top of the small hill. There, framed through the leaves and branches of the trees was a large, perfect cove carved out of black rock. The water was a cool gray-blue and white mist was rising off it. Seagulls careened and dipped over the placid surface of the cove and Haina's heart soared in delight. "What a beautiful place," she breathed.

"It is," came Chance's deep voice. For a moment she had forgotten his presence.

"Really, Chance," she said dismissively, "I have arrived at the cove safely. You may go now."

He looked at her, his green eyes assessing. Then he smiled, and she shivered slightly for it was a predatory smile. "Aah, *Chummuss*, but the best part is yet to come. You must bathe. And I will stay to see that you get back to the village safely."

"What do you want from me?" she hissed. "Why did you take me captive?"

A long brown finger reached out and lifted her already proud chin. He looked deeply into her eyes and repeated softly, "What do I want?" He leaned closer. "Why *Chummuss*, I want you."

Mesmerized by his glance, Haina went still. His lips touched hers gently, then he surged against her and his arms pulled her closer. She raised her hands to push him away, but her futile efforts went unnoticed against his strong body. His lips were tasting, exploring, then consuming hers and she grasped the heavy fur of the bearskin across his chest. Her fingers kneaded the fur and then she was scraping her nails across his bare chest. He groaned and pulled her closer. "Aah, *Chummuss*. You taste so sweet."

"Let me go," she heard herself plead.

"Never." And he bent his head to her again, his eyes closed, a look of contented bliss on his face.

Her hard slap caught him unawares. In an instinctive reaction he had lifted his own large hand and was about to slap her back when he caught himself. There was no twinkle in his eye now, she saw with satisfaction.

"Let me go, Kyuquot dog," she hissed. "You will not find me easily won over by sweet words and kisses."

Anger blazed across his face. "And you will not find me an easy master," he snarled. Grabbing her upper arms, his fingers left bruises she would still have days later. Pulling and cursing, he dragged her down to the beach.

"Let me go, you fool," she cried struggling against his iron grip.

Chance paid her struggles no attention. When he reached the water's edge a cruel smile formed on his mouth. "I will let you go," he muttered. And he seized her about the waist and began wading out into the deeper water.

"No, no! Put me down!" she screamed as his intent became obvious. "Chance, put me down!"

"As you wish." And he dropped her, splash! into the gray-blue sea.

Haina screamed but no sound came forth. Her mouth opened under water, and she swallowed a large gulp of the salty fluid. She surged to her feet, choking and sputtering, kutsack wet, hair dripping, dark brown eyes flashing.

"You animal!" she croaked and lunged for his blond head. He ducked but too late. She caught him off balance and together they fell back under the waiting sea. Chance held tight to the writhing woman on his chest and then they both pushed to the surface.

Haina drew large wonderful breaths of air into her aching lungs. Chance snapped his head back, flicking the dripping wet hair out of his eyes and wiping his face with both hands. He was just in time to see her lunge for him again, both arms straight out as she pushed him back into the chilly liquid. He thrashed about, trying to regain his footing, but by the time he was steady on his feet, the woman was running through the shallow water, racing for the beach.

"Come back here!" he bellowed. But Haina kept running. Grabbing up the cedar blanket she had dropped in the struggle, she raced for the trail. She darted up the trail and, not hearing his footsteps, she risked a glance behind. She halted her flight and turned to stare fully at the wet, dripping figure of Chance, waist-high in the water, still bellowing for her to come back. His bearskin looked bedraggled, his hair dripped around his ears and suddenly Haina could not stop herself from laughing. Her loud peals of merriment burst through the enraged roars of the man and he watched her in sudden, stunned silence.

"Laugh at me, will you, wench?" He cursed and began to wade slowly out of the clinging gray fluid.

Doubled over helplessly, Haina watched the enraged man come towards her until, finally, weak with laughter, she managed to make her shaky legs totter along the trail. She had to get away from him, one part of her realized. He was not used to being laughed at, and seemed to take very poorly to the idea. Still doubled over, and holding her stomach, she chortled to herself as she ran along the trail, hearing the angry man behind her slamming at bushes and tripping over roots. He was getting closer and the clumsy noises he was making were getting louder. He must be very enraged, she realized, to be making so much noise.

A small side trail appeared to her left, leading away from the beach. Hide, she warned herself, hide until he calms down. She darted down the side path.

Chance was muttering furiously to himself as he careened along the trail. "That woman will wish she had never set foot in my village," he snarled, conveniently forgetting that he himself had brought her to his home. "Laugh at me, will she? Spurn me, will she?" That was the part that really made him angry. And he crashed on through the bushes, carelessly bypassing the small trail Haina had dashed down.

He returned to the village beach, dripping in his sodden clothes. Concerned villagers ran up to him, only to be angrily waved away.

It was a sly Beachdog, still miffed at the loss of

Haina, that dared ask, "Where is your hostage, Chance? Did I not see you go off with her towards the forest? And now you come back, alone and soaking wet. How odd." His smirk did nothing to restore Chance's usual good humour and the midday meal for the men was unusually strained.

When Haina silently reappeared later that afternoon, no one commented on her absence or the trade dress she wore. The garment, which must have come from the *mumutly*, was made of a soft, light material, and clung to her shape. The tiny white flower pattern on a red background was most pleasing to Haina's eye. She wondered how such a garment had come to be in this poor village, but asked no questions when Aunt Salal searched through her one cedar trunk and generously handed over the dress.

And now that good woman was too busy fluttering after the men reconstructing the village buildings to question Haina's constant presence inside the longhouse, or wonder why her unexplained 'guest' should insist on helping with so much of the housework, and be so cheerful about it. Why, the girl was positively humming to herself as she went about the onerous tasks of sweeping fish bones and animal refuse off the dirt floor and carrying armloads of smelly, used clamshells outside the longhouse.

As for Haina, on her several trips outside the longhouse to the clamshell dump, she kept a sharp eye out for a glimpse of Chance. And everytime she saw him she chortled to herself, causing the inhabitants of the longhouse to wonder pityingly if perhaps the pretty 'guest' in their midst was not just a little simple.

Chapter 7

It should only be a little further, thought Haina, as she hurried along the forest path. She had wheedled the directions out of the preoccupied aunt, Salal Woman, pleased to have discovered that worthy's name at last. Haina could not make herself bathe again at the gray-blue sea cove, not after what had happened with Chance. Now she was hurrying to a second bathing place.

It had taken awhile to escape Chance's watchful eye, too. Ever since their 'swim' yesterday, he had been regarding her steadily and measuringly with those beautiful green eyes of his, and she did not like it. But she had managed to slip away without being seen.

Aah, there. She could hear the rushing noise of the falls now. She hurried and soon she burst into a clearing, a beautiful glade of green-tipped alder trees swaying gracefully around a small but deep pool carved into the black rocks. Pouring into the pool was a white waterfall, taller than three men. The water rushed over the steep side of the moss-covered rocks and cascaded down, down, into the deep green pool. Stunned at the beauty of it, Haina could only gape open-mouthed at the lovely sight.

At last she could wait no longer and dashed ahead to the pool, peeling off her cedar kutsack as she ran. The water was cool to her heated body, but she did not mind. She ran headlong into the pool and splashed into the water. Haina came up for air, then plunged into the emerald depths once again. Aah, it was so refreshing, so invigorating. Her senses were alive, her skin glowing. Birds chirped in the distance and the world was a wonderful, marvelous place to be.

She swam about, then stood in the cool water, staring at the cascading falls in fascination.

And that is how he found her. Chance stood transfixed on the trail to the pool, unable to take his eyes off the beautiful woman standing hip-deep in the water. Her long black hair spread down her back like a black cape, and her lightly tanned form glistened in the slanting sunlight cutting through the glade. He could see her smooth, long legs through the crystalline depths of the water and he knew he had to have her. No more waiting, no more taunts from his men when he had already claimed her publicly, and no more worries of what that would do to her hostage status. He had to have her. Now. He felt his manhood rise, engorged with blood. No woman had done this to him since he was an untried boy. He took a deep breath as he continued to watch her, feeling like a wolf stalking its prey. She was so graceful, so free. Desire pushed him forward.

Chance shed his bearskin in one lithe movement, and dived cleanly into the shallows of the pool from the side. Haina whirled at the sound of the intruder, but it was too late. Chance surfaced beside her, a predatory twist to his lips. The fear in her large dark eyes only made the game more enjoyable, he thought.

Haina stared into the green depths of his eyes and

she could see the lust there, the wanting. He would show no mercy. She turned and tried to run, but the force of the water held her back. Arms outstretched, she scrabbled frantically against it's weight.

Chance reached out and grasped her arms. She tried to shrink from him, but he held her easily. Her warm skin against his grip only enticed him further.

For Haina the strength of his grip was merciless. He pulled her back into his heated frame. She could feel the hard muscles of his chest and stomach as he pressed her against him. And against her buttocks she could feel the hard shaft of his desire. She struggled frantically in the water. "Please let me go."

He could feel her trembling. Suddenly the chief's proud daughter was not afraid to beg.

"Please do not—"

Her murmured pleading served only to increase Chance's impassioned state. That she should recognize his power over her was a heady stimulus. "I will be gentle, *Chummuss*."

"No, please, let me go!" She was ready to cry and beg and plead. Anything to be set free. There were tears in her eyes as she turned to gaze at him. She saw that her pleas were merely inflaming the large man holding her. "Please," she tried once more.

"You are not leaving," he said huskily, his hands climbing up her torso to cup her full breasts. A chill ran through her slender frame at his touch. She could feel the rough calluses of his fingers playing across the tender tips of her breasts, first one, then the other. He massaged them gently and she felt herself sag against his hard body. She should be fighting him! He had cruelly stolen her from her people. He was her enemy! But her body was surrendering so easily. What was happening to her?

"Let me go," she cried out, fearing the way her body was responding. By now, her nipples were hard little nubs and her stomach sucked in at the sudden touch of his fingers there. "Please let me go," she faltered.

"Not this time." And he easily lifted her small body into his arms and carried her, struggling, to the soft, moss-covered bank of the pool.

"I must have you, Haina," he murmured, looking into the dark depths of her wide, frightened eyes. "I have tried to stay away from you, but I cannot." And he bent his head and pressed his lips gently against hers. Had his kiss been vicious or violent, she would have struggled, but this, this sweet gentleness caught her unawares and she heard herself moan softly. The tip of his tongue sought entry into her warm mouth and she did not deny him. He battled her tongue for possession but he had already won the territory, she thought hopelessly. He tasted so good, so warm. And his arms were so strong. Just a little longer, she told herself. One more kiss cannot hurt.

The taste of Haina, so clean, so fresh, washed through Chance's body like lightning and he knew he could not, would not let her leave this glade until he had satiated himself on her defenseless body.

Groaning, he forced her back onto the spongy moss and she went slowly with him, as caught up in the kiss as he was. His hand tenderly touched her breast, stroking the nipple gently, then he bent his head and suckled there.

Haina flung her head back as she melted into his embrace. If only this feeling would never stop. She arched herself shamelessly into his waiting, wet mouth. Enraptured, she wrapped her fingers in his coarse hair and tugged his head closer. His answering moan only set her further afire.

Now his hand was wandering tantalizingly down her soft inner thighs, and she closed her legs reflexively.

"Easy," he murmured soothingly. "I just want to

touch you." He pushed his strong hand against one inside thigh and she was open to him again.

Haina heard his ragged breathing and then heard her own echoing his. She relaxed against him and let his hand continue to stroke her gently. It felt so good! When he touched the hidden, intimate bud of her womanhood, she stiffened, but his marauding lips and gentle hands easily overcame her feeble objections. She moaned again and he slid an invading finger closer to the center of her being. Then his finger was inside her, probing, feeling, owning. "Mmm," he whispered. "You are so warm, so wet. So ready for me."

"Let me," he murmured when she tried to push his hand away. "Let me come inside you, Haina. I can make you feel so good. Even better than you feel now." Dimly she heard his words but it was the soft tone, the cajoling tone, that convinced her to let him continue. He buried his nose in her fragrant hair and groaned as he gently rubbed her. Haina stretched her legs, toes curling, sinking into a blissful lethargy. She wanted more and arched against his large hand.

Now he was kissing her neck, her shoulders, her face, as his hands continued to do wonderful things to her body. He was learning every part of her, claiming her, making her his own and she could not stop him. His lips were hot and his breathing ragged as he covered her with impassioned kisses. Now his lips were skimming over her breasts and drinking of the hard pebbled tips. Haina thought she had never felt such ecstasy. She gasped as those firm, masterful lips moved down towards her stomach.

It was all Chance could do to contain the hot pounding of his body screaming for release. Easy, he warned himself. He had her gentled and ready and melting in his arms, right where he wanted her.

Haina felt his lips on the curve of her stomach. "Please," she gasped, pulling him closer. "Please!"

"What do you want, Haina?" he murmured. "Tell me what you want."

Murmuring incoherently, she tried to clutch his big body closer but he held her off, poised over her quivering frame. "Tell me what you want, Haina," he demanded. And still his hand was massaging her there, rubbing in gentle circles until she thought she would scream in an agony of pleading and frustration. "Please," she moaned weakly.

She felt him trembling and wondered at the restrained power of him. Suddenly she realized he was not as in control as she had thought. He wanted her, too. His hips ground against hers and she felt his hard shaft rub against her, so close, so close to the center of her desire. Oh, yes, he wanted her, very much!

Her new-found knowledge gave her courage. "Chance," she said tremulously. "I want you." She tensed slightly in his strong arms. "Almost as much as you want me!"

Her dark eyes met his widened gaze and then his eyes narrowed. With a slow, leisurely movement he was pushing at her entrance. "Let me in," he whispered huskily. "Let me in, *Chummuss*. Now!"

His eyes watching hers seductively, he penetrated her slowly and lingeringly. He was only partially enveloped in her velvet sheath when he stopped, halted by a soft barrier. Virgin! screamed his brain. She is a virgin!

He moved to withdraw, but Haina grasped his rounded buttocks and dug her sharp nails into him. "So you want me, my little virgin," he murmured hoarsely.

"Oh yes!"

With that, he cast restraint aside and slowly, inexorably pushed his way into her, murmuring love words in her ear. Oh, how he wanted to plunge his hot length deep inside her. But this first time was for her and he would be gentle.

He stared into her half-closed eyes as he took her. She gazed back at him, lethargically watching his every move, a beautiful sensual smile on her face.

This was her first time with a man, and oh, what a man! He was gentle, strong, forceful. . . . Haina smiled into his eyes knowing it could never be like this with any other man. No other man could make her feel so wonderful, so cherished.

Then he was moving inside her, his hips pumping against hers. She was his, and the thrusts he made into her body told her she could never get away from him, ever. Eyes closed, she sunk deeper into the moss as Chance plunged into her again and again. Soon Haina was moving with him, matching his eager thrusts with tentative movements of her own.

Then he halted deep within her, inflexible. He poured forcefully and finally into her. His unrestrained cry as he climaxed caused Haina to open her eyes in surprise. What was the matter?

"Aah, beautiful Haina," he soothed. Then he was touching her womanhood's glorious bud again and moving gently against her. She closed her eyes and strained against him. His fingers worked their spell on her and soon she was caught up in her own rapturous climax.

Slowly floating to earth after her ride into the sky, Haina looked into the eyes of the man who still lay in and on top of her. She smoothed back his hair from his forehead and kissed him gently. "Thank you, Chance," she murmured. "That was truly beautiful."

Her simple statement woke Chance out of the sexual haze he had fallen into after his release. He rolled off her and then propped himself so that he could gaze down into her softened eyes. No woman had ever given herself so generously, so lovingly, as Haina had, he thought in awe. For long, golden moments he stared at her, marveling at the wondrous gift they had shared.

89

Then he pulled her tightly to him and his breath came out on a long sigh, like the wind. "Aaah, Haina." A frown suddenly marred his handsome face as he unwillingly imagined this woman being torn from him. "You are mine," he whispered sternly. "Mine." She smiled and cuddled closer to him.

Exhausted and spent, the two lay side by side on the green moss, each with their own thoughts.

A peaceful lethargy settled over Haina and she placed her arms around the man who had aroused such strange new desires in her and then miraculously satisfied those desires. She wanted to stay in his warm, secure arms forever. For in Haina, in her strong, honest heart was born a love for this man and she looked at him with new eyes. No matter that he was a commoner, that his people and her people were enemies. She realized in that moment that he was the man she had been waiting for, the man who would give meaning to her life, and she would let nothing and no one come between them.

Chance rubbed his nose affectionately against Haina's cheek, watching lazily as she gazed intently back at him. How beautiful she was. How wonderful their lovemaking had been.

He sighed contentedly. Yes, he would keep her with him. She belonged to him now. Small matter that he had taken her as part of his family's vengeance. He had possessed her in the most primitive way a man can possess a woman and he would not let her go from him. Not yet. He would keep her and they would spend many wonderful days and nights together until her father could ransom her. His previous plans to harm her family intruded on Chance's blissful reverie. Ah, well, he sighed dismissively. Plenty of time to worry about that later. For now there was only Haina, and himself, and the lovely forest glade they lay in.

Incredibly, he felt his manhood stir again with

desire for the beautiful woman at his side. He rolled onto her, slipping easily into the warm nest he had left only moments before. A surprised Haina welcomed him eagerly. Soon they were caught up in the ancient dance of passion.

Later, a sleek and very satisfied Chance withdrew and rolled off Haina. He clutched her to him, and they both fell asleep.

Much later, Chance awoke. The glade had darkened, the spring air was chill. He nudged the slumbering woman in his arms. "Wake up," he whispered. "Wake up *Chummuss*."

He stared into the beautiful, drowsy brown eyes that Haina tried to focus on him. "Wake up, *Chummuss*. It is late. We must leave here." Soon the night spirits would be walking through the forest and Chance, brave man though he was, had no wish to encounter them.

Then he grinned and ran a large gentle finger down Haina's cheek. His finger continued its leisurely pace down the length of her slim body until it came to a small, dark birthmark at the top of one shapely thigh. Circling the mole slowly, he reached around suddenly and gave her firm buttocks a squeeze. "Are you always this difficult to awaken? Or only after making love?"

Haina blushed. His chuckle at her discomfiture was maddening, but then she found herself grinning along with him.

They got dressed in companionable silence. Haina slipped the barely wrinkled kutsack over her head. She fumbled with the tie at the waist because she was surreptitiously watching her lover casually drape the black bearskin over his broad shoulders.

They started along the darkened trail that led back to the village. As Haina followed hastily along behind her protector, one nagging thought threatened to destroy the peaceful lethargy of her body in the wake of

Chance's lovemaking. What, she wondered, what will happen to me now?

Chapter 8

Haina followed Chance through his aunt's long-house. He marched over to the palette where Haina had spent the previous night. Wrapping his arms around her, he pulled her closer. "Get your things," he murmured into her dark hair. "I want you to come with me."

Haina pulled away to look at him. "What things?" she asked with an amused gleam in her eye. She plucked the front of her kutsack with both hands. "This is all I have. You should know that."

"What about that red and white dress I saw you in yesterday?"

"Oh. That."

"Mmm-hmm. That." He pulled her back to nuzzle the top of her head. Her hair smelled so fragrant, so womanly.

"That was a dress your aunt kindly lent me until my own kutsack was, um, dry." She pushed away a little and looked up into his eyes. She could not keep the laughter out of her voice as she remembered the awkward picture he had presented, stomping wet and dripping out of the water yesterday. Had it only been yesterday? So much had happened since then, she mused.

"She did not give it to you? Never mind, I will see that you have other clothes. . . ."

"I have no need of your clothes, Kyuquot." The haughty chief's daughter was back.

"Very well. Easier for me," he replied, his eyes laughing as he pulled her close again. "I do not know where in this village I would find you the kind of clothes you deserve."

There was a wistful note in his voice that was not lost on Haina. Mayhaps he did care for her. Mayhaps he would learn to care for her. She touched his chest gently. "Chance," she murmured. "It is all right. I do not need fine clothes. I am happy with you." He looked at her in astonishment. She blushed at his searching gaze. Had she revealed too much too soon? "That is, I —I am satisfied with my own kutsack." She sought to change the subject. "Perhaps your aunt will let me weave another dress?"

"Hmm? Oh, yes, yes, of course. I am sure she will not mind if you wish to make your own clothes." He stared at her thoughtfully a moment then released her. "This way," he said briskly.

He led her to the highest status corner of the longhouse. "These will be your new quarters," he announced.

She started in surprise. "Here? But—but this is where a chief should live."

"I live here."

"But—but you are just a commoner. Why does your aunt let you live here?"

His sardonic gaze swept her. "Still the mighty chief's daughter, Haina? Did you think I lived with the slaves? My, my. How difficult it must have been for you to make love with *me*, a mere commoner." He lifted her chin. "Well, get used to it, *Chummuss*. You will be staying with *me* while we are here. You, a chief's daughter, will be warming *my* bed—the bed of a mere commoner," he sneered. The look he gave her was contemptuous and knowing. "Excuse me, I have work to do." He turned on his heel and left.

What had gone wrong? Haina asked herself. She had not meant to insult him. It was true there was a status difference between them, but she would overlook that, for his sake. Did he not know how she felt about him? And he had been so insulting about the wonderful lovemaking they had shared. She looked sadly around her new living area. She must remember how sensitive he was about the difference in their families, Haina decided. It would not do to keep reminding him of that, if she wished to make him love her. Love? Was that what she really wanted? For Chance to love her? Yes, whispered a small, honest voice in her heart. She wanted Chance to love her as much as she loved him.

Chance stepped out of the longhouse into the cold night air. Damn the woman! Her snobbish games were beginning to grate on him. Who did she think she was? Who did she think *he* was?

At first, it had amused him to let her believe he was a commoner, but she needled him about his status at every opportunity. Such overconcern with status did not bode well, Chance thought. It tended to make one slight the very real, very hard work done by slaves and commoners. If it were not for their labor, his Nootkan society would cease to exist and Chance was wise enough to realize that. It irritated him that others, like Haina, could not see this.

Why, the people she so looked down upon were the very ones responsible for the food she ate, and the clothes she wore and the canoes she rode in. And, what did she think those people were? Dirt beneath her dainty feet? He had had to leave before he felt the urge to shake her.

Chance strode around the village for awhile until he calmed down. Seeing the decrepit buildings turned his mind to planning further repairs for the village.

Still, the memory of Haina's warm body sidled into his thoughts. That was really why he was angry, he realized. He had been more affected by their lovemaking than he had wanted to believe. She was beautiful and he wanted to have her over and over again.

He halted in his pacing when he realized he was loathe to ransom the wench. Making love to her had merely whetted his appetite for her.

This must stop! he chided himself. She was merely a captive Ahousat woman, an enemy, not the love of his life. He could play with her, satiate himself with her and then casually let her go. He *must* remember that! She was pretty, yes, and spirited too, but far too haughty for his tastes. She would be easy to forget, he assured himself. His only concerns should be how well she responded to him in bed and how much ransom he could get for her. Clinging to these thoughts, his blood cooled and he turned his steps back to the longhouse.

The fire had gone out in the hearth, so Haina decided to light it. There was a small stack of wood next to the firepit, and some moss. She searched around for matches—her family always used matches to light their hearthfires—but could find nothing to light the moss and thin slivers of wood. By now Chance's quarters were dark. The sun had set some time ago and no lamps were lit in his area, either.

"Where can those matches be?" she muttered to herself as she fumbled through baskets and boxes in the dark, trying to feel for a package of the kind of matches the traders sold. Nothing. "Ouch." All she got for her trouble was a sore finger. She sucked at the small, stinging cut. There must be knives in that box, she decided.

"Going through my possessions already?" came a jeering drawl. "I had heard that Ahousat nobles liked to steal."

Haina bristled at Chance's taunting voice. Oh, why was he being so hateful? "No, Ahousat nobles do not like to steal," she snapped. "But neither do they like to sit and grow cold in the darkness when they might light a fire to keep warm and some lamps to see by. Where are your matches?"

"Matches? We do not have any." He nodded negligently toward the neighboring living area. "Go to that firepit and get a light."

Haina stomped off to do as she was bid and returned shortly bearing a small burning cedar stick. Kneeling in front of the firepit, she studiously ignored the watching man, and concentrated on lighting the slivers of kindling and moss. There! The flames caught and soon she had a warm fire burning.

Next, she went to the lamps. They were the old-fashioned kind: large, oil-filled clamshells with a twist of fiber for a wick. Back home, her family used candles they had bartered from the white traders and for special occasions her mother brought out their one precious kerosene lamp. In Chicklesit there were only clamshell lamps—how primitive! But Haina did not voice her thoughts aloud.

"I am hungry. Get me some food, woman."

"Get your own food, Kyuquot." The nerve of the man! After making love to her, he now treated her like a —a slave!

Suddenly her arms were caught in a tight grip and she was swung around to face an angry Chance. His words came out in a low, arrogant warning. "Do not push me too far, little cougar. You will not like the results."

"You push *me* too far, Kyuquot," she snarled. She fought back the tears she could feel pooling in her eyes. She shook his hands free and ran to where she knew the aunt's new quarters were. Perhaps Salal Woman would help her.

Chance watched her go. A shadow of regret stole across his face so fast it might not have existed.

There was a rustling sound and Chance turned to observe a stout, middle-aged woman boldly entering his quarters. By the look of her unadorned, red cedar kutsack, she was a commoner. "Who are you?" he asked wearily.

"Bitter Cherry," she answered. "Mistress Salal Woman sent me to look after your needs."

"Get me some food then." She started to move away. "Wait," he said. "Why did you let the fire go out? Why did you not light the lamps? I do not like to return to a cold, dark house."

"Yes, noble sir," she began hesitantly. "It will not happen again. Only—"

"Only what?"

"It is my daughter, sir. She—she is in childbirth. I have been with her all day." The woman was wringing her hands and Chance narrowed his eyes.

"Prepare my meal," he said, his voice softer. Childbirth could be dangerous, he knew. The woman hurried over to where the dried fish hung and then bustled about getting the food. "Once you are done here, Bitter Cherry, you may return to your daughter," he said gruffly.

"Oh, thank you, sir," she answered, her tense face relaxing with relief. She had not expected kindness from a visiting tyee.

Haina walked calmly into the living area. As calmly, that is, as her shaking knees would let her. Mistress Salal Woman had proven to be no sanctuary for the distraught girl and had waved her away.

Deciding it was easier to face Chance than to wander aimlessly through the longhouse at the time of the evening meal, Haina had returned. Chance said nothing, merely ate the meal the older woman served him. Without even a glance at Haina, he left the longhouse.

Haina stood staring after him. What was the matter with the man? Why was he treating her like an old cedar mat? A slight cough from the other woman interrupted her reverie. "Yes?" Haina inquired politely.

"Would you be having some supper, mistress?"

"Yes, please."

Haina sat down to the meal the woman had prepared. "Mmm, cinquefoil, my favorite vegetable." Haina happily munched on the slim roots, steamed and then cooled by the conscientious Bitter Cherry.

The older woman smiled. "It is one of my favorites, too." She held out a platter of split, dried salmon.

Haina took two pieces, thanked the woman, and then inquired politely as to her name.

When told, Haina asked, "Bitter Cherry, did I hear you say your daughter was giving birth?"

"Yes, mistress."

"How long has she been laboring?"

"The pains started after midday."

Haina nodded. Then realizing she was keeping Bitter Cherry from being with her daughter, she said, "Go, go. Your daughter needs you."

With a grim smile the woman hurried away.

Intending to lie down for a short while after the evening meal, Haina sought out her new sleeping chamber, the one she was to share with Chance. The bed consisted of a wide plank platform wedged into the corner. A carved cedar box that looked to be very old was stationed at the foot. Several furs, in a variety of shades from brown to dark black, were heaped upon the planks and well-woven cedar mats covered the dirt floor in front of the bed. Gingerly lying down on the edge of the bed, she resolved she would but close her eyes for a moment.

It was morning when she woke to find herself curled around Chance's warm body. Mortified, she pulled away, only to have him draw her back. She looked at him, and noticed his eyes were still closed. Was he reaching for her in his sleep?

She relaxed and took the opportunity to study him, though the light was dim. Her eyes roved over his face, centering on his lips. They cracked into a smile and she started. He was awake! "And do you like what you see, *Chummuss*?" he breathed intimately.

She scrambled to her knees. The arrogant oaf had been toying with her. "I have seen better," she snapped. It was not true, of course, but she was not going to encourage him!

He chuckled, not at all offended by her insult. Where had the angry man of last night gone? she wondered, bewildered. "I—I must get dressed."

"You already are."

She looked down at her kutsack in chagrin. "Ooooh," and she flounced off the bed. Glancing over her shoulder at his magnificent naked body, she sniped, "*You* should get dressed, too."

"Why? You liked me this way yesterday, at the waterfall."

"Did I? I was merely amusing myself with you." The boldness of her words surprised Haina. Then she thought, let him think he means nothing to me.

Haina's words struck too close to home. That was how he was supposed to feel about her. Chance growled and rose from the tousled fur bed. He was no longer feeling so amiable.

"Get my breakfast," he said curtly. Haina sighed. Chance was back to his angry frame of mind. She did not answer, unwilling to provoke him further.

She combed her fingers through her long, thick hair and tied it back with a cedar strip. Chance watched her, unable to keep the hungry look out of his eyes, but Haina ignored him and walked over to the fire that had been allowed to go out in the night.

"Where is that woman?" asked Chance irritably.

"Bitter Cherry? I assume she is with her daughter," answered Haina calmly.

Chance's grunt was not encouraging, so Haina left for the neighbors' hearth and another borrowed light. When she returned, Chance was nowhere to be seen, so Haina bent over the fire pit and devoted herself to starting the fire. Soon flames were licking at the crackling wood. The welcome warmth took the chill off the morning air.

She heated some rocks in the fire, and found an old, bent-cedar box to heat water in. Did these people not even own one iron pot? she wondered. Here she had to do things the old-fashioned way: heating the rocks then plunking them into the water-filled box.

She steamed some left-over cinquefoil roots for breakfast and found a seal bladder half-filled with oil. Fish or whale oil was served with every meal as a tasty accompaniment to fish and vegetables. Haina sniffed the bladder and made a face. The fish oil was rancid.

"Planning on giving that to me?" asked Chance, seeing the disgusted look on her face.

"Why, yes," she smiled sweetly as she prepared a platter of cold smoked salmon and the now cooled roots. "I heated water for tea."

"Tea? Where do you think you are? Ahousat?"

"My family always has tea in the morning," she explained. "We get it from the traders."

"And pay dearly for it, no doubt," he sneered. "Forget it. You are a hostage now." Seeing her lips tighten, he relented. "Besides, Yuquot is too far away. Nobody from here travels that far, not even for tea."

"Nor for iron pots, nor matches, nor candles . . ." added Haina, grimacing.

"None of those are necessities."

"Tea is," muttered Haina. She had come to like the aromatic brew and especially enjoyed it with sugar in it. Sugar. That was something else she would have to do without while she was in this forsaken place.

"My people do not need such trinkets from the white man. The Ahousats are getting soft to want such things."

Haina gasped at his taunt. "The Ahousat people are not soft," she warned. "They are the most powerful tribe on the west coast and soon even you, ignorant Kyuquot, will realize that."

Her words stung. While his status was equal to hers, the wealth of his family was not and her words rankled his pride. "Threats, fair Ahousat? Your father cannot even find you. That does not speak of a powerful man or tribe. Please do not scare me so."

"Oooh, you conceited sea slug! Even now my father is searching for you and when he finds you. . . ."

"I know, I know. He will cut out my heart and feed it in little pieces to the sharks." He yawned. "Is my breakfast ready yet?"

Haina practically threw the platter at his head. "Here!"

Chance chuckled and sat down to enjoy his breakfast, happy to have bested the haughty wench.

"By the way," she sidled up to him, a sweet smile on her face once more. "I forgot to give you this."

And she threw a cupful of the rancid fish oil right in his face. Then she burst out laughing.

Haina was laughing too hard to be able to run from the dripping man.

Chance sat there in shock, oil dripping off the end of his nose. "You, you—!" Words failed him at this important moment. Instead, he lunged to his feet, reaching blindly for her but she evaded his hands.

She did not run far, however. She was too weak from laughing.

Nearby neighbors were looking over at the pair to see what was so funny. They quickly shifted their curious gazes away when they saw their tyee with oil dripping down his visage. No one wished to cause the proud tyee to lose face.

Haina had no such care. By now she was doubled over with laughter and Chance easily caught her. "You think this is funny?" he roared in an awful voice.

Haina, still doubled over and holding her aching stomach, nodded weakly. With eyes shut tightly, she did not see Chance's next move until it was too late. But she felt it—wet, cold, smelly fish oil oozing over the back of her head and all through her hair. "Chance!" she screamed and struggled to get away.

"Aaah, no, *Chummuss*. Not so fast. Stay and enjoy the bath I have prepared for *you*."

"Let me go," she was wriggling frantically. The horrid oil was now running down the neck of her kutsack, and all the way down her back. "Let me go!"

By now, the watching spectators were agog with the doings of the new tyee. Chance glanced up at the gaping audience and casually waved the seal skin at them. He then went back to pouring what was left over the struggling Haina.

"You smell terrible, Ahousat woman. Do all Ahousats smell like rotting oil?" he asked innocently.

"You—you—" sputtered the sodden Haina. She stood there, frozen, with the cold, stinking oil covering her hair, her neck, her chest, her back. Her kutsack was soaked through with the stuff.

When Chance had poured the last drop over her, he let her go and Haina dashed out of the longhouse. Chance guessed where she was headed and called to

Bitter Cherry. That woman was doing her best to keep a straight face in front of the tyee, but his sharp eyes noted that she paused once or twice to wipe at her eyes, and when she answered him, her voice choked.

"What ails you, woman?"

"Nothing, Tyee, nothing," gasped the woman. "It is just that I have never seen such a funny sight." And she could no longer hide her mirth as she burst into loud guffaws.

Chance waited patiently until she had finished laughing, then he handed her a clean cedar mat. "Take this to the waterfall. She will need it." The woman turned away to do his bidding. "Oh, and take that red trade dress with you. She will surely need that, too."

"Yes, sir." Bitter Cherry hurried off to catch up with Haina.

"No need to search for her," he called after the woman. "Just follow the smell."

He turned to his waiting audience and dismissed them with a wave of his hand. "Back to your breakfasts," he ordered sternly. He must not let them think he was too easy a tyee. "The woman has been punished enough for her gross violation of my dignity."

Murmurs of agreement reached Chance's ears as the people drifted away. There would be no need to give a feast and gifts to all the witnesses to save his face, after all.

He settled back to eat the fish, ignoring oozing oil spreading over his face. Yes, he thought smugly, he had taught the Ahousat wench a good lesson: Never cross Chance Gift from the Sea. She would only lose.

Chapter 9

Haina bent over the green pool, scrubbing madly at her hair. Oh, she moaned, would she ever get that smelly stuff out? If only she had the hair wash her mother always made . . .

The pounding of the waterfall kept her from hearing the approach of another person. It was only when she looked up from her odorous task that she saw the bare feet standing beside her. "Who?" she started. She raised her eyes. "Oh, it is you, Bitter Cherry. You scared me."

"Forgive me, mistress." She held out the dry cedar mat. "It is for you to dry yourself."

"Thank you." Haina gratefully took the mat. The fine weave cloth had soft thistle down interwoven throughout to make it fluffy. Haina vigorously toweled her hair, but she could still smell the rancid oil. "Damn! This stuff will not come out."

Bitter Cherry squatted down on the green moss beside the pool and watched her. "I could make a hair wash for you," she suggested.

"How kind of you to offer. But no, I will make my own. My mother always made hers and I think I remember how to do it."

The older woman shrugged and stood up. Haina was reluctant to let her go. She felt the need of a sympathetic presence after what she had just been through. "Has your daughter delivered her baby?"

"No." The older woman's face suddenly looked drawn. "I must go to her. I have been away too long."

"Of course. How selfish of me to keep you. Please go." Haina watched the woman's retreating shape. "Let me know if there is anything I can do to help," she called after her, but Bitter Cherry did not turn around. The pounding noise of the waterfall had drowned out her words.

Haina stripped off her oily kutsack and tossed it near the cedar mat. She noticed the red and white flowered trade dress she had worn yesterday. How thoughtful Bitter Cherry was to bring it. Not like some people she could name!

Haina stepped gingerly into the cool water. Bitter Cherry's daughter was in a fight for her life while Haina only had to worry about how to get rid of the awful smell on her body and in her hair.

Haina glanced up at the weak sun filtering through the trees. Almost mid-day. The daughter had been in labor for almost a full day. That did not bode well for the birth, Haina thought grimly.

She waded slowly out into the cleansing water, stopping often to scrub herself with some of the fine sand lining the bottom of the pool. Her skin reddened from the vigorous scouring she gave herself and she was relieved to note that most of the rancid oil smell was coming off her skin. If only she could get it out of her hair . . .

As she scrubbed, she thought back to how her mother would make a hair wash. Sarita picked some kind of plant and would make a tea of it and let that cool. Sometimes she added buds or something to make it smell nice. Yes, that was it. Haina knew she would recognize the plants her mother used. Hopefully they grew in Chicklesit territory . . . .

Wait. Did her mother not have a childbirth recipe as well? Dimly, it came to Haina that her mother had often been called to the bedside of laboring women. Now, what was the plant she used?

Still musing, Haina absently dried herself off, slipped the colorful trade dress over her head and set off to wander the trail, looking intently for the plants her mother had collected.

Sometime later Haina returned to the longhouse. Her scratched arms were loaded with branches and leaves and the roots of various plants.

Chance had obviously been watching for her because he appeared behind her moments after she entered. He sniffed the air and did not have to feign the comical look that came over his face when he smelled her hair. "What is that terrible smell?" He sniffed again and pretended to choke. "There must be an Ahousat wench nearby."

Haina turned to glare at him. "I am surprised you seek to blame others, Kyuquot. That terrible smell is from your own hair and skin." She deposited her armload of foliage beside the fire and looked about for the bent-cedar box to heat water in.

"What a good idea!" exclaimed Chance. Haina looked at him questioningly. She followed his gaze to the plants.

"What is a good idea?"

"I presume you brought these plants to air out my quarters. It was beginning to smell fishy in here."

"You presume too much, Kyuquot. Have you not better things to do than harass poor Ahousat captives? You could be building more longhouses or repairing canoes or catching fish." She looked at him blandly. "We *do* need fish oil."

Chance snorted. "Bah, woman. Your jokes are as stale as the oil you threw at me."

"As are yours."

Chance stomped out of the longhouse. Why had he bothered to talk to her at all? Why had he bothered to bait her? He ignored the small voice that answered, Because you just cannot keep away from her. His men needed his help. To hell with contrary Ahousat cougars.

Haina industriously set to work, heating water and peeling leaves off branches. She hummed softly as she worked, content for the first time since her capture.

If the hairwash turned out well, she might, just might, be brave enough to make the childbirth potion. It was supposed to make the child come quickly. Her mother had sworn by it, she remembered now.

But first she would make the hair wash. When the water was hot, Haina poured some of it over the hairy stem and leaves of the common bedstraw plant. She let the tea soak in a small, watertight cedar box until it had cooled. Yes, it smelled just like her mother's recipe, she thought, taking a deep breath of the sweet scent emanating from the infusion. She would go to the waterfall pool and use this aromatic hairwash. Anything to get rid of the rancid fish smell.

Now for the childbirth potion. Haina took a deep breath. She held up the thin, flexible pieces of water parsley she had managed to find near the pool. The skinny root was the valuable part. She soon pounded the few onion-like roots she had found into an unrecognizable, pungent-smelling mass. She could offer it to Bitter Cherry for her daughter.

Taking a small cup of water and the mashed Water Parsley root, Haina headed for the birthing hut. She wended her way along a narrow trail to a quiet, rather dark part of the forest. There Bitter Cherry and her attending women had constructed the birthing hut. Made of brush and cedar mats, it was large enough to hold several women. A small fire burned in the hut to keep the occupants warm.

Arriving at the small dwelling, Haina tensed as she heard the muffled cries of the laboring woman. Looking inside, she saw Bitter Cherry holding the straining woman's hand and wiping the sweat from her forehead with some soft moss. Bitter Cherry leaned over and murmured encouragingly to the younger woman who now lay limp and exhausted between contractions.

"How is your daughter doing?" asked Haina.

Several women looked up. Bitter Cherry eyed Haina speculatively. "Hummingbird Plume still labors," she said brusquely. "What do you want?" Bitter Cherry dispensed with politeness on her own territory, Haina noted.

Two or three of the attending women shifted uneasily as they watched Haina. Haina could understand their uneasiness. These women did not know her, she did not know them. They could only suspect she was satisfying idle curiosity and nothing more.

The laboring woman froze again as another contraction seized her distended abdomen. A harsh cry escaped her lips and the women bent over her solicitously, murmuring family chants and prayers.

"The babe does not want to come," moaned the mother. She was a young woman, her brown face tightly grimacing during contractions, unlined when relaxed. Her hair hung in lifeless black strands. Her lips were dry and cracked and her forehead was beaded with sweat. She sat on a cedar mat on the floor, propped up by her mother. Piles of shredded cedar bark and soft cedar mats lay scattered about, ready for the baby's arrival.

"Hush," murmured Bitter Cherry. "He will come. He is only taking his time being born. You, yourself, took a long time to come into the world, as I recall." She chuckled to lighten her words, but no one in the hut responded. They were all too worried.

Haina watched the young woman tensing and gasping through the next several contractions. The other women appeared to have forgotten her presence until she asked, "Is the babe in the correct position?" She remembered Sarita, her mother, had sometimes checked for this.

Several heads nodded absently. Then the women, in unison, held their breaths as another tremor shook the young woman's straining frame.

But no baby's crown appeared. Haina grew tired of squatting on her heels near the door. She stood up and stretched, looking around for the father. Usually the anxious husband hovered nearby or looked in often on the laboring wife, especially in a first birth. No husband. Where was he? Haina wondered angrily. Had he no care for the agony he was putting this good woman through?

A fresh breeze wafted across Haina, blowing her loose hair back from her face. Behind her, the woman's muffled scream tore through the air.

No longer able to listen to or watch the mother's pain, Haina approached Bitter Cherry. "Please," she said urgently, taking the mashed roots out of her pocket. She held up the cup of water. "Will you not try this root? My mother uses it in childbirth and gives it to others. It shortens their labor."

Bitter Cherry looked at her, her eyes carefully screening her thoughts. "Why do you do this, Ahousat woman? We all know you have no love of the Chicklesits, or the Kyuquots for that matter."

Bitter Cherry's blunt words took Haina aback. "Why—why—your daughter is in pain. I only want to

110

help."

Bitter Cherry eyed her warily. "I wanted to call the *shaman,* but we have nothing to pay him with. We have nothing to pay you with, either."

"I ask for nothing," assured Haina. "The recipe is a family one. I share it with you gladly." Seeing Bitter Cherry's disbelief in her eyes, Haina plunged on. "Hummingbird Plume must swallow a little bit of water with the root," Haina said hurriedly, afraid Bitter Cherry would reject the offering. "She must keep it in her stomach. If she throws it up, give her a little bit more. Soon after she takes the root the child will come. In about the time it takes a mother to nurse a babe, the child will come."

Bitter Cherry took the root and nodded shortly. Haina fled, unable to face the doubting looks of the other women, or the suspicion in Bitter Cherry's eyes. Haina was only trying to help!

The hurting cries of the laboring mother followed Haina back to the longhouse. Once inside, Haina sought the privacy of Chance's quarters. She clapped her hands over her ears to block out the cries she could still hear echoing in her brain. Oh, why did women have to suffer so? Would her own babies be so difficult to birth? At the thought, she blanched. Why, she could be pregnant even now. She shook her head. No, no, it must not be. She, Haina, could not go through such torment. She must not be pregnant!

To distract herself from such unwelcome worries, she decided to wash her hair once more. She grabbed a cupful of the hair wash tea she had made. Picking up the soft cedar mat she had used to dry her hair once before, she raced out of the longhouse.

She encountered no one on the trail to the waterfall. Once at the pool again, she looked around the clearing, marveling to herself at the beautiful place where she had become a woman.

111

Haina contented herself with scrubbing her hair mercilessly until her scalp was throbbing. Drying her hair more leisurely, she took the time to sniff. Good, the awful rancid smell was gone. Her hair wash was a success! Surely the childbirth medicine would be, too.

She walked slowly back along the path to the village. It was a beautiful day and the singing birds entertained her as she strolled. She arrived at the village only to be greeted by more cries from the laboring woman. What was the matter?

Haina hurried over to the birthing hut once more. She set down the wooden cup and towel she was carrying and poked her head inside the hut. "Does she still labor?" Haina asked, incredulous that the childbirth potion had not helped.

Several pairs of worried dark eyes met her wide ones. "She still labors," muttered Bitter Cherry. "It is not good."

"I do not understand. That medicine should have worked!"

Bitter Cherry glanced quickly away and Haina's eyes narrowed. "Did you use the medicine I gave you?"

The woman reluctantly shook her head.

"Why not? I am sure it will help her," Haina said indignantly. Then her manner softened. Bitter Cherry looked tired, her straining daughter looked exhausted and the surrounding women worried, indeed.

No one answered. The women merely looked at her and remained silent.

Haina held out her hand to Bitter Cherry. "Please. Give the root to me. I will show you how the medicine should be given."

Taking the cup of water, Haina confidently pulled off a little piece of root and placed it on Hummingbird Plume's tongue. Another contraction came just then and Haina waited patiently, gritting her teeth against the other's obvious pain. When the contraction subsided, Haina held the cup of water to the young woman's lips.

"Please drink, my daughter," encouraged Bitter Cherry wearily. She sounded like she had given up. Haina hoped that Hummingbird Plume had not.

Hummingbird Plume gagged on the strange taste, but she swallowed the stuff. "Good," murmured Haina. "Soon the baby will come."

Her confidence seemed to give new strength to the exhausted girl, who managed a weak smile. "Thank you."

Bitter Cherry regarded Haina thoughtfully, then shrugged. What was done, was done, she seemed to say.

Several more contractions shook the small frame of Hummingbird Plume, and each time her mother held her hand and stroked her forehead lovingly. Haina's heart ached for them both. But it would not be long before the pain would be gone and the babe would be born, she encouraged herself.

And indeed, soon the crown of the baby's head appeared and a joyous yell went up from the waiting women. "It comes! The babe comes!"

Bitter Cherry and one of the older women hastily changed places, the older woman propping up Hummingbird Plume and wiping her forehead. Bitter Cherry positioned herself in front of her sitting daughter, ready to catch the newborn. In a low, calm voice, she encouraged her daughter to push. At the next contraction, Hummingbird Plume pushed hard, sending the baby's head farther out into the world. In three more contractions the baby was born.

"The babe comes!" Haina heard the cry echoing outside the hut and down the trail to the village. People started to gather a short distance away, careful not to violate the mother's privacy. Happy murmurs sang through the crowd of mostly women and children. It suddenly struck Haina that there were few men in this village.

"Where is Hummingbird Plume's husband?" she asked one of the waiting women.

"Dead."

"Oh." Haina could say nothing to that so she contented herself with watching the exhausted woman rally.

The baby was placed on the mother's warm stomach. Hummingbird Plume ran her fingers eagerly over her infant, feeling his soft skin and slack little muscles. Bitter Cherry cooed to the baby, indeed all the women were crooning sweet words to the little one, but Bitter Cherry was also watching the pulsing umbilical cord, a mussel knife in her hand. She would have the honor of cutting the cord.

Haina watched the naked, shivering, crying baby and was humbled at the miracle of birth.

The cord was cut and the baby placed at the exhilarated mother's breast. Tears came to Haina's eyes at the happiness she saw radiating out of that tired face. "My babe," murmured Hummingbird Plume exultantly. "My babe!"

Suddenly Haina knew that she, too, would welcome the pains of birth if she could but hold her own little babe. An intense longing swept over her, one so strong she had to bite her lips to keep from crying out.

All about her, the women were laughing or crying, depending on their temperment. Bitter Cherry was calmly massaging her daughter's stomach to expel the afterbirth.

Hummingbird Plume was still running her hands over her child, examining the little limbs, fingers and toes. "My son," she murmured, "Oh, my son." She inspected his ears, his genitals, his whole body. He was healthy, not deformed in any way. Tears of happiness ran down her cheeks and she murmured a prayer of thanks to the Spirit-Over-All, Naas. "Oh, my beautiful babe," she murmured over and over.

Bitter Cherry caught the afterbirth in a cedar mat and placed it carefully outside the door of the hut. There it would stay for four days and then be ceremonially disposed of. She turned to Haina and clasped the young woman's hands between her own wrinkled ones. "Thank you, thank you so much. You saved my daughter's life and the life of my grandson. I can never pay you enough."

"No payment is necessary," soothed Haina. She smiled and gave the tired old hands holding hers a squeeze. Bitter Cherry smiled too, the guarded look gone from her face.

"What goes on here?" came Chance's drawl. "Is the baby born?"

"*Hoowhay,* yes," answered a chorus of happy voices. "The baby is born, at last! A healthy boy!" The whole village seemed to be hovering about the birthing hut. Chance pushed his way through the waiting crowd.

"I am happy for you, Bitter Cherry. And you, new mother." He bowed to the glowing women, then turned to Haina. "What are you doing here?"

"She helped us," explained Bitter Cherry before Haina could say anything. "She gave Hummingbird Plume some medicine that brought the baby." She smiled at Haina. "We are very grateful to her."

"I see," said Chance. "Would you come with me, please, Haina?"

His formal use of her name unnerved Haina for a moment, but she stepped to one side with him, curious as to what he would say.

"And just how did you know what you were doing? You are hardly old enough to be a midwife or to know about birthing babies." His knowing eyes ran up and down her slim frame and Haina felt her face grow hot.

"I will have you know that my mother has assisted at many birthings. I simply used a plant that I have seen her use before." She smiled mockingly at Chance. Let him answer that!

"Oh, she taught you about what plants she used?" His voice was cautious.

"Not completely," Haina felt obliged to explain. "I picked some plants for a hair wash and then I searched for the plant that looked like what my mother always used for women in labor. And I found it," she said triumphantly.

"I see. You mean you guessed you had the correct plant?"

"Well, yes. But I was fairly certain. And the hair wash turned out so well, I was sure the other—"

"Enough, Ahousat!" roared Chance. "Do you realize how much you endangered that woman's life? And the life of her son?" His eyes were flashing angry sparks. "Do you have any idea of the risk you took? What if she had died? What if it was the wrong plant?"

"But the hair wash—"

"Damn the hair wash! You took a terrible chance, risking their lives and your own, you fool."

"My—my own?"

"What do you think would have happened if Hummingbird Plume had died?" His voice was low and harsh. "Have you any idea what would have happened to you?"

Haina hesitated, considering the prospect for the first time. "Well, I suppose they would have been angry . . . ."

"Angry!" He snorted. "Furious is what they would have been. And I would have been, too."

He grabbed her arms. "You little fool," he gritted through clenched teeth. "The village people would have demanded your death."

Haina looked at him, shocked.

116

"And I would have been forced to go along with them." Chance's look was bleak. She did not stop to ask him why the thought of her death would upset him so, but a vague feeling of happiness crept over her. She reached up and stroked his cheek gently.

"But everything turned out fine," she reminded him.

"Do not ever, ever," emphasized Chance through his clenched teeth, "*ever* give out medicinal herbs again. It is too risky. Let the shaman, or the old women do that."

Seeking only to soothe him, she caressed his cheek again. "Very well, Chance Gift from the Sea," she said meekly, that warm feeling still with her. "Very well."

Chapter 10

"Move that plank," ordered Chance.

"Move it yourself!"

Chance dropped the rock he had been lifting and slowly straightened. He eyed the defiant young man curiously. Chance wiped a hand across his sweating brow while he pondered on how to deal with the youth. "It's hot work," he murmured conversationally. "But then patching up longhouses usually is." He wiped his hands across his chest and took off the heavy bearskin. Summer would be here soon, he thought absently. Tossing the robe to one side, he asked casually, "What's your name?"

The youth merely glared at Chance.

Taken aback at the young man's obvious hostility, Chance looked more critically at him. Barely out of boyhood, he judged. Chance wondered what he had done to set the youth so against him, then shrugged and looked around. Work had stopped and his men were eyeing the youth. "Get back to work," ordered Chance. Reluctantly, the warriors went back to their carpentry tasks and Chance signalled the young man to one side, out of hearing of the others.

With a careless shrug, the young man sauntered slowly over.

"Have you got a complaint?" asked Chance.

"No complaint," sneered the youth but he was still glaring. "Surely you know you are not welcome here."

"Oh? And why is that?"

"What makes you think you can come to this village and take over?" snarled the youth and Chance was surprised at the vehemency in his voice.

Chance looked assessingly at the younger man. "Tell me what this is all about," he said.

"It is as I said," answered the younger man, his mouth a tight line and his eyes a hard black. "Who are you to arrive at Chicklesit and start giving orders?"

"I am the tyee of this village."

The youth gave a loud snort. "You don't care about this village and your chieftainship or you would have returned a long time ago." The young man turned to the longhouses and his arm swept through the air as if presenting Chance with the scene. "Look at it. This pitiful village is barely surviving. Where were you when your people needed you?"

Chance winced at the question that came so close to his own thoughts. Where, indeed, had he been? Staying at the cozy village of Kyuquot, eating the fish his brother fed him and sleeping in the warm, well-built longhouse his brother housed him in.

And all the while his mother's people had been going hungry and cold. His mother's people, the very ones who had taken him in and fed him and clothed him and yes, loved him when he was a helpless babe, those people he had left to flounder as best they could. They needed him, he knew that now, had always known it in a small corner of his mind. Guilt made his voice harsh as he answered, "Why are you so con-

119

cerned stripling?"

" 'Stripling' am I?" snarled the youth. "Stripling I may be, but I can see with my own eyes and speak the truth with my own tongue. You have neglected this village for too long. Go back to Kyuquot. Leave us here, to fend for ourselves as we have done."

"And poorly," Chance could not resist the taunt.

The young man's eyes were hard and contemptuous. "At least we stayed with our families, and fished for them, and hunted for them as best we could. We didn't desert our women and children when they were in need."

Chance was beginning to grow angry. "I did not desert you."

"No? What do you call it?" sneered the young man. "The old people kept saying, 'Wait, wait, our tyee will return. Ocean Wave's son will not forget us.'" He spat on the ground. "Well, I, for one, got tired of waiting for the great tyee to return."

Chance hesitated. Should he defend himself from this young pup's ridiculous assertions or should he put him in his place? Opting for the latter, he said, "I still do not know whom I have the pleasure of addressing."

The youth stood straighter, his chest puffing out. "Whale Hunter is my name."

"An honored name," said Chance through narrowed eyes. "You are too young for such a noble name."

"Young I may be," snarled the youth, "but my heart is strong and my mettle has been sorely tested. It is I," his thumb struck his chest sharply, "who have kept this village alive. It is I who have organized the men—the few there are—to go hunting, to go fishing. It is I who Salal Woman has relied upon to keep her people fed."

Chance stared at the man in astonishment. He had wondered how the old woman had managed. It made sense that she'd had someone like this youth to help her. "But you are so young . . . ."

"Twenty summers," boasted the youth. "I am a man."

"Yes, I can see that," acknowledged Chance. New respect was in his voice as he asked, "But I have been gone that same length of time. How did the people manage—?"

"My father," interrupted the youth proudly. "My father was the tyee of this village, in fact if not in name," he added bitterly.

Understanding began to dawn. "Your father died?"

"Drowned on a seal hunting expedition."

Chance nodded. "And you took over running the village."

"*Hoowhay*, yes. For two years these Chicklesit people have looked to me, Whale Hunter, for their meat. And now you come. You, who will leave them as soon as you can to return to your soft nest at Kyuquot." Whale Hunter spat at Chance's feet. "You had better leave soon, Kyuquot—while you are still alive." And with that, the young man turned on his heel and stomped away.

Chance stared after him. A slow grin curled his lips. The pup had courage, he thought. And deep feeling for his people. A man like that would prove a valuable ally. Chance continued to stare thoughtfully at Whale Hunter's retreating back.

Haina wiped her brow as she bent and added more alder wood to the fire. Thick smoke belched up from the small flames. A stilt-like, cedar fish rack was fashioned over the fire and held the split pink carcasses of several fat salmon. It was Haina's job to smoke the fish to preserve the flesh for winter. Other women, commoners and slaves, worked at similar smudge fires nearby. The salmon catch had been plentiful.

Haina backed away from the fire. She was new at this task. Her eyes were stinging, her nose and lungs filled with smoke. She bent over, coughing heavily to force the aromatic smoke out of her lungs. She looked up, eyes watering, and there stood Chance. He *would* pick such a time to seek her out. To save herself embarrassment, she tried to stop the coughs but that only made her body heave and her eyes water all the more. Wretchedly she gave in to her body and coughed until she could cough no more. Holding her chest, she croaked at him, "What do you want?"

"I brought some more salmon for you to smoke. You do it so well." His innocent look and light tone did not fool her. He was laughing at her and she hated it.

She took the basket he held and swung away from him. Presenting her back to him did not deter the man. He stepped behind her and wrapped his arms around her waist. He swept the hair from the back of her neck and placed his lips on the sensitive skin there. His small kisses covered her neck until she tried to shrug him away. "Please," she hissed. "People might see!"

Her argument carried little weight with him, he merely kept on kissing her. "Chance," she murmured, irritated. "Stop that."

"It's been so long since I've held you."

"It was only this morning," she whispered angrily.

"That's what I said, so long," he murmured. "Come away with me. Now."

"I can't," she said in exasperation. "I'm busy smoking fish."

"Forget the fish."

"Salal Woman set me this task and I'm determined to do it right. Besides, it's daylight."

Chance lifted his head from her delectable skin and looked avidly about. "So it is," he agreed, then he went back to nibbling her neck.

"Chance," she scolded, pushing at him with an uplifted shoulder. "Don't do that with everyone staring at us."

He did not lift his head. "Is everyone staring?"

She glanced hesitantly around. "Yes," she sighed. "They are."

"Then come with me to the longhouse. There's more privacy there."

"For what? So everyone will know for certain what we do?"

"Come with me, Haina."

"No."

He stepped back then and a flash of anger crossed his handsome face. "Ahousat bitch," he said and walked away.

Haina stared at him in surprise as she watched him go. Once more her eyes filled with hot tears, but not from smoke. She wanted to call him back, to ask what she'd done to offend him, but she had pride, too. She heard some snickers from the women nearby and her back stiffened. Let him be like that. She didn't care!

Chance was muttering to himself as he walked away from Haina. "Damn her! I must be bewitched by her. I can't stop thinking of her, watching her. . . . She's only a Hesquiat. An enemy! She's here to see to my needs. 'Stop that, Chance'," he mimicked. "'Go away, Chance'." He kicked angrily at a piece of kelp on the beach. "Who does she think she is? It is not her place to say 'no.' She's mine, to do with as I will."

A part of him thought he was being foolish in his anger. He had work to do, it was not time to be stealing off to a longhouse and making love. But, damn it, he wanted her. She was his, and she should come to him when he wanted her. And it wasn't as if she would always be there for him. They only had a short time together, just until he returned her to her family for ransom. The thought of her leaving sent a pang through him. He *had* to stop feeling anything for her. She was only a hostage, a tool for his family's revenge. Nothing more.

Beachdog, following at his heels, interrupted Chance's thoughts as he stalked the beach. "Chance, did you still want that stage built in the large longhouse? The performers need somewhere—"

"*Hoowhay*. Go and do it!" Chance whirled on the unfortunate man and barked, "Do I have to do all your thinking for you?"

Beachdog stopped and backed away, looking uncertainly at Chance. "Nevermind, I'll talk to you later," he said gruffly and started back up the beach to the longhouses.

A wave of self-disgust passed over Chance. The woman was getting to him. Now he was shouting at his own men when they but asked a harmless question. He shook his dark blond head slowly. Better to leave her alone for awhile until he could think clearly. Yes, he resolved. That would be best. He would stay away from Haina until he could treat her like the hostage she was, not the lover he wanted her to be.

Haina sauntered down to the beach. Dusk was one of her favorite times of the day. As the sun slowly crept down to meet the sea, it threw out pinks and purples to paint the clouds. The vastness of the evening sky never failed to awe Haina. For a short time, the world was just Haina and sky—the few trees, pitiful houses, and small mountains faded into insignificance.

A feeling of contentment stole over her. She sank down onto a sandy patch of beach and stared out to sea. She let herself relax for the first time in days.

Ever since she had refused to sneak away with him in the middle of the day, Chance had been too busy to even speak to Haina. He would arise early in the morning, leave the longhouse without partaking of breakfast and only return late in the night. His actions were inexplicable because for all his attempts to ignore her, she still caught him watching her when she'd turn her head quickly in his direction. Just as swiftly he'd look away. Yet when he came to her bed, late at night after the families in his longhouse had retired, he certainly did not ignore her. Quite the contrary. He made sweet love to her all night long. Then the next morning he dragged his body from their bed and kept himself so busy that she saw little of him through the rest of the day.

Haina shook her head, unable to fathom Chance's peculiar behavior. She tried to explain his actions to herself as those of a busy man, but she could no longer hide from the truth.

She picked up a small stick and drew idly in the sand. He only wanted her body. It was as simple as that. But he didn't want *her*, Haina, the woman she was, the hopes and thoughts and feelings that were the essence of her. It was true he took his time with her. He was a skillful lover and he made her cry out for his caresses, but when he was done and she'd given him her heart and soul along with her body, he'd merely roll over and go to sleep. She'd lay there, bereft, as she watched the even rise and fall of his chest through her tears.

But at least she had that much, she thought sadly. At least she was with him, though he did not love her as she loved him. Where is your pride? A part of her asked. Gone, she answered, blown away on the wind.

Gently wiping away a tear from her eye, Haina glanced seaward, striving again for the calm she had felt only moments before.

Suddenly she was on her feet and running toward the longhouse. "Chance! Chance!" Her voice carried the panic racing through her. Before she could reach the longhouse, he was there. Right behind him were several men, some of them grasping weapons. She ran into his arms. "Chance, oh, Chance!"

"What is it, little cougar?" It seemed eons since she'd heard tenderness in his voice. "What alarms you?"

"Chance! Look!"

She pointed out to sea. "Lights," he exclaimed. "What is it? A ship!"

Haina could only stare breathlessly at this, her first sight of a white man's ship. The proud ship sailed slowly, majestically into Chicklesit harbor. Against the lavender evening sky, the ship's sails were displayed in full regalia.

"It is beautiful," she breathed.

"Get my canoe ready," ordered Chance. "I'm going to see what they want."

Haina grabbed his hand. "Do you think you should? It's dark, they could capture you. Why not wait until morning?"

Chance looked at her, surprise etched across his face. "Such concern for me," he murmured.

She flushed in the dusk, but hoped he could not see. "It's not concern for you. I just don't want anyone getting hurt or killed. . . ." Her voice trailed away weakly. She *was* concerned about him, but she certainly wasn't going to admit that to him!

When she did not explain further, Chance took her in his arms and hugged her tightly. Then he set her from him and walked down to the beach. She watched him go, the light almost completely gone now. Several men tramped in his wake.

"Be careful, Chance," she whispered into the velvet night. "Be careful."

Chapter 11

"Och, but it's a clear night t'night, Cap'n."

"Aye, Burns, it is that," Captain Daniel Jasper agreed. The two stood at the railing of the ship, *Lady Boston*, and looked out into the gathering dusk. "You know, Burns, this part of the coast always leaves me restless . . . uneasy."

"Aye? 'Cause o' that ship the Indians burned so long ago, I suppose."

"No, it's not that." The captain sighed ruminatively into the night air. He watched as several dark dots with torches broke away from the shore and moved slowly, bumpily out towards his ship. Like fireflies they were, he thought, like the fireflies he used to catch as a child back on the farm, so long ago. . . .

"I been sailin' wi't ye nigh on half a score o' years, and I've no' heard ye mention feelin' uneasy around here." The grizzled mate waited patiently for his captain's answer. He knew not to push the man, something else he'd learned in the ten years he'd spent with Jasper.

Daniel looked at his first mate closely. "We've been friends a long time, Burns," he said at last. "What I am about to tell you is between you and me. It's something I've not thought of for a long time, but it's always there, festering. Do you know what I mean, Burns? Have you ever had something bothering the back of your mind every day of your life? Something you live with, the sad thoughts becoming a part of you, until they're almost old friends, or enemies. Sometimes I don't know which."

"Aye, Dan'l," came the soft answer. "I know of what ye speak. I have me wife and daughter to remember. They haunt me at times." Burns shook his head. "I shoulda been there for them. The fire—Och, but I been over it afore." He looked at the captain. "I know what ye mean," he repeated softly.

Neither spoke for awhile, they contented themselves with watching the bobbing canoes, for that's what the fireflies were, bobbing canoes.

"It was twenty years ago . . . no, twenty-four years ago, now." Daniel sighed heavily into the cool night air as he watched the slowly approaching canoes. "I had a sister, once."

Burns was silent, but Daniel knew he had the older man's full attention. "Eleanor was her name. Eleanor of the sweet temper, Eleanor of the bright red hair, Eleanor, who loved to play pranks. Somewhere around here, under this godforsaken sea, lie the bones of my only sister."

Burns flinched at the stark words.

"She's never aged in my memory. She's forever young. And very pregnant," he added wryly. "This area of the coast raises her specter for me."

When Daniel did not continue, Burns asked, "Ye say she was young and pregnant? What was she doin' out here, mon? Ye were daft to be bringin' a breedin' woman aboard ship."

Daniel shook his head. "She was married to my best friend. Insisted she had to be with him. Mitch—Mitchell Fleming—his name was." Daniel paused, reliving the memories. "We ran away to sea together, Mitch and I, when we were but boys. Later, he met my sister and, well, all I can say is I've never seen a man so besotted. And she with him. He married her a month after he met her."

Daniel was lost in reverie. "We shipped together, all three of us. Mitch had some fool notion that he was going to show Eleanor the world, or some such thing. That was fine with her. Nowhere she'd rather be than with Mitch. They were a pair!"

Daniel shook his head again, coming out of his reverie. He frowned. "We had shipped out of Boston. Came around the Cape. Up the coast of Mexico. Headed north for some godforsaken place called Yuquot where there were furs, enough sea otter furs to blind men to all else but the gold they could get for them. Traders were making huge fortunes selling furs to the men of China, sometimes to the Russians, too."

"Then there was a storm, a terrible storm. I hope to God I never encounter another storm like that one. I've never seen such a blow; such waves." His hands gripping the railing were white-knuckled. He looked down into the dark depths of the calm water. "We were blown far off course. We made it about this far, by my calculations." He spread one arm wide, taking in the shadowed water, the tree-lined shore.

"Mitch and I were topside in the storm. We were trying to tie down some of the cargo left on deck. Eleanor had somehow—to this day I don't know how—but somehow she had climbed up on deck. The ship was reeling from the weight of the wind and the waves and the fierce rain blowing onto us. What a terrible night!" He paused thoughtfully. "Mitch yelled at her to go below. Next thing, she was washed overboard. She was so big with child she was unwieldy, in water or out of it. She was gone before I could call her name into the blackness." He shook his head, unable to believe she had gone from him, from Mitch, so quickly. "I had to hold Mitch back. He wanted to throw himself after her. If I hadn't held him, he would have drowned too."

"And so you lost your sister and the wee bairn," said Burns softly. "It may be none o' me business, but at least you saved one, mon. Don't be torturin' yerself about it."

"Saved him for what?" snorted Daniel. "Saved him so he could end up dead and broken in some old fleabag hotel in Boston, you mean."

Burns heard the naked pain in his companion's voice.

"After Eleanor was gone, poor Mitch took to blaming himself for her death. And me. Said I should have let him go to her." Daniel lifted a hand to clasp the back of his neck. "Sometimes I think he was right."

"Ye did what ye had to, mon. Ye did what had to be done."

"Aye, I did that. One evening, maybe two years after that storm, I was in Boston. Heard from some sailors that Mitch was there, too. I looked him up." The hand clasping his neck went back to the rail. "I wish to God I hadn't."

Burns braced himself for what was coming next. "Ye found him, I suppose."

Daniel stretched his body to relieve the tension he felt. "I found him, that I did. He was laying stiff and stark naked on a dirty bed in a cheap hotel. Dead, he was. Laid out like a dead codfish on a slab at market. For a winding sheet he had a tattered old rag, and for company he had an empty bottle of rotgut wine and a big snarling rat in the corner. Nary a cent in his wallet, either."

Daniel sighed again. "Poor Mitch. I can still see

him. His face was white, hollow. It must have showed every minute of the empty life he'd lived since he'd lost Eleanor—and the babe."

"Ye don' have t' be tellin' me this, mon. . . ."

But Daniel could not stop. "The stench of death was thick in the room, Burns. Mitch must have been dead for days. And you know what really bothers me about it all, Burns?" he said, swinging to look at his first mate with anguished eyes. "What really bothers me is there was no dignity to his death. Just as there was no dignity to his life—after I saved him."

When Burns met his gaze in compassionate silence, Daniel added, "Oh, I'd heard stories. The women, the drink, the low companions and lower places he'd taken to frequenting. But I hadn't seen it. Not until I looked into his cold, dead face. Turns out my sister was the fortunate one, Burns. She died a clean death. Quick, clean." Daniel looked down into the silent depths of the sea again. "May God forgive me," he said hoarsely. "May God and Mitchell forgive me."

Burns felt the words of consolation die in his throat. He patted his friend gingerly on the shoulder. Words would be useless at a time like this. Silent friendship would have to suffice.

The Indians were closer now. The two men at the railing focused their gazes on the canoes. Daniel shook himself, as if waking up suddenly in a different world. He took several deep breaths, trying to restore a calm. He needed his wits about him for trading with the newcomers. He wiped clammy hands on his blue pantleg.

The lead canoe glided to a stop and torches were doused. An Indian reached out to catch the rope a sailor tossed from the ship.

The Indians crowded onto the deck and Daniel sized up his visitors with a practiced eye. He was back to being the hardened trader.

"Ye know enough o' their language to get by, Cap'n," said Burns in a low voice. "And what ye dinna ken . . . I just might have in me trusty notebook here." He patted his back pocket. Recently Burns had taken to writing down the Nootka words he heard. More than once, Daniel had consulted with Burns and his dog-eared notebook about the meaning of a certain word or its pronunciation.

"Ye'll make short shrift o' these natives, Cap'n. Green about the gills, they are. Wet behind the ears, too." His comments elicited the chuckle from Daniel that he'd hoped for and Burns stepped away from the railing to watch the Indians from a discreet distance.

Some of the Indians, all men, were naked while others wore cedar kutsacks, a shift-like garment Daniel was familiar with from past trading expeditions to the coast. Many of the Indians had knives stuck in the belts at their waists.

Daniel waited impatiently as his uninvited callers straggled on deck. He wanted to get this meeting over and done with so he could go below and have a hearty swig of whisky to wash away the grim memory of his sister and her unhappy fate. And to wash away the gruesome memory of his brother-in-law, too, come to that.

Interest sparked in his hard gray eyes when one of the visitors stepped forward. The Indian, taller than the rest, wore a black bearskin tied at one shoulder. Against the black of the fur, his hair looked blond. A blond Indian! Daniel frowned into the deepening gloom as he peered at the man. Why, give the Indian a suit of sailor skivvies and he'd look like a white, he thought in amazement.

The Indian approached confidently and greeted Daniel. Through hand signs and a few words of guttural Nootka, Daniel was able to make the natives understand he was looking to trade for furs. In return he'd give good blankets, cloth, pots and guns. Especially guns.

Usually Daniel traded farther to the south, around Yuquot, but the furs were all dried up there. Maybe here, farther north and more isolated, he could get his hands on some of those fine sea otter furs. Prices were still high enough that he'd retire a rich man. And if it meant trading guns to the Indians to become rich, he'd do it. He had done it before. He had to ask the tall, blond Indian to repeat himself.

Chance looked at the older, gray-bearded man. The trader's thoughts seemed to be flying elsewhere, mayhaps in the sky, thought Chance. Was he truly here for trading or was there some other reason he had chosen to stop at Chicklesit? Chance tried his question again, but the graybeard's knowledge of Chance's language was not fine enough to grasp the nuances of what Chance was asking.

Chance gave up in disgust. He did not trust these white men. Graybeard was looking at him strangely though, Chance sensed, not unkindly. Chance determined to take his men and leave the ship quickly once his curiosity was reasonably satisfied.

It interested him to know that the trader had guns. What else did he carry? "Rum?" asked Chance, the foreign word feeling awkward on his tongue. The trader shook his head.

"He's not going to get rich very quickly," smirked Whale Hunter. "Ask him if he will take women in trade." At Chance's questioning look, Whale Hunter shrugged. "Some of them do," was all he said.

"*Klutsma*, women?" When Chance put the question to him, the trader shook his head again.

"How do you know so much about trading?" asked Chance. Whale Hunter just shrugged again, a half-smile on his face. Chance turned back to Graybeard.

133

Between gestures and words the two managed to make themselves understood. They parleyed for several minutes longer and it became obvious to Chance that no trading would be done because the Chicklesits did not have the furs that Graybeard wanted. He must set some of the men to hunting sea otters, Chance decided. The village could use some of the iron and metal that the traders offered. He'd make sure the Chicklesits would have furs to trade on the next visit.

Daniel too, was reaching the same conclusion. He'd get no furs from this group tonight. A silence developed as both sides realized the impasse.

Chance sheepishly pantomimed someone drinking and fluttered his fingers over the imaginary cup. He did this several times. No one seemed to understand. Finally he said, "Tea." He felt foolish asking for such a frivolous item, but Haina *had* wanted some.

"Tay! Och, the mon wants tay!" blurted Burns.

In his head Daniel ran through the stores and provisions the ship carried. He shook his head, "No tea. Sorry. Next time." He'd make a note of it, for sure, Daniel thought in amusement. An Indian who wanted tea, way out here, of all things. Must be from the Yuquot area. Lots of traders there. He could have picked up a liking for tea there. Daniel frowned. If that was so, maybe the Indian was some trader's by-blow. He looked carefully at Chance again, scrutinizing the blond features carefully. No, he still looked like a white man dressed as an Indian. His frown deepened. "Burns, go to my cabin. Get my personal stash of tea . . . Don't look at me funny, man. Get the tea."

Burns scrambled away.

"No trade now," Chance informed the older man in Nootka. "Maybe later."

"Do you speak English?" tried Daniel. The Indian looked at him blankly. "I could have sworn . . ." muttered Daniel.

Daniel knew there'd be no trading tonight but he was reluctant to let the young Indian go. He admitted he was intrigued. He leaned closer and in the flickering light could make out green eyes. Green eyes! What manner of Indian was this?

"Here's the tay, Cap'n."

Daniel held out a brown leather pouch to the Indian. "Here you go, chief. Tea. A gift with my compliments."

Chance took it, looking bemusedly at Daniel the while. Suddenly Chance reached for a stone knife at his belt. He grinned when Graybeard took a wary step backward.

Still grinning, Chance slowly removed the knife from his belt and handed it, hilt first, to Graybeard. Cold gray eyes stared into green. Slowly the captain smiled and his eyes warmed in understanding.

"Thank you, chief," Daniel said eyeing the sharp weapon curiously. The knife was made of fine-grained black slate, the blade sharpened to a razor's edge. The handle had been wrapped with leather and was well-worn from the Indian's grip. Daniel stroked the knife gently. "Mighty nice present, chief. Thank you." He clasped Chance's forearm.

Chance did not understand the words, but he was satisfied from Graybeard's manner that he was well-pleased with the gift.

They conversed awhile longer. At last satisfied that the trader was just that, Chance signalled to his men to leave. They crowded after him.

Chance caught Beachdog trying to lift a loose piece of iron from the ship's deck when he thought no one was watching. "*Wik*, no," admonished Chance sharply. Beachdog just grinned, but he desisted after meeting Chance's stern gaze. Chance did not want to provoke these strangers. Let them keep their pieces of metal.

135

Once in his canoe, Chance and his men pushed away from the ship and paddled for the village. Unaccountably, Chance turned around in his seat and looked back at the ship, now outlined only by it's lanterns. He'd had a strange feeling when looking at Graybeard, and the feeling puzzled him. He shrugged. Doubtless it was just that he'd met so few white men.

Chance held up the brown leather pouch. Haina would be surprised in the morning when he gave her the tea. But not as surprised as tonight when he made sweet, passionate love to her! His body hardened at the mere thought and he bent to his paddling with a will.

Behind him, a curious Daniel stroked his full, salt-and-pepper beard. A blond, green-eyed Indian. How strange . . .

"Glad to see the last o' that crew, Cap'n. Gonna seek me wee bed. G' night."

Daniel pulled himself from his lost reverie for a moment. "Eh? Oh yes, good night, Burns. See you next watch." The grizzled old seaman was gone, leaving Daniel to his pensive meanderings. It was a long time before he turned his steps downward to his cramped little cabin, and longer still before he fell asleep.

Chance strode into his quarters. Most of the inhabitants of the longhouse were asleep and fires burned low. A single clamshell lamp lit his bed area and he could see Haina in the warm glow. Her dark hair fell about her shoulders and her dark eyes glistened.

Late as it was, Haina had lain awake with worry for Chance. Suppose something had happened to him? Suppose the trader took him prisoner, or killed him? When she heard his heavy tread enter the sleeping area she sat up, clutching a fur blanket to her breast. Her eyes were large and soft in the lamplight as she gazed at him.

"It went well?"

Chance tossed a small pouch into a corner and shrugged out of his bearskin kutsack before answering. "Well enough," he grunted. "The trader was looking for furs." He sat down beside her on the low plank bed. It groaned under his weight. He picked up one of the seal skins blanketing the bed and stroked it thoughtfully. "I told him we did not have any furs for him this time. I hope he stops by again." He stared at the flickering lamp pensively. "I think it would be a good thing for my people to get sea otter furs. Then we can trade for useful things." He slanted a glance at her. "Useful things like iron pots, knives and fish hooks."

"And tea, and sugar . . ."

He swung around and planted his hands on either side of her. He leaned into her and kissed the tip of her nose. He nibbled on her neck. "Ah, fair Ahousat with your taste for the white man's foods, you make a man forget himself," he murmured. And then he was beyond speaking. Haina held him closely and soon she too was lost to the wonderful bliss of his lovemaking.

Afterwards, as they both lay satiated, Haina ran her fingertips through the blond hair of his chest and ventured, "Chance?"

"Mmm?"

"Don't go to sleep yet, Chance. I want to talk to you."

He roused himself sufficiently to say, "Speak then, *Chummuss*. Soon my body must rest from your greedy demands."

She rapped him on the chest with her fist and laughed. "Proud Ahousat, it's *my* body that is exhausted.

"I expect no less. Come here."

Haina went into his arms again and for long moments they kissed. Snuggling up to him, she said, "Chance, why have you been leaving me to myself so much?"

137

She felt him go still. When he didn't answer, she said hurriedly, "Have I displeased you? Said something to anger you?" She waited, holding her breath for his answer.

He moved his arm from around her and sat up. "It's nothing like that, *Chummuss*."

"Then what is it? Tell me, please, Chance."

He sighed heavily. "*Chummuss*," he began carefully. Dare he tell her that when he brought her to this village, he thought he could take her body and walk away from her when the time came to ransom her to her father? No, he could not tell her that. He could not give his enemy's daughter such power.

Instead he said, "There is much to do in this village. I have neglected it and the people for too long. I must help while I am here."

Haina felt a curious disappointment. Mayhaps it was too soon for her to hope that he cared for her. Still, she knew her feelings for him were strong.

She sat up and reached gently for a lock of his hair that fell across his brow. She pushed it back from his face and smiled into those beautiful green eyes. Their gazes locked. Haina was afraid to disturb the moment with words so she gently touched his lips with hers. Something unspoken but loving passed between them and she was satisfied. They slept.

The next morning, Haina woke just as Chance returned, dripping wet, from his morning ablutions and prayers. He rummaged through a cedar box. "Here it is," he murmured.

Haina sat up in bed, unable to take her eyes off Chance. He looked so handsome, so strong. She sighed happily to herself.

He took out a long, metal knife. He began scraping it against his damp cheek, stopping every now and then to curse.

Haina could not restrain her curiosity. "What are

138

you doing, Chance?"

More curses. "I'm shaving this stubble off."

"What is that knife you are using to do it?"

"A razor," he answered. "It's a white man's razor. My Indian father gave it to me when I was younger. He wanted me to be able to keep my beard growth down. He didn't want the other boys mocking me."

"And did they?"

Chance smiled his slow smile. "Only once."

Haina heard the rough scraping as he drew the sharp blade over his cheek and she winced. "Do you do this often?" she asked.

"Every day if I can. Otherwise my beard grows in. One of the disadvantages of being born a white." He so seldom mentioned his white heritage that she did not know what to make of his comment. Then he looked at Haina and his eyes twinkled.

"I will make a skin softener for you to put on your face," she decided at last. She could no longer stand the rasping, rough sound as he scraped away at his chin. She wondered why he did not walk around with a broken, bleeding face every day after subjecting himself to this treatment!

Haina was as good as her word. The following morning, she presented Chance with a sweetsmelling lump of rendered deer's fat. She had carefully rendered the deer's fat, mixed in some pine pitch for scent and then molded the fat in a bulb-shaped bull kelp float she'd found on the beach.

Chance was about to start his morning shave when she presented her gift. He looked at her, sniffed the fat, looked at her again, then slapped some on his cheeks and slowly slid the razor through the oily mixture. The smooth ride of the sharp blade felt good. He slapped some more fat on. At last, when he had finished his shave, he said gravely, "Thank you, *Chummuss*. I am glad you made this for me."

Haina smiled shyly in response.

In the many days that followed, Chance and Haina were as newly married lovers are. Nothing was said, but both felt the difference. Their eyes touched and glanced away only to return to the beloved. Their hands reached out and stroked one another of their own accord. Haina had only to think of Chance and he appeared. Drawn to each other by bonds stronger than any either had ever known, they laughed and played together or worked into the night together. They went fishing together to replenish village food supplies, went swimming together, Chance even lowered himself to pick berries with her one time. When his men saw him and Whale Hunter chided him for doing woman's work, Chance merely laughed and shrugged off the good-natured taunts. He was happy, happy beyond belief, and he knew it was because of Haina.

Mudshark, Beachdog, Chance and several other men stepped out of their small, two-man canoes and onto the beach. Chance wiped a hand across his sweating brow. Summer was upon them and he welcomed the hot days.

He reached for the big ling cod he'd caught and watched as the others hefted several silver salmon out of the canoes.

"Good catch?" greeted Whale Hunter.

He was not so defiant now. He occasionally accosted Chance in conversation. At other times he was aggressive and contemptuous but he was gradually beginning to accept Chance's leadership. Still, Chance was not one to impede the young man's progress from enemy to friend. In fact, he was doing all he could to bring the young man around.

Chance nodded. "Several big ones," he said pleasantly. He pointed into the distance. "We caught them off that cape."

"What my cousin means," explained Mudshark heartily, "is that *we* caught the salmon. He only caught that puny little ling cod." He playfully punched Chance on the arm. Chance winced from the blow and almost lost his balance. He dropped the ling cod and lunged for Mudshark. Soon the two were down and wrestling on the beach sand.

Whale Hunter joined in the general laughter. This tyee was different, not pompous like he'd first expected.

When Chance finally let Mudshark rise, the two brushed the wet sand off themselves. Whale Hunter cleared his throat. "There's good fishing just off the island south of that cape," he volunteered.

Chance glanced skeptically at him. "That so?" he said politely.

Whale Hunter nodded. "I've caught big salmon there every time I've fished it."

Chance almost chuckled aloud at Whale Hunter's characteristic boasting. "We must try there next time," Chance offered with a straight face. Whale Hunter looked pleased that Chance obviously appreciated his good advice.

The men continued up to the longhouse and went their separate ways. Chance carried the large ling cod through the village until he came to his aunt's longhouse.

He bent at the door and stepped inside. Evening meals were being prepared and small children played underfoot.

"Aunt Salal Woman," he greeted when the old woman came to greet him.

"Chance Gift from the Sea," she acknowledged. "Please sit down and visit. What brings you to my dwelling?"

Chance had seen her eyes dart to the large fish; she knew very well what brought him to her dwelling.

"Ah, Auntie," he said as he sat down on the cedar mat she had indicated. He placed the fish beside him and pretended not to notice her hopeful gaze. Had this village been so desperate for fish before he arrived? He felt a stab of guilt.

"It is good to visit with my mother's sister."

Salal Woman sighed and sat down across from him. For a few minutes there was silence. Then she said, "I miss your mother so. She was a good sister to me." Her hand went to her cheek and she wiped away a slow tear.

Chance shifted uncomfortably. He hadn't intended to bring up sad memories for the old woman.

Salal Woman added, "Your father was a good man, too. How he had hated to see Ocean Wave lying about the longhouse, her face swollen from crying for her dead babe. When you were born," here she wiped another tear, "it was a wonderful time for both of them."

Salal Woman wiped her face with her hands and looked up at him. "I know you've heard the story many times, but humor an old woman."

Chance smiled and nodded that he was listening.

She continued, "Your mother's face lit up with such joy when the midwife placed you in her arms." Salal Woman sniffed and her wrinkled face softened at the memory. "She cooed over you and loved you from the moment she saw you." Her own face shining at the memory, Salal Woman added, "We all did. Now that your mother is gone, I feel I must take her place." She gently touched his forearm. "Were she here now, I fear there is something she would warn you about."

This was so unexpected that Chance could only stare at her.

"Yes," nodded Salal Woman. "There is something I must tell you. It concerns your brother."

"Throws Away Wealth? Come now, Auntie, don't

look so solemn when you speak his name."

"If I look solemn," rejoined his aunt, "it is because I have good reason."

Chance merely raised an eyebrow questioningly.

"Ah, young man," she sighed. "I see this is going to be more difficult than I had thought."

"What is, Auntie?"

"Your brother, Chance, is not what he seems."

"He's been a good brother to me," said Chance stubbornly.

"I have no doubt that he has—for his own reasons," she stated slowly. "But should you cross him, or appear as a threat—"

"Me? A threat? Please, Auntie, you joke with your poor nephew."

"Chance, I am serious. Throws Away Wealth is a dangerous man. Do not take my words lightly."

"Why, Auntie," he mocked. "Have you knowledge of any words he's spoken against me? Any deeds he has done against me?"

Salal Woman looked uncomfortable. "No, it is more a feeling. . . ."

"A feeling? You see fit to condemn my brother because of a feeling?" His voice was stern.

"Chance," she scolded. "I have known him all his life. I have never seen him do something that did not serve his own ends. My purpose is to warn you. Guard your back, my nephew. Guard your back. He is sneaky. And cruel. When he was a boy I saw him torture puppies and—"

"Auntie, you forget yourself," Chance's voice held nothing but reproach now. "It is my brother we speak of. I will not have him slandered. If all you have is that he accidentally hurt a puppy when he was a child . . . ."

"He did not 'accidentally' hurt a puppy. He purposely tortured several of them. . . ."

"Nevertheless, it was a thing done as a child. Long ago. Do not hold it against him. He is a man long grown and he has been nothing but kind to me."

But his aunt would not stop her words. "Chance, please listen. When he offered you a home after your mother died, it was to watch you, perhaps to have you killed."

"Killed! What madness is this, woman?" He lowered his voice. "He offered me a home at my mother's death because no other family would have me!"

"He told you this?"

"He did, yes."

"He lies. *I* would have given you a home. I, and the Chicklesit people would have taken you in."

Chance refrained from the retort that sprang to his lips. Chicklesit was too poor to take in any orphans. One more mouth to feed would have proved too much for the poverty-stricken village. No, he could not say that, even though his old aunt maligned his brother terribly.

He regained his temper. "Auntie, I know you think to do the best for me, and I thank you. But understand that Throws Away Wealth is my brother. He has stood by me since our parents died—"

"Bah," she spat. "He has separated you from your family—us—and kept you soft and powerless in that village of his. Were you to be *our* tyee our people would follow you willingly. You are the heir to your mother's family. It was a strong family, a rich family—"

"It is now a poor family," said Chance, brutal in his irritation with her. "Understand, Auntie. It is poor! There is no wealth in this village. These people could not help a chief to potlatch and gain a name for himself."

"And why is it so poor, Nephew?"

Chance shrugged. "I don't know. These things

144

just happen. . . ."

"This village is poor because your brother made it that way!" The old woman's eyes were spitting fire.

"Come now, Auntie, I can't believe that."

"Believe it, Puppy, because it is the truth. When we had rich fishing and many sea otter furs and much deer meat, your brother visited us. He took the sea otter furs—to potlatch he said. He never repaid them, even after we requested repayment. He never gave a potlatch here. He never asked any of *our* noble families to join him when he went to other potlatches."

The old woman was almost spitting, she was so angry. "We had slaves—No, you listen to me, young man. We had slaves, many of them. He took them, oh, to 'borrow' them for sure. But he never returned them. He took our wealth. Stole it as surely as I sit here."

Chance shook his head, unable to believe the accusations. "Auntie, Auntie, I cannot believe this. My brother would not seek to weaken a small, insignificant village as this. It makes no sense."

"It makes sense," she said wearily. "But I can see that nothing I say will matter to you. Go, my nephew, leave an old woman in peace."

Chance rose to his feet. "I go, Auntie, because I believe you are not feeling well today. I will forget this conversation and the slander of my brother. I leave this ling cod as a parting gift," he said politely and took his leave.

Salal Woman watched him go, her shoulders sagged and her face was sadder than before. "I tried to tell him, Ocean Wave. I tried to tell him."

She closed her eyes, exhausted from the emotional exchange. "He must find his own way now."

Chapter 12

It was a cool evening. Chance and Haina sat watching the sun set into the sea. The sky was lit with soft colors of red and yellow and pink, all washed into each other. A pleasant breeze stirred Haina's dark hair and caressed her cheek. The soft sand of the beach had pillowed her for too long. She stood, ready to return to the longhouse.

"Come," she said. "I will make your evening meal."

"Such a good woman," he murmured, seizing her hand and pulling her to him. "Don't go yet. I am not done with you."

"Now, Chance," she cautioned. "We *are* in front of the whole village."

He let her hand drop but she could see he was not irritated with her. They had been so loving to each other these many days, it seemed they had never differed, never fought.

Chance narrowed his eyes against the failing light. He had watched the approaching canoe for some time.

Idle curiosity, he supposed.

"You go ahead," he said easily. "I'll wait for our visitor."

Haina glanced seaward in surprise. Chagrined that she had not noticed the approaching canoe earlier, she merely nodded and ran up the beach to the longhouse. Chance turned and watched her go, his eyes following her hungrily.

When he swung his gaze back to the water the canoe was quickly pulling into the harbor. He could see that it was only manned by one person, a large man. Strange that a man would paddle these parts alone. Strange, but not unheard of.

The man pulled his canoe up onto the beach. The craft grated noisily across the gravel and sand. Chance remained where he was, back against a log and watched the newcomer.

The man grunted from the effort of lifting the canoe and headed towards the longhouses. Spying Chance, he veered toward him.

"What do you want?" Chance asked lazily. The man was a slave judging from his kutsack. It was wellworn but presentable, as was his canoe.

"I'm looking for Chance Gift of the Sea," the stranger stated.

Chance nodded once. "I am he. What business do you have with me?"

"My name is Dog Shadow," said the other politely enough, though Chance was wary of the man. Why, he didn't know.

"Your brother sent me," explained Dog Shadow. He squatted down beside Chance and wiped his brow. Chance had seen the man a time or two around Kyuquot so he knew the slave probably spoke the truth. "Throws Away Wealth said you should come back to Kyuquot now."

Chance sat up straighter. This was news indeed.

"Back to Kyuquot?" he asked. "Why? What has he heard of the Ahousats? Of Fighting Wolf?"

The stranger smiled and Chance noticed his eyes for the first time. He had eyes like cold hard pieces of flint, and his smile, rather than softening his face, was merely a stretch of facial muscles. The man looked keenly at him for a moment then said, "Fighting Wolf has given up the search."

"So easily?"

The man shrugged. "He came sniffing around Kyuquot a few times, but your brother sent him on his way. Fighting Wolf knows nothing."

"Do not make the mistake of misjudging Fighting Wolf."

"He knows nothing, I tell you," said the slave impatiently. There was something in his tone that made Chance pause. It was almost as if the slave were *daring* him. But to do what?

"My brother sent you," Chance repeated, stalling for time. "Come to my longhouse. I will have a meal prepared for you." Such courtesy to a slave was highly unusual but Chance welcomed the news to return to Kyuquot, didn't he? Besides, he wanted to pursue questioning this slave. Something wasn't quite right.

Haina served Chance and his lowly guest their meal of fresh caught salmon and steamed cinquefoil roots. She would have liked to offer potato, a large root vegetable that her family grew near their longhouse in Ahousat, but of course such things were unobtainable in Chicklesit. She sighed. At the end of the meal she presented the two with fragrant blackberries, berries that she and Chance had picked on the hillside only yesterday.

As the men ate they made no secret of what they talked about. Chance planned to return to Kyuquot. Haina's heart plummeted like an eagle dropping upon a salmon. But a salmon had all the sea to evade the eagle's sharp talons. What hope had her poor heart of eluding Chance? His talons had already seized that poor bleeding organ and it only remained for him to tear it to pieces.

The slave ate noisily and with a great deal of lip smacking while Haina only picked at her delicious meal. So, it had come to this. Time had run out for her, and for Chance. The time had come to return to Kyuquot, to become a hostage, a prisoner, again. She pushed flakes of salmon listlessly around on her wooden plate and never looked at Chance through the whole meal.

Chance, for his part, could not ferret out any new information from the slave. The man did not seem to know much, only repeating what Throws Away Wealth had told him, but it was the manner of his repeating it. He fidgeted, would not meet Chance's eyes. He was curt, surly almost, whenever Chance questioned him about Kyuquot. Chance shrugged off the gnawing uneasiness.

Later in the privacy of their bed, Chance whispered sweet love words to Haina but he failed to stir her passions. "What is wrong, *Chummuss*?" he asked at last.

"Will you forget me easily when I am gone?"

He sighed and sank back onto the furs. "So, that is what ails you."

She refused to answer. What good would talking do now? He would return her for ransom and that would be that. That he would think of her no further rankled her fine spirit.

"*Chummuss*." He dragged her hands from her face. "Look at me. Please." Reluctantly, she dropped her hands.

He lifted her chin and gazed into the sorrowful, beautiful brown eyes that he never failed to get lost in. A clamshell lamp sputtered for a moment, sent a burst of light to outline her face and hair and he knew he could not part with her. Her beautiful face was set, her lower lip trembled and a tear coursed down her cheek. He kissed the trail and gently enfolded her in his arms.

"I cannot let you go, Haina. Do not ask it of me."

She swung her arms around him. "Oh, Chance. I do not ask it of you. I want to stay with you. I love my father, my family, but I—"

She stopped. She could not declare her love for him. He might be using her, trying to make her return to Kyuquot willingly. She had seen his ruthlessness before, when he had first captured her, and she had not forgotten that part of him. Perhaps once she was in Kyuquot, he would blithely cast her aside or return her to her father. No, not yet, she cautioned herself. Wait, wait and see. Wait before revealing your love. Wait and see if he is worthy.

Thus she fortified herself. She pushed herself from his warm arms. Wiping a tear from her eye, she smiled tremulously up at him.

At the sight Chance's heart went out to her. He could not, would not let her go. No matter what Throws Away Wealth asked of him, he could not do this one thing.

They made love that night as if they would never love again and the passion each brought to the other was a wondrous gift. Never had lovemaking been so beautiful, so all-encompassing. But for Haina, never had it been more desperate.

They awoke early in the morning. By mid-morning they were paddling out of Chicklesit harbor, flanked by a contingent of young, strong warriors. Chance's Kyuquot men had been joined by the Chicklesit youths and men and the force numbered twenty men in all.

Haina cast a backward glance at the small, impoverished village. So happy, she murmured, she had been so happy there.

Resolutely, she turned in her seat and faced the front. Kyuquot, and trouble, awaited.

Chapter 13

Haina stared wearily at the longhouses of Kyuquot. The trip south had been slow and a constant drizzle of rain had long ago soaked the men and single hostage in the Chicklesit canoes. Chance had tossed Haina a cedar cape. She'd donned it over her head to keep her hair dry and it had worked fairly well as a hood. But the red and white trade dress she'd chosen to wear on the morning they'd left Chicklesit had proven to be little protection against the rain. Her legs and arms were cold and shivering, only her hair and shoulders had been protected by the cape.

And now she was back in Kyuquot, a hostage, she thought miserably. Even the rain had conspired against her. Chance had spoken no more than ten words to her on the whole voyage and she knew it was because he was going to ransom her back to her father, despite what he'd told her. He probably did not want to even be reminded of the passion that had passed between them, she thought sadly.

The canoes crunched up onto the beach gravel in

front of Kyuquot village. It was early evening and most of the inhabitants had retired to their longhouses to outwait the rain. No one came to greet the Chicklesits and Haina took a perverse pleasure in that. Chance was obviously unimportant, unworthy of her. She could not wait to be returned to her noble father, she assured herself.

Chance and most of his men headed for the largest longhouse. With but a glance over his shoulder, Chance called out to her to go to the quarters she'd stayed in during her first visit. Irritated at being so casually dismissed, she grabbed her small basket with its few possessions and splashed her way out of the canoe. She stomped up the beach, muttering dire imprecations down on the blond head of the unsuspecting Chance.

She had but reached the overhang of the longhouse when suddenly someone grasped her arm and she was swung around to face Beachdog. This was the final indignity! "Unhand me," she demanded. "At once!"

"Silence," he hissed.

"What do you think you're doing, Beachdog? Unhand me, I say!"

Beachdog looked furtively about before turning his full attention to her. He loosened his grasp. She shrugged her arm away. "What is the meaning of this?"

Clearly he had expected her to be cowed by his action. Well, he was in for a surprise. She was a war chief's daughter and fighting ran in her blood.

"Keep quiet and I won't hurt you."

"You won't hurt me," she repeated incredulously. "Go find someone else to play your strange game with. Let me pass!"

She moved to walk past him. "Not so fast, my little Ahousat flower," he said. "I think you'll be interested in what I have to tell you."

She looked at him intently. "I doubt that very much, Beachdog." She sighed. "I suppose you'll keep annoying me until I hear you out."

He nodded.

"Very well. Speak."

Sure that he had her attention, he crossed wiry arms over his thin, hairless chest and leaned back against the longhouse. "Chance is going to ransom you."

"I know that," she said sharply. "Now if you'll excuse me . . ."

"Are you so sure your family will pay the ransom? Many families refuse to take back a daughter who's been a slave."

"I am *not* a slave! I'm a hostage. There's a big difference."

"Is there? To your family?"

"My family will stand by me," she said stubbornly. "Now, if you are done . . ."

"Not yet." He pushed himself slowly away from the building and said in a low voice, "Chance doesn't want you any more, does he?"

"What do you mean?"

"He ignored you for most of the trip down here, didn't he? Chance is tired of you. That's why he's going to ransom you. If he really wanted you," Beachdog insinuated slyly, "he'd keep you, or marry you."

Beachdog's words caught her unawares. What he was saying was too much like what she had been thinking. Was it so obvious then? If Chance's own men were assuming he wanted nothing more to do with her, then she must prepare for the worst. "Don't trouble yourself . . . dog," she rejoined. She gave a toss of her head. "I go home to Ahousat. I need have no dealings with Chance Gift from the Sea—or with the likes of you."

"Ah, yes. So proud, little Ahousat flower. Still, should you find yourself in a . . . shall we say awkward . . . postion, you can always come to me."

The audacity of the man! Haina could hardly believe her ears. "Beachdog," she said as evenly as she could, "do not worry over me. I will take care of myself!"

She stormed past him and entered the longhouse. He called after her, "Do not take my words lightly. You may be in sore need of my protection."

Haina stuck her face out of the entry way and answered, "Go and find Kingfisher, Beachdog. Perhaps *she* needs your protection. I, however, do not!"

Fuming, Haina marched through the longhouse until she found the living quarters of the young matron she had stayed with on her earlier visit. Haina threw down the small basket and sat down on a cedar mat placed next to the cheerfully burning fire. The young woman looked up from cutting a piece of fish and said politely, "Welcome, mistress."

"I don't suppose Chance told you I would be staying with you," said Haina as calmly as she could. Somehow the domesticity of the scene was soothing to her. The two small children played nearby as they had the first time Haina had visited and the old grandmother dozed on a cedar mat in the corner. Haina felt as though she'd never been away.

The young matron continued cutting the fish. "Yes, he did mention that you'd be here." Even her voice was soothing, thought Haina.

Haina looked around, pleased with her reception. "I see you have fish this time," she said. Then could have pinched herself for her lack of tact. Surely the woman did not want to be reminded that she could provide little food for guests.

The young matron glanced at her and Haina thought she saw a sparkle of mischief in those calm brown eyes. "The village prospers," she said. "Many of our men have had much success with the salmon and there is great abundance in our village and in my

155

home."

"I am pleased for you," said Haina politely. "What is your name?" she continued. "When I was here last I was too upset to remember names, manners and the like."

"My name is Kelp Woman, mistress."

"And your children's names?"

"My son is Bird Catcher, my daughter is Pine Cone."

"Those are good names," complimented Haina. Of course they were baby names and the children would be renamed before adulthood.

Kelp Woman caught Haina's curious glance at the old woman dozing on the mat. "Old Granny likes to nap at this time of day," she explained.

Haina nodded. She relaxed, feeling at ease with this small family. "I don't know how long I will be staying with you."

"You are welcome to stay as long as you wish," said Kelp Woman politely.

Pleased with her hostess' answer, Haina confided, "It is not up to me, I am afraid. How long I stay depends upon when my father arrives to pay my ransom." She did not feel like pretending that all was well.

Haina began to think of her family. It seemed so long ago that she had seen them. Had they given her up for dead? Surely Chance's forthcoming ransom message would correct that error!

Haina allowed her thoughts to dwell on her family until Kelp Woman moved past her to the fire to cook the fish she'd been slicing. Wrapped in several layers of fern fronds and leaves, the fish was put in hot embers to steam. Haina's mouth watered at the delicious smells wafting upwards from the fire. Soon the meal was ready and she sat down to eat.

"Much better than the fish soup you had on your

first visit, my lady?" asked Kelp Woman slyly.

Chance sat with Throws Away Wealth while his brother's wives served the evening meal.

For the whole trip down from Chicklesit, Chance's mind had whirled with wild plans of how to prevent his brother from ransoming Haina. Throws Away Wealth would not like Chance's change of plan, Chance knew that instinctively. But for all his pondering, Chance had not yet found a way other than to bluntly tell Throws Away Wealth of his change of heart and proceed from there.

The meal over with, Throws Away Wealth held up a bottle and slurred, "Chance, have some of this good rum. It'll make you a man."

Chance pushed the waving bottle away. "Thanks, brother, but I have had enough of that stuff. Perhaps you have, too."

Throws Away Wealth drew himself up to his full, unimpressive height while sitting on a mat in front of his hearth. "Do not insult your tyee," he said, all hint of a slur gone from his voice. "I do not need some young pup like you to tell me what to do." Tipping the bottle up, Throws Away Wealth took another drink. He wiped his mouth with his arm. "Aaah, that was good."

Chance sat impassively, a muscle in his jaw twitching as he kept from uttering a sharp response to his brother's words. "Very well, Tyee."

"That's better," sneered Throws Away Wealth. "You should know your place. A young pup like you should know your place." He took another drink from the bottle and nudged Chance with it. "Drink, you young pup."

"No." It irritated Chance that first his aunt, and now his brother, had called him a pup. Didn't these relatives of his see him as he really was? He sighed in exasperation. "Do you want to discuss the hostage or not?" he asked impatiently. He half hoped his brother would say 'no'. Throws Away Wealth was too difficult to reason with when he was drinking the white man's rum.

"What about the hostage?" asked Throws Away Wealth stupidly. "What hostage?"

Chance sighed. "Never mind. I'll come back in the morning." He got up and walked away.

"Morning? What morning?" muttered Throws Away Wealth but Chance was too far away to hear. Throws Away Wealth took another swig from the bottle, then licked his lips. "Good stuff."

Suddenly a crafty look came over Throws Away Wealth's face when he realized there was no one there to watch. He set the bottle aside and called out in a loud voice to his first wife, "Woman, fetch Dog Shadow."

His timid wife did as bid and returned with the slave in tow.

"You called for me, master?"

"Sit down, sit down," said Throws Away Wealth gesturing expansively to the cedar mat Chance had so recently vacated. "Here, have a drink."

Dog Shadow tipped the bottle up and took a long drink. He handed the bottle back to his chief.

"Do you like that rum, slave?" asked Throws Away Wealth. Dog Shadow nodded.

"Want some more?" asked Throws Away Wealth holding out the bottle. Dog Shadow nodded and reached for the bottle.

Throws Away Wealth snatched the bottle back. "Uh-uh, not so fast. There's more of this for you, but only after you do what I tell you."

Dog Shadow dropped his hand, watching the chief narrowly. "What is it?" he asked suspiciously.

"It's easy," assured Throws Away Wealth. "Not like some of the other things I've had you do." He laughed, but Dog Shadow did not join in. He merely sat there, stiff-faced. Throws Away Wealth stopped laughing and leaned closer. "Go to Fighting Wolf," he whispered. "Tell him that his daughter is here. Tell him that Chance Gift from the Sea has her." The chief chuckled. "That ought to bring him running."

Dog Shadow stared hard at his master. "Why?" he asked.

"'Why?' You dare to question me?" asked Throws Away Wealth in surprise.

"I do. I am tired of doing your dirty work for you."

"Silence, slave. You will do anything I tell you."

"What can you do if I refuse?" sneered the slave.

"How dare you talk to your tyee this way," snarled Throws Away Wealth. "I can have you killed."

"I dare, because I have nothing to lose." Dog Shadow was angry now and careless words rolled off his tongue. "Who will kill me? Not you. *I* do all your killing for you." The slave's contempt was obvious. "I care little what you do. You can only kill me once."

"Aaah, so that is it." Throws Away Wealth toyed with the knife at his belt. He always kept the iron blade honed to a sharp point. The iron handle was wrapped with braided cedar bark and fitted his hand well. The knife was one of his favorite possessions and he liked to finger it to reassure himself that it was there, close at hand.

"You must be tired of living," Throws Away Wealth said conversationally, and smiled.

The slave watched him warily. "I am sick of doing your killing. Of arranging 'accidents'."

"You mean the seal hunting 'accident' when you killed that would-be tyee in Chicklesit for me? Bah, he was nothing, I tell you!"

The slave glared sullenly at Throws Away Wealth. "Him, and some of the others you've had me kill. That noblewoman—"

"Her?" Throws Away Wealth shrugged. "She should have married who I told her to. She was mere dogmeat. Less than nothing!" He smiled for a moment, then his smile vanished. "Make no mistake, slave. You are not the only one I own. There are others who will gladly do my bidding."

The slave snorted. "I am sure you can force any number of men to your will, as you have me."

"Are you tired of hiding the truth, of what you really are?" The conversational note was back in Throws Away Wealth's voice.

"Aye, I am tired, Tyee. Tired to the point that I do not care any longer who knows."

"You would be in severe trouble if you let it slip," warned Throws Away Wealth.

"I don't care anymore, I tell you."

"Your life would be worthless if others should know you practice evil rites and witchcraft," the chief taunted. Throws Away Wealth pretended to shiver even as he said it.

Witches were feared in Nootka society. Enough so that a charge against a man as a witch was enough to condemn him to death. This hold had worked on Dog Shadow for several years but Throws Away Wealth could see that the man was either tired beyond caring of his chief's blackmail or worse, had some plan of turning on his master. He could not trust Dog Shadow. The slave was aptly named. He was like a dog, a vicious dog, only good to his master as long as the master was in control. One little slip and . . .

Throws Away Wealth licked his lips and said, "How about that drink?"

Dog Shadow nodded and accepted the bottle held out to him. He took a swallow and handed it back to Throws Away Wealth who only pretended to take a drink.

Back to Dog Shadow went the bottle.

"Take your time, take your time," said the chief generously. He must learn what Dog Shadow was about. "Have some more," he encouraged. Throws Away Wealth smiled beatifically. "It seems so long ago that I found you in the forest, doing your magic."

Dog Shadow looked bitterly at the chief. "I remember the very day," he said. "I don't suppose it does any good to tell you I was burying my dead baby son—not practicing sorcery."

Throws Away Wealth shook his head and pretended to take another drink from the bottle. "No good at all. I saw the black feathers you scattered on the body. I heard the words you spoke, calling out for the death of that midwife."

"I was angry. You would be, too, if your son died because a midwife was careless."

Throws Away Wealth shrugged. "What do I care? If I cannot have sons, why should you?"

He dismissed the dangerous look in Dog Shadow's eye. The hatred lurking there would have frozen a lesser man.

"It is too bad the midwife died so soon afterward," pointed out Throws Away Wealth blithely. He was enjoying this. He loved to tell and retell the story of how he had entrapped Dog Shadow. Aah, but there was something else, something Dog Shadow did not know, though the fool should have guessed by now.

"Yes, very suspicious, wasn't it?" The slave took another swig from the bottle. "The midwife was found washed up on the beach, her body barely recognizable, a black feather twisted in her hair."

"I never told you how easy it was," hinted the chief. Seeing the surprised look on Dog Shadow's face, he nodded happily at his victim. "It was easy to push her into the water and hold her under until she stopped breathing. The feather was clever, don't you agree?" He wanted to laugh at the furious hate contorting the slave's dark features.

"So!" exploded the slave. "My suspicions were true. You killed that woman!"

Throws Away Wealth did laugh then. "Yes," he crowed. "I did."

"All those years—! All those years you said you thought I was a sorcerer. That one word from you would be my death!" The slave choked on his words. "Sometimes even I thought—" He recoiled visibly from the tyee, and started to rise to his feet. His face twisted with hate, his breath whistled through his gritted teeth. "When I think of all the men I've killed for you, you—" The slave could not get the words out, he was so enraged. "I ought to kill you for this. Here. Now!" He lunged at Throws Away Wealth.

The chief whipped the knife he had been playing with from his belt and held it's sharp tip to the neck of the furious slave.

"You won't though, will you?" said Throws Away Wealth softly. The slave glared at him, hatred a palpable thing in the air.

"What's to stop me now that I know the truth about you?" he hissed. "The truth that you let me think all these years that one word from you and the people would call me sorcerer."

"They would!"

"You almost had *me* believing that *I* did it! Many times I thought of that feather. How it could get from my son's grave to that old woman's hair—"

"You are a fool," snorted Throws Away Wealth.

"Not too much of a fool to kill you," snarled the enraged slave.

The tip of the chief's prized iron knife pushed against the slave's throat. "Get back," warned the chief. "Get back or I will kill *you*!"

They glared at each other for several long moments. Then with a low growl, the slave subsided. In a daze, he noticed the several slaves who had come running to their master's aid. Throws Away Wealth watched Dog Shadow closely, then, satisfied the man was well and truly cowed, he waved the slaves away. Dog Shadow collapsed on a mat near the fire. He held his head in his hands.

When they were left alone again, Throws Away Wealth said, "You are in too deep to back out now. I still need you, the work you can do for me."

"What do you mean? I can get away from you. I am sick to death of you and your sly killings."

"That may be, slave, but you did them for me. Too many men, and women, have died at your hand. Betray me now and you will not live to see the sun set on this day."

"What do I care, you vicious excuse for a chief? All these years, I did your killing, hurting people because if I did not, my own life was at stake. . . ."

"You enjoyed it. You loved the power that came with it. The fear. I've seen you with the other slaves. . . . You're in this just as much as I am."

The slave shook his head. "No. No, you forced me to kill, to maim. . . ."

"You make me sick. You never cared before about the men—or women—I had you kill. And you don't care now."

"I've had a bellyful. A bellyful of you, of your sickening orders . . ."

"Quit now, and you are a dead man."

"How? Another accidental drowning?" Dog Shadow sneered.

Throws Away Wealth sat back, breathing heavily from the heated exchange of words. "Your family will pay, then."

"What about my family?"

"Your poor wife. How would she manage if you weren't around to feed her and all those brats you sired on her? Nine, isn't it? *Hoowhay*, yes, and those two other brats off that other slavewoman. Oh, don't look so surprised. I know all about you and your family—families, I should say."

"Why you—!"

"Uh-uh, must not attack your tyee." Throws Away Wealth fastidiously removed the slave's clawed hand from around his neck but he was in no real danger from Dog Shadow now and they both knew it. "Must not have that. Something might happen to your precious families. I'll see to it, myself." He looked Dog Shadow straight in the eye.

The other held his gaze for a terrible moment before dropping his eyes. "Damn you, damn you," he hissed.

Throws Away Wealth could feel the man's pent up hatred and he shivered in excitement. He thrived on hate, lived on it. He laughed, exultant in his triumph. Then he relaxed. It was going to be all right. He shook himself, foolish to have thought a mere slave could challenge him, he who was so much smarter. . . .

"Have a drink," he said, smiling beatifically. "You can leave for Ahousat in the morning."

The slave grunted and accepted the bottle. He took a long, deep swallow. The two took turns drinking until the bottle was empty and Dog Shadow lay comatose on the floor.

Throws Away Wealth called over two husky slaves. "Take him to his quarters," he said and kicked the prone figure lying at his feet. The slaves dragged Dog Shadow away.

"Throws Away Wealth stretched, ready for his bed. *Hoowhay*, it had been a good night's work.

Chapter 14

Chance lay on his back staring up at the cedar plank ceiling. Dawn's light fingers crept across the sky, but inside the longhouse it was still dark. He'd slept little through the night. It had been late when he'd left his brother, too late to go and disturb Haina in her new quarters. He had no desire to fuel talk and speculation about her among the longhouse occupants, so he'd quietly sought out a bed in his brother's quarters. He sighed heavily, his thoughts somber on this morn.

Throws Away Wealth was a good man, but it was getting difficult to talk with him. Was it the rum? Chance pondered. His brother had always been difficult—for others, not for Chance.

Chance stared at the ceiling and watched little fingers of light creep through the cracks between roof planks. He wondered what to do. Maybe a move would do him good. He would move out of his brother's quarters. Today. He needed his own living quarters, now that he had Haina with him. The thought of Haina filled him with renewed vigor and he rose lithely from the bed.

Once dressed in his favorite bear robe, he dug through his clothing until he found the little leather sack he was searching for. He hefted it's light weight in his hands and smiled to himself.

No one was awake yet in his brother's living area, so Chance decided to find Haina.

The wailing cry of a hungry baby pierced the early morning stillness. The quiet longhouse was slowly awakening.

Chance walked through the middle of the longhouse until he came to Kelp Woman's living area.

He had known Kelp Woman a long time. She was the widow of one of his best friends, a commoner, and she had been very beloved by the man. Chance always tried to make things easier for her, giving her a fish whenever necessary. Not that Kelp Woman ever asked him for anything. Far from it, she was grateful for whatever he gave her, but never imposed on his good will. An unusual woman, Kelp Woman, he smiled to himself with an ironic twist to his lips.

No one was awake at Kelp Woman's living area, either. Chance knelt at the fire pit and placed slivers of cedar wood on the smoking embers from last night's fire. He soon had a crackling fire burning. He put three big chunks of wood on the blaze. Next he filled an old iron pot with water, then set it in the flames to heat. He chuckled to himself as he imagined Haina's delight with the little surprise he planned for her.

"Wake up, *Chummuss*." He leaned over the sleeping woman. Haina stirred from a dream of passionate love-making with Chance. Suddenly he was there, his warm lips on hers and it was no dream. She awoke at once, her eyes wide and staring into his dancing green ones.

He kissed her again then sat back on his heels. "Awake at last. Come, I have something for you."

Haina was tempted to tell him to go away and let her sleep. Instead she waved him away and reached for her clothes. She'd despaired of ever again seeing him gentle and soft like this. When he had not sought her out last night, she'd known he no longer wanted her.

So what was he doing here this morning? He was looking so pleased with himself. Probably had arranged a high price for her ransom, she thought morosely as she dressed. The red and white trade dress, as much as she liked it, was still damp from the rain yesterday. She put on a traditional cedar kutsack, tied her long black hair back with a cedar thong and walked over to the fire pit. She sat down next to Chance.

"Here," said Chance, as he thrust a steaming mug at her. Haina took it reflexively then gazed into the dark depths. She inhaled the fragrant steam.

"Tea! Oh, Chance, tea!" Excited, she took a sip, but it was too hot and she burned her lip.

"Easy, *Chummuss,*" he cautioned. He leaned over and gently kissed the burned lip. "There."

She smiled up at him, her dark eyes twinkling. "Where did you get this tea? Surely you did not paddle all the way to Yuquot and back in the night." She knew there was no way he could have done such a thing—the distance was too great. She was happy about the tea of course, but happier still that he had surprised her with it. A man who was tired of a woman would not try to please her with such a gift, would he?

"I got it from the trader at Chicklesit."

"Oh, Chance, it's so wonderful to have a cup of tea in the morning." She took another sip. The slight bitterness on her tongue tasted refreshing; the aroma drifted to her nose and she sighed. Her sigh was contentment itself.

Chance watched her and sipped his own mug of tea. He smiled easily, unwilling to say anything to disturb her obvious happiness at tasting the smoky

167

brew. He liked to see her happy he decided. How could he let her go? He could not, and that was that. He'd speak to his brother and tell him something, anything, but he was not going to let Haina go. He knew that now.

They finished their tea in silence, Haina with a look of bliss on her face. "More," she demanded, holding out her cup.

Chance chuckled and obliged her as he made a second cup for them both. They again drank in companionable silence and Haina thought to herself how nice it would be if every morning were like this: Chance, herself and a cup of delicious tea. She did not even mind that there was no sugar to sweeten it. Surely life could not offer anything better!

Kelp Woman approached, with a sleepy Pine Cone perched on one hip. "How honored we are to have the tyee's younger brother join us for breakfast," she said graciously to Chance.

He acknowledged her greeting with a regal nod of his head.

"'Tyee's younger brother'?" echoed Haina, looking at him, askance. Any question she had died on her lips as she saw Mudshark approach.

"Greetings, cousin," said Mudshark. "Mind if I join you?" And he sat down without waiting for an answer.

Kelp Woman went to fetch another cup.

The men talked about fishing while Haina helped Kelp Woman prepare breakfast. "It is most fortunate that Old Granny and Pine Cone went digging for clams yesterday," murmured Kelp Woman as she scooped cooked clams out of the hot water in the iron pot. At last the two women spread broad leaves on a cedar mat. They piled the food onto the leaves: cold fish from the night before, fresh blackberries, and the clams. Haina set out small bowls of whale oil as a condiment. It would not do to offer food without the delicious whale oil to pour over it.

The four adults talked through breakfast while the two children nibbled at their meal and then played. When Chance said, "I want to go catch some cod, or mayhaps some salmon," Haina perked up.

Mudshark agreed to go with him.

"I would like to come too," said Haina. "It has been too long since I went fishing. It is one of my favorite things to do."

Chance looked at her. "I remember the first time I saw you, you were fishing . . . ."

He broke off when he caught Mudshark's eye and the two men grinned as though they shared some secret joke. Haina's cheeks flushed. She knew very well what the joke was, but it was not funny to her. She had been fishing when Chance had kidnapped her.

Haina ate quietly and let the other three talk. Her thoughts drifted from the kidnapping to the words Kelp Woman had let drop. 'Tyee's younger brother'. What did that mean? How could Chance, a white man, be the brother of Throws Away Wealth, an Indian? And yet, if he was, then she, Haina, had been vastly mistaken about Chance's status. For if he was the tyee's brother, then Chance was a nobleman.

Haina cringed inside as she remembered her haughty words to Chance when she believed him to be a mere commoner. How he must have laughed at her! Or hated her—noblemen were proud men. Mayhaps that explained his strange behavior to her, warm one time, cold the next.

Finally the interminable meal was over and Chance rose to his feet. Mudshark, too, rose and thanked his hostess for the food. He watched her keenly as she poked at the dirt floor with her big toe. When he left, Kelp Woman's eyes followed him. Pine Cone's cries brought her attention back.

Haina started to clean up and Kelp Woman went over to the bed to nurse Pine Cone. As Haina straightened with a half-full bowl of oil in her hand, Chance tipped her chin up. "You may come fishing with me anytime you want to," he said arrogantly. Seeing her raise the cup and the dangerous gleam in her eye, he held her hand stiffly away. "Oh no, you don't. No more baths in oil for me."

He started to bring her hand with the cup in it closer, closer to her own face until she shrieked his name. Laughing, he let her go and sauntered away. "I'll let you know when we're leaving to go fishing," he called over his shoulder and then he was gone.

"Arrogant man," muttered Haina as she slammed pots and mugs about. Kelp Woman looked over at her questioningly and Haina restrained herself. Why did that man do this to her? One day she flew high with love for him, the next she plunged to the depths with fear he no longer wanted her. What to do, oh, what to do?

Chance roused Throws Away Wealth from bed. His brother sat up, groggy, eyes red-rimmed, thin body bowed as he clutched a handful of furs. "I'll wait for you at your hearth," said Chance. "That will give you time to get dressed."

When his brother finally put in an appearance at the hearth, Chance almost felt sorry for him. He looked like he'd spent the night wrestling spirits of the dark, and Chance said as much to him.

"Bah," muttered the older man. "Too damn early in the morning to be up and about." He waved a slave over and helped himself to the smoked fish on the platter the slave carried. "What do you want?"

Chance fought down his annoyance at Throws Away Wealth's bluntness and came directly to the point. "You are the one that called me back from Chicklesit.

What do *you* want?"

"Ah yes, I did, didn't I?" Throws Away Wealth grew silent. Finally he said, "I called you back because enough time has passed that Fighting Wolf has given up looking for his daughter."

"Oh? Is that a guess?"

"Certainly not. I happen to know that his family had a funeral service for their dear, departed daughter." These last words were said in a sneer that curled Throws Away Wealth's lip in a most unbecoming manner. "My informants assure me that he thinks she is dead."

Throws Away Wealth was watching Chance closely. Chance merely nodded. So, the father had given up the search. He relaxed, satisfied. Now Haina was his, all his, should he decide to keep her. Of course, Haina would not be too pleased to find that her family thought she was dead. Doubtless she would try to get some word to them, but he would deal with that when the time came. It was enough that for now, he had her to himself.

"About the hostage, Haina," Chance began.

Throws Away Wealth stopped chewing. He looked alert for the first time. "What about her? You still have her, don't you? She hasn't escaped, has she?"

Uneasy at the thread of alarm he detected in his brother's voice, Chance hastened to reassure him. "Yes, yes, she's here. I've kept her with me."

Throws Away Wealth grunted and seemed to relax. He went back to picking at the fish. He looked around with a disgusted frown and then waved another slave over. "Oil," he demanded and the man hurried away.

"What about the hostage?" Throws Away Wealth asked when the slave had fetched a kelp bulb full of oil.

"I want to keep her," stated Chance evenly.

For a moment Chance thought his brother was going to have some kind of a seizure. "Keep her?" he screeched. Seeing the house slaves turn at the sound, he lowered his voice. "Keep her? What are you talking about? Have you lost your wits?"

"Not at all, brother," Chance grinned at his tyee's shocked face. "It is merely that I have no wish to return Haina to her father."

"But we can get a good price. . . ." said the older man, recovering himself.

"Price be damned," exploded Chance. "I want to keep her—with me! I do not want to ransom her. I do not want to return her to her father. I do not want to let her go. Do you understand?"

Throws Away Wealth gazed calculatingly at the younger man. So, that was the way the wind blew, was it? Well, he mused, Chance's impetuosity could be used against him. He smiled craftily. Let the pup keep his toy, he thought. Fighting Wolf would find his daughter soon enough when the slave, Dog Shadow, told him where to look. And Fighting Wolf would be so enraged he would kill Chance for daring to kidnap that bitch of a daughter. . . .

Chance watched Throws Away Wealth as he smiled to himself and absently rubbed his hands together. What was going on in his brother's mind?

Throws Away Wealth gazed into the fire, trying to hide his glee. Yes, let the pup keep his toy. It would only be a few days before Fighting Wolf would be here, pounding down the longhouse doors to get at Chance . . . to kill him! A surge of power raced through his thin frame. Yes, it was a good plan. It mattered little what Chance did, whether he kept the daughter or tried to ransom her. In fact, keeping her would work into his plans very well. Very well indeed.

Still, it would not do to let Chance have his way too easily.

"But my dear brother," he whined, "it was all your plan to kidnap the bi—wench in the first place. Surely you can see that your original plan was a good one. We could enrich ourselves by many slaves were we to ransom her." Throws Away Wealth's voice was wheedling. Not for nothing did he love to be in the winter plays and dramatics his people loved so well. He always let his followers convince him to play the lead roles—heroes and the like. Like now.

"I am sorry for that, Tyee," said Chance. "I sincerely meant to ransom her when she first fell into my path. But now, now that I know her, well, it is not as easy as I thought to let her go." He hesitated a moment. "It is not easy for me to admit such a thing, my brother. But I know you will understand. I trust you with my thoughts."

Throws Away Wealth's face lit up. "And well you should, younger brother. Well you should." He smiled beatifically at the younger man. "You can always trust me."

Chapter 15

Chance was pleased with the way the talk with his brother had gone. It had not been easy, but he had finally convinced Throws Away Wealth to let Haina stay at Kyuquot. He hurried off to find her.

Haina was not in Kelp Woman's quarters. When he asked the woman where she had gone, Kelp Woman could only shrug.

At first he had merely searched the village for Haina. Then growing alarmed, he had made a fool of himself asking any and all throughout the village if anyone had seen her. At last Mudshark had taken pity on his distraught state and reported that he had seen Haina paddling due west in the small, one-seater canoe. She was certainly off to the fishing grounds. Chance had not stayed around to challenge the wink and the smirk on his cousin's face. He had rushed after her.

All this came back to Chance as he approached the woman leaning over the side of her dugout canoe. He stopped paddling and rested the pointed paddle athwart the canoe. The prow of his craft bounced nose-to-nose with Haina's dugout. He gripped the paddle shaft with white knuckles as he ground out, "And just what do you think you're doing?"

Now that he had found her he wanted to swamp her canoe and drag her back to the village with him. "You should not have come out alone! It is too dangerous. What were you doing? You were trying to escape, don't deny it!"

Haina looked at him, dumbfounded. "Escape?" she stuttered, bewilderment written large across her face. "No, I—I was merely fishing."

Chance glowered at her. Desire and anger fought in his gaze.

"I got tired of waiting for you to take me fishing."

"Still, you should have waited for me," Chance bit out.

"Why?" She waved her hand casually. "I am perfectly capable of taking care of myself. I know how to fish. I do not need you to tell me when and how to do it." She bent over her line again and gave a small pull, hoping to attract a large cod off the bottom of the sea floor. When Chance said nothing, she glanced up at him, shielding her eyes against the glare of the sun. "Well?" she asked.

"Well, what?"

"Now that you are here, aren't you going to join me? I already have two big ones," and she pointed to the pair of gasping gray cod in the bottom of her canoe.

"Why do you always make me feel like gnashing my teeth, woman?"

Haina giggled delightedly, knowing that his temper was abating. "Is that what I make you feel like doing? Mayhaps I will make you toothless."

"Mayhaps. And soon, too." He looked over the side into the depths of the green water. There was only a small roll to the sea. "Leave some fish for me, woman," he ordered, that slow smile that Haina loved curving his lips.

Haina ducked her head. "Find your own, Kyuquot." And the rest of the afternoon was spent in desultory conversation and companionable fishing.

Chance and Haina had just finished thanking Kelp Woman for the delicious evening meal when a slave approached.

He bowed and said, "My master, Throws Away Wealth, wishes to see you."

Chance wiped his mouth with the back of his hand and stood up. "Very well, I will come now." He started to walk away.

"Excuse me, sir," interrupted the slave. "The tyee wishes you to bring the woman hostage, also."

Chance frowned. "Are you certain, slave?" he asked. There was no need to involve Haina in any talks with Throws Away Wealth.

"That's what he told me, sir," the slave answered, swallowing. Perspiration stood out on his brow though the room was not warm. He rubbed absently at a large bruise on his upper arm. "Please come, sir. The tyee does not like to be kept waiting."

Chance heard the urgency in the man's voice and wondered at it. He touched the slave's bicep where the ugly purple bruise lay dark against the man's tan skin. "How came you by that mark?"

Eyes fixed straight ahead, the slave repeated, "The tyee does not like to be kept waiting, sir."

Chance gazed thoughtfully at the man. It was possible the slave had obtained the bruise by some innocent means such as wrestling, or he could have been beaten. Chance's lips tightened at the thought. Brutality to slaves was a common enough practice in Nootka society, but he himself did not countenance the beating of helpless men and women.

"Very well, then. Come along, Haina."

She got to her feet and followed Chance through the longhouse. "I want to speak to this tyee," she said, her chin tilted at a precarious angle.

"Oh?" Chance cocked an eyebrow at her. "Do you hope to plead your case in front of him?"

"Would it do any good?"

"Probably not." After a moment, he asked, "And what would you ask, *Chummuss*? Would you ask to be ransomed?" He had been reluctant to tell her she was to stay with him. Now he wondered if he had been wise to keep quiet.

"What would you have me ask?" she shot back. Did he want her to go, or to stay? For herself, she wanted . . .

"Coyness does not become you, *Chummuss*." His voice sharpened. "Just answer me. Would you ask to be ransomed?"

She slanted a glance at him. He was staring straight ahead as they walked through the longhouse. His jaw muscles clenched briefly, then were still. "I would stay," she whispered softly, so softly he had to lean close to hear her.

He stopped walking and turned to face her. "Good," he grunted. "I have already made arrangements for you to stay. The tyee has agreed."

"Then why does he want to see me?"

Chance shrugged. "I'm curious to see why, myself." He had no opportunity to say more because just then a woman came up and tugged on his arm. "Please, sir, won't you help me?"

"What do you want, woman?" Chance halted and gently unwound the woman's fingers from his arm. Haina waited quietly at his side, curious to see what would happen.

"Please, sir. It is my neighbor." At Chance's nod, she hurried on, "She lives in the space right next to me. Every night she has people in her home. I do not object to that. It is just that they are loud, and laugh and talk until the sun is ready to come up. I can get no sleep and have four children to look after each day. My old husband has told my neighbor and her guests to be quiet, but they just laugh at him and keep on singing and dancing. Please, please, can you not stop them?"

"When does your neighbor start her visiting?"

"In late evening, sir."

"I will visit your quarters later today. I will talk with your other neighbors and make a decision at that time."

"Very good, sir. Thank you." The woman bowed herself away.

Haina watched the whole scene with her mouth open. Just then a middle-aged man pushed himself forward from the small crowd clamoring for Chance's attention. The man's angry voice was raised as he told of how he had been cheated by a white trader at Yuquot. Chance heard him out, then suggested quietly that the man be more careful in this next time. There was nothing Chance could do in this particular case and he told the man that. The man was still angry but he seemed to accept Chance's words.

Haina watched closely as several people, of varying ages, approached Chance. She was surprised to see how respectfully they treated him. One woman tugged on his arm, he disengaged her carefully, but listened to what she had to say.

Chance made a brief comment to the woman. She nodded and left with a satisfied look on her face. Several people waited patiently for their turn. Haina marveled that he gave each one his complete attention before making judgements. What manner of man was this?

Throws Away Wealth watched Chance and Haina's slow progress towards his quarters. His eyes narrowed in hatred as he saw the people, *his* Kyuquot people, seeking the younger man's advice. So they thought Chance's judgement was better than his own, did they? From the intent look on Chance's face, Throws Away Wealth could tell the white man was puffed up with his own importance as the people begged his help. How sickening! Throws Away Wealth clenched his teeth as he thought of Chance's bold bid for the chieftainship. He thought to win the people over, did he? He, Throws Away Wealth, would have to do something about that! He would die before he would let his people set him aside and choose that— that—*white man* for tyee. Throws Away Wealth's upper lip curled.

At last the crowd dispersed, and Haina and Chance walked the short distance to Throws Away Wealth's living space.

Haina glanced around the tyee's quarters. The floor was bare, hard-packed dirt. Several iron cooking pots were set near the fire. Empty burden baskets were stacked near one wall, empty berry cake frames next to them. The tyee must have many slaves to fill so many baskets and frames, thought Haina. Baskets of herbs lined the other wall just in front of the plank beds mounded high with white man's trading blankets.

This Throws Away Wealth must be a wealthy man, thought Haina. Indeed, his name meant that he was so rich he could afford to throw away his wealth and still have much left over. She mused on his name. It tickled at the back of her mind. She'd heard of him before. But where? The thought nagged at her but she couldn't quite remember. Ah, well, it could not have been important.

"Sit down, sit down," urged the older man seated beside the fire. Chance and Haina sat.

Haina surveyed the tyee through lowered lashes. His narrow chest was naked, a blanket draped his lap, and he had an empty cup clamped in one hand. Haina could see the veins and bones of his hand stand out. When she raised her eyes to his face her eyes widened. Deep set eyes stared back at her like the glittering eyes of a hawk. She shivered and dropped her gaze.

When she looked up again, his attention had shifted to Chance.

"So this is the Ahousat wench. Kind of scrawny looking, isn't she? Little, too. She's not going to get sick on you, is she?" Throws Away Wealth observed.

Haina squirmed under his scrutiny but her small chin shot high in the air. "I can assure you that I am not easily sick. And you need not talk about me as though I were not present."

"Ill-tempered, too, I see," taunted the tyee. He regarded her a moment longer. "She's not the woman her mother was," he assured Chance. "Not at all."

Suddenly it came to Haina where she had heard this tyee's name before. Of course, he was the one who had been briefly pledged to marry her mother so long ago! Several things began to fall into place. His cold glances towards her. Her capture. She knew a tentative truce had existed between the Kyuquots and her people, the Ahousats, but it had never taken much for her father to voice his suspicions of the Kyuquots, especially this man, Throws Away Wealth. She must tread very carefully with him.

The older man gazed at her thoughtfully. "We Kyuquots do not like our hostages to get sick."

"Tyee, we agreed that she was no longer a hostage," interrupted Chance. "If you have changed your mind, I'd like to know about it. Now."

Throws Away Wealth eyed him. "Ah yes, you wanted to keep her. Very well, she is your slave."

Startled, Haina turned to Chance. "What—? I am to be your slave?" Haina tried, albeit not too hard, to keep her voice from rising to a shriek.

"Tyee, no mention was made that she was to be a slave," said Chance, ignoring Haina. "We agreed that she was no longer a hostage."

"Yes," agreed Throws Away Wealth. "I just naturally assumed that if she was not a hostage, she was a slave. Surely," he added smoothly, "you could not think to free her?"

"That's exactly what I thought to do."

Throws Away Wealth shook his head. "I am afraid that such a thing cannot be," he sighed. "If she were free, she would be free to return to her father, and once he heard that you had captured her—no matter the circumstances now—he would want full revenge. That would mean war!" He shook his head again. "No, I cannot allow it." He was proud of the regret he let creep into his voice.

A slave! With no hope of freedom! Haina could not believe what her ears were hearing. Far better to be a hostage, than a slave.

Chance sat, stunned.

"You *did* tell the wench why you captured her?" murmured Throws Away Wealth. He was enjoying his guests' shock. They both looked sick. Ah, but the white dog had not squirmed enough, in his opinion. The puppy was soft on the woman. Mayhaps he could wreak some damage there. Throws Away Wealth gazed innocently at Haina. "He did tell you why he captured you, did he not?" he persisted.

Haina turned glazed eyes to him. She shook her head, her thoughts in a turmoil. "No. I thought—I thought it was for the slaves you would get in ransom."

Throws Away Wealth chuckled. "Oh, you are a delight, Ahousat wench." He shook his head, vastly amused. "No, not for slaves." He gestured around his living quarters. "I have many slaves. Many. I do not need more." He smiled benignly. "He captured you for revenge."

Haina looked at Chance. He was watching the tyee. "Revenge?" she echoed.

"Mmm-hmm. Revenge for the loss of your mother. She married the Ahousat instead of *me*."

"But that was so long ago. . . ."

"True, but we Kyuquots have long memories," answered Throws Away Wealth.

"Revenge," murmured Haina. She looked at Chance as if seeing him for the first time. "Is that true?"

"Yes, but—"

"And I suppose the love you declared for me was all part of that revenge, wasn't it?" Her voice was raised, slaves were staring, but she was beyond caring who listened. "You Kyuquot bastard! All you thought of was your plans of revenge!"

Throws Away Wealth hugged himself delightedly. "We Kyuquots would not allow Ahousats to get the better of us," he said loftily.

Haina swung on him. "You keep out of this, you pompous oaf!"

"Unmannerly wench! I'll have you taken to the slaves' quarters," threatened the tyee nastily.

"Haina, *Chummuss*—"

"Don't you 'Haina, *Chummuss*', me! All this time you had planned for revenge! Didn't *I* mean anything to you? Anything?" She got to her feet, her voice shaking, chest heaving and eyes flashing. "I never, never, want to see you again, Kyuquot bastard!" she cried and turned on her heel and dashed for Kelp Woman's quarters.

Chance watched her go, his heart in his eyes. Throws Away Wealth observed him intently.

"Let her go," he advised. "She will cool down and come to accept her lot."

Chance looked at him. He, too, rose to his feet. His eyes on his brother were unreadable. "I must take my leave," he said politely. He bowed out of the tyee's presence.

Throws Away Wealth smiled in satisfaction. The visit had gone better than he had hoped for. Now, all he had to do was wait for Fighting Wolf to arrive. . . .

Chapter 16

"Come, Haina," panted Chance, dragging her towards him by the hand. It had taken him all day and into the evening to find her. "We can't speak here."

"I do not, *do not*, want to speak with you ever again!"

"Haina," pleaded Chance. "Let us get out of this longhouse. Everyone can hear our every word in here. This will be bad for your status."

"Bad for my status!" she shrieked. "What status? I have no status! I am only a slave!" Her voice rose on the last word and her eyes flashed.

Chance looked at her helplessly. How to explain this mess? "Come," he encouraged. "We will walk outside as the sun sets over the sea and discuss this."

"Discuss? Discuss? There is nothing to discuss. I demand to go home! I demand to be ransomed!"

In exasperation, Chance reached for her. He threw the startled Haina over one shoulder and marched for the door.

"Let me go! Let me go!" Haina beat at his

shoulders with her fists, but Chance kept striding towards the door. "Put me down!" she howled.

Behind him, he heard the murmurs of the watchers, but he knew he had to get Haina away from there and cooled down.

They reached the deserted beach. It was a calm evening, that moment of sunset when the whole world is still and perfect. Purples and oranges lit up the sky. A gentle tangy salt breeze brushed the hair from Chance's hot face.

"Now, my little cougar," he panted as he placed her carefully feet first onto the beach, "you can scream all you want!"

Haina wanted to take him at his word, she was so enraged. But somehow she knew that mindless screaming would not help her any. She settled for stating her anger in no uncertain terms. "I want to go home. You have made me a slave. A slave!" She glared at him. His blond hair was tousled and moved easily in the wind. His green eyes watched her warily.

They stood like that for many heartbeats. She wanted to lash out at him for all that had happened to her. And it was all his fault!

"Haina," he said quietly. "I know this has come as a shock to you. But it has been a shock to me, too. I did not know when my brother agreed so readily that he had slavery in mind."

"Oh, so now you blame your brother," she jeered. "How easy that is to do." She conveniently forgot that she herself had been happy to blame Chance just moments before.

Chance said nothing. It was a useless thing to do, he thought. Still, he wished his brother had been more straightforward. . . .

"Oh, Chance," Haina moaned. "How could you?" Tears welled in her eyes and she dashed them away. "How could you make sweet love to me and then turn me into your slave? Your revenge is complete!"

"Haina," he took both her hands in his. "I did not make you a slave. I swear it. Throws Away Wealth surprised me, just as he did you. I had no intention but to make you a free woman!" He sought her downcast eyes. "It's true," he said softly, "that it was in revenge that I led the raid to capture you. But revenge is not so important to me now. . . ."

He added softly, "Haina, I love you. I don't wish to hurt you. Ever."

Dare she believe his words? It was so what she wanted, longed to hear. "But, but how—?" she croaked. "How am I to be free?" She swallowed and gave a bitter chuckle. "And here I thought—" She fell silent.

"Thought what?" prodded Chance.

"Thought that you and I—" She broke off. "When I found out that you were a nobleman, I dared to hope that you—that nothing stood in the way of—"

"Of what?" He stroked her black hair gently. When she said nothing, he said, "Of us?"

She nodded. *Of our marriage*, she thought silently. She reached for him.

He enfolded her in his arms. "Aah, Haina. I love you so."

They stood together a long time, the gentle breeze tugging at their hair, the water chuckling at their feet as each wave touched the shore. They watched as the sun sank into the sea and still they stood there.

"Come," Chance said at last. "Let us walk along the beach. The light of the moon is enough to see by." Indeed, it was true. Haina could pick her way carefully along the beach by the light of the bright halfmoon hanging above the earth.

Chance took Haina's hand and led her along the slippery rocks near the water's edge. Soon they rounded the corner of the beach and the village was hidden from view.

The night was so beautiful with the stars winking down at her, and Chance leading her along the beach, that Haina thought there had never been a night as full of wonder as this one.

And Chance loved her! He had told her so. Somehow that made up for the revenge he'd taken. And if he loved her, he'd see her free. He could do no less. He loved her! Oh, how long she had waited to hear those words, to know that all the love she had for him was returned. Together. They could be together at last!

"Where are we going?" she asked. She did not recognize this section of the beach. She had only walked the beach in front of the village, not ventured this far away.

"I'll show you," Chance promised and continued to lead the way, stumbling sometimes against a stone. She walked slowly behind him, trusting him to lead her to a safe place.

"Here," he said. "This is the spot I was searching for." By now he was leading her across the beach to the high tide line. An alder tree had fallen across the upper beach and she could see its ragged branches entangled with dried seaweed.

Big logs crisscrossed the top of the beach. Floating in on winter storms, they'd been abandoned by the sea to the merciless rain and wind. Weathering over the years had given them a smooth gray, patina. Darker gray shadows lay between the logs—patches of sand, Haina knew.

Chance found a spot behind one of the logs and sat down on the sand. "Here," he said softly. "You'll be protected from the wind here."

Haina walked slowly over, knowing what would come next. She knelt down beside him and looked intently into his eyes. "Chance?" she asked.

He was taking off his knife belt. "Mmm?"

"Chance, how will I be freed?"

He took off his bear robe and laid it out on the sand beneath him.

"You will never be a slave, Haina. That I promise you." The grimness in his tone convinced her that he spoke the truth. "I will tell my brother that. He cannot keep you as a slave, and I certainly won't. You are a free woman, free to stay with me."

He watched her solemnly. The moonlight struck her dark hair and made it blue. Her eyes were hidden as she watched him and he wondered if she realized he had said nothing about her freedom to go. . . . He was not willing to part with her.

The moonlight made his hair even lighter, Haina decided. He was watching her so intently, even now. Did he not know that she loved him? Wanted only to stay with him? She smiled. "I love you, Chance Gift from the Sea." She thought she saw him relax.

Then he reached for her and she came into his arms willingly. They held each other closely and it was as if they had newly discovered how precious the other was. Long ardent kisses were soon replaced by heated, passionate touches. And Haina met him with all the love that was in her.

Later, as she lay sleeping in his arms, it was Chance's turn to wonder. He must make his brother understand that he, Chance, wanted this woman and that he would do anything, brave anything, to keep her.

Chapter 17

"Did you want some breakfast?" asked Chance.

Haina looked up from the fishing line she was holding over the gunwale of the gently rocking canoe. "Breakfast? No, no thank you. I'm—I'm not hungry." Nausea twisted her stomach. "I don't even know why I'm fishing this morning. I certainly won't eat anything we catch."

Chance looked at her strangely. "Why—?"

"All the more for me," came Mudshark's hearty voice. "I've never seen a woman who could catch so many fish. How do you do it?"

Haina smiled weakly over at Chance's cousin. "I do all the proper rituals," she said.

"Hmmph. So do I, but the fish don't come to my line like they do to yours."

"Are you still complaining?" joined in Beachdog. He sat in his own canoe. Whale Hunter and another man were with him and their craft bobbed gently on the swell of the sea. Beachdog peered over the side into Chance's canoe. It was common knowledge that

Chance called his canoe "Overflows With Fish" whenever he used it for fishing.

"You have a long way to go before your canoe lives up to its name," Beachdog said jovially to Chance. "You only have three fish." Beachdog held up five young salmon, their silver scales glinting in the rosy dawn. "I have five—five big ones." He laid them carefully back on the bottom of his canoe. "The woman caught all of yours, didn't she?"

When Chance and Mudshark did not answer, Beachdog guffawed, his two companions echoing him.

Haina had seen the stranger with him before and she did not like him. Once she'd seen him tormenting a slavewoman.

"You need a woman to teach you how to fish, you weaklings."

The two in the canoe with Beachdog chuckled at his wit. Whale Hunter looked especially amused at Chance's discomfiture, thought Haina.

Chance and Mudshark ignored the jibes and patiently continued to study the water where their lines disappeared into the green depths.

Beachdog was still watching them.

Mudshark said, "Why don't you go fish over there?" He pointed. "I saw a sea lion there awhile ago. He'd like a plump loudmouth for his breakfast, I'm sure."

Haina giggled.

Beachdog frowned at that. With a snort, he raised his line. The two with him pulled in theirs. They'd caught no fish. Beachdog paddled away, but not in the direction indicated by Mudshark. They settled at some distance and Haina watched them drop their lines once more.

Then her attention was distracted by a tug on her own line and she felt a thrill of excitement as she held on to the now taut line. Taking her time, she pulled a still struggling cod into the boat. She beamed with pride.

Chance watched her, a slow smile curving his lips. She looked so beautiful in the early morning light. Her hair was blowing loose and free; her eyes held a glow.

She caught him looking at her. "Another big one," she chortled. "When are you going to catch one, Chance?"

"I'm in no hurry," he said yawning. "They'll bite soon."

At the stern of the canoe, Mudshark shifted slightly. "I'm going to take a nap," he announced and soon they heard gentle snores coming from him.

Chance smiled that slow smile. "Now there's just you and me," he said. He crawled closer to Haina.

She watched him come and smiled into his eyes. She was beginning to feel better. He looked so handsome this morning, she thought, with his dark blond hair and—she sniffed a whiff of pine scent—his clean shaven cheeks. She was pleased to see that he was still using her deer fat mixture to shave with.

The canoe suddenly shuddered. She warned, "Don't tip the canoe."

"I've been in canoes all my life," he retorted. "I know how to move carefully."

Now he was behind her and he wrapped his arms around her. She glanced down at the cod, still flopping on the bottom of the canoe. She felt Chance's warm lips on the nape of her neck. "Mmmm," he murmured. "I'm hungry for breakfast, even if you aren't."

She elbowed him in the chest. "Chance," she whispered. "Someone will see. . . ."

"Mudshark's asleep," he said, continuing his maddening assault on her neck.

"Beachdog . . ."

"Beachdog is too far away to see anything."

Haina glanced in the direction the Kyuquots had

gone. Now Beachdog and and his companions were drifting farther away, the waves pushing them slowly in the direction of the village. She could not see it; they had paddled for a long time to get to the fishing grounds.

Haina relaxed and let Chance hold her. They sat like that for a while, Haina with her eyes closed, Chance kissing her softly.

A seagull screamed overhead and broke Haina's gentle reverie. She sat up straighter. Mudshark woke up and looked around. Haina glanced towards Beachdog's canoe. He was paddling back towards the village. Fast. "Chance?"

He looked up. He followed the direction of her gaze. "What the—? Beachdog's paddling as if a sea lion were chasing him." And indeed the three men were barely visible on the horizon.

Chance scanned the sea all around them. "Oh, no."

Mudshark was instantly alert. "What?" He turned in the stern to see what Chance was staring at. He groaned. "Trouble."

Several dark canoe shapes were speeding towards them. The canoes was fast approaching and Chance could see guns from where he sat. He shaded his eyes and could make out the markings on the canoes. They were not Kyuquots.

"Father!" cried Haina.

Chance grabbed his paddle and plunged it into the water. The canoe lurched ahead. Mudshark hastily reached for his paddle. "Pull up the lines!" ordered Chance. Haina jumped to obey.

Chance's paddle strokes were strong and sure, but a crisp westerly breeze blew against them, holding them back. It was soon clear to Haina that they could not outrun their pursuers. The village was too far away and the strangers were gaining too fast.

"Chance!" cried Hainā, worried. "Chance, it's my father!"

"I know that," he gritted. "We've got to get away! If we can't, we'll have to fight. Beachdog had better bring help!"

"He won't bring help," ground out Mudshark. "He's only interested in saving his precious—" He broke off and glanced sheepishly at Haina. "Sorry," he mumbled.

"Just paddle," snorted Chance.

Haina looked at her paddle lying on the bottom of the canoe. Should she help outrace her father or not? She felt torn. She wanted to see him, but she feared what would happen to Chance were her father to catch him. Fighting Wolf could be fearsome. His ferocious reputation up and down the coast was richly deserved. Perhaps if she and Chance made it safely to the village, her father would be content to rescue her and not hurt Chance. She picked up the paddle and sliced its pointed tip cleanly through the green water.

The three paddled hard and fast but their pursuers were still gaining. Then a musket shot echoed over the water and they heard a plop in the waves nearby.

"Halt!" came the cry.

Chance and Mudshark kept paddling. Another shot exploded like thunder, and this time Haina heard a whistling noise close to the canoe.

"He's shooting at us!" Haina shook with fear. Surely her father had gone mad!

"Halt!" came the cry again, much closer.

Chance scanned the sea frantically. Beachdog had disappeared. Mayhaps he would bring reinforcements. If he did not . . . Chance looked over at Haina. She was watching the other canoes, her hand to her mouth, her eyes wide. "If we run," he said to Mudshark, "they may shoot Haina by mistake."

Mudshark nodded. "We all risk getting shot,

cousin."

"I don't want her hurt. Stop paddling!"

Haina watched Mudshark. His eyes met Chance's, held briefly; then he lifted his paddle out of the water and laid it across the gunwales. No one said a word as the Ahousats closed the gap in triumphant silence.

I couldn't risk it, Chance told himself. If she was shot, or killed, it would be too terrible. This way, at least she'll live. At least she's safe. And what about you and Mudshark? came a chiding voice. He'll die. And so will you. Her father won't let you get away alive. Not after kidnapping . . .

Haina watched Fighting Wolf's canoe come closer. He looks tired, she thought. Dark circles marked her father's eyes, and the lines in his face looked deeper. Even his hair looked grayer than before. Why, he's getting old, she thought. Oh, *Nuwiksu!*

Then she saw her brother, Sea Wolf, sitting in the canoe behind her father's. She let out a cry of gladness. I know it's dangerous for Chance, she thought, but I am so glad to see them. I missed them so. Mayhaps I can convince *Nuwiksu* to let Chance go. Mayhaps Sea Wolf will help me. . . .

But the grim look on her brother's face was not encouraging. After he knows how much Chance means to me, after he knows how much I love him, he'll help me, she encouraged herself.

And then her father was speaking. "Haina! My daughter!"

Her father's deep voice was both sad and wonderful to her ears. She could see the relief in his eyes. She reached out and touched his canoe. "*Nuwiksu,*" she said simply. "Father. I'm so glad you found me." She smiled at him and at Sea Wolf. "I missed you so," she said. "Thank you for coming to get me. I knew you would."

"Sea Wolf, help your sister into your canoe," said

her father without acknowledging her welcoming words. She looked at him again and saw his steadfast gaze on Chance. Chance was staring back, no fear on his face. Haina looked wildly around at the men in the other canoes. They were her father's warriors, all of them, men she had known since she was a mere child. And every one of them had a grim, forbidding look on his face. Haina's heart sank a little. Oh Chance, I did not want it to come to this.

She sought to help him. "*Nuwiksu,*" she said softly, "This man, this man helped me when—"

Her father raised his hand to stem her words. "He is our prisoner. You, and you," he pointed to two Ahousat warriors, "lash his canoe to yours, bow and stern."

Chance's canoe was quickly tied in place. Mudshark and Chance still sat silently, jaws locked, faces tense.

"You will both come back to Ahousat, there to meet the anger of the Ahousat people," was all her father said. He turned his back and the entourage started the return trip to Ahousat. The westerly wind pushed at their backs and they skimmed across the sea.

Haina glanced over at Chance but he was staring straight ahead, jaw clenched. Mudshark would not meet her eyes, either. She sighed and glanced back in the direction of Kyuquot village. No canoes, nothing; the horizon was empty. So, she thought. Mudshark was right. Beachdog did just want to save his precious— self.

She swung around and faced forward. The warriors paddled quickly and quietly for home, for Ahousat.

Chapter 18

The small flotilla of canoes continued all day until the Indians stopped to make camp in the lee of an island. A fire was soon burning and one of the warriors staked out six big salmon to be cooked for the evening meal. Haina merely sat on the beach, too tired and too afraid to do anything else.

The whole day she had watched her father, and what she saw boded very poorly for Chance. Fighting Wolf had been glaring at Chance throughout most of the day. Mudshark he ignored. Sea Wolf had been no better. Once she saw her brother raise his fist to Chance, though the blond man towered over him. Sea Wolf had only lowered his fist when he'd caught Haina watching him. A small measure of satisfaction went through her when she realized her father and brother were trying to contain their violence because she was there. For that reason, she stayed as close as possible to Chance and Mudshark once they landed, though her father had expressly forbid her to talk with either of them.

After Haina had managed to choke down the evening meal, she went over to sit beside Chance and Mudshark. They were each tied to a spruce tree by long leather ropes. Their hands were tied in front of them and Haina could see that Chance's fingers were becoming swollen and red.

He's tied too tightly, she thought. She looked around to ask her father to loosen the bonds, but he and Sea Wolf had walked down to the far end of the beach. They were obviously caught up in deep conversation.

Seeing her standing beside the prisoners, some of her father's warriors wandered over. "Keep away from them, my lady. They're dangerous men," warned one of the older men respectfully.

Haina deigned to smile and nod her thanks. "It's quite all right. I am in no danger."

One of the men said something she could not hear and the others chuckled. Haina smiled uncertainly when she saw them looking at her, some curiously, some strangely. Then another man, a youth, looked at Chance and said casually, "I wonder how he'll look after Fighting Wolf is done with him." Seeing he had the others' attention, the youth continued in a loud voice, "Oh, yes. Fighting Wolf has plans for these two. They won't get away with stealing our noblewomen." He bared his teeth at Chance and said, "We'll kill you, big man. But we'll hear you scream and beg for mercy, first!"

"Enough of that," Haina said sharply. Some of the men moved away at her words, intent on finding something else to do on the beach, but a small knot of men formed around her and the prisoners.

Haina glanced around for Sea Wolf and her father but they were still at the far end of the beach, their backs to the campsite. She wanted to call out to them, but she was not going to let these fools see she was nervous. Now the men were crowding closer and she could smell their bodies, sense their fear, and see the hate in their eyes.

"Damn Kyuquots. All they know how to do is fight and raid and steal women!"

"We'll fix these two so they'll never look at a woman again!"

"Ha, ha. Let's cut them up now. Let's not wait till we get to Ahousat!"

Haina was surprised at those words. She had not thought about what would happen once the two Kyuquots reached the safety of Ahousat village.

"No, we have to wait. Fighting Wolf gave that order."

"He'll thank us for taking a piece off this big fellow here." A man was reaching for the sharp knife that dangled at his side.

"*Wik!* No! Fighting Wolf won't want his daughter to see what a mess this big one is when we're done. I say we should wait."

"He stole our tyee's daughter. Death is too good for him."

"Aah, he won't die—right away. We'll carve him up a bit first." Another man was fingering his blade.

The youth, a young man of noble family who had once asked for Haina's hand in marriage, sneered contemptuously at her. "He's probably had her seventeen different ways, including upside down and in front of his village," said the young nobleman.

Haina was mortified. Several of the men guffawed and their laughter and coarse leers hurt her more than she had thought possible. These were her father's own men—men she had known and respected all her life.

Then Chance hurled himself at the nobleman. But the strong bonds tying Chance's hands held and he only made it to the end of the leather thong.

The young nobleman stepped back a pace. Then,

seeing that the rope held, he laughed in Chance's face. Several of the men crowded around now, knives out.

Haina could wait no longer. The men were out of her control. *"Nuwiksu!"* she called. "Come quickly!"

She was relieved when Fighting Wolf looked up. He and Sea Wolf started towards her. She swung around to face the men. "Go!" she said imperiously. "Leave these prisoners alone. You are not to hurt them."

One by one the warriors moved away. The young nobleman was the last to leave. He lowered his voice, but Haina knew that Chance and Mudshark could hear his words. "Next time your father won't be around to help you, bitch." He turned hate-filled eyes on the Kyuquots, then turned back to Haina. "He had you, didn't he? Didn't he?" Haina gasped at the man's words. "You're no noblewoman. You're nothing but a Kyuquot whore now. And to think that I once wanted to marry you." He spat. "Your father could never pay me enough to soil my hands with you now!"

Chance lunged again at the nobleman. Again he was brought up short by the leash. The nobleman turned on him, teeth bared. "As for you, Kyuquot, you are a dead man. I'll see to it, myself." The young nobleman stalked off.

Haina watched him go. She was shaking.

"He'd better kill me," gritted Chance in a low voice. "Because if he doesn't, I'll kill him!"

Haina threw herself at his chest and clutched him. "Chance, oh Chance, what have they done to you?" she moaned. "All this talk about killing."

He pushed her away with his bound hands. His chest heaved in anger. "Stay away from me, Haina. Stay away from me or those bastards will kill you, too."

She looked at him, aghast. Chance, her Chance, had become like another man—one she didn't know.

"He's right," chimed in Mudshark. "They'll take

their hate for us out on you—when we're gone."

"Gone?" echoed Haina. "Gone where?"

Her father approached. "Get away from those prisoners, Haina. I told you not to speak with them. I meant it."

Haina gasped. "But *Nuwiksu*, your men . . . They meant to hurt Chance, hurt Mudshark. I stopped them —this time. You must tell them to leave the Kyuquots alone." She clutched her father's arm tightly. "They mean to hurt them, even kill them."

"They will not touch the prisoners until we get to Ahousat. I promise you that."

"What—what are you saying? What will happen at Ahousat?"

Her father looked at her and she thought she saw pity glint in his eyes. "Leave it be, Haina," he said. "Leave it be."

She looked at Chance. He, too, was looking at her with something akin to pity. "What—?" she began. No one spoke.

"Mudshark?" Her voice was weak and trembling.

"They mean to kill us, Haina," he said softly.

"Kill?" Her head was swimming. The figures in front of her were swimming. She felt herself shaking. "Kill?"

"Yes, but before they do," and a bitter note crept into Mudshark's voice, "they mean to torture us. With your father's approval."

She sank into the blessed relief of darkness.

When she awoke, she was back by the campfire and two burly warriors were guarding her. "These men will stay with you now," said her father evenly. "To keep you safe." He looked over to where the prisoners were tethered and muttered under his breath. "And to keep you away from those two."

It had taken them four full days and nights to

reach Ahousat village. Haina was exhausted by the time she crawled from her brother's canoe to stand on the beach in front of Ahousat village. She'd made it. She glanced over at Chance and Mudshark. They were being kicked from the canoe.

Haina rubbed her arms, shivering in the evening rain. She stumbled onward to her father's longhouse—she could no longer think of it as hers. They had arrived at night. The torture would start tomorrow, she thought dully.

Her foot slipped on a wet stone, but before she could fall one of the bodyguards caught her. He lifted her easily to her feet. She shook her arm free of him. "I can walk by myself," she said haughtily. The man said nothing, only stepped back with a barely perceptible bow. Haina ignored him and straightened her spine. She walked unaided the rest of the way to the longhouse.

She'd almost reached the door when a white dog launched himself at her.

"Stinky! Oh, Stinky!" Haina fell to her knees and hugged the squirming, wiggling animal. She laughed as he jumped up on her, his tongue licking, his tail beating frantically. "Oh, Stinky, how I missed you!" She buried her face in his dear, squirming back but he moved around too much. She hugged and patted the dog until he finally quieted down. She got to her feet. "Come on, Stinky," she murmured and stepped into the long-house.

"Haina!" Her mother's arms enfolded her.

"*Umiksu!*" Haina wanted to weep her cares and fears away in that loved embrace.

"My daughter, I'm so glad you've returned! We—we feared you were dead!" Sarita's voice was breathless with emotion.

Haina hugged her mother tightly. Both their faces were wet with tears. "I'm here now," she said. "Oh, it's so good to see you, *Umiksu*."

The two women retired from the curious eyes of a few onlookers to the family living area. The two bodyguards followed discreetly. Sarita went to wave them away and Haina watched to see what would happen. Exasperated, she stood there as neither man moved. They just leaned against the wall and crossed their arms across their broad chests.

Surprised, Sarita ordered, "Please leave. My daughter and I wish privacy."

"So sorry, mistress," said one, the one that had helped Haina when she stumbled on the beach. She thought of him as Squashedface because his face was very flat; he looked like he'd been in too many fights. She wondered where her father had found him, for she did not remember seeing him before. The other bodyguard, whom Haina knew slightly, was named Spit. Because he was a slave, he had an insulting name and Haina thought that Spit summed the man up wonderfully well. She would certainly have liked to spit on him. Her mother's words drew her back to the conversation.

Squashedface's big feet were planted firmly on the ground as he politely declined to leave Sarita's living area. "We are to guard your daughter, mistress. The master appointed us to the task, and we cannot leave." Spit grunted his agreement.

Sarita looked at the two and turned away. "Your father shall hear about this!" she promised. Haina almost felt sorry for her father. Almost, but not quite. It was he who would be allowing the warriors to torture her beloved.

Haina turned her back to the two men and whispered her story to her mother. She told of the kidnapping and watched the anger ripple across her mother's face. When she came to the part about falling in love with her captor, Haina saw her mother's frown soften for a moment. "Do you really love him, daughter?"

"Very much. He—he's been very kind to me." Haina toyed with a long strand of her hair, winding and unwinding it from around her finger. "He loves me, also," she said, her voice so low Sarita had to lean forward to hear.

Sarita stared at her daughter thoughtfully. "Does your father know of your feelings?"

Haina shrugged. "I think he has guessed." She rolled her eyes in the direction of her bodyguards and saw understanding light her mother's eyes.

"Whom do they protect you from, daughter?"

Again Haina shrugged. "Myself? The Kyuquots? Our warriors?"

"Mayhaps all three." Sarita's eyes narrowed. "What does your father plan for the Kyuquots?"

"Why don't you ask him?"

"I already know, daughter. He plans to have them tortured and then killed."

Haina nodded. "And if he does that, I'll hate him for the rest of my life."

Sarita was silent. "It is our way," she explained at last. "Our enemies must not be allowed to live and wreak destruction upon us."

Haina nodded. "I know this, but Chance is not an enemy, *Umiksu*. He is the man I love!"

The bodyguards shifted restlessly and Sarita whispered, "Your father does not see it that way." She waved a slavewoman over. "Bring us some water and food. Those berry cakes we made yesterday will suffice." The slave nodded and hurried off.

"Haina, I must tell you that your father was heartbroken when you were taken. He tried to hide his fear for you and be the strong war chief the Ahousat people expect him to be, but I could see it. He aged overnight."

"*Nuwiksu* does look older," agreed Haina.

"Now that he's found you—" Sarita broke off and looked at her daughter. "I know it is difficult for you," she said gently. "But it is our way."

Haina knew her mother referred to the torture. "That does not make it right, *Umiksu*."

"True. But it is the way we act and the way our people expect your father to act."

Haina tried another tack. "Did you never go against the ways of our people, *Umiksu*?"

Sarita was silent. Then she nodded. "Yes," she said softly. "Yes, I did—when I was much younger." Her golden eyes took on a dreamy look and Haina's curiosity grew.

"What did you do?"

"Well, it was a long time ago," began her mother. Sarita thought back to when Fighting Wolf had stolen her from her people. She had escaped and he'd come after her. When he'd caught up with her, he had asked her to marry him. She had thought it a trick and had refused. It was only when she saw him walking away from her, accepting her refusal rather than forcing her to accompany him, that she'd realized she truly loved him and wanted to be his wife.

Presently, Sarita focused on Haina and sighed. She could not tell her daughter *everything*. But, she could remember how it was to love when one was young. Aah, how intense everything is when you are young, she thought.

Aloud she said, "It was when I was pregnant with your sister, Fire-on-the-Beach Woman." Haina nodded. "I was not married to your father at the time and my father, your grandfather Thunder Maker, dead these many years, was not pleased about it. He did not want a grandchild born out of wedlock. His people looked down on me for this and because I had been your father's slave. It is the Nootka way," she said simply. "I did not like the things my father's people said about me or my baby. I had to stop and think about what was best for me and my growing baby, not about what was best for my father and his people. *That* was when I went against what the Nootka people expected."

Haina smiled in satisfaction. "So! You *did* go against the ways of our people. Mayhaps I can go against the ways of our people, too."

Sarita looked at her thoughtfully, then continued, "By then, your grandfather was trying to marry me off to the Kyuquots, to Throws Away Wealth."

Haina nodded. "That's the man I talked with in Kyuquot. He is Chance's older brother."

Sarita frowned. "But they don't look like brothers. In fact, I must say that this man, Chance, does not even look Indian. Of course he speaks our language very well, but—"

"He's not Indian born, mother, but he *is* Indian." At Sarita's doubtful look, Haina told her how Chance was found and given to Ocean Wave to raise as her own.

At the end of her tale, Sarita said, "My daughter, I find it very difficult to believe that story. I think perhaps Chance did not tell you the truth—" She held up her hand to stop Haina's flow of words. "Or perhaps he was lied to. I cannot believe such a tale. It is too unlikely. His mother washed up on shore to give birth to him . . ." She shook her gray head. "No, it is impossible."

Haina started to laugh. "I agree it sounds strange, *Umiksu*. But he is convinced of the truth of the story. Now, what were we talking about?"

"My thoughts tend to wander somewhat as I get older," acknowledged Sarita. "We were discussing your feelings for the young man," she added shrewdly.

"Your thoughts may wander but your curiosity is as strong as ever, I see," answered Haina dryly.

Now it was Sarita's turn to laugh. The slave woman arrived with the refreshing drinks and the berry cakes. The two women sat talking, catching up on family matters since Haina's kidnapping, and oblivious to the two bodyguards hovering in the background.

At last Haina steered the conversation back to Chance. "I worry about him," she confessed to her mother. "I do not know what to do to help him. But if I do nothing, he will die."

Sarita nodded. "Yes." She turned to Spit. "Please go and see what is being done about the Kyuquots," she said imperiously. Seeing his hesitancy, she waved her hand. "Surely one of you is enough to guard my daughter. After all, she is not so very big."

The man sheepishly left the longhouse and Haina and Sarita glanced at each other, smug smiles on their faces.

When Spit returned, however, their complacency vanished. "Mistress," the man said importantly. "They are tied to stakes in the beach and the Ahousat people are stabbing at them with sticks. A large bonfire is being built near them, probably for more torture, and the people amuse themselves with insults. They insult them one moment and promise them freedom the next if they will but—" Seeing the noblewomen watching him he remembered his place. "If they will but do one or two, ah, humiliating acts."

Haina jumped to her feet.

"Haina, stay here!" ordered her mother.

"No, I must go to him!" She would have rushed from the longhouse had not Spit and Squashedface held her back. Stinky barked madly. "I must go to him!" cried Haina, desperately struggling against the brawny arms that held her. Still barking, Stinky darted in and out amongst the slaves' legs. Spit kicked the dog out of the way when sharp teeth pierced his ankle.

Sarita felt torn. To let Haina go to the Kyuquot

could very well endanger Haina's own life. The people's mood was cruel at the moment. But she could understand Haina's desire to do something to help her man. "Haina! Stop this at once," Sarita ordered in a strong voice. "When you are calm, we will make plans."

Haina's strugglings gradually ceased and she looked at her mother, her chest still heaving from her exertions. Stinky circled Haina, growling.

Seeing that Haina was calmer, Sarita waved the bodyguards away. Spit went to the doorway to watch the activities on the beach. Squashedface backed away to the wall, out of earshot. Haina straightened her clothing and sat down once again. Stinky came over and sat beside her, whining and snuffling.

"I hate him," Haina said under her breath.

Sarita knew she meant Fighting Wolf. This terrible incident with the Kyuquots would leave lasting marks on the family if she, Sarita, did not do something. But what?

Chapter 19

Haina lay on her blankets, Stinky beside her, waiting for the bodyguard on duty to fall asleep. She had decided she must rescue Chance, and Mudshark too, if possible. If only Spit did not take so long to fall asleep, she thought desperately.

It had been quiet outside for a long while; there was no more yelling and no more cruel laughing. Whatever was being done to them had not made Chance cry out, nor Mudshark. This worried Haina. She knew Chance was very brave and would never scream for mercy despite the terrible things being done to him. Unless—unless he could no longer scream! That thought launched her from the bed.

Stinky got to his feet, ready to follow his mistress. "Stay," Haina whispered to the dog. He lay back down on the bed and whined softly. "Quiet!" she hissed.

The sight of Spit still slowly nodding in time to the pounding rain outside was the only thing that kept Haina from running out of the longhouse at top speed. All night long it had rained.

Spit and Squashedface were taking shifts guarding her. Squashedface was now snoring in the corner and it was Spit's watch. He took his duties seriously. Although he had stayed alert for a long time, he was starting to relax, even closing his eyes a little as he leaned against the wall.

But he was not relaxed enough for her to safely tiptoe past him, she thought. She crouched tensely beside the bed. Dawn would come soon and with it new torments for the two Kyuquots. She had to see Chance. She just had to!

Spit's whole body looked limp as he sat against the wall. He was drifting in and out of sleep now, his body jerking awake when he fell too far to one side or the other. If only he would lie down, Haina thought, her teeth clenched.

She slowly straightened beside the bed. No response from Spit. She took a stop towards the door. Still no response. Another step. Still no movement from the sentry.

Haina took a third step. Spit was still nodding, but he seemed asleep. Stinky whined softly. Spit snuffled in his sleep.

The sound grated on Haina's already strained nerves. Just a little farther, she told herself. Be patient. You'll get to the door. She tiptoed closer.

She could not take her eyes off Spit. Sleep, sleep, sleep, she chanted inwardly to him. Sleep. She was two steps from the door. She poised herself to race through the doorway.

At that moment Squashedface rolled over in his sleep. He awoke immediately and took in the scene: Spit asleep on duty, Haina sneaking out the door. With a bellow Squashedface was on his feet and charging at the frightened Haina.

Stinky started barking.

Spit snuffled and woke, startled. Then he too was

on his feet. Between the two of them, the slaves carried the kicking, shrieking woman back to the bed. A barking Stinky darted in and around their legs, almost tripping them. The slaves carefully placed Haina on the tousled blankets.

"You are to stay here, mistress," ordered Squashedface. Then he rounded on Spit. "What the hell were you trying to do?" he growled. "Get us both killed?"

Spit shook his head in denial. "I fell asleep—"

"I can see that, you fool. Fighting Wolf will kill us if she gets away! Think about that the next time you feel sleepy!"

In disgust, Squashedface stomped back to his blankets on the floor. "Do you think you can stay awake?" he sneered. At Spit's shamefaced nod, Squashedface rolled over to face the wall and was soon snoring again.

Haina lay upon the blankets of her bed. Stinky lay beside her, whimpering softly. She cried her heart and soul into his curly, damp fur and then fell into an exhausted sleep.

Spit stayed wide awake the rest of the night.

Outside, Chance lay in the beating rain. His body ached all over from the punches and pokes and prods the Ahousat people had delivered. He felt like one giant bruise. But he knew he could expect worse when morning arrived. The Ahousats had plenty of time in which to torture him. They would make full use of that time, he thought grimly.

Chance looked over at Mudshark. "Mudshark? Mudshark, you awake?" he whispered. Mudshark moaned, his bruised face cut and swollen. He struggled to sit up straight, but soon gave up. Both men's arms were behind them, their wrists tied together and bound to a stake. They could not move. The leather bonds had shrunk in the rain and cut into the skin of their wrists.

Their legs were free but what good did that do? Chance asked himself. They couldn't kick their way to freedom.

He was tired, thirsty, and in pain. He knew there was little hope of getting away alive but he strained against his bonds anyway. He hoped to wear them down by rubbing them against the wooden stake. A long time had passed, it seemed like all night, but they were as strong as ever. And his wrists ached.

His broad shoulder slumped. It was no good. He'd never get free, never see Haina again. Haina. He wondered if she were thinking of him. He loved her. He was glad he'd told her that the last night they'd made love.

He sighed. What rotten timing. It was almost as if Fighting Wolf had known where to find them. . . . His thoughts were interrupted by a rustling behind him, coming from the direction of the longhouse. Who—?

He tightened his muscles in preparation for a blow from some zealous Ahousat with a personal grudge against the Kyuquots. If he ever got out of here, he'd . . .

"Chance?" His name was almost lost in the wind and rain beating against him.

"What?" he answered guardedly. "Is that you, Haina?" She'd come to him, his heart sang. She'd come to see him one last time.

A knife was pressed to his throat and his heart sank. No, it was not Haina. He waited, knowing a quick death to be more merciful than what the Ahousats had planned for him.

A woman's voice whispered in his ear. "I am going to cut your bonds. You must not move." Another rustle and she was facing him.

He had never seen her before. She was an older woman, gray-haired, with Haina's eyes and face shape, but she was bigger than Haina. "You're her mother?" he guessed, his whisper hoarse. His dry throat longed for water.

The woman nodded, still holding the knife to his throat as if she did not trust him. She was correct not to trust him, he thought, watching her carefully. He waited for an opening to make his move and wrest the knife from her grasp.

Then she lowered the knife and crept behind him and began sawing at his bonds. "How do I know this is not an Ahousat trick?" he whispered.

"It's no trick."

"You could be cutting my bonds to let me think I'll escape. Then the rest of your bloodthirsty village could jump me. Is that your plan? Is it?"

"Silence," she hissed. "I don't do this for you, fool. I do it for my daughter."

He felt one wrist free but did not move it. He did not want to scare her before she finished cutting him loose.

He could feel the blood coursing painfully into the free hand and he cursed softy. The woman was almost done on the other wrist. With a final jerk, she cut through.

He whirled on her and grabbed the knife with his good hand, his warrior's reflexes faster than hers. He pressed the knife to her throat, but she did not flinch. Incredibly, she laughed. "My daughter has chosen well," she said, her voice low.

Chance looked at her for a long moment. She held his gaze serenely. He lowered the knife and got slowly to his feet, looking around. No one moved in the rain.

He squinted into the rain, but still could see nothing, certainly no movement. He listened, heard only the wind. He bent down and sliced through the bonds holding Mudshark. He shook him. "Wake up, Mudshark! Wake up!"

Groggily, Mudshark came awake. "What—?"

"Someone may have seen me," whispered Sarita urgently. "There was a noise in the longhouse when I left." She glanced back but could see nothing in the darkness and rain.

"Quick! We must leave. Now!" Chance shook Mudshark again.

Mudshark got to his feet and tenderly rubbed his wrists. "I'm ready."

"Hurry," said Sarita. "There's a canoe. Food. Water. You'll need it."

Chance swung to face her. "She's right." He studied her. "Why do you do this, woman?"

"To keep peace in my family, Kyuquot. My daughter loves you. My husband would see you dead. Should you be killed, she would hate her father the rest of her life."

Chance nodded. "Let's go," he said to Mudshark.

"The canoe awaits at water's edge," Sarita added. A flash of lightning lit the sky and she saw their haggard faces. They turned from her.

Before Chance could take many steps, Sarita called out, "Kyuquot!"

He turned.

"Do not come back, Kyuquot. Never return—on pain of death! My people will kill you. My husband will order it. And I will not go against him a second time."

"Thank you for the warning." His voice was gruff as he bowed to her. "And thank you for our freedom." He walked quickly towards the beach.

Another jagged flash of lightning cracked through the black night. Chance turned around and saw her watching them. "I love your daughter!" he called back and the wind carried his words to her.

Suddenly there was a commotion at the longhouse door. People were running out of the house; lights flared in the darkness. "After them! After them!"

came the shout.

"Run!" cried Chance. "We've been discovered!"

Sarita faded into the trees lining the beach and watched the mad chase as several warriors ran after the fleeing Kyuquots. Barking village dogs pranced at their heels.

Chance and Mudshark raced for the water's edge. They commandeered a sleek canoe they saw bouncing offshore on the choppy sea. Chance lifted the stone anchor and placed it in the craft. The waist-high water lapped at him. Mudshark was right behind. Chance threw one leg over the side of the canoe and fell into the tippy craft.

Mudshark frantically pushed the canoe into deeper water. He glanced over his shoulder at their pursuers. The Ahousats had reached the waterline. Mudshark jumped against the heavy water and tried to climb over the gunwale at the stern. But all he could do was cling to the churning canoe.

"There they are!" yelled an Ahousat.

"Help me, help me," gasped Mudshark. Chance grabbed Mudshark's heavy torso and heaved him into the canoe. The canoe tipped crazily and they almost fell into the sea.

On shore the Ahousats clambered into canoes and pushed off after them. No one fired any shots and Chance prayed no one would. "Hurry!" he cried and thrust a paddle into Mudshark's hand.

But their excited efforts forced the canoe to swing wide. Chance lashed at the water with his pointed paddle as he frantically tried to straighten the boat. At last it was pointed in the direction of the open sea. "Paddle!" he cried and they fell to paddling with a desperate will.

Their frail craft sped through the waves and Chance thanked *Naas* that the woman who had helped them knew about canoes. This one, besides being stocked with provisions and extra paddles, was built for maximum speed. They had only to touch their paddles to the water and the craft shot ahead.

The distance between pursued and pursuers began to lengthen once Chance and Mudshark established their paddling rhythm.

The Ahousats called foul names after them and ordered them to stop but Chance and Mudshark kept paddling. They were both panting from their exertions.

Neither man had eaten for two days and their bodies were stiff and sore from many beatings. But they kept paddling. They knew they'd get no second opportunity.

Sarita watched the scene from behind the graceful cedar branches of the tree where she'd sought refuge. When she could no longer see, she walked slowly back to the longhouse. At the next crack of lightning, she turned and looked towards the sea. They were gone.

Chapter 20

"Escaped! They've escaped!" Fighting Wolf was in a rage. He paced back and forth in front of the cheery fire burning at the hearth.

Haina sat quietly on her plank bed, her arm around Stinky. Her eyes were swollen and she shuddered involuntarily every once in a while, spent from crying. But her heart was glad. He was free. Chance was free. Her hopes soared to the roof of the longhouse. She'd never see him again, but he was free!

The slave that brought Fighting Wolf the news cowered on the floor holding his hands over his head. "Go! Get from my sight!" the furious man told the frightened slave. The slave rose, still cringing, and ran for the door. A warrior stuck out a foot as he ran by and the slave crashed to the floor. He lay sprawled awkwardly on the dirt floor amidst the rough guffaws and chuckles of the men. The chuckles died in their throats when Fighting Wolf's harsh bark brought them to order. The slave limped, unheeded, out the door.

"How did they get away?" Fighting Wolf turned

accusatory eyes on Haina, but she faced her father squarely. Spit and Squashedface hurriedly assured him she had been in her bed all night.

Slowly some of the Ahousat warriors sidled into the longhouse, their faces grim in defeat. "How did they get away?" yelled Fighting Wolf. One of the warriors, a taciturn man, spoke up. "We tried, sir—"

"Tried! Not good enough! Not by far!" A string of curses followed that made even the seasoned warriors wince. "That Kyuquot stole my daughter! He did who knows what to her! He must pay!"

Fighting Wolf rounded on Haina and glared fiercely. Her cheeks flamed at his frank words in front of slaves and warriors. She put her hands to her hot cheeks to cool them but said nothing. Her heart was still singing that Chance had escaped.

The watching warrior cleared his throat. Fighting Wolf swung back to him. "What is it, Cod Killer?"

"Sir, they had help. We examined the bonds. They were cut." He, too, glared at Haina. She met his eyes and her small chin rose a fraction.

Squashedface and Spit straightened. "He and I were here with her the whole time, I tell you," blustered Spit. Squashedface merely nodded, his big arms folded across his broad chest. The listening warriors shifted nervously.

"The Kyuquots had help. Someone cut those bonds," insisted Cod Killer. "Someone who—" He broke off, aware all of a sudden that he, a commoner, was about to accuse a chief's daughter. He turned back to Fighting Wolf. "Sir, they took the best canoe, the fastest one."

"My canoe!" gritted Fighting Wolf. "They took *my* canoe!" A pained look crossed his face. "Not *Slider*?"

Cod Killer nodded. "Afraid so, sir. We couldn't catch them. They were just too damn fast."

"My best canoe!" exclaimed Fighting Wolf. He shook his head in disgust. "He'll pay for that."

Sarita came to stand beside her husband. She put her hand on Fighting Wolf's arm and he straightened. He turned to Cod Killer. "Take two men and search the village for the culprit that helped them get away. When you find him, bring him to me."

Fighting Wolf's jaw clenched momentarily and those watching sent up silent prayers of thanks to *Naas* that they had not been the ones to help the Kyuquots escape. "The rest of you, go back to bed!"

The people lingered, reluctant to leave such interesting events. "Go on! You're dismissed!" shouted Fighting Wolf. Finally, the men and women dispersed to their living areas, leaving Fighting Wolf and Sarita standing alone. Haina and her bodyguards sat in the background.

Sarita led Fighting Wolf back to their fur-covered plank bed.

Haina sank down on her own blanketed bed and laughed with relief into the bedclothes. "He's free," she murmured into the rough wool. "He's free!" And whoever helped him would get her help, she vowed. She too, would be watching for the 'culprit.' But for a different reason than her father's!

The next morning Haina awoke early, exhilarated by the memory of Chance's escape. She rose, dressed, and ignored her sleeping bodyguards as she made her way to the family cooking area. She would surprise her mother and make breakfast, she decided.

Instead, her mother surprised her.

Sarita lay stretched out on a cedar mat near the fire. A large brown bearskin covered her and only her gray hair poked out where the bear's head should have been. Haina smiled at the amusing sight, then she grew thoughtful as she wondered why her mother was sleeping next to the fire and not in her plank bed with Fighting Wolf.

Haina worked quietly preparing the breakfast for her family. She thought that small oysters, gathered the previous day by slaves, would roast up well in the hearth fire and make a suitable morning meal.

Three female slaves soon joined her and Haina let them finish the task. She took a cup of strong tea and squatted by the stoked fire. She sipped the hot drink carefully, screwing up her face because she had no sugar to put in the tea. She sighed, but took another sip of the brew. She sank back on her heels in contentment and stared into the flames.

Behind her came a rustling and Haina turned to see that her mother was awake and sitting up. Before Haina could ask Sarita about her strange sleeping habits, she noticed that Sarita's eyes were puffy looking and swollen, almost as if, thought Haina, she had been crying. What goes on?

Haina offered Sarita a cup of the tea and her mother gratefully accepted. The two women sat without talking, gazing into the fire and sipping their hot drinks.

They had just finished their tea when Cod Killer approached their living area. Sarita got to her feet and greeted him politely, then dutifully went to fetch Fighting Wolf.

He came out of their alcove, Sarita behind him. He ignored Sarita. Haina noticed the two did not touch or glance at each other. Fighting Wolf marched up to the waiting warrior.

Haina's curiosity was piqued by her parents' manner with each other. It was further piqued when Fighting Wolf waved the warrior away. Cod Killer's jaw dropped as he realized his war chief was not even going to listen to his report on the night's activities. Haina managed to keep her jaw from dropping, but just barely.

"But—but, sir," protested Cod Killer. "Don't you want to know that we have not yet found the culprit who freed the Kyuquots? We only need a little more time and I'm certain—"

"Leave me, I say," cut in Fighting Wolf harshly.

Cod Killer bowed stiffly and said, "Very well, sir. Do you wish us to continue the search for the culprit?"

"No. Just leave."

The man bowed again and left, muttering to himself about the vagaries of war chiefs. Haina saw him cast her a suspicious glance and heard him add daughters to his list, but she smiled sweetly at him, too pleased that Chance had escaped to care about what he, or anyone else, thought of her.

During the next two days Fighting Wolf and Sarita continued to treat each other carefully, like two strange dogs, evenly matched in height and weight, warily circling each other for the first time, thought Haina in amusement. The third night she noticed that they were again sleeping in the same bed.

As for the 'culprit,' no more was said, but Haina once glanced thoughtfully at her mother, wondering, but not daring to ask, if she knew anything about how Chance had won his freedom.

Always Haina's thoughts would drift to Chance. She yearned to see him, though she knew to do so would jeopardize his very life. Oh, but how she missed him!

Then one day Haina found other things to concern herself with. She was pregnant.

Chapter 21

Kyuquot Village

For Chance, the trip from Ahousat to Kyuquot passed as if in a dream—a bad dream. It was fortunate he had Mudshark to help him, Chance realized later, or he would never have survived the journey. A man alone, beaten and wounded as each of them was, could never have paddled the long distance. As it was, whenever they were too exhausted from the endless paddling, they would point the canoe into a bay or a cove and let the tide push them into shallow water. There they'd roll out of the canoe, totter onto the beach and sleep where they fell. Once or twice they were fortunate and did not have to crawl too far to fresh water.

Chance's body, aching from the cuts and bruises inflicted by the angry Ahousats, was in constant pain. Mudshark was in no better shape, noted Chance when he thought to look. His cousin was a mass of purple welts, turning to a putrid yellow and black. Chance never even noticed the hot summer sun beating relentlessly down upon them.

The food supply that Haina's mother had stuffed into the canoe ran out two days before they reached Kyuquot. They paddled the last day and night with no food except for handfuls of huckleberries they'd found near a brackfish stream at one of their forced stops. They carried some of the salty-tasting water with them in a wooden container Haina's mother had packed and that was their only nourishment until they fell, sick and hungry and exhausted, onto the beach at Kyuquot village.

When Chance and Mudshark were finally discovered by the village dogs, the slaves that came running at the loud barking had to pry the canoe handles out of their desperate grasps. Even then, a delirious Mudshark, not realizing where they were, managed to strike down two slaves with the pointed blade of his paddle. It took three more men, all commoners, to hold Mudshark down and wrest his weapon away from him. By that time, Mudshark had fainted. Chance, his wits still about him, managed to move his swollen tongue and ask hoarsely for water. A slave ran to fetch it, only to return to find that Chance, too, lay insensible.

The two unconscious men were carried to the longhouse and laid down in Chance's quarters. It was after two days of sound sleep that Chance finally awoke. Several women slaves waited upon him, waving hearty soups under his nose to entice him to eat. Or if they were not doing that, they were exposing his bruised, tortured flesh to curious onlookers as they tried to wash his wounds. Chance waved the hovering women away and looked around.

Mudshark lay on a plank bed across from him. The gentle rise and fall of his chest beneath a thin blanket told Chance that his cousin still slept the sleep of exhaustion.

Chance sat up and sniffed the air. His own scent

was mixed with the unfamiliar scent of dried herbs. Not only had he been partially bathed, but someone had put herbal poultices on his injuries, and he saw the dried leaves stuck to his skin in several places.

Chance crawled from the warm coccoon he'd spent the last days in and got shakily to his feet. The longhouse was quiet; roof planks had been pulled back to let in sunlight. It must be afternoon. No one stopped him, or helped him either, as he made his way on shaky legs to the longhouse door. He tottered out the door and down to the beach. The happy cries of laughing children splashing in the water greeted his ears, but he thought if he did not concentrate on placing each step carefully, he would never make it to the water's edge.

The cool sea water surrounded and soothed his bruised, aching, stiff body. The warm sun revived him and he soaked and floated on the buoyant waves until he felt his palms starting to wrinkle.

Renewed, he made his way back to the longhouse to see how Mudshark fared. Before Chance could reach the longhouse, Beachdog sauntered over and greeted him politely.

Chance glared at Beachdog. "Thanks for the help when I needed it, good friend." Sarcasm laced his voice.

Beachdog had the grace to flush and the dark red stain stood out unbecomingly against the brown of his skin. "I went to get help," he defended himself.

Chance laughed, but there was no humor in the sound. "Help from who? Your gossiping wife?" He eyed Beachdog contemptuously. "What did you do, Beachdog? Stop for a meal before you returned with your 'help'?" The tone of Chance's voice was scathing, reflecting his anger. "You left me to face the Ahousats alone! And you know it. You're a good man to have at my back—" he sneered—"running away."

Chance turned on his heel and walked away.

Beachdog's hostile eyes bored into his back.

Beachdog sauntered after him.

"It wasn't like that, Chance. Be reasonable. I went to get help. I got several warriors together—you can ask them. But when we returned to the fishing grounds you were gone!"

Chance stopped and faced Beachdog. "Then why didn't you come after us? You knew what those Ahousats would do to Mudshark and me when they caught us."

"We tried! We didn't have enough provisions. Or water either. And they had too far a head start on us."

Chance turned away. "Leave it be, Beachdog," he said evenly. Truly, he did not know what to think. It would have been hard to follow the Ahousats. And Beachdog, even if he had had several men with him, would have been badly outnumbered, as well as unprepared for a long chase.

Chance was irritable, tired from his ordeal. Mayhaps he was not thinking clearly yet. "I am tired, Beachdog. I wish to rest." It was an excuse. Beachdog accepted it and left.

Whale Hunter leaned against the silvered, weathered wood of a longhouse and watched the two men. Though he was some distance from him, their angry voices had carried clearly in the still air. "How interesting," he murmured aloud. "Beachdog plays Chance for a fool. And that one is too sick or too stupid to know it."

Whale Hunter squatted down on his haunches and picked up a smooth beach pebble. He idly tossed it up and down in the air several times.

When Beachdog and Whale Hunter had returned to the village, it had been merely to visit at the fireside of one of Beachdog's friends for awhile. Then, as if it was an afterthought, Beachdog had mentioned that the Ahousats had chased Chance and Haina and Mudshark.

Several of the listening men had immediately wanted to leave and rescue the missing three. The warriors' pointed looks at Beachdog had told Whale Hunter that he had fooled no one with his jealous trick. At the time, Whale Hunter had thought it was just that —jealousy. Beachdog had acted properly abashed and the others had said little, though their grim faces had left Whale Hunter feeling uncomfortable.

Later, Whale Hunter had decided to go along with the rescue party, just to see what would happen. When they got to the fishing grounds, of course Chance was gone. In that, Beachdog had told Chance the truth. But, Beachdog had intended them to be gone.

Now Whale Hunter was intrigued. Was Beachdog merely jealous of the handsome white who was so well-liked by the people? Or did Beachdog have a larger plan? Certainly his attempts to ingratiate himself with Chance despite being caught acting the coward seemed to hint at a larger plan.

Whale Hunter had seen the hostile look on Beachdog's face when he'd glared at Chance's back. It was obvious that Beachdog did not like Chance. If so, he was a possible ally against the man who had taken Whale Hunter's own chiefly position at Chicklesit village away from him. Whale Hunter did not take that loss lightly.

The whole situation bore watching, Whale Hunter told himself. And he was good at that. Watching and waiting, then striking. He was not called Whale Hunter for nothing. He smiled.

"How did he get back here alive?" demanded the enraged Throws Away Wealth. "He's supposed to be dead!"

Broken bottles and plates littered the tyee's living area, evidence of his recent temper tantrum.

A lone slave stooped to pick up broken glass. The other slaves and servants and wives had fled their tyee's fury.

Throws Away Wealth flung a chunk of wood against the wall of his apartment, and watched as it bounced off the wall and slammed into the slave. The slave howled and ran out of the longhouse. Throws Away Wealth laughed. "Serves him right!" He wheeled around and faced his luckless guest. "Why did you let him return to this village alive?" he hissed.

"I—I didn't know he'd escaped the Ahousats! I swear I didn't!" There was a loud crack as the tyee's open hand connected with the unfortunate one's face. The man sucked in his breath to hide his surprise and distress. "My Tyee, there's no need . . ." he protested.

"Silence, dog! Be glad you escaped with that insignificant tap. I could have your head for this!"

"But I did not know he would escape," the man whimpered.

"No, but you could have killed him when he and that useless worm of a cousin of his collapsed on our beach. You were there!"

"Kill him in front of witnesses, Tyee?" The man was horrified. "Surely you know not even *I* could get away with such a thing in front of witnesses!"

Throws Away Wealth drew back his foot and kicked his questioner, hard. "What am I paying you for, dog dung?"

The man winced and held his aching shin.

"Pay attention!" The tyee leaned closer and his fish breath hit the man full in the face.

The man did not even flinch. "Yes, Tyee."

"I want you to follow that piece of rat meat that calls himself my brother. Follow him day and night. And then, I want you to kill him!"

"That's not so easy to do," protested the man, rubbing his sore leg. "He's always got friends with him, his cousin . . ."

"I don't care who he's got with him! Or how you kill him or even when you kill him. Just kill him! One of these times he'll be alone. And when he is, you'll be there, waiting—with a knife, or a musket or a spear. Anything! Do you understand?"

"Yes, Tyee."

A sly grin crossed Throws Away Wealth's seamed face. "There will be many women for you. Young, beautiful women. Furs, too. And I will give you slaves. You will be rich. And powerful. Do we understand each other?"

"Yes, Tyee."

"Good. Now get from my sight, dog dung!"

The man left and the tyee hurled another empty bottle of rum at the wall. "Incompetents! Fools! Why do I surround myself with incompetents and fools?"

"Greetings, brother," said Chance as he limped over to the fire pit of Throws Away Wealth. Chance was supported under one arm by a young male slave. The slave carefully seated him by the fire, then Chance dismissed him with a wave of his hand.

Throws Away Wealth looked up from the meal of smoked salmon he was eating and a sour look crossed his face. He grunted and went back to his meal.

Chance politely accepted the platter of smoked salmon that Throws Away Wealth's oldest wife placed in front of him. "More oil?" she murmured. A sad expression crossed Chance's handsome face.

"Oil?" Chance shook his head. "Not unless you have rancid oil," he said with a wistful note in his voice.

The old wife shook her head. "Nobody I know eats rancid oil," she murmured, "but I will get you some if you insist."

"'Tis but a joke," answered Chance. "And a poor one at that. Forgive my bad manners." She nodded and left the two men to themselves.

The two ate in silence. Throws Away Wealth was irritated. Nothing was going right, and here was this, this *man,* the biggest threat to his chieftainship, alive and well and sitting next to him. Damnation!

Chance reminisced about Haina and the day they had thrown oil on each other. He could laugh about it now. Instead, he sighed and stared into the fire. How he missed Haina. More than he'd ever thought possible. When he'd paddled away from Ahousat, he'd left part of him behind. Haina. His heart. He wondered if he would ever get over the beautiful Ahousat woman and be able to live a normal life, free to take a wife or another woman again. He sighed doubtfully. Probably not. There was no one else like Haina.

"Why all the sighs?" demanded Throws Away Wealth snidely. "Did the Ahousats give you belly gas?" Then he laughed.

Chance looked at his brother. "No," he said calmly. "They gave me bruises and cuts but no gas. It was a long paddle back here and I was just remembering the voyage." Somehow he did not feel he could confide in Throws Away Wealth when he was in such a mood. "And you? Any sign that the Ahousats followed Mudshark and me?"

Throws Away Wealth shook his head. "I sent my men out to scout the fishing grounds. No sign of the Ahousats. I think you got clean away." Unfortunately, he added silently.

Chance shook his head. "I thought Mudshark and I were dead men when those Ahousats had us on that beach."

So did I, thought Throws Away Wealth. Aloud he asked, "What happened? How did you get free?"

"Haina's mother freed us," answered Chance. "She cut our leather bonds and let us go."

Sarita! Damn her! Why couldn't that bitch leave

227

well enough alone? Always she's interfered in any plans I've made, raged Throws Away Wealth inwardly.

Outwardly he tore at his smoked salmon with his teeth and a large leathery strip came away in his mouth. He gnashed his teeth into it and almost choked on the meat. He managed to spit out the mouthful and start over again, still tearing at the salmon.

Chance stared into the fire, seeing Haina's face dance in the flames. He would never see her, or hold her or be with her again. He knew that as surely as he knew he was sitting safely at his brother's hearth. She was gone from his life. Her father, Fighting Wolf, would kill him on sight and would keep Haina close to Ahousat.

Chance perked up. Mayhaps if he and some of his warriors were to try to rescue her. Ahh, but it was too much effort and too late. His body was too tired. What had the Ahousats done to him? he wondered. Had they sapped his very soul and life from his body? Why could he not overcome this lethargy, this despair? His body was healing slowly, the shaman healer had told him that. So why this slowness? He pondered this for some time then looked up to see Throws Away Wealth gnashing his teeth into the salmon.

"What are you doing?" he asked the tyee. "That salmon is already dead. You don't have to kill it again."

Throws Away Wealth growled in response and choked the mess down. "Why don't you go on a voyage?"

"A voyage? Why should I do that? I just got back here."

The tyee waved his hand. "I know, I know. But it seems to me that you could use a rest. Far from here."

And far from my men. That way you won't be around to stir up trouble, Throws Away Wealth added to himself. Then mayhaps Dog Dung can find an occasion to kill you.

Chance looked into the flames again. There was merit in the tyee's suggestion. Mayhaps a change would help. He could recover from his wounds and plan what he would do next. Yes, the tyee's idea was a good one. Chance could already feel life flowing into his veins again. Yes, he would get away. Get away and see some new sights, forget the hard times. Forget Haina? asked a small voice. No, not that, probably not that. Still, it would not hurt to try.

"There is truth in what you say, brother," he answered and saw that the tyee relaxed. "I must get my thoughts straight. I have not felt well since the Ahousats finished with me."

"Indeed," said Throws Away Wealth. "Those dogs are enough to make anyone sick." He clapped his hands and a slave came running. "Bring me some rum."

The slave returned with a bottle and worked at the cork with a long mussel knife. At last, he got the bottle open. "Have some?" asked the host.

Chance shook his head. "I'm befuddled enough, thanks," he said.

Throws Away Wealth laughed. Not as befuddled as I'd like you to get. That old shaman used a powerful herb to keep you docile, my *brother*. But now that your strength returns, it is time to get rid of you again. "Perhaps you will take some of your men with you," he suggested. "Mudshark, some of your friends, let's see, Beachdog . . . who else?"

Chance nodded. "Yes, I'll take a few warriors with me. I've always wanted to go to Yuquot and see the white traders. Mayhaps I'll go there."

Throws Away Wealth nodded. "Seems as good a place as any." To die, he added silently. He watched Chance out of narrowed eyes.

Chance stared into the flames of the fire. Haina was there, trying to tell him something. But what? She beckoned. Now she was fading. Gone.

"Haina?" He reached out to the flames, then dropped his hand. "She's gone."

Throws Away Wealth shook his head in amusement. Whatever it was the old shaman used, he knew his business. The white bastard was seeing things and talking to people who weren't there. Oh, too rich! He wanted to laugh aloud but instead plugged his lips with the bottle.

"Mayhaps you should lie down?" Throws Away Wealth suggested. "Let me call your slave."

As the young male slave led Chance back to his quarters, Throws Away Wealth chortled to himself. "What a fool you are, my fine brother. What a fool!"

Directly across the longhouse, two slaves, a male and female, watched the scene with interest. "Your father is up to something, my love," whispered the male.

The female slave nodded. "Yes, may his flesh rot and all he holds dear perish with him!"

Chapter 22

Chance limped through the dim longhouse. One leg was still sore but he was glad that he no longer needed a slave to support him as he walked. It was evening and he felt groggy. He would go to Kelp Woman's living area and have some food. She would feed him, yes, she would, the widow of his old friend.

He shook his head groggily. Since his return from Ahousat he had not been thinking clearly. What had the Ahousats done to him? He could remember no blow to the head, but it was possible one of them had hit him and knocked him unconscious, he supposed. *Something* must have happened to him to explain his strange thinking these days.

As he walked along the main path in the center of the longhouse, his thoughts, when he could focus them, were on Haina. Suddenly she was ahead of him, her small slim body hurrying, her long black hair flying behind her.

"Haina!" he cried. "Haina! Wait!"

She turned, saw him and ran. He limped after her.

They were running past the slaves' quarters now, soon she would stop at the wall, there was nowhere else to go.

"Haina? Wait!"

Before she reached the wall, he caught her. He held her close, his arms clasped around her waist, lifting her off the floor. He crushed her to him and kissed the nape of her neck.

"Ahh, Haina!" he said. "Why were you running from me? I've missed you so!"

She turned to face him then and he stared, openmouthed. It was not Haina.

Clumsily he dropped the woman and almost lost his own balance. "I'm sorry. I," he swallowed, "I thought you were someone else."

Midnight black eyes gazed up at him. Her form resembled Haina, her face less so. There was a large purple scar covering one cheek. And her eyes, her eyes, were cold. Not Haina at all.

He stepped back. "Excuse me," he said. "I've mistaken you for someone else." He bowed to her formally, despite her obvious slave status. She wore an old kutsack that was frayed at the edges. He recalled having seen her before, but never having really noticed her. She must live in one of the other longhouses, he thought.

Her voice interrupted his thoughts. "Quite all right, sir," she simpered, but there was a cunning look in her eyes. "I feel honored that such a fine nobleman, should think me worthy of his pursuit." She laughed and he stepped back, repulsed. There was something odious about her; he felt the hair on the back of his neck stand up.

She stepped forward. "Do not leave, kind sir." She took his hand in hers and Chance wanted to pull his hand free. Her skin felt cool, smooth, lifeless. Like a lizard's skin, or a newt's, he thought. Or a snake's. She was watching him, those midnight dark eyes impaling him as if ferreting out his darkest secrets.

He stepped back. She no longer looked like Haina. He was surprised he had ever thought there was a resemblance.

"I must go," he said evenly. "Again, I apologize for my error." He turned on his heel and walked back along the main path through the longhouse. He walked as straight as he could, but he wanted to run and inwardly cursed his sore leg from preventing him.

He didn't turn when he heard her low laugh follow him and swirl around his head to lure him back. "You must visit me sometime, kind sir. Ask for Sea Cucumber!" She laughed throatily and he repressed a shiver. It would be a desperate day when he'd visit the likes of her, he thought.

He kept walking and her laughter tapered off. When he peeked over his shoulder she was gone. He had a bad taste in his mouth and he swallowed to rid himself of it.

"Sea Cucumber is it?" he muttered. "I'll paddle clear of the shoals in those waters!"

Chapter 23

Ahousat Village

It was early morning. Haina had managed to escape from the longhouse without anyone watching her. She thought. As she sat by the gurgling little stream holding her stomach, then wiping her mouth, she heard the soft approach of slow footfalls.

She waited, a sick, hunted thing crouched there on the banks of the small stream. When old grandmother Crab Woman tottered into view leaning on her stout stick, Haina thought she would faint with relief.

Her next feeling was disgruntlement. Grand-mother Crab Woman was a most difficult old woman to get along with. Haina's mother had kindly invited the old woman, who was her step-mother, to live with Fighting Wolf's family after Grandfather Thunder Maker had died. Rather than live at Ahousat year round, Grandmother Crab Woman had chosen to visit Ahousat regularly and stay at Fighting Wolf's long-house. To keep an eye on things, she explained. At Hesquiat, she lived with Abalone Woman, Grandfather

234

Thunder Maker's other wife.

It was Haina's misfortune that the old woman had arrived recently on one of her lengthy visits. She had to make sure that everyone was doing the proper rituals for catching fish and digging roots. Grandmother Crab Woman was most insistent that everyone in Fighting Wolf's longhouse should follow the correct, that is ancient, ways of bringing up the children. Which of course, no one was.

Crab Woman walked with halting steps, feeling her way with the stick, for she could barely see—at least with her eyes. What she saw with her mind was, by common consent in the village, found to be amazing.

The old woman threw down her walking cane and sank with a thump beside the crouching girl. "So this is where you've taken to spending your mornings, my sweet," she mumbled.

Haina would have liked to ask Grandmother Crab Woman to go away and leave her alone but she knew the old woman would never understand such a thing, that it was disrespectful, and that it would in fact hurt her terribly. So Haina said instead, "I trust you enjoyed your walk, Grandmother."

The old woman snorted and said, "It was a lot of work, girl, and well you know it."

"It is a fine morning," tried Haina again. When the old woman sat there, slumped, breathing wheezily, and saying nothing, Haina thought that she must have fallen asleep. "I wonder what the old bat is here for?" she whispered to herself.

"Ehh, Ehh?" Crab Woman stirred herself. "What am I here for? Ehh?"

Haina put her hand to her mouth in mortification. The old woman could not see, but how could Haina have forgotten how well she could hear?

"I'm here," said Crab Woman stoutly, wide awake now, "to see where you've been sneaking off to every morning. You have been most disciplined about your morning ablutions and prayers. It is not like you. I approve of the change."

Haina rolled her eyes. "Then why do you say I've been 'sneaking off'?" Haina asked, slightly exasperated.

"Because you have, dear child," answered Crab Woman. "And," she added, peering down at the stream bed and the evidence, "you've been sick. I want to know why!"

Haina cringed. Of all the people in the village, Grandmother Crab Woman was the last one she'd have wanted to guess her secret. But she didn't have to say the words. The crafty old woman was ahead of her. "You're pregnant!" she crowed. "You're pregnant!"

"Shh, Grandmother," pleaded Haina. "I wish it to be a secret."

"Hmmph, some secret," muttered the old woman. "Does your mother know?"

When Haina did not answer, she persisted, "Does your father know?" At Haina's silence, she chortled, "Your father doesn't know! Hee, hee. Fighting Wolf doesn't know his nestling is pregnant. Ho, ho. That is rich! Fighting Wolf doesn't know!"

"No, and you are not to tell him," said Haina sternly.

The old woman kept chortling to herself, finally breaking down into a coughing fit.

"Besides," added Haina, "I fail to see what is so funny."

"You wouldn't know, dear," chortled the old grandmother. She broke into another fit of coughing. "I'll tell you when you're older. Hee, hee."

"I fail to see how I can get much older," answered Haina. "I'm going to have a baby. You can't get much older than that!"

The old woman wiped her eyes. They were running

tears from laughing so hard. "Who's the father?" she demanded suddenly.

"Chance," answered Haina, caught off guard.

"The Kyuquot that stole you?"

Haina nodded, looking down at the mossy bank of the stream.

"Hmmm, not so good," muttered the old woman. "People will talk."

Haina sighed heavily. "They talk anyway, Grandmother."

"Too true. One of the penalties of being a noble. Everyone loves to talk about you. Especially when you're pregnant." She sat there, shaking her head from side to side.

Haina stared into the stream. She did not hear the gurgling water as she mused upon Chance. He was gone, gone from her as if he had never been. He could never return to Ahousat. Her father's people would kill him. She could never go to Kyuquot to visit him. To take such a trip was unheard of for a lone woman. He was as gone from her as if he'd been spirited away by the Wolves in a ceremonial dance, and never brought back.

She sighed. At least she had known him for a little while. She had loved him, too, loved him with all her heart and still did. Oh Chance, she thought. How could life be so cruel? To meet you, to love you and now to have you driven from my side.

The old woman sitting next to her shifted and Haina suddenly remembered her presence.

"Tears, my sweet?" The old woman gently rubbed a gnarled thumb on Haina's clear, unlined cheek and followed the wet track down her face. "So sad," she murmured. "So sad." She sat looking at Haina quietly and Haina thought in surprise that the old grandmother was really quite kindly. She wondered why she had never noticed it before.

"Your tears tell me that you despair. Is it so?" Crab Woman asked gently.

Haina shook her head. "Not really. It's just that he's so far away and I can do nothing. . . ." She choked on the words and wiped at her tears.

"Enough of this crying and moaning." Crab Woman was clearly back to her usual self. "I suppose you're going to just give up."

"Give up?" echoed Haina. "I haven't given up."

The old woman snorted. "Hmmph. If you say so. I thought old Fighting Wolf's daughter was made of sterner stuff. Looks to me like you're just going to sit there and cry all day. Let me tell you a story."

Haina dutifully sat up and wiped her eyes. She expected to hear a story about folk heroes like Raven, or the Wolves, or mayhaps even the Salmon People. Instead, Crab Woman spoke of Sarita and Fighting Wolf.

"Did you know your father stole your mother?" the old woman began.

Haina nodded.

"Well, it was not some gentle capture, some love-sick swain stealing his beloved in the night, let me tell you," said the old woman. "It was a violent, angry taking and many were killed."

Haina looked at Crab Woman, aghast.

"No, you didn't know *that*, did you?" the old woman taunted. "You can be sure Fighting Wolf never told his daughter the real story of what went on." She snorted in disgust. "Pap. That's all the younger generation feeds their children these days. Pap. No truth, all gentle lies. Hmmmph. I've a mind to not tell you a thing."

"Oh please, Grandmother Crab Woman," implored Haina, "don't stop now. I must know. What went on?"

The old woman shifted her bulk more comfortably

238

and leaned against a tree. "It all began when your Grandfather Thunder Maker decided to marry his daughter, your mother Sarita, off to the Ahousats. It was for peace, he said. Oh, I warned him. But in those days we both had eyes only for wealth and," she shook her head sadly, "the Ahousats promised us much wealth. They knew our weakness, oh yes, they knew.

"When your father, Fighting Wolf, arrived, I recognized him for the trouble-maker he is, always has been." At Haina's frown, Crab Woman leaned over and patted her hand. "There, there, child, only an old woman speaking her mind."

Haina nodded and Crab Woman continued. "We had games for them. Games handed down through your Grandfather's family, games to outdo those wily Ahousats, but they beat us at all of them. We had many silver salmon and roots to feed them with. Strangely, the Ahousats arrived without their womenfolk—we were to think much of that later. At the time we only thought to entertain the men well, and we did have many slave women about. It was during the feasting to celebrate the joining of our two great tribes, that your father's men leaped up and began slaughtering our men and warriors. Our warriors were at a disadvantage from eating and drinking too much." She nodded sagely. "We Hesquiats could always do that, eat and drink. We're very good at that." She patted her belly under the old-fashioned kutsack that she always wore. She insisted that a kutsack was the only proper clothing for a Nootka noble grandmother to wear.

"Our men were quickly slaughtered and wounded and many of our loveliest women taken captive. Your father then marched them off to canoes and took them away, your mother included. The few warriors we had left could not follow because your father had sunk their canoes." She snorted again. "Never again were we Hesquiats caught off guard like that, but that one time—" she shook her head, "that one time was too terrible."

"Didn't you save Uncle Feast Giver somehow? I thought I heard something about that."

The old woman snorted. "Oh, I threw an old cedar mat over his head to hide him from the Ahousats. Not that it helped! I thought he was dead, but I was not going to let those—" she caught herself, glanced sheepishly at Haina, "those Ahousats take his body. They found him anyway and tied him up with your grandfather." She put her hands over her face. "Even now it shames me to think of it. Fighting Wolf shamed us all."

Haina shifted uncomfortably. "I didn't know—"

Crab Woman recovered herself. She coughed, then continued, "Your mother was held captive for a long time, long enough to get pregnant." Here Crab Woman glanced slyly at Haina. "Then she escaped your father's clutches and returned to us, but she was a changed woman, in more ways than one. She sat around the longhouse, mooning and sighing and sitting in front of the fire. She wouldn't work—your mother never was one for work," Crab Woman added sharply.

At Haina's patient sigh, Crab Woman hastily continued, "She missed *him*, if you can believe it. Fighting Wolf, the one who stole her. I never could understand it myself, but there you go. Some people can't be reasoned with." She shook her head and missed Haina rolling her eyes heavenward.

"Then much to our surprise, he came for her. Paddled into our bay with a horde of his dirty Ahousat warriors and demanded, no asked for, her hand in marriage. We told him 'no' of course, but he would not accept that." She shook her head. "Stubborn man. He deserved her," these words were muttered and Crab Woman was certain Haina had not heard her. "He finally prevailed upon your mother to marry him and she moved here. They've been together ever since, though it's not something I ever expected to last. I was sure he was too sneaky and she was—well, enough of that.

"Tell me, does that story help you with your own situation?"

"No." Haina looked, and felt bewildered.

Crab Woman stared at Haina. "Why not? Think about it, girl. There's a truth in that story for you."

"If there is, you have to explain it to me," said Haina pouting.

Crab Woman snorted. "Next you'll have me paddling after that young fool myself to bring him back." She got slowly to her feet, then leaned on her stick. "I'll leave you now," she said. "I've shared enough wisdom for one day."

Haina walked down to the beach, Stinky padding at her heels. The beach was deserted as the evening sun sank low on the horizon. Haina arranged herself on the beach and patted a place beside her. The dog sat down next to her.

She nibbled on some smoked clams she had carried in a little basket. The dog looked at her, large brown eyes following her every chew. She held out a clam. He sniffed at it delicately, took it gently into his mouth and gulped it down. Then he watched her expectantly, waiting for more. She laughed and patted his white head. "Ah, Stinky, at least you haven't changed. You want only simple things from me."

She continued to pat him idly as she watched the setting sun. "The rest, they want my heart from me." The bitterness in her tone caused the dog to tilt his head curiously at her.

She gazed into his eyes intently. "Did you know, Stinky, that this is the only time of day when I can keep any food down?" she asked conversationally. "This morning, if I had tried to eat these clams, aargh!" The sputtering noise caught Stinky's attention. "It would have all come up."

Woman and dog sat quietly for a while.

"What am I going to do, Stinky? I'm pregnant and alone."

The dog whined softly.

Haina corrected herself. "Oh, not completely alone. I have my mother and father and friends and slaves here. And you, Stinky. But I'm still alone, because there is no one to help me."

The dog lowered his head to the beach and moaned.

"But I thought you understood, Stinky." She scratched the top of his head. The white, curly hair was wiry. She could remember when he'd been born in her family's longhouse. He'd been a rambunctious puppy.

"So what shall I do?" she asked again. She remained silent for a while and the dog closed his eyes. "Don't go to sleep," she warned and prodded him gently. "You have to help me make my plans." Stinky opened one eye, saw she was serious and closed it again.

"Well, it *is* Chance's baby. He should be here with me. He's the father, he should help me to raise the child! Besides," she whispered into the pointed ear parked beside her. "I love him. I love him so and I miss him more than I can say."

The dog moved his body restlessly and Haina patted his white back until he calmed down. "I've decided what to do, Stinky," she informed him. "I've been thinking about it for days but talking to you has convinced me."

She smiled secretly. "Sit up and listen," she ordered. The dog lay unmoving. "Up! That's better."

She put her arms around his neck and the rank odor of unwashed dog mixed with rotting bear or deer meat tickled her nostrils. "Pheww! You are well-named. What did you roll in? Let's go down and play in the water."

After several attempts to hold Stinky's back under water so that she could rid him of his offensive odor, she finally succeeded in plastering two handfuls of sand on his back and scrubbing away the terrible smell. "It seems I must spend my life scrubbing smells out of hair," she mumbled to herself.

Stinky broke away from her and galloped to shore. He raced around, stopping to shake vigorously. Droplets sprayed everywhere. "Oh, Stinky," laughed Haina. "Now I'm wet, too!"

He ran in a big circle, shook himself one last time then came over to Haina. "You're a good dog. Now listen carefully." Stinky sat down and cocked his head to one side as he watched her solemnly. Haina squatted down beside him and lifted his muzzle into her palm. She stared into his eyes.

"I'm going to fetch Chance, Stinky. I'm going to paddle to Kyuquot and demand that he marry me!"

The dog whined.

"I am. It does no good to protest. My father and mother won't know that's where I'm going." Stinky stuffed his nose in her hand and waggled. "No, you can't come with me. I go alone." He licked her hand in earnest entreaty. "No, Stinky. It does no good to beg."

To soften the blow of her refusal, she added, "You liked those clams, didn't you? Here's another one." She tossed it high in the air, there was a snap of jaws and the clam was gone.

"I'm going to pack plenty of clams for my trip, I can tell you. And water. And berries. I won't have time to stop. Once I return with Chance and tell my parents I'm pregnant and he's willing to marry me, they'll have to agree to the marriage."

Stinky was pushing at her hand. "More clams? They're all gone." She pushed his nose away and clapped her hands. "Oh, it is just too perfect! I'll have the man I love, my baby will have his proper father and my mother and father will accept Chance and grow to love him, just as I have. They'll forget all about their anger at my kidnapping."

Tired of being pushed away in his search for clams, Stinky laid his head in her lap. "I can tell you like my plan, old one. So do I." She patted his head and he dozed quietly. "Thank you for your good advice, Stinky. We Ahousats are fortunate to have someone as wise as you." She laughed.

The old dog snorted as he dozed.

"I stand corrected," agreed Haina. "I should never have doubted your wisdom." Stinky whined softly.

They sat there, the drowsing dog and the musing woman. Later, the dark of night was joined by wind and a drizzle of rain that began to fall. Haina prodded her companion. "Come on, Stinky. Time for you to go to the longhouse and time for me to go and search out the man I love."

Chapter 24

Getting away from Ahousat had been a problem, thought Haina as she paddled the medium-sized canoe through the ploughing waves. Splashes on either side of her reminded her of her unwanted traveling companions, Squashedface and Spit, as they, too, dipped their paddles into the green sea.

But getting to Kyuquot would be an even bigger problem, Haina decided, squinting her eyes the better to see against the light mist. A buffeting wind at their backs propelled them forward. While normally such a wind would help to speed Haina's trip to Kyuquot, today she was uneasy. The wind had been gathering steadily since morning.

When Haina had told Fighting Wolf and Sarita that she was going to visit an aunt that lived up the inlet, only one day's travel away, they had adamantly refused to let her go alone.

Haina's pleadings and rantings had availed nothing. Her parents stood firm. They had insisted that after what had happened the last time she was in a canoe—did she forget so soon that she had been kidnapped by that Kyuquot dog? demanded her father —that she must have guards with her at all times when away from the village.

And so here they were, all three happily paddling for Kyuquot, thought Haina grimly. What a struggle it had been. She'd finally gotten those two big bears into the canoe. The amount of food the two large slaves needed for the one-day trip she ostensibly planned was of such a quantity that she needed a larger canoe. She'd stood back and watched in awe as they carried bales of smoked fish and dried clams down to the beach and loaded up her father's second favorite canoe, *Tames the Waves*. They'd filled up two baskets with berry cakes, courtesy of her mother, and Haina heard whispers that Sarita was getting old and soft to be giving slaves such fine food. But it really did not bother Haina. The generosity reflected well upon her mother, and Haina was secretly proud of her. Besides, pointed out Sarita practically, any leftover salmon or berries could be given to Aunt Purple Winkle as a gift.

Tames the Waves had finally been loaded, Haina had hugged her mother and father good-bye and seated herself in the middle of the canoe. The two slaves had pushed off from the beach.

And then the trouble began. They had paddled out of the bay, straight out to sea and out of sight of the village when both slaves had stopped paddling and demanded—yes, demanded of *her*, an Ahousat noblewoman—to know where she was heading. This was not the way to Gooseneck Inlet, where Fighting Wolf had ordered them to paddle her. Gooseneck Inlet was south. Why did Haina have them paddling north?

Irritated with Squashedface's questioning, and feeling guilty because the slaves were correct to question her, Haina had been unnecessarily short with them. When her rudeness had still not moved them from their demands to know what was going on, and where she was going, she had finally told them she had no intention whatsoever of visiting Auntie Purple Winkle in Gooseneck Inlet. Her real destination was Kyuquot and they could either come with her or . . . She had hesitated to threaten them with death, because she knew now she would never carry out such a threat. Watching what had been done to Chance and Mudshark had been enough to cure her of flinging loose death threats around.

Fortunately, Squashedface, for some odd reason of his own, had recognized her desperation. He explained to Spit that it was better to accompany her than to have her return to Ahousat only to escape alone. He reasoned that they were bound to follow Fighting Wolf's instructions to accompany Haina and keep her safe. This they would do, whether in Gooseneck Inlet or Kyuquot.

Haina had regarded Squashedface thoughtfully after that and found that she did not dislike him quite so much as she had first thought. After all, the fact that he was not pleasant to look at should not be held against the man. Obviously he had a good brain in his head.

Once the details had been decided upon, the three had paddled swiftly enough for Kyuquot. It was only since the morning of this, the third day, that Haina had become nervous.

The weather was turning and not for the better. Summer storms could arise swiftly along the west coast. The heavy winds and rain from the southeast, while hurrying the small canoe upon its way, could also turn into a terrible lashing storm, driving all before it to seek shelter.

Were they to get caught in such a storm, Haina feared for their lives. It would not take much to swamp the canoe and the three paddlers were not strong enough to contend against the powerful surges of the sea. But she paddled on, hoping for the best. Kyuquot was still another three days' travel northward.

But the wind roared strongly and rain pelted down. The howling winds created a dread in Haina's heart that she would never see dry land again. Spit and Squashedface paddled frantically now and the canoe sped on into the waves. The craft balanced precariously on the crest of a huge wave, then dipped down into the trough. Another huge wave picked them up again. The slaves' paddles seesawed in the air, groping for water.

Haina, sitting in the middle of the craft, stuck her paddle out the side of the canoe and waggled it uselessly but could not touch water.

Each time the canoe plunged down into a trough, the bow hit the water and a vast spray drenched her and Spit. With each plunge a loud 'smack!' resounded and scared Haina.

The canoe was completely out of control now. The fierce waves could be pushing her farther out to sea for all she knew.

The slaves shouted back and forth at each other. They tried various paddling tricks in hopes of finding some way to guide the boat. All Haina could think was that it was hopeless. Squashedface, at the stern, leaned this way and that with his paddle out, desperately trying to steer the boat. A sudden frothing boiled beneath the vessel and they were tossed dangerously once more. Despair knifed through Haina. They were going to die, she knew it!

Spit, at the bow, ceased paddling, whether giving up or taking a rest, Haina could not tell at first. She watched as he rose to a crouch and hung on precariously to the prow. What was he up to? He started yelling into the darkness around her. His words were whipped away.

When Haina heard Squashedface roar his approval, she spun around, openmouthed. What manner of men or beasts was she trapped with? Did these slaves know no fear? At the height of a terrible storm, when her life was dearest because it could be snuffed at any moment, these two fools were screaming their heads off and . . . and laughing!

She gaped at them, unable to believe her eyes and ears. They were all going to drown and these two slaves, *slaves* mind you, were hurling terrible words—she could understand the words now—into the face of the storm.

Unable to account for it, and feeling helpless, she, too, raised her voice to the din and screamed her defiance and fear to the wind. Immediately she felt better. Hanging onto the sides of the pitching boat, she let loose a yell that caused the intrepid Spit at the bow to turn around and stare with admiration. She grinned at him and let loose with another yell. He laughed and added his own bellow to the noise.

And so they continued, their canoe tossed about, the human occupants screaming and bellowing sometimes in stomach-sickening fear, sometimes in heady exhilaration.

Just as her voice was beginning to give out, Haina spotted a light. There, over to one side where only blackness had been before. She stared, her whole being focused on that light, but it was gone.

For a long time she gazed into the darkness but could see nothing. The rain pelted, the wind howled and all around was black despair. When she finally decided she'd only imagined the light, she saw it again. There, steadier, for a longer time. She tried to croak out a word, then gave up and merely pointed.

Squashedface followed her finger and saw the light too. Suddenly he started yelling and Haina turned to him, marvelling that he could still make a sound. Excitedly, he pantomimed to Spit to head the canoe in the direction of the light. Haina and Spit obeyed and after several tries they managed to get the canoe pointed in the right direction.

Now all they had to do was paddle, thought Haina grimly. And paddle they did. The three paddled as they never had before in their lives. They made slow headway because the waves kept pushing them off course. But the three pushed doggedly onward.

At last the sea seemed to tire of its game with them. As if in salute to the daring humans who had challenged it and won, the sea let the wind push them swiftly to their destination. The waves died down a little and the canoe shot forward to the light—several lights in a cluster now.

It was a boat, Haina saw, but a boat like no other. A white man's ship! It bounced up and down slowly in the storm, its stout anchor holding the bow firmly.

The ship lay in a sheltered cove. Beachward, Haina could see more small lights.

Why, this must be Yuquot, she breathed. The town of the white traders!

Chapter 25

Yuquot Village

Haina woke and stretched and sat up on the plank bed. The fur covers slid off her shoulders and the chill morning air bit at her skin.

She looked around at the unfamiliar chests and hanging mats in the strange longhouse. Ah yes, Yuquot. She could hear the rain drumming on the roof and battering at the sides of the longhouse. Wind whistled through cracks in the wall and added to the din. She thought of sliding back under the covers, then chastised herself. She was in Yuquot, a new town to her—a whole new town to explore!

She patted her gently rounded stomach. "Sleep, baby," she whispered. "Sleep and grow big. Your mother loves you."

She thought she'd only breathed the words but she heard a stirring beside her on the floor. Squashedface was awake, Spit still snored. She sighed. Ah, her faithful companions, she thought ruefully. How could she have forgotten them?

They'd been fortunate to find a place to sleep under a dry roof last night. They'd beached the canoe high above the tide-line then ran for the nearest longhouse. The inhabitants had found them a place to sleep and Haina had been grateful. Of course, mentioning her father's name had not hurt. The longhouse dwellers had seemed more enthusiastic and hospitable once they realized it was the war chief Fighting Wolf's daughter they were hosting. She smiled. People were so amusing sometimes.

Later, she politely thanked the woman next door to the sleeping area. They had given Haina and her slaves breakfast, then respectfully answered Haina's questions about the village.

She found that she was distantly related to one of the lower chiefs in another longhouse and decided she would spend the next night there. The drumming rain told her it might be several more days and nights before the storm spent itself. While it might be amusing at first to impose upon strangers, she did not think her good humor, or theirs, would extend over a several-day visit.

She felt no such qualms about staying in the quarters of a cousin. She had not met the distant cousin but she had heard her mother speak of him and his wife and their gaggle of children. And after all, should the cousin ever visit Ahousat, she, Haina, would naturally extend every courtesy. That's just how things were done with nobles, she thought with smug satisfaction.

It bothered her a little that her trip to Kyuquot was delayed. She desperately wanted to find Chance and tell him about their baby and her marriage plans but she was no fool. A storm was a storm. It could not be stopped and she was certainly not going to risk her life, and her baby's, in a storm that would blow over in a few days. When peaceful waters were restored and soft summer breezes blew once more then she and her slaves would paddle out of Yuquot, but not until then.

She surveyed the longhouse once more. Nothing new here. But the ship that she had seen last night, with its many bobbing lights, now *that* would be worth exploring!

She dispatched Squashedface to find a canoe for them. He returned, breathless. "Mistress, there is a crowd leaving for the ship this very moment. Come quickly and we can board the ship with them."

"Squashedface, I thank you for your news," Haina said. "But I must insist that you stay here. I do not want you to come with me."

"Not come with—!" He moaned. "Mistress, do not do this to me, to yourself, to poor Spit." He pointed to Spit who nodded vigorously. "Only think of the traders! They're strange to us. Their ways are strange to us. Do not go alone. Let us go with you. Let us protect you!"

Squashedface's pleadings struck a strange note in Haina's breast. The man was sincere. He did not want her to come to any harm. Haina marveled at the devotion of a slave to one who held him captive. She had never really put herself in the place of one who was born to the lower ranks of her society. No, she had not thought of it even when she herself had been so close to slavery at Chicklesit and Kyuquot.

Squashedface's flattened face scrunched up in concern. "Think, Mistress, your father—what would he say?"

Haina flinched to think what her father would say. "There is no point in arguing, Squashedface," she said with a stern note in her voice. "I go, and I go alone."

He held her gaze for a short time then he blinked. "As you wish, Mistress," he said in a low voice.

"And do not try to follow me," stated Haina.

Squashedface started visibly.

Ah ha, so he was thinking to outwit her. She smiled to herself. Her father had chosen well after all, in his selection of companions for her. Still, they were a nuisance and she did so want to go and see the ship without their added presence.

"Just a little trip out to the ship," she cajoled. "Then I will return and nap for the afternoon. That should please you!" She smiled but he did not smile back.

"Yes, Mistress," he intoned.

"You and Spit stay here," she repeated and Spit bobbed his head. Squashedface gave him a hard look but said nothing.

She wrapped a cedar cloak around her shoulders and placed a pointed, woven cedar hat on her head. Her long hair hung far below the hat and draped over the cloak. Her locks were sure to get wet but she was undisturbed by the thought.

She edged to the door where she turned to regard the slaves once more.

Spit's mouth hung open as if he could not quite believe she was really going to go out among the foreigners without him. Squashedface merely stared after her with a stony expression. Well, there was no help for it.

"You stay!" she warned, and slid through the door, the words ringing in her ears as though she had spoken to Stinky. What was the matter with her? They were only slaves. How foolish to let two *slaves* make her feel guilty for leaving them behind.

A solid sheet of rain poured down from the skies onto the small crowd of curious onlookers that stood on the beach. Haina huddled among them and peered through the gray curtain. The little she could see of the ship was indeed wondrous.

Like a big bald eagle, the ship bounced up and down slowly on the choppy waves of the bay. The hull was painted a shiny black, and the sails were white rolls plastered tightly to the booms. The tall masts, like trees growing out of its deck, reached to the very skies.

It looked like nothing she had ever seen before. She remembered the ship she had seen at Chicklesit with its full sails poised against the setting sun and she wondered why this ship did not have its wings spread full. Then she shrugged. From the little she had gleaned from the talk around her, the foreigners were strange creatures, not always doing things for a reason.

The people around her shifted, waiting for a turn in one of the canoes being plied between shore and ship. The torrent of rain from the sky ceased and Haina blinked. The respite would be short, she knew, because the wind still howled.

At last a canoe was ready and Haina stepped into it. A slave sat at the stern of the boat, his paddle ready.

Haina waited as five others climbed into the canoe, three women and two men. The slave paddled them slowly out to the ship and Haina could feel her body tense with excitement. Her first opportunity to see a ship! Her first opportunity to see white men!

"This bay used to be full of ships," said one of the men. He was older, his hair done in the old style, knotted on top with a spruce branch. He clutched a fresh-caught salmon under his arm. It fixed Haina with a glazed eye. She looked away. "Now only one or two ships call here in a season."

"Why is that?" asked a high-pitched voice. Haina turned to see one of the women, young and pretty, watching the older man appraisingly.

"No sea otter furs left," answered the man. "That's why all the ships came to us . . . for furs." He glanced at the woman and smiled. "Is this your first visit to a ship?"

The young woman nodded. "Yes." The other two women murmured that they'd been on a ship before. Haina smiled to herself. Many people were so curious about the traders that they would go back again and again.

A guttural order from the other man in the canoe quickly silenced the women. Haina slanted a glance at him. He was a middle-aged man wearing a trading blanket; he must be a chief, thought Haina. She looked more closely at the young women with him. Their faces and skin looked to be scrubbed clean, their cedar cloaks were plain and well-worn. Her stomach started to churn. She wasn't sure she wanted to know what was going to happen to them.

Putting such thoughts aside, Haina watched the boat loom closer and excitement filled her once more.

A rope ladder dangled over the side of the ship and the gruff middle-aged man caught it. He helped the young women climb aboard, then followed. Spruce-knot went next and Haina last.

She stood on the gently rocking deck and looked eagerly around. There were heavy ropes coiled along the sides of the ship and rope ladders leading up the heavy masts. She tilted her head back and stared up at the great masts until she felt dizzy. A light mist kissed her face.

The ship creaked and groaned. The wooden decking was discolored and worn smooth from many footsteps. A large ship's wheel was located towards the stern of the vessel. A long, low cabin graced half the bow. Open doors and stairs led down into the black bowels of the ship. Haina could smell funny smells, food smells, issuing forth. She wondered what the strange men ate, then remembered the salmon the Spruce-knot had brought on board.

Haina counted twenty Indians, men and women, standing about on deck. They all carried things of value to trade: furs, carvings, berries, fresh roots. Haina craned her neck around them, anxious for a first glimpse of the white strangers.

There were about ten *mumutly*, white men, standing on deck. They wore heavy sailor pants with big coats. When they walked, their boots clumped heavily on the deck.

A big white man talked earnestly with Spruce-knot. It was obvious to Haina that they bargained for the salmon.

Haina centered her gaze on four white men leaning against the rigging, their eyes on the Indians. One of them held a strange little weapon casually in the crook of one arm. It looked like a tiny curled musket. She'd seen muskets before when her father and his warriors prepared for raids and war. But she'd never seen such a tiny weapon as this one appeared to be. The handle curved to fit the palm of the user and the other end was pointed. She did not think an Indian had much to fear from such a little weapon but still she gave the man a wide berth. She wondered idly if her father would be interested in such a tiny device.

Her gaze fell on five other white men standing near the open doors. They huddled around the three young women and the middle-aged chief. He was waving his arms and talking loudly. One of the white men was waving a string of blue beads and shouting back. The women giggled.

Just then, another man, smaller than the others, stepped out of the ship's doors. He had brown eyes and brown skin and looked to be Indian. Haina wondered why an Indian was dressed as a white man. One of the whites waved to him and he clumped over to the huddled men.

Haina unashamedly eavesdropped. The newcomer was speaking in Chinook, the trading jargon. Several Nootka words threaded through his speech and she could understand some of what he said.

"White man want to give three bead strings for one woman. Three bead strings, not six. Six too many." The interpreter held up three fingers.

"No, no!" cried the middle-aged chief. "Not enough. *Klutsma*, woman, very good." He grasped the arm of the young, pretty woman Haina had spoken with earlier in the canoe and pulled her forward. The chief held up the woman's plump arm. "Very good *klutsma*."

He pulled the shoulder cape away. The woman's shoulders and bare arms were exposed. The men sucked in their collective breath.

"F-four," gulped one of the men. "Four strings of beads!" He was tall and thin and clean-shaven. He appeared to be all elbows and knees. Haina noted in fascination that his prominent adam's apple bobbed up and down as he spoke. He could not take his eyes off the pretty woman.

The chief snorted in disgust and proceeded to ignore the offer. He smiled as he tugged gently at the knot under the woman's chin until her kutsack opened. He peeled away the top of the garment until one firm breast was exposed. "See." The men stared at the lovely globe and the brown nipple and Haina thought they would all reach for the woman at once.

"Five!" came the ready cry.

The chief sighed in satisfaction as he saw the longing, desire and plain lust etched on the five faces before him. He carefully tucked the inviting breast back into the kutsack and smiled. "Six strings."

"Yes, s-six," came the hoarse response as the thin man with the bouncing adam's apple dug into his pockets and handed over several strings of beads to the chief. "Six. Now, I take her." He grabbed the woman's arm and led her towards the stairs.

The chief beamed as he watched them go. He turned back to the others. "Now, what offers for second woman?"

Haina turned away as the interpreter and the

remaining men bargained heatedly for the favors of the other two women.

A wave of sadness washed over Haina as she reflected upon the scene she had just witnessed. She was indeed fortunate she was not born a slave. She supposed that many chiefs had discovered a ready way to gain the white man's goods: by selling slave women's bodies. The thought sickened her.

She walked to the side of the ship and breathed the fresh sea air into her lungs. She felt her mind clear as she stared down into the slate-green depths. It was such a long way down, she thought.

Mudshark was careful not to stare too long at the woman bending over the side of the white man's ship. She might sense his eyes on her and turn to see him.

He slid back into the rest of the crowd of Indians. He did not want Haina to see him. He had noticed her earlier, standing in the crowd on the beach but had managed to keep hidden from her. When he'd seen her he'd almost approached her to ask her what she was doing in Yuquot. Then, he decided against it and settled for merely following her to see what she was up to. He chuckled to himself as he thought of what Chance would say when he found out his beloved woman, Haina, was also in Yuquot.

Mudshark conceded to himself that he was glad indeed to find the Ahousat woman in Yuquot. Mayhaps she could do something to bring Chance out of his gloom. Mudshark certainly could not. Ever since their return from Ahousat, Chance had been miserable to be with. If they had not been cousins, and close friends, Mudshark doubted that he could have withstood the miserable man Chance had become.

Chance had taken longer to recover from his wounds than he had expected and seemed to blame everyone around him for that. He kept talking about people who weren't there, notably Haina, and Mudshark was getting tired of it.

Chance once muttered that he had seen Haina in Kyuquot village and then later denied it. Mudshark knew the woman had been nowhere near there.

Something was very wrong with Chance and Mudshark was baffled. He was becoming very concerned about his friend's state of mind. He would have done anything, tried anything to get Chance back to his usual cheerful self.

When Chance had casually mentioned that getting away from Kyuquot might help him to recover, Mudshark had leapt at Chance and hugged him. Beachdog had joined in and the two of them had convinced the ailing man that a visit to Yuquot would cure his ills.

Later, Mudshark had worried that Chance, not so groggy now as he'd been at Kyuquot, was still imagining things. Chance had complained that the previous night someone had tried to kill him. He'd pointed to a spot on the longhouse wall where he claimed a bullet had just missed his head and entered the wood instead. In the dark of the longhouse, Mudshark had not been able to verify the marks as made by a bullet but he had promised Chance he would look more closely at the wall once it was daylight. Instead, he'd hurried out the door early in the morning, needing time to get away from Chance for a little while. He dreaded what he would find when he checked the wall. He knew there would be nothing.

Haina straightened at the rail and Mudshark decided not to put off meeting with her any longer. He started across the deck towards her but before he could reach her, two large white men descended upon her. One of them grabbed her arm and swung her around to face him.

When Haina first felt the grasp on her arm, she had tried to shrug it off, thinking someone had mistakenly reached for her instead of another. There was no one she knew in Yuquot and she certainly never expected to be accosted.

Yet here she was staring up into the face of the largest man she had ever seen. And right next to him stood an even larger man! Haina wrenched her arm free of his grasp and swung her head haughtily. "What do you want, insolent one?" she demanded.

"Aww, ain't she purty?" said the one she'd freed herself from. The other nodded happily.

"I do not understand your language, fools. Leave me alone."

"What's she sayin'?"

"Danged if I knowed. Let's call that interpreter fella over. Hey, Bob!" Haina had to steel herself to keep from jumping back when one of the men reached out a big arm and waved it in the general direction of the other white men on the ship. "C'mon over here. This little gal wants to talk to us."

"I fail to see why you are both standing there grinning at me like fools. Leave me alone, I say!"

The Indian dressed as a white came clumping over in his big boots. At least he was of a size Haina could approve. She looked him straight in the eye and said evenly, "I am a noblewoman. Get these dogs away from me!"

"Now, now, princess," said the interpreter. "Just calm down. These men want to know who you are."

"I will tell these dogs nothing. Tell them to leave!" Haina turned back and looked over the railing at the village which, alas, seemed so far away.

"She says she is flattered by your interest."

"She is? She don't look it." The biggest man was eyeing Haina in a friendly manner when she turned back from the railing.

"Are you still here?" she demanded imperiously. "Leave my presence!"

"What'd she say?" asked the second largest man. He had a large brown wart on one cheek and Haina noticed a hair sprouting out of it. She looked at it in a kind of sick fascination.

The interpreter scratched his chin thoughtfully. To tell the two men that this haughty Indian woman rejected them outright and wanted nothing to do with them would not help him. He had to sail with them. It was hard for a half-Indian interpreter on a ship of whites. He was usually ignored and left to himself. He felt barely tolerated among these men and some secret part of him longed for their acceptance. If he got this woman to go with them, perhaps these two would treat him better.

His decision made, the interpreter smiled with one corner of his mouth and said, "She says she likes you, but she wants a lot of pretty things to wear before she will come with you."

"I'll be right back," promised the largest man. He stomped off.

"Thank you for getting rid of him," said Haina politely. "Now tell this one to leave, too."

The interpreter smiled. It was a kind of lop-sided smile, Haina decided. "*Seix*." He touched his chest. "Friend."

Haina was not so sure that this man was a friend but she waited, watching.

"Are you hungry, Princess? Thirsty?"

"*Wik*. No. I just wish to be left alone, thank you."

"Come, Princess. Come downstairs. We have good food for you. Good drink." The interpreter's eyes were narrowed as he watched her.

Haina stared right back. So, this *friend* wanted to give her food and drink, did he? She could just imagine where that would lead! Aloud, she said, "*Wik*."

The large white man beside the interpreter shifted uneasily. "She said 'no,' didn't she? What'd you ask her? Don't she wanna come with me and my friend?" he asked plaintively.

"She want to come," assured the interpreter. "She just don't know it."

A sunny smile broke out on the large man's face. "Oh good. Mayhaps she just wants to play at saying 'no,' huh?"

The interpreter nodded agreeably and the large man continued to stare at Haina, smiling, obviously pleased at how well he knew women.

Haina looked at them both. Time to leave, she decided. She started to inch towards the rope ladder hanging over the side of the ship. It was several lengths away, but she thought she could easily make it if these men would only stop watching her.

The large man reached out and grasped her shoulder. "Hey, there, girlie. No need to leave just yet. Me and my friend gonna visit with you." He leaned closer and Haina steeled herself not to shrink away.

She removed his hand from her shoulder. She had had enough of these white lice! She was leaving. She marched smartly towards the ladder, not caring what they thought.

"Princess, come back!"

"Hey, missie, don't go!"

Neither plea particularly moved Haina. She kept on course and was only a few steps away from the ladder. She breathed a sigh of relief at having gotten out of a difficult situation. Just then a large hand clapped itself firmly on her shoulder. Again. "Aww, don't leave, purty gurl! We was just gettin' to know ya."

Haina swung around angrily. "Leave me alone!" she cried.

It was the largest man—he was back. She only had time to notice he looked ridiculous with several strings of beads, red, blue, white, green, draped around his neck. Two lengths of coarse cloth, dull red and purplish blue, cascaded over one of his arms. As she stood there gaping at him, wondering why he was dressed so strangely, he suddenly picked her up in his arms and started marching across the deck with her. He was headed towards the open doors.

"Put me down, you louse!"

"Haw, haw," laughed his watching partner. "She sure can kick!"

Haina could punch, too. She landed a first right on the large man's chest and he never even flinched. He just looked at her out of little mild blue eyes that crinkled at the corners and he kept walking. Haina flailed her arms at him. "Let me go!"

By now the others on deck, whites and Indians, had stopped their various business transactions to watch the show. Out of the corner of her eye, Haina saw a flash of brown and realized someone had dived over the side of the ship. She heard the splash, but was too caught up in pummeling the foolish man's hard chest to wonder about anything else. "Let me go!"

"Calm down, Princess." This said soothingly by her good *friend* the interpreter. "You won't be hurt."

Haina began to kick and scream in earnest then.

"Dagnab it, Henry, can't you keep her quiet?" demanded the other white man, tagging at the heels of the first. "She sure do make a lot of noise."

"Aww, she just havin' a little fun," assured the man with the kicking, screaming, clawing bundle. "She sure do fight, though. Like one o' them wild cats—cougars. Know what I mean?"

"Sure do, Henry, sure do."

"Princess, no say such rude words!" scolded the interpreter, secretly impressed by the woman's amazing vocabulary of curse words. Where had she learned such phrases?

Haina kicked and screamed her way all the way to the open doors. Those on deck could still hear her screaming as she was carried down the stairs and into the hold of the ship. Then the doors slammed behind her and all was silent.

Chapter 26

Mudshark swam as though an angry bull sea lion were chasing him. The big ship receded as he stroked closer and closer to the village. He waded ashore, running in big clumsy steps until the water was knee high. Then he raced for the longhouse where he had last seen Chance.

The loud drumming of rain had started again on the roof and Chance listened to its lulling beat. He watched the flames dancing and thought lazily of Haina. He wondered how he could get to see her. Since he'd arrived in Yuquot, he'd felt his thoughts clear and now he almost felt like doing something to pursue his heart's longing for Haina. Almost. He still felt a strange lethargy in his veins and in his muscles but he knew he was getting better.

He thought back to the night before. He'd been asleep in his furs in the strange longhouse that he, Mudshark, Beachdog, Whale Hunter and his other warriors were staying in. He'd woken suddenly as though someone had snapped their fingers in his face.

Instantly alert, he'd seen a heavy black shadow creep towards his sleeping place. The shadow, somehow familiar—had he seen it in a dream before?—pointed a dangerous stick at him. This time his slow moving body had obeyed his lurching mind's command to roll away.

The night exploded around him and he heard a deadly whine whip past his ear. Something buried itself in the wall above his head. Then all was quiet again.

When he looked up from his furs, he saw nothing and no one. The shadow was gone. All around him lay sleeping people. No one had even awakened. He remembered that earlier in the night many of the longhouse inhabitants had been drinking rum—it was easy to get at Yuquot—but surely *someone* had heard. But no. All was still and silent.

He'd turned then, to Mudshark's sleeping place but his cousin was gone, still visiting friends in another longhouse.

Tired, but wide awake from the jolt of fear he'd had, he wondered if he'd imagined the whole thing. He got up and went to look for his cousin. When he'd brought Mudshark back and told him what had happened, he'd seen the disbelief in his cousin's black eyes. Enough! He'd lain down to sleep again, sick at heart, and in body. . . .

Now he sat wondering again if he'd only dreamed the shot, and the bullet missing him. He was waiting for Mudshark to examine the walls with him. Mayhaps he had not been dreaming after all . . .

As if conjured up by his very thoughts, a dripping Mudshark stood before him.

"Odd time to swim, Mudshark," observed Chance, noticing the soaked clothing hanging on his cousin's frame.

Mudshark, gasping, showed no inclination to bandy words. "Come—it's Haina—" he gasped.

Chance sat up straighter. "Haina? What about Haina?"

"Come—" Mudshark wiped his mouth with the back of his hand. "She's—she's here."

Without hesitation, Chance was on his feet and tying his bear robe around his shoulders. "Where?"

"On the ship." Mudshark's breaths were more regular now. "Trouble."

Chance tightened his belt and tucked several lethal looking blades at his waist. "What kind of trouble?" he asked evenly and Mudshark was almost able to believe it was the old Chance come back—the one he'd known before all the trouble at Ahousat.

"White men. They've taken Haina. Down below. Into the ship."

Chance paused. A sick feeling twisted his gut and he fought the feeling of hopelessness that he was too late. "Let's go."

He reached for a pistol, one of a brace he'd acquired two days previously.

"Where'd you get those?" asked Mudshark in surprise.

"I won them, gambling with old Gaptooth. A white tyee from a ship gave them to him for a present. I have none of the black powder that is supposed to go with them. Nor do I have the little round balls that go in here." He pointed.

Chance held up the pistol for Mudshark's perusal.

"Beautiful," murmured Mudshark. The curved handle of the pistol was of a dark, polished wood. The barrel, as long as a man's forearm, was overlayed with gleaming metal.

Chance looked grim. "I like them, even if I can't fire them. I like to wear them. They make me look fierce!"

"They do," agreed Mudshark admiringly as Chance tucked one of the pistols into his belt.

Mudshark picked up a lance leaning against one wall of the longhouse. "There are many white men," he warned.

"I do not fear them. All I want is Haina, not trouble with the white men. But if they give me trouble . . ." he shrugged, "they will not take her easily." Those were the last words he spoke until they got to the beach.

There, several of Chance's warriors were walking up the beach, two carrying a dead deer between them. Chance and Mudshark hurried over to them. Chance quickly told them what happened. The deer was dispatched by slave to the longhouse and the Kyuquots raced for the canoes.

There was no time to search out the sleek black Ahousat canoe that Chance had brought with him. He and Mudshark picked a heavy, plain, work canoe and Mudshark grunted as they carried it to the water. Ignoring the rain on his skin, Chance jumped into the bow of the canoe and Mudshark pushed off at the stern. They surged out of the harbor to the ship.

Chance paddled against the strong waves and felt life returning to his body. Haina! Haina was out there, on that ship. Suddenly he had the strength of two men and his canoe leapt ahead of the others. Mudshark roared with exhilaration as they sped towards the ship.

Chance touched a sharp metal knife at his belt for reassurance. He hoped he would not have to use it. His mouth thinned. If he had to, he would use it. He would brave anything for Haina.

They arrived at the ship and clambered aboard. Several Indians huddled on deck and four white sailors stood about watching them. One of the sailors tried to get Chance and his warriors to give over their weapons but Chance merely laughed.

"Where is *klutsma*, my woman," he demanded.

Several of the sailors looked blanky at him until one thought to call for the interpreter. "Bob! Tyee

269

Bob!"

The small man came running up the steps when he heard his name.

"I come for *klutsma*," Chance told him, eyeing him sternly.

"*Klutsma*," shrugged the man, his eyes shifting quickly about the deck. "Many *klutsma* here. Cheap, too." The little man smiled and Chance did not like it.

He touched the butt of the pistol. "Take me down into the ship."

"Why do you not speak English?" asked the interpreter in that language. "Why is a white man like you dressed like an Indian?"

Chance merely stared at him. Getting no answer the interpreter shrugged. "Have it your way," he said. "Though I do not see what is to be gained by playing the Indian."

Chance was getting tired of the interpreter's incomprehensible mutterings. "*Klutsma*," he said again. He tapped the front of Tyee Bob's coat with one big finger. His voice was full of menace. "Now."

Suddenly the interpreter realized which woman this big, blond white man dressed and speaking like an Indian was after. He blanched.

Chance smiled ferally when he saw the other's fear. "You know," he said. "You know who I mean."

The interpreter looked dazed. The Princess! He should have thought. . . . Of course, she would have protection. She was a noblewoman, not a prostitute putting on airs like he'd thought. His gut turned over as he looked at the fierce man standing before him. Not even Henry and Lars could fight this lot, he thought, his stomach sinking.

He stalled for time. "Many pretty *klutsma*. You like? Mayhaps food, drink? Good drink, you like." If he could get them drunk, mayhaps the sailors could pour them off the ship later. "Good rum," he cajoled in a sing-song voice, his throat tightening.

But the blond Indian was looking at him with contempt. "No, white-man's-speaking-boy, no want drink. Get woman. Now."

When the interpreter merely stood there, Chance pushed past the man who could not, or would not, help him. His warriors filed past after him.

"You can't go down there, bucko."

Chance turned when he felt a rough hand graze his back. The man who had accosted him looked different from the others. He appeared to be a sailor who scorned sailor's clothes. Instead he wore leather— leather jacket, leather pants, leather boots—and no hat on his head. His loose brown curls dripped with moisture. Across his chest he'd strapped two belts, and he had a powder horn swinging at his waist. Hostile dark brown eyes gazed into Chance's green ones.

"Tyee Bob!" he shouted into Chance's face, "tell this fool Injun that he's not welcome downstairs. No Indians allowed down there!" Here the man's lips curled in a sneer.

Tyee Bob eyed the man in leather with hate, knowing the buffoon was laughing at him, telling him that he, Tyee Bob, best interpreter on the west coast, was not wanted downstairs either. One of these days I'll get you sons of bitches, thought Tyee Bob.

Tyee Bob spoke in rapid Chinook jargon. "No go down."

"I go down," Chance said evenly. "Or this man dead!" He gestured to the knives belted at his waist.

"I understand him," said the big man, cutting off Tyee Bob's flow of words. He stepped aside. "Where's the captain? He should be here to stop this Injun. What's he doing?"

"Captain's sick, sir," answered Tyee Bob sullenly. "Been sick all day."

The man in leather laughed. "Sick, is he? Why that

puling coward is lying in his bunk again! Happens two times a year, regular as clock-work. Can't seem to make up his mind whether he wants to be a captain or a priest! So, his oh-so-tender conscience struggles with him twice a year—once in summer, once in winter." The man spat on the deck. "He makes *me* sick."

"So why you still here, Layverley? Why ain't ya trappin' for those precious furs you done tole us about?"

"Who asked you, loudmouth?" The blond man turned on the speaker, a slovenly sailor lounging against some ropes. "Get your butt downstairs, afore I kick it for ya!"

"Shut up, Layverley. Don't start no fight wit' me. I ain't ascared o' the likes o' you."

"You should be. I've beaten up better men than you and spat 'em out. Before breakfast, too."

"You shouldn't be on this ship!" spoke up the sailor.

"Comes with bein' a friend o' the good captain's family, like," taunted Layverley. Then he stuck out his chin belligerently. "So put me off it, loudmouth."

The slovenly sailor did not move and the two glared at each other. Seeing no more threat from that quarter, Layverley turned back to Chance. Then he threw back his head and laughed. "So, it's up to me to handle this son of a bitch, is it?" They were of a size and eyed each other carefully. "Seems to me this Injun needs to learn to do as he's told."

"Leave him alone," Tyee Bob cautioned. "All he wants is his woman."

The brown-haired man rounded on the interpreter. "You tellin' me what to do, boy?" he said softly.

Tyee Bob backed down. "No, sir," he answered.

"Good. I like an interpreter what knows when to keep his mouth shut." Layverley laughed uproariously at his own joke and Chance glanced questioningly at the interpreter.

Tyee Bob shrugged. Chance turned back to his opponent. "*Klutsma*," he said.

Layverley circled Chance slowly, keeping his eyes on the blond Indian. He stopped when he stood between Chance and the stairs leading to the ship's hold. "Ain't no klootsmuuuhhh here, Injun. Go back to your village." He waved in the general direction of the village but neither man looked. They would not have seen the village anyway, not through the heavy mist.

Chance tried once more. "Interpreter," he said. "Tell this man," here he sneered and Layverley sneered back. "Tell this *man* that I want my woman. Give her to me and I go peacefully. No fight." He nodded in the direction of his warriors. Beachdog, Mudshark, Whale Hunter and the others stood watching grimly.

Tyee Bob translated and Layverley laughed. "You one dumb man, Injun or white or whatever the hell you are." He stopped laughing and stuck his face in Chance's. "Get off this ship afore I throw you off." His breath hit Chance and made him want to gag.

Chance said evenly, "I do not leave this ship without my woman." Tyee Bob dutifully translated and when he'd done, Chance added, "Step aside, white dog."

"Don't bother," Layverley held up his hand to stop the interpreter's words. "I know what he said. Some kind of Injun insult." And before Chance could move, Layverley followed through with a blow that knocked the side of Chance's head. Chance went reeling across the deck.

Immediately Mudshark, Whale Hunter and the others had their knives out and were moving towards Layverley.

"Fight! Fight!" called the sailors. They gathered round, jostling each other for a frontal position to the fight.

Chance got to a kneeling position on the deck and shook his head groggily. He staggered to his feet. He ran his fingers over his temple and winced at a tender spot. He pulled his heavy knife out of his waistband and advanced on Layverley. The white dog would die!

"Here he comes! Get out of the way!" Sailors and Indians scattered between the two antagonists, leaving Chance a clear path to Layverley.

Layverley had a knife out too, balancing the hefty, vicious looking weapon in one hand. "Come on, Injun." The brown curls bounced on his head as he laughed, showing big white teeth.

A wave of anger rushed over Chance and he wanted to bury his blade in the tanned throat of the white man in front of him. Then cold reason intruded. He stopped. Haina! He had to get to Haina. It would not help her to kill this man, it would only keep her from him. If this man were killed, the surrounding sailors would make sure Chance never got off this ship alive. Haina would be doomed, doomed beneath the decks of the rocking ship.

When he saw Chance stop, Layverley taunted, "Come on, come on, Injun. Fight!"

Chance threw his knife down on the deck and drew himself up. "I will not kill a man just because he is stupid. Interpreter, tell him!"

Tyee Bob glanced from one to the other. He hesitated, then translated Chance's words.

Layverley flushed red as he heard the words. He raced at Chance and shrieked, "You gawdamn coward, fight me!"

Chance braced himself for the madman's charge.

"What is going on here?" roared a voice.

Layverley stopped in midstride. Chance swung his head to see who called out. A thin, graying man in a dark blue uniform, his hat slightly askew stood at the top of the stairs, opening the doors. "Layverley," the apparition barked. "Who are you trying to kill now?"

Layverley sheepishly dropped his head and the knife clattered to the deck. He stooped, embarrassed to pick it up and mumbled, "This Injun's makin' trouble."

"That so?" The man turned to Chance. His sharp eyes glittered on either side of his beaked nose, took in Chance's unarmed stance, his knife on the deck. The man turned to Tyee Bob. "What goes on here?"

Tyee Bob hurried over, almost tripping in his haste to get to the man. "Captain, so sorry you were disturbed." He bowed and Chance recognized that the thin man in the dark suit was the tyee of the ship.

"This Indian," Tyee Bob was saying, pointing at Chance, "wants to go downstairs to find his *klutsma*, woman."

"So what's stopping him?" asked the man, irritably.

Tyee Bob glanced at Layverley. Layverley was glaring at him, daring him to say anything. The captain followed his glance. "Nevermind. I think I know," he sighed. It was a long suffering sigh. "Layverley, put your knife away. I don't want any blood shed on my tidy, clean decks."

Sullenly Layverley tucked his knife back at his waist. "Yes, sir," he mumbled and turned to go.

"And Layverley . . ."

The man in leather turned.

"Leave the Indians alone, would you? It was for starting little fights like the one with this man here," the captain nodded at Chance, "that I agreed to take you on in the first place. Those trappers would have killed you if I hadn't taken you away from them in time. Remember?" he prodded. "After I rescued you, you agreed to stop getting into trouble." He sighed. "Our families have known each other for a long time,

Layverley." The captain took off his cap and ran his hand through his thinning gray hair. "But even friendships have their limits. I'm running out of patience, Layverley."

Layverley grunted and turned away. He walked to the stern of the ship and stared out over the rail.

Chance's eyes followed him, then he turned back to the ship's tyee. The captain was motioning Chance towards the stairs.

"Tell him he can find his woman, Bob," the captain sighed. "I'm going back to bed." He disappeared into the darkness once more.

Tyee Bob nodded to Chance. "He say go find your woman," he translated.

Chance nodded and stepped towards the stairs.

It was dark down in the hold of the ship. Chance flinched at the overpowering stench of greased rope, pitch, tar and and dark greasy substances.

He squinted into the gloom. Ropes lay coiled everywhere and men's clothing was scattered about. Sea chests lined the sides of the ship. When he got to the bottom of the stairs he banged his head on the low ceiling. A rat scooted ahead of him and disappeared into the dark. Where was Haina?

A lantern threw a soft golden glow ahead. Behind a stout wooden support he could see tall squirming shadows against the wall. His eyes were adjusting to the dark now.

He stood, listening carefully. The voice he longed for and never thought to hear came out of the gloom.

". . . tear you into little pieces and throw you to the sharks!"

Haina, beloved Haina, and still making threats. She was alive! He was not too late. For a moment the memory of when he first captured her and heard her lovely voice say those same brave words washed over him. Then he clenched his fists. Now was not the time for his mind to wander. He must bring it back for the work at hand.

"All I want is just one li'l kiss," cajoled a gruff voice.

Loud hoots echoed throughout the cavernous depths of the ship and Chance looked about, trying to determine where the sound came from. He glanced back at the squirming shadows. There, it had to be there. He stepped forward, still hidden from the noisy occupants by the stout wooden pillar.

Haina's heart pounded in fear, yet she refused to let these white lice see how afraid she was. They'd dragged her downstairs. She'd fought free of them and raced for the stairs. The man she thought of as Sprouting Mole had grabbed her before she set foot on the first step. The largest man she thought of as *Katsa*, Three, because he was the size of three men.

Katsa had seized her about the waist and hauled her back to where there was a big table and benches on either side of it. She'd fought on, terror giving her the strength of a man. Katsa had hugged her close to him as she'd fought for breath. When he'd lain his foul lips on hers she'd bit and shrieked and clawed his face. Her nails had scored him, three long red streaks graced one cheek. *That* had given them pause.

They'd backed off then and talked to each other in their funny bird language. She wished she could understand their words but she knew they spoke of her and how to subdue her.

While they were thus making plans, she looked about wildly for a weapon. She spotted two long, flat broadswords decorating one wall. Swords were not weapons she knew, though she had seen them before, again with her father. Still, a sword would do, she thought, fear twisting her bowels. If she could only reach one, she'd have something to defend herself with.

They were watching her, though—Katsa and Sprouting Mole. Tiny little eyes peeking out of now flushed, red faces. She inched towards the sword. Their little eyes followed her but they made no move, still talking between themselves. She made a quick movement to the other side and they both jerked towards her. So, they were alert. She feinted the other way, they lunged for her and grabbed thin air. She drew back and threw herself against the wall and tore a sword from its resting place.

"Aha!" She cried out triumphantly and her voice echoed in the stinking, cavernous depths. They leaned back, then scrambled to get away from her and the long sword she held out in front of her.

She laughed exultantly. All the fear she'd been flooded with turned to heady, sweet victory. "I have you now, my fine sailors," she cried. She began to beat Katsa over the head and shoulders with the flat of the sword and he threw up his arms to protect his head. She laughed and pounded with the sword some more.

"And then I will tear you into pieces and throw you to the sharks," she yelled. To one side, Sprouting Mole was bending over, holding his sides, and shaking with fear. And well he should! she thought. "When I get done with this one, you are next!" she promised Sprouting Mole and she showed her white teeth in a ferocious grin. Yes, she was very much her father's daughter!

She paused in beating Katsa to grip the sword more firmly in her two-fisted grip. A sword made an awkward club, she noted. Then she glanced at Sprouting Mole. It was not fear he was shaking from, she realized, aghast. No, not fear—laughter. Laughter! What strange manner of men these were, she thought with one part of her mind. The other part continued to direct her beating efforts with the sword.

Chance appeared out of the gloom. "Haina."

She looked up from her battle to see him and could not believe it was him. "Chance! What—"

"Go on, Indian. This is our party," snarled the man Katsa when he realized he was no longer being hit. He grabbed for the sword but Haina whisked it out of his reach. She centered the pointed deadly tip right at his heart.

Chance stood in the door, a pistol pointed at the same chest. He hoped the *mumutly* would not know the weapon was useless. He frowned ferociously.

Katsa subsided; a big, hulking heap, waiting. He eyed the pistol aimed at his heart. "Hold on. We was just havin' a li'l fun—"

"Haina! Come with me," demanded Chance. He ignored the big hulking brute that was standing in front of Haina.

The big hulking brute eyed the pistol in Chance's hand. "This purty gal don't want to go with you," he said.

When neither Chance nor Haina reacted to his words, the man looked at his friend. "You gonna let this funny lookin' Indian take our woman?"

The man with the mole looked from Chance to Haina and back to Chance again. His eyes, too, centered on the pistol. "Yep," he said evenly.

The other man snorted. "You chicken shit."

Chance watched the two men. Haina carefully laid the broadsword on the table. She dusted off her hands. "I come now," she said. She stared defiantly at Katsa, daring him to stop her.

He contented himself with a small sad smile. "We coulda had fun, purty gal."

"Let's go. You first." Chance indicated the steps. He kept his eyes, and pistol, on the two big men. When Haina had climbed the stairs, he backed carefully up himself.

Haina sniffed and walked away without a backward glance. Sprouting Mole and Katsa longingly watched her leave.

The air felt fresh and clean when Haina stepped back on deck. "Whew, that place smelled strong," she told Chance as he clambered up behind her. On deck, there were still a few Indians left bargaining with one or two sailors. The rest had been rushed off the ship after the near-fight between Chance and Layverley.

Beachdog, Mudshark, Whale Hunter and the others stood along one side. Mudshark grinned when he saw Chance. Haina's eyes widened when she saw the Kyuquot warriors. "How—?"

"Later," said Chance. "Let's just get you off this ship."

The warriors could not wait to leave the ship, either. They quickly filed down the ladder to the waiting canoes. Beachdog reached up to help lower Haina into the canoe he was in. Just as she reached for his hand her foot slipped on the wet rope and she slid towards the water.

"Aeeii!"

Beachdog grabbed for her but she hung on tight to the ladder with both hands. The rope cut into her palms and the small craft bounced up and down in the waves, a mere handsbreadth away. She sought desperately with her feet to feel the canoe under her and Beachdog finally clutched her ankles and placed her feet on the cold, wet wood. Thankfully she collapsed onto a wet seat and huddled into a small ball. Her cry had immobilized Mudshark and Chance, the last two on the ship. Chance had tucked away his pistol. He held a knife in one hand to guard their backs. When he saw that Haina was safely seated, and when he sensed no threat from the sailors, he replaced his knife.

Mudshark had just thrown his leg over the railing and was about to step on the first rope rung of the ladder when a voice boomed behind them.

"Injun! We ain't done yet." Layverley stalked towards them, his fists clenched into huge hams.

Chance groaned and rolled his eyes at Mudshark. "It was too much to hope," he muttered, "that we'd get off this white man's ship without any trouble."

He turned to Layverley. "What do you want?" he asked in Nootka.

"None o' yer gibberish, Injun," sneered the brown-haired man. His recent humiliation was still fresh in his mind, judging from his swaggering walk.

Chance took his pistol out of his belt and handed it to Mudshark.

"Take this, I don't want it getting damaged. It is too valuable."

Mudshark shrugged and added the pistol to the other side of his belt. He knew he looked fierce. He set his jaw belligerently. If this trouble-making white man got the best of Chance, he, Mudshark, would see to it that the white dog never picked another fight again.

"I jest wanted to see you off, ha ha," jeered Layverley. "Too bad you don't speak English, you stupid son-of-a-bitch."

"He doesn't have to Layverley," piped up Tyee Bob stepping from behind one of the masts from where he'd been watching the confrontation. "I'll tell him every sweet word that falls from your lips."

"Yer getting damn cocky, my little bantam rooster," sneered Layverley to the interpreter. "When I'm done with him, I'll start on you next."

Tyee Bob swallowed once, hesitated, then hurried away.

"Hah!" snorted Layverley. "Now let's settle this, Injun. Just between us." He assumed a boxing stance. "Come on, come on." He jabbed the air in front of his face.

Chance watched the strange antics of the large

white man. Obviously the white man was spoiling for a fight, but what did punching the air have to do with it? Must be some kind of white man's war ritual, thought Chance. He balled his hand into a fist and jabbed at the air in front of his face. There, let the white fool know that he, Chance, would meet him and beat him!

Layverley dropped his fists and stared at Chance, disconcerted. "What—?" he asked. "That's the funniest kinda boxing I've ever seen. What kinda man are ya anyway? Are ya Injun or white?" He shook his head. "Ya act Injun and ya look white. And ya sure don't know how to box!"

"Your people are cannibals!" answered Chance in Nootka. "I will stick your head on a pole!"

"Don't talk to me in no gibberish," said Layverley. "Ya won't be doin' no talkin' once I beats ya around a little!" He rushed at Chance.

Chance had been expecting something like that. He waited until the big white man was almost upon him, then he wrapped one leg around the white man's foremost leg and tripped him off-balance. Chance was positioned against the rail and with one large heave, he threw Layverley up and over the railing. Down, down into the depths of the sea plunged the startled man.

The watching Indians let out a whoop of joy. Chance stood, arms akimbo, on the deck and gazed down at the floundering white man.

"He can't swim! He can't swim!" Beachdog and Whale Hunter were laughing uproariously. Haina noticed that Beachdog almost fell out of the canoe, he was laughing so hard. She watched the white man's struggles and found them amusing—at first. Then his gasps and frantically flailing arms spelled out to her the real trouble he was in.

Unintelligible gurgles, sounding something like "hlp ee" came from his mouth. Then more water poured in and he went under again.

"Chance!" Haina cried, her voice shrill above the wind. "He needs help! He's drowning!"

"Let him," answered Beachdog. Mudshark sat on the rail, one foot still poised over the rail and laughed down at the white man. "It looks serious," he told Chance. "If you don't want to help him, he's a dead man."

Chance's eyes narrowed against the heavy mist and he watched the floundering man. Chance realized then that if he wanted it, the man would drown. Not one of the watching Indians would lift a finger to help the man if Chance was against it. And not one of the whites on the ship knew of their comrade's predicament.

Then Chance's eyes shifted to Haina. She was the very picture of horrified womanhood; one hand covered her mouth, the other she pressed to her heart. Her whole being seemed concentrated on the drowning man.

Chance knew that to do nothing was to let the man die. At that moment, Haina turned her horrified gaze full upon Chance. He met her gaze and for a heartbeat their eyes locked. Then Haina's eyes swung back to the drowning man and she began to fumble around the canoe.

Chance wondered what she sought until she suddenly held aloft a paddle. A paddle! Oh, no! His fearless Haina was at it once again. She was going to rescue that drowning white man singlehandedly!

"Out of the way," he ordered Mudshark and that one scrambled aside. Chance climbed down the swaying rope ladder. He stepped into Beachdog's canoe and kneeled beside Haina.

She was stretched out holding the canoe paddle towards the panicking man. Layverley had grabbed the paddle and was now pulling frantically on it. Haina refused to let go of the paddle and she was already half out of the canoe. Chance barely had time to grasp

Haina about the waist to save her from falling into the sea. "Give me that," he muttered and took the wooden paddle from her grasp.

Haina would not let go, not until he assured her he had a strong grip on it. "Oh, Chance," she breathed. "Please save him."

Chance looked into her eyes then and knew he could refuse her nothing. He did not stop to ask why it was so important to save the drowning *mumutly* who had been so insulting and who had demanded the fight. All he knew was that Haina, his gentle Haina, wanted the man's life spared and so he, Chance, would do it. He would do anything to see that love in her eyes.

The floundering man was tiring now. He hung heavily onto the paddle and Chance pulled him closer to the canoe.

Fortunately the paddle was thick and strong. Otherwise it would have snapped under the strain of Layverley's grip. Coughing and sputtering he leaned his head on the wide part of the paddle and let Chance pull him to the canoe. But before Chance could lift him into the canoe, a wave lashed Layverley in the face and he slid off the paddle. He coughed and started to sink again.

Chance grabbed for him then, bending dangerously over the side of the canoe. A handful of brown curly hair was all that kept the white man from the ocean's watery welcome. Layverley thrashed weakly, risking Chance and the others with a dunking.

"Easy," cautioned Chance to the panicking man.

"Help me!" gasped Layverley when his head cleared the water.

But Layverley was too tired from all his frantic splashing around before. His eyeballs rolling, grasping blindly for the canoe, he struggled to climb aboard. Just as Layverley would have tipped the canoe, and Chance, Beachdog, and Haina into the sea, Chance hit the floundering man sharply across the head with his fist.

Layverley was now a dead weight. He would have sunk like a stone if Chance had not held onto him by his hair. Straining, for Layverley was a big man, Chance pulled the unconscious man half into the canoe. Haina leaned towards the other side of the craft to balance out the heavy weight of the near-drowned man.

"Help me," gasped Chance, his arms wrapped around Layverley's shoulders. "This white man is heavy."

Beachdog tried to reach around Chance, but to no avail. Whale Hunter maneuvered his canoe closer and pulled Layverley's legs out of the water. The unfortunate man was suspended between the two rocking canoes and Haina feared he would fall between them back into the cold green depths.

Whale Hunter pulled his canoe closer by pulling on the gunwales of Chance's canoe. The two craft were now alongside each other and with a last heave, Whale Hunter rolled the lower half of the unconscious Layverley into Chance's canoe.

Everyone gasped in relief. The giant was out of the water. Haina looked at Chance with her big, beguiling eyes and all of a sudden he was glad he had saved the white dog, irritating though the man was.

"Hey, down there," called out Tyee Bob from the deck. "What goes on?"

"Come and get your friend," called Chance.

"He is not my friend," answered a sullen Tyee Bob.

"He is from your ship, then. Come and get him. He almost drowned."

Tyee Bob peered closer at the Indians upon hearing this. He quickly called out some words to some sailors and they were soon scrambling down the ladder to reach the unfortunate Layverley.

After the unconscious man was carried onto the deck, Tyee Bob called to Chance, "The ship's tyee will be very pleased that you have saved his friend. No one here knew he had fallen into the sea. Our tyee will thank you and give you many gifts."

Chance waved the man's words away. "He fell into the sea because he wanted a fight. I gave him one. He would be a drowned man now if it were not for this woman." Chance pointed to Haina. "Give her your thanks."

Tyee Bob called down more compliments, but Haina did not understand them. She too, waved away the words. "Let us go back to shore," she said. "I have had enough of the *mumutly* for today."

Chance, Beachdog and Mudshark obligingly put themselves to the paddles and soon the ship was left behind.

Chapter 27

Chance and Haina stood on the beach, arms around each other, oblivious to the wind and rain that drummed at their bodies.

"Chance," murmured Haina, "I'm so glad you're here. I missed you so much." She hugged him closely and rested her head on his chest.

"Aah, Haina," he answered, "it is I who am glad of you." He let out his breath in a gentle sigh. "I've so longed to hold you, to touch you. . . ." His voice broke at the last and Haina held him tighter.

"Come," he whispered huskily. "Let us get in out of the wind and rain." Arms around each other, they ran to the nearest longhouse.

Chance shook droplets of water from his tousled blond mane. Then he pulled off the cedar cloak he'd borrowed in his haste to rescue Haina. She, in turn, pulled off her cloak; she'd lost her pointed rain hat somewhere on the ship.

Chance led Haina over to an unoccupied bench along a sidewall where they could have some privacy. She carefully laid the cloak on the bench as she wondered how she should word her proposal of marriage. Now that the time had come the blood pounded through her body and her hands trembled.

Before she could seat herself beside her sodden cloak, Chance took her in his arms and nuzzled her ear. "How is it that I find you here in Yuquot? I thought I would never see you again. Aah, Haina," he murmured, holding her close to him. "If I had not been driven away—"

She searched his face, her beautiful dark eyes reflecting the flames of a distant fire. "I thought never to see you again, dearest one. My father—"

"Hush, *Chummuss*." He kissed her lips gently, so gently. "You are here. I am here. That is all that matters."

She clung to him as if she would never let go. Then, slowly, they broke apart. "Chance, I missed you so."

"And I, you." He looked down into her beloved face and squeezed her tighter. Then he glanced around. No one paid any attention to the two strangers seeking shelter from the storm.

He nudged her to sit down. When they were seated, Chance took her hands in his. "So tell me what causes you to journey so far from your home?"

She looked into his eyes, those green eyes the color of the sea on a hot summer's day, and for a moment her courage failed. What if he did not want her? Or their child?

He saw her falter and wondered at it. For his part, Chance could only gaze hungrily at her, feeling whole for the first time since his ordeal started. "Aah, *Chummuss*," he stroked her heavy black hair, "you are so beautiful it brings tears to my eyes."

She smiled softly at that. "Chance," she said gently. "I am in Yuquot because I was searching for you."

"Me?"

She nodded and looked at the floor. It was dirt, beaten smooth by hundreds of footsteps. Bits of wood and pieces of bone lay scattered about but Haina did not see them. How to ask him to marry her?

"I-I," she swallowed. "I—"

"What is it?" Chance asked. He watched her and knew then that she could kill him with a single word if she chose, so much did he love her. "What is it, Haina? Are you all right? Sick? Injured in some way?"

"I-I," this was much harder than she had ever thought it would be.

Panic flared in him. He ran his eyes and hands over her desperately searching for a sign, any sign, of what ailed her. "Someone has hurt you. Who is it?" He lifted her chin. "Who is it? Tell me, Haina! I'll kill him!"

She gazed into his green eyes. The intensity in him scared her. "Oh, Chance," she moaned, "it's not that . . ."

"Then tell me!" he cried. "Haina, it scares me to see you like this," he admitted hoarsely.

She knew she had better say something quickly. He was obviously distraught over some imagined pain to her and she marveled that he should feel that way about her.

Reassured, she took a deep breath and laid one small hand on his arm. "Chance," she blurted at last, "I am pregnant with your child."

She hesitated, wondering how to word her marriage proposal now that the time had come. Should she say, Please marry me? Or, Would you marry me for the sake of the baby? No, not that. She wanted him to want her for herself. Drat, why had she not given more careful thought to this? But so much had happened on the short voyage to Yuquot, she had not had time . . .

Lost in her thoughts, she came out of her reverie when she noticed Chance looking at her oddly.

"Pardon me," she said ruefully, "I was not listening. Could you please repeat that?"

Chance now had a cold, implacable look on his face.

Haina wanted to shrink away from him. He looked as he had when—when?—when he and his warriors had first swooped down on her and captured her. Whatever was the matter with him? she wondered. Did he not want her? Not want their baby?

Tears rose unbidden to her eyes and she swallowed. There was a painful tightening in her chest. No, it could not be that he did not want her! "Chance?"

"I said," Chance repeated painstakingly, "that you must marry me." He felt his whole being awaiting her answer. He, a man who had given up hope of ever being with the one woman he loved, had suddenly been given hope. If he could marry her, have her for his wife, what a happy man he would be. Her father could not refuse marriage now, not with Haina pregnant. It was Chance's hope, his only hope, the only way he could have Haina to wife.

Then he saw her hesitate and his heart fell. She did not want him! In all his dreams he had not imagined this. For a moment his life stretched in front of him, bleak and lonely. No, he would not, could not accept her refusal!

Very well, he had no choice. He would force marriage upon her. Coldly, calculatingly he would see to it that she had no other choice. He smiled grimly. He almost pitied the poor, beautiful butterfly caught in his palm—almost.

Haina felt her heart contract and realized that it was with relief, relief and yes, love.

Chance, seeing her touch her breast, gently clasped her hands in his. He held them tight and would not let

290

her pull away.

"Haina," he warned. "If you will not come to me willingly, I will steal you. You will never return to Ahousat again!"

She looked at him, her mouth gaping. "But Chance—"

"It does no good to protest. I have spoken my mind on this matter. We will be wed."

She smiled down at the dirt floor and replied meekly, "Yes, Chance."

He looked at her, suddenly suspicious that she had surrendered too easily. He waited for her to speak but she continued to stare at the floor. At last he nodded. "That is settled then. We will go to your parents and tell them you have agreed to marry me."

"Yes, Chance."

"I warn you, Haina! It will do no good to plot and wriggle your way out of this. You are caught like a fish on a hook. We *will* marry, and your family will not stop us. Do you understand?"

"Yes, Chance."

"Then we will come back to Kyuquot to live." He thought for a moment. "Or perhaps Chicklesit. Would you want to live at Chicklesit?"

"Wherever you say, Chance." Her voice shook.

He heard it. He leaned over and peered at her more closely. She was laughing. The wench was laughing!

"Haina!" he roared. "You anger me. You *dare* to laugh at my marriage plans?"

She reached out and placed a small palm over his mouth. She looked into his furious green eyes and choked anew on her laughter.

"Hush, Chance," she said softly. "Know that I love you. Truly, I do."

He pushed her hand away, frowning ferociously. "Then why the laughter?"

"Because—" she snickered again, "because I had

planned to ask *you* to marry *me*!" And she burst into another gale of laughter.

Chance stared at her, then he too started to laugh. Soon the two were howling with laughter.

Two curious women, inhabitants of the longhouse, crept closer to see what the noise was all about. Seeing only a man and woman laughing so hard that they had to prop each other up, the women shrugged at each other and silently crept away.

Chapter 28

"Chance?" Haina's voice quavered. "Mayhaps you should wait in the canoe. Mayhaps I should go to him and mother and talk with them first."

Chance looked at Haina, sitting in the bow of *Slider,* the sleek black canoe he had escaped in. The smooth manner in which the well-made craft slid through the water gave it it's name. Behind him, in the stern, paddled Spit and Squashedface. They towed behind them the big canoe that Haina had paddled to Yuquot.

Throughout the whole trip the two slaves had kneeled on cedar mats in the stern and paddled silently. Chance was grateful for their silence. It was almost as if they were not there, except for the large quantities of food the two consumed.

Chance was amazed by that. Never had he seen men eat such prodigious amounts of food, yet he could not deny they used it well. They'd reached Ahousat village in half the time it normally took.

"Chance?"

He had thought that returning the valuable canoe, *Slider*, to Fighting Wolf might make the older man more amiable to his and Haina's marriage plans. Now doubt crept in. The old man would probably take back the canoe, *and* his daughter. And, if Chance was fortunate, Fighting Wolf would attack him with only one-half of the Ahousat warriors!

Coming alone might not have been the best idea, Chance conceded. When discussing the matter in the safety of Yuquot village, Chance and Haina had thought that coming alone would show Chance's sincerity about the marriage plans. But now, the closer he got to Ahousat village, the more Chance doubted the wisdom of that thinking.

"Chance?"

When he spoke his voice was gruffer than he intended. "What is it?"

Haina sighed. Sometimes this man she loved could be so exasperating! "Do you wish to wait in the canoe?"

"Let's get this over with, Haina. The sooner we convince your father to let us marry the sooner I can go back to Kyuquot and arrange for the wedding gifts."

"You want to be rid of me so soon, Chance?"

"You know it is not that, Haina. I merely want this difficult part past us and the marriage to take place. Then you are mine, in front of everyone."

Here his voice took on an almost vicious quality, Haina noted in amusement.

"Everyone will know you are mine! Including a little skinny nobleman who thinks he can fight me." It still rankled when Chance thought of the young Ahousat nobleman who had been so insulting when Chance was tied up.

"*Nuwiksu* won't let us hold the wedding at Kyuquot, Chance. I'm sure he and my mother will want it held here."

Chance sighed. Another concession he'd have to make, he supposed. "As long as he lets us marry, I don't care if he demands that the wedding take place in the middle of the sea lion breeding grounds," he answered with some asperity.

Haina giggled. "The sea lion breeding grounds, you say," she mused. "An appropriate place to celebrate, my lusty bull sea lion!" She thought a moment then frowned. "But do not think to take as many wives as a bull sea lion. I will not let you."

Her fine chin was pointed high in the air and he bit back a smile.

"Only one mate for you, my love. Me!" she exclaimed.

He laughed. "You are all I want, Haina. All I need," he added softly so the slaves would not hear.

She smiled then. "Oh, Chance, I love you too." The sunlight caught on his dark golden hair and the highlights glittered. He looked so handsome, she could not ask for a better man. His green eyes held hers and she lost herself in them. A discreet cough came from the stern—it was Squashedface. "As for my father," she added in a louder voice, "he is not that unreasonable. He only wants what is best for us."

That remains to be seen, thought Chance, but did not say so. Better not to upset Haina if he could help it. She was, after all, carrying his child. Everyone knew that a pregnant woman should think sweet, soothing thoughts. Not ugly, violent thoughts, like the kind buzzing through Chance's head. Should Fighting Wolf decide against the marriage, he'd arrange a torture session for Chance that would make the previous time look like a potlatch compared to a bone thrown to dogs.

He stopped paddling. Mayhaps he should have let Mudshark, Whale Hunter and the others come along as they had clamored to do. He was getting soft in the head. And now he was alone, about to face the enemy.

Chance shook his head, wondering at his stupidity in coming alone. He was completely at the Ahousat's mercy. And everyone knew the Ahousats had none.

He went back to his paddling. He and Haina continued to paddle in silence. The village was coming closer and closer.

The afternoon sun shone on the soft chop of the sea and Haina felt that she was being welcomed home. "Look, Chance!" she exclaimed. "There's *Umiksu* and *Nuwiksu*!" She leaped to her feet, waving at the tiny figures on the beach, and the canoe tipped dangerously.

"Sit down, Haina!" cautioned Chance. "And we're too far away to tell if it is your parents or not," he added gruffly. He was tense and he knew it.

"Her father will not be pleased to see you," added a voice from the stern. "He thinks she went to visit her aunt."

Haina turned to Squashedface. "Oh hush. I'll convince them I had no choice. I *had* to find Chance."

The slave said nothing, only rolled his eyes in silence and Chance felt a strange kinship with him. Chance wondered if he himself was as trapped in all this as the slaves. For they were surely trapped. If Haina did not convince her father about the slaves' innocence in her decision to paddle to Yuquot, Fighting Wolf would have the two killed.

No more was said until the canoe and its occupants were floating in knee deep water in front of the village. Chance knew better than to grind the fine, sleek canoe onto the beach gravel. Prized canoes like *Slider* were treated carefully.

He, Haina and the two slaves got out and Haina waded to shore. Chance and the salves lifted the canoe out of the water and carefully carried it up the beach. They placed it gently on the soft sand above the high tide line. Chance turned back to watch Haina.

She was bent over, hugging an excited white dog who wiggled and beat the beach with his thumping tail. Her greeting to the dog over, Haina threw her arms around her mother, then went to her father and hugged him. She pretended not to notice the frown that creased Fighting Wolf's brow. Instead, she chatted excitedly about how pleased she was to see them both.

While she chattered, Chance guardedly watched the white dog as it approached him with a stiff-legged walk. The dog circled him warily, sniffing intently. Chance turned with the dog as it circled him. When the dog growled low in its throat, Chance slowly reached out a hand. The dog froze, sniffed his hand cautiously, then slowly wagged his tail.

"Stinky, come here!" ordered Fighting Wolf.

The dog dashed back to where Haina and her parents were gathered.

When neither of her parents answered her, but continued to stare at her grimly, Haina began to realize that something was wrong.

"How was Auntie Purple Winkle?" asked Sarita. Her golden eyes had narrowed as she asked the question and Haina knew it was a trap.

Haina shrugged her shoulders in an attempt to look unconcerned. "Oh, I didn't go to visit Auntie," she answered. She absently patted Stinky's head.

She thought she saw the shadow of a smile on her father's face, but when she looked again it was gone.

"You didn't go to visit Auntie," repeated Sarita. "Perhaps you had better explain."

Haina studied the pebbles beneath her feet with intense concentration. A small red crab scuttled sideways across the rocks.

Haina hesitated. She had not thought she would have to tell her parents of her trip to Yuquot so soon. She looked up to see her father's eyes slant towards Chance and back again. Haina noticed her father's clenched jaw and his crossed arms and her heart sank. It had been she who had talked Chance into coming to the village unarmed and with none of his warriors. What if she had been wrong? What if he was hurt, or worse, died because of her advice? All of a sudden Haina realized this was deadly serious. It was not a playful game where a few airy words would clear things up between her, her parents and Chance. Her brave spirit faltered and she wondered at her earlier blindness.

"Haina?"

Haina took a deep breath and riveted her gaze on her mother's dear face. "I did not go to visit Auntie," she began, "because I wanted to go to Kyuquot."

"Kyuquot!" exploded her father. "Is that were you've been all this time? Your mother and I were very worried when—"

Sarita's upraised hand warned him not to continue. Uncharacteristically, he subsided, waiting impatiently for this youngest daughter of his, this most exasperating daughter of his, to further explain herself. "Continue," he said and Haina heard the restraint in his voice.

"I-I did not make it as far as Kyuquot." Haina was finding the explaining to be more difficult than she'd thought it would be. "A storm came up and blew us into Yuquot."

"Yuquot! That terrible place! Disease. White men. All manner of wretches looking to buy and sell anything or anyone!" Her father caught himself again. "What did you do in Yuquot? How did you even get that far? Those slaves I insisted you take with you should have brought you back home at once! I shall have them killed."

Haina winced. She was scared now. First her father demanded the death of the slaves. Next, it would be Chance.

"Please, *Nuwiksu,* do not do that. It is my fault. I ordered them to paddle me to Kyuquot on threat of death."

Her father snorted. "Threat of death! You expect me to believe that? Two big slaves against one tiny girl? Why, they could have killed you and thrown you overboard and we'd have believed you drowned. Threat of death!"

"It is true, *Nuwiksu.* I intended to go to Kyuquot to find Chance."

"Ah yes, the Kyuquot warrior. I was wondering when you would tell us about him." Haina should have been on guard when she heard the deliberate note in her father's voice.

Seeing them turn his way, Chance walked up to where Fighting Wolf, Sarita and Haina stood. Chance wanted to defend Haina against her father, and he knew he walked into a dangerous situation when the man was so furious.

Haina held out her hand to him. He reached to take it.

"Seize him!" cried Fighting Wolf. "Take him to my quarters and tie him up."

"No!" screamed Haina. "No!" Stinky started barking.

Four men, two commoners and two slaves, wrestled a struggling Chance away. Stinky ran after them, still barking.

"*Nuwiksu,* no!" Haina's hands flew to her flushed cheeks in terror. Stinky raced back to her. "You can't do this! He trusted me." She was sobbing. "I said he'd be safe here. That you wouldn't hurt him." Haina lifted her tear stained face proudly. "I will do everything I can to free him! You can't hold him!"

Her mother shifted uneasily beside the angry Fighting Wolf. She laid a hand on his arm. "Fighting Wolf, we must find out why she went to find him. I have a terrible feeling about this."

Fighting Wolf nodded grimly. "Very well. Tell me, daughter, why did you search this young man out? You knew I would have killed him when he was here. If he had not escaped earlier," here Fighting Wolf slid an unreadable glance at Sarita, "he would have been tortured to death."

Haina's and Sarita's gasps disconcerted Fighting Wolf, somewhat. "It is true, Daughter," he continued. "You knew that, yet you went and searched him out. You brought him back here. For what? So I may finish the work?"

Haina stood proudly. "I brought him here," she said, "so that you would give your approval to our marriage."

"Approval!" exploded Fighting Wolf. "To your marriage! I cannot believe what I am hearing!"

"What is this, Haina?" asked Sarita. "Surely you do not mean to marry this man! You know how we feel about him, about what he did—"

Haina's mother broke off when she saw Spit and Squashedface staring openmouthed at the three of them. She noticed then the small crowd that had gathered to eavesdrop on their conversation. "Come, let us discuss this elsewhere," interrupted Sarita.

Haina and Fighting Wolf looked at the surrounding people. Reluctantly they followed Sarita to a log a little way off. Stinky padded after them.

Seagulls screamed overhead, warm sunlight beat down on them, and little children laughed as they splashed in the warm shallow water. Haina had been too caught up in the talk with her parents to notice anything else.

"What is this about marriage?" demanded her father when he had placed one foot on the log. "I refuse permission. Surely you must know that."

"Hear her out, my husband," cautioned Sarita.

"Do not make a decision yet."

Haina smiled gratefully at her mother. She was rewarded with a frown. She frowned in return. For courage, Haina firmly grasped the short curly hair on Stinky's head. "Yes, well, you see," Haina's tongue tripped over the words. "I—I," she swallowed. "I carry his child."

"I knew it!" roared her father. "I knew it would be something like this!" He grabbed a large stick off the beach and beat the log with it in frustration. "Damnation!" he howled at the sky. "Why did this have to happen?"

Sarita sat down on the log, far enough away from Fighting Wolf that she would not be accidentally hit by the flailing stick. She looked pale and shocked. Stinky ran over to her.

Haina watched her two parents and felt pity for them. And for herself. What a mess.

She did not know what to say. 'I did not plan it'? 'I did not wish it to happen'. Ah, but she did. She was glad she was pregnant with the child of the man she loved. For a moment her heart went out to her parents that they could not see the good in this.

"I will kill him for raping you!" cried Fighting Wolf.

Haina started. She had not anticipated that her father would think that! "But—but *Nuwiksu*. He—he did not—"

"What?" roared Fighting Wolf again.

Haina noticed his voice sounded slightly hoarse. All the shouting, she supposed.

"You let him—! You let him do that to you? Haina! How could you?" Haina wondered what was passing through her father's mind. He seemed so, so furious. More furious than she'd ever seen him. "How could you?"

Haina's mother stood up, face bloodless, watching

her husband. "Fighting Wolf," she said. "Please come with me. We must talk."

Without waiting for an answer, Sarita began walking further down the beach, away from the two and further away from the longhouse.

Fighting Wolf gave one more furious glance at Haina and muttered, "You will not marry that Kyuquot. I will not have him in the family!"

Then Fighting Wolf strode after his wife. "Well?" Haina could hear him demand. Then she heard only the low murmur of her mother's answer and she wondered if anything would ever be right again.

She reached blindly for Stinky. "Chance! I must go to him!" she said aloud. "I must assure him that all is well, when it isn't! Oh, Stinky, what am I going to do?" She hurried off, the faithful animal at her heels.

"Well?" Fighting Wolf demanded again. "What is it you have to tell me? You might as well know you're wasting your time, Sarita. Nothing will convince me that our daughter, raised as an Ahousat noble, should marry that—that foul Kyuquot!"

Sarita continued walking along the beach. She stopped to pick a clam shell up off the beach. "You are right, my husband," she answered at last. "We are too angry now to discuss this matter. Later, when we have cooled, we can talk about our daughter."

Fighting Wolf raised an eyebrow. "You work me as one of our master wood carvers works soft cedar wood, Sarita."

A slight smile crossed her lips, then vanished. She said nothing.

"I know," he stated, "that it is not you that is raging in anger. Therefore, it must be me. Let us walk a little way and then we shall discuss this matter."

Fighting Wolf stomped along the beach and Sarita wandered along behind him. When she noticed that he no longer seemed to be pounding his feet so hard in the gravel and sand mixture of the beach, she caught up with him. Seeing that he was no longer as angry, she ventured, "We must be careful, Fighting Wolf, about one thing."

He grunted but kept walking. "And what might that be?"

"We must be careful not to allow our own mistakes from the past to intrude on our decisions today."

He lifted his brow again. "You speak in riddles, Sarita. I am a simple man. You must speak simply with me."

Sarita smiled to herself. "You are anything but simple, Fighting Wolf."

Even he had to smile at that. "You are right, wife. I am not simple." As they walked on, he added, "Please explain what you meant about our mistakes from the past. And, how do they effect our decision about our daughter? I do not understand your meaning."

Sarita hesitated. At last she replied, "I know for myself that I still have many sad, angry, fretful feelings about our own marriage and courtship."

"Courtship? There was no courtship," he stated. "I saw you and I took you. It was as simple as that. See? I am a simple man."

"Fighting Wolf, that you joke about this tells me that you too are battling your own discomfort about the topic of marriage." When he said nothing she continued. "When you held me as a slave. . . ."

"Do not say it, Sarita," he begged. "Do not say you were my slave."

"It is true, Fighting Wolf," she returned gently. "I was your slave. You captured me and carried me to your village. I had no other status."

"I know, Sarita, I know. To this day, the thought plagues me."

"Aah, so you too are bothered by old memories."

They walked on in silence. "We made love many times while you kept me in your longhouse."

"When I escaped back to my village, it was my pregnancy that brought you to me."

"I came for you, Sarita, not the baby."

She touched his arm and stopped walking. She looked into his eyes and he saw all her love for him shining in those beautiful golden eyes and he was warmed. "I know you came for me, Fighting Wolf. But the babe hastened your visit."

"Perhaps," he acknowledged, caught up in his love for her. He leaned over and kissed her gently. "It is a good thing for you that I came to get you. You would have had a hard time raising our child alone in your home village." He thought for a moment. "Your own father was against the babe. He wanted it dead. You and your child would have had a very hard time of it."

Sarita decided not to remind him that her father had already chosen a husband for her: the Kyuquot chief, Throws Away Wealth, older brother of Chance the man Fighting Wolf now held tied up in the longhouse. Aloud she said, "It was a very good thing that you came for me. And for the babe. Look at the good life we have had together. Seven fine children. Many potlatches. Our name is respected on the coast. We have had a good life together, my husband."

"*Naas,* God, has been good to us," agreed Fighting Wolf. "But how does all this fit with Haina and that dreadful young man? Where are you leading me, wife?"

"I think, Fighting Wolf," she said thoughtfully, "that we are still angry about what went on at the start of our own marriage. I think that perhaps my own fears of being left abandoned and pregnant enter into my decisions about Haina. I do not want to see her abandoned when she is pregnant. For that reason, I feel it is hard for me to decide if this Kyuquot is really a good man for her or if I see him as rescuing her and their babe. I do not wish to hand our beloved daughter over to a bad man."

Fighting Wolf was silent. After awhile he said, "I, too, feel sad about our own start in marriage. I feel that I forced you to marry me. You were pregnant and helpless." He sighed. "It has not been on my mind these many years, for I have been very busy. But now, when Haina is pregnant and alone, I think of how I did to you the very thing I accuse the young Kyuquot of."

He gazed into Sarita's eyes. "Some of my anger at him is really anger at myself. I treated you badly, my beloved, and I deeply regret that."

Tears came to Sarita's eyes. "Oh, Fighting Wolf, I love you. I have never worried about your treatment of me. I loved you even when you first kept me as your slave, well, mayhaps not at the very first," she amended. "But I grew to love you. As for my first pregnancy," she wiped her tears away, "I have always been grateful for our first child, our daughter, Fires-on-the-Beach Woman. Never, never have I regretted her or my marriage to you." Sarita threw herself into her husband's arms. "We've had many long, happy years together, Fighting Wolf. Out of the anger and hate and revenge of our forefathers we brought love and life. Let us be thankful for that!"

Fighting Wolf held her close. "Where, oh where," he asked, "did I ever find such a beautiful woman as you?"

"I am not beautiful. Have you looked at me lately? I am old, I have lines on my face. I have gray hair. I walk slowly."

He gazed into her golden eyes. "I see your real beauty, your kindness, your wisdom," he answered. "You are more beautiful with the passing years. The fiery woman I stole has become the wise, compassionate, loving woman who has given me children, raised them in love and stood unswerving by my side these long years. That is true beauty. That means far more to me than any unlined face, no matter how beautiful."

He kissed her gently. "Aah Sarita, it is good we had this talk. It helps me to know how much you mean to me." He pulled back to gaze at her. "Our love has been good over the years, but now I think it is even stronger. I am glad *Naas* sent you to me."

Sarita hugged him and they stood together a long time. After a while they turned to walk back to the longhouse. As they walked the beach, Sarita stopped every now and then to pick up shells. They were both very quiet, each content in the presence of the other.

At last, as they approached the longhouse where Chance was tied, Sarita asked, "Fighting Wolf, are you still against the marriage of the Kyuquot to Haina?"

Fighting Wolf was silent. Finally he said, "I think we must be very careful to see what our daughter wants. And what the young man wants. He may be a very good husband for her. Or he may be challenged by her family's opposition to him. Such a man would throw away a woman once he has won her. We must watch and wait and see whether he is sincere about our daughter."

Sarita nodded. "I think Haina loves him. She has always been an honest girl and, I think, knows her feelings. That she risked her life to go to Kyuquot to find him speaks strongly of her love for him."

"Yes, she is ready to defy us, her parents, who she has always loved, for him. Her love for him must be very strong. Let us hope he can return it in full measure."

Chapter 29

"Untie him!" Haina cried out when Fighting Wolf walked into the longhouse. Sarita peeked over his shoulder and had to stifle a gasp at what she saw.

Chance lay on his side on the floor, his arms twisted back and tied behind him. His blond head lay on the dirt floor and a scrape on one cheek had bled and turned a wretched brown against his tanned skin.

Haina sat over in one corner, crying. Stinky sat beside her, whimpering. It was obvious that she had tried to get to Chance, but the four men that Fighting Wolf had ordered to take Chance away must have seen their duty as guarding him from others, including Haina.

Sarita went to her daughter and knelt beside her. It was not often she saw this brave one brought to tears and her heart went out to her daughter. She put her arms around Haina and hugged her. Haina turned to her mother and sobbed into her shoulder.

Then she lifted her head. "He's hurt!" she cried. "He's dirty. He's bleeding. *Nuwiksu*, please untie him!"

"Untie him," Fighting Wolf repeated her words gruffly.

Haina dried her eyes and straightened when she heard her father give the order. The four guards moved to do his bidding and Chance was untied.

He sat up, groggy. Haina wanted to run to him. He looked awful. He groaned. Stinky hovered nearby, whining.

"What are your intentions?" asked Fighting Wolf sternly. He was looking at Chance.

Chance, who had never expected to be freed after being tied up, could hardly focus his thoughts to answer. He was now sitting at the hearthside of the one man and woman who had most reason to kill him. And his enemy was talking with him. Talking! By now, Chance had expected he'd have been screaming for mercy from the Ahousats' various crafty torture methods. What had happened? Or was this an Ahousat trick to put him off his guard? They were sneaky, these Ahousats. He must be careful.

Chance cleared his throat. "I have come here, sir," he began carefully, "after rescuing your daughter from the *mumutly*, white men at Yuquot."

Fighting Wolf nodded but said nothing. He waited. Chance took courage and continued, "I also have come to ask for your permission to marry your daughter." He sat back and waited for the explosion.

It did not come.

"Why?"

Fighting Wolf's terse question threw Chance. "Why? Because I love her; I want her for my wife. Because she carries my child."

Fighting Wolf answered, "Yes, she told us she carries your child. How did she get this way? Did you force her?"

Haina felt the blood rush to her cheeks and she

fastened her eyes unwaveringly at Chance. How, indeed?

"I—uh, I—" Chance swallowed.

"He did not force me, *Nuwiksu*."

"You keep quiet." He swung back to Chance. "Well?" he demanded.

"I did not force her, sir." Chance replied. "It is true that I could have. I had her at my mercy. But I did not force her."

Fighting Wolf glared at the younger man. "Well, we'll never know, will we?" he snorted in disgust. "And so you want to marry her, you say."

"Yes, sir."

"How many other wives do you have?"

"None, sir."

"Children?"

"None."

Fighting Wolf's gaze swung to Haina. "And what are your thoughts on all this, Daughter?"

"I love him. I want to marry him. I travelled to Kyuquot to find him and marry him." Haina met her father's eyes and he was the first to look away.

Fighting Wolf sat thoughtfully for a long while. His daughter was very determined. If he and Sarita were to deny their permission, Haina would marry the man anyway. He knew that much about her. As if reading his thoughts, Haina announced, "I *will* marry him, *Nuwiksu*. With or without your approval."

Fighting Wolf raised an eyebrow and glanced at Sarita. So, it had come to this. Sarita tilted her head slowly at him. She would not go against his decision.

"And you, young man, are you content to let a woman speak for you?"

Haina gasped and Chance sat up straighter. "It is not my habit to let a woman speak for me. I wish to marry your daughter. I have come here for this purpose. To show my good intentions, I have brought no warriors and I come unarmed."

Too late Chance saw Fighting Wolf glance at his pistols, tucked carefully at his waist. "They are valuable pistols, sir," he said. "I did not wish to leave them behind when I left Yuquot. I will not use them against you." He flushed. "There is no powder or shot."

Fighting Wolf grunted and eyed the young man. Brave words, backed up by equally brave actions. The young man had come to Ahousat with no warriors. He seemed sincere. "What names and entitlements do you have to offer your children? You look white. How can a white man give his children proper names?"

Chance cleared his throat. All his life it seemed, outsiders had thrown his white blood at him. "I am Nootka Indian, sir," he said proudly. "I do not know the ways of white men. I have had little contact with them. As a babe, I was born on a beach. My white mother crawled out of the sea after a storm. She gave birth to me and then died. She left me my life and a small bracelet, which I cherish deeply. My Indian mother, Ocean Wave, and my father, a Kyuquot chief, raised me. I have songs and dances from my mother's side. I have territories from my father's. My brother, the great Kyuquot chief, Throws Away Wealth, is also a man of great importance. One you would not wish to offend, I am sure."

Fighting Wolf glared at Chance. "Threats, young man? We have already offended Throws Away Wealth. Long ago. But you need not worry. Throws Away Wealth knows that the Ahousat people are his friends."

Chance smiled. "There should be no problem uniting our tribes," he said smoothly.

Fighting Wolf sat staring into the fire. At last he spoke, "An alliance with the Kyuquots would be a good thing," he said at last. "But I am still angry with you for stealing my daughter. That was very wrong."

"I did it for my brother," said Chance at last. "I thought to revenge him for the loss of Sarita as his wife."

Sarita looked surprised. "His wife? I never intended to be his wife. I told him that, to his face."

"That may be, but he always bemoaned your loss. Many nights he would sit in the longhouse and mourn for you."

"For me? I cannot believe such a thing. Why would he mourn for me? I was as nothing to him!"

"Not so. He mourns your loss to this day."

"Surely you speak of some other woman. I never gave Throws Away Wealth cause for such sadness. He only wanted to marry me to have an alliance with my father. He did not want me, except perhaps to beat me."

Chance was getting angry now. "I tell you he never got over the blow you dealt him when you refused to be his wife! It was for this terrible blow to him that I robbed you of one of your children. I sought to avenge my brother's hurt."

Fighting Wolf spoke up. "We tell you true, young man. An alliance was contracted with the Kyuquots but I broke it. I married Sarita when I learned she was pregnant with my child. Had he married Sarita, your brother would have killed the child."

"My brother does not war with babes!"

"He does! He told me himself that he would not allow the child to live." Sarita's flashing eyes dared Chance to say her nay. "I would never marry a man who would kill my child!"

Chance sat, stunned. Throws Away Wealth did nasty little tricks to people, yes, but surely, surely, he had never threatened to kill a baby. Yet these people were saying he had. How to learn the truth?

There was silence for a while as all pondered. Finally Fighting Wolf said, "Mayhaps you should ask Throws Away Wealth about this."

Chance shook his head. "It will do no good. It is as I have told you. He bemoans the loss of Sarita. In recent years he has gone so far as to say that she loved him, and wanted him."

No one knew what to say. At last Sarita sighed and said gently, "It is sad that he thinks this. I tell you true, I never loved your brother. I never would have married him."

"You say that now. How do I know what you promised him so long ago?" Chance demanded.

Sarita looked at him thoughtfully. At last she said, "Look to Haina, Chance. She is pregnant with your child. Can you see her marrying somebody else after she has said she loves you and wants to marry you?" She hesitated, then added, "It was the same for me. I did not care for any other man but Fighting Wolf."

Chance sat staring into the flames, saying nothing. There was nothing he could say. Haina would not marry another man after declaring she loved him. He knew that, felt it.

His mind was in a turmoil. Had his brother lied all these many years? The thought was too awful to believe. And if Throws Away Wealth had lied, then what did that make of Chance's own foray to revenge him?

He did not notice when the others got up from the hearthside and left him some privacy. He did not notice that he sat staring into the flames for a long time. He only knew that he had sought revenge for a man, and a cause, that was beginning to appear false. He groaned wretchedly from deep in his body.

At last Chance stood up and wandered through the longhouse and out the door. A light rain was touching everything and night was coming on. He wandered down by the sea and his thoughts were troubled. So much had happened. He'd thought he was right to avenge his brother. He'd based all his actions on the thought and training that it was honorable to avenge those you loved, those who'd been hurt. But now? What about now, when he knew that his actions were based on a lie? Not his lie, his brother's lie, but a lie nonetheless. What was the honorable thing to do then?

Chance's torment continued long into the night. No one approached him as he paced the beach or sat on a log and gazed into the night. No one bothered him. He did not know that Fighting Wolf had warned others to keep clear of him, to give him time to think through his turmoil.

When morning came, Chance had decided. He had had a hard time, had faced things about himself he did not want to face, but he knew he must do something to right the terrible wrong he had committed in abducting Haina.

And his brother, what of him? If he lied to others, he also lied to himself. Was Chance also infected by the same weakness? Chance feared he was.

A great weight lay on his heart and he wished he'd never come to Ahousat. Never found out the truth.

Then he looked up from where he was sitting and saw Haina. She was leaning against the doorpost of the longhouse, watching him. The morning sun touched her hair and glinted in her dark eyes. She smiled and held out her arms to him. He got up and walked towards her.

Out of the worst mistake he'd ever made in his life had come the best gifts in his life: Haina and her love. Before, he had been without her and had not known what he was missing. Now, if he were to live through his life without her, he knew the loss would be insurmountable.

He reached her and took her in his arms. They stood together like that, arms around each other, as the new morning sun filtered down through the clouds and touched them.

At long last Chance murmured into her ear, "Come. I would speak with your parents."

Chapter 30

When Chance and Haina got to the longhouse it was to find that Fighting Wolf had already gone to the river to do his daily bathing ritual and pray. Sarita, however, was at the fireside directing breakfast preparations. Stinky dozed near the fire.

Haina sat down on a cedar mat. Chance groaned as he, too, sat down.

"Oh, Chance," Haina murmured. "Are you hurting?"

Before he could answer, Sarita crisply ordered a slave, "Fetch water and a cloth." The slave hurried away and returned promptly with a bowl of cold water and a soft cedar cloth. Haina dipped the cloth into the water and wiped at Chance's forehead. When she came to his scraped cheek, she examined it carefully.

Sarita saw her concern and got to her feet. She returned with a small dried plant. "Let us steep this in warm water," she said. "Then you must bathe his cheek with it. The skin will heal well and he will have no scars."

"Thank you," murmured Haina gratefully.

When Haina had finished tending to Chance, Sarita offered them some tea. Both accepted politely. They had not been seated long before Fighting Wolf entered the longhouse to partake of his meal. He nodded a greeting to Chance and Haina but no word was spoken until after the delicious breakfast of smoked salmon, roots and tea.

Finally the breakfast platters were cleared away and Fighting Wolf turned to Chance. "So? What is your decision?"

Chance cleared his throat. He almost did not know where to start now that the time had come. How could he tell this man that he, Chance, had grievously wronged him and wished it had not happened. And that he still wanted to marry Haina?

But Sarita and Fighting Wolf were gazing at him, expecting an answer.

Chance began, "I was wrong to steal your daughter. I regret it."

There was a long pause as if Fighting Wolf and Sarita were waiting for him to say more. Chance fidgeted. "Very deeply."

Still they waited. Chance fidgeted some more but said nothing. Then Fighting Wolf nodded slightly in acceptance.

Heartened, Chance said, "We Kyuquots value honor. We believe it is honorable and just to avenge a raid, a war, the taking of a slave. We are taught this from the time we are small children. You Ahousats, too, are taught these things. I believed myself to be doing an honorable thing when I stole your daughter. I was avenging my brother's suffering." He sighed heavily.

"I see now," continued Chance, "that I was wrong." He swallowed. "My brother suffered, it is true. But he suffered because he did not choose to look at what really happened, at the truth: the truth that he did not love Sarita nor she him. He believed a lie, and was content to believe that lie." He shrugged. "For what reason I do not know."

"When I stole your daughter I was acting on a lie. I, too, looked no further. I believed that my brother had been wronged and so I sought to avenge that wrong. I based my action on a lie. Therefore, I believe my action was wrong. And what is worse, hurtful. I have hurt you and yours with my actions. You Ahousats share our Kyuquot idea of honor. Therefore, you have every right to avenge yourself on me."

Fighting Wolf nodded.

"However," returned Chance, "I ask that you do not."

Fighting Wolf raised an eyebrow in question.

Chance coughed. "If you avenge yourself on me, and I am killed, my Kyuquot people will be forced to take hurtful action against you. Many of your people will be killed. You will then act against us in turn, killing Kyuquots. We are caught in a circle, a never-ending circle from which we cannot escape."

"Very true," nodded Fighting Wolf. "Perhaps we can just avenge ourselves a little. You know, hurt you, leave you crippled, but not dead." He did not take his eyes off Chance. "Or, if that's not to your liking, we could let you go free, walk away a free man, and instead we'll attack the village of Kyuquot and slay a few people." He nodded as if to himself. "Yes, I like that. After all, what are the Kyuquot people to you? You are white."

"*Nuwiksu*!" shrieked Haina. "You cannot—!"

"What do you say, Kyuquot?" Fighting Wolf grinned ferally. "You say you were wrong. Are you willing to submit yourself to our torture, our honor, our fairness? To those things we do to our enemies who hurt us and steal our daughters?" He grinned again, showing his teeth. "Or shall we go and slaughter a few useless Kyuquots?"

There was a long pause. Chance groaned inside. So, it had come to this. So close he'd come to having Haina, his beloved, the wife of his heart. He blinked back tears for his naive dreams. All was lost. He shuddered under the onslaught of those lost dreams. And now, this.

His heart heavy, he talked with himself. His honor, the very thing that made him a man, his sense of right and wrong, was being questioned. He'd always prided himself that he knew Kyuquot ways, right from wrong. He'd never questioned his own judgement in avenging his brother when he'd first set out on that ill-fated mission to capture Haina.

And now, this same honor was demanding that he follow through when he was the one in the wrong. Now he must follow his man's honor to its fatal end. He would have meted out death to a man in his place.

And what of loyalty to his people, to his brother? nagged a quiet voice. That was another Kyuquot value. How loyal a brother was he now? Here he was admitting that his brother, Throws Away Wealth, the one man who had stood by him when he was but a boy, had lied. Worse, Chance had gone on to embrace the cause of his brother's enemy. Had believed the enemy over his own brother. How noble was that?

And, continued his inner voice, how loyal was it to bring the vengeance of the Ahousats down on the heads of the unsuspecting Kyuquots? Which is what would happen if he refused Fighting Wolf's savage offer of crippling. Somehow he knew that Fighting Wolf would not be satisfied with the death of "a few" Kyuquots. No, Chance could not lie to himself. The whole village would be in danger of a sneak attack. One that could kill most of the Kyuquots—men, women and children.

Chance could see no way out. Honor demanded he

meet Fighting Wolf's vengeance. Loyalty to his brother demanded that he fight with everything at his command. Loyalty to his people demanded he sacrifice himself. But loyalty was weakening. His brother had lied. Where did that leave him, Chance? Still protecting his people, the Kyuquots, the very people who had taken him in when he was but a nameless babe. They'd fed him, loved him, accepted him as one of their own. And now their well-being lay in his hands. He could sacrifice them all and retain a whole skin or he could give in to Fighting Wolf's vicious demand for honorable vengeance. And to do so, of course, meant a crippled, broken body for the rest of his days. He had no illusions about that.

With a sorrowful sigh he met Fighting Wolf's watchful gaze. Slowly he nodded.

"It shall be as you say," Chance answered at last. "I will stay." His heart was heavy. He would be a broken man with nothing to offer Haina when the Ahousats were finished with him, he knew. He had lost her.

"*Nuwiksu!*" shrieked Haina.

Fighting Wolf looked at the tearful eyes of his beautiful daughter. His gaze swung to his wife. Her golden eyes were sorrowful and sad as they met his. Surely she could not be sad for him, Fighting Wolf? The thought shocked him and he turned back to the quiet Kyuquot.

"Take him away," Fighting Wolf ordered gruffly. "Tie him to a stake on the beach." Two brawny slaves jumped at his command and dragged Chance away.

Chapter 31

"*Nuwiksu*!" cried Haina. "What are you doing? Do not do this, I beg of you!" Haina held her arms out to her father, beseeching him. "Do not cripple him, I beg of you. Do not do this terrible thing!"

"Quiet, Haina!" Her father rose to his feet unable to bear the sight of his pleading daughter. He turned away too, from the look in Sarita's eyes. "I do what I must do," he said and stalked out of the longhouse.

His wife got to her feet and ran after him. "Fighting Wolf," she pleaded, grabbing his arm and turning him around right there on the beach in front of all his people. Word travelled fast in the Ahousat village and many had turned out to watch the torture of the strange Kyuquot. "After all we talked about, how can you go and do this thing? To torture and destroy that young man will be a thing most foul. I will have no part of it!"

"Silence, woman," cautioned Fighting Wolf. "You know not of what you speak."

Sarita dug her heels into the sand, preventing him

from taking a step farther. "I know you intend to torture that young man and I cannot, will not, stand by and let it happen!

"Fighting Wolf," she implored. "I am her mother. I was hurt too, when she was stolen! But she is back now. Safe. To hurt this young man whom she loves, the father of her babe—"

Fighting Wolf tried to jerk his arm out of her grasp. She would not let go. "Silence, woman," he said again. "Do not defy me. I will have slaves haul you away, too!"

Sarita let go of his arm then. One hand flew to her mouth to keep from crying out. "I do not know you," she whispered, watching Fighting Wolf walk away, towards the bound man on the beach. "All these years with you and I do not know you." She turned and fled to the longhouse.

As he stalked along, Fighting Wolf wondered at this course he had chosen. It hurt him to see Haina so distraught and he could not bear to examine how he felt when he'd turned away from his beloved wife's pleading face. He must be steady, he cautioned himself as he approached the small gathering encircling the Kyuquot. He must be steady, for Haina's life rested in the balance. He could not, would not, give her to a man who was weak in body or soul.

He approached the crowd. "Stand him up," he ordered the two brawny slaves who'd bundled Chance out of the longhouse. They obeyed and Chance was hauled to his feet, his arms bound behind him. A large stake was driven into the ground behind him and the two slaves busied themselves binding Chance to it.

"Prepare the stick," Fighting Wolf said succinctly and a murmur of anticipation rippled through the crowd. They *would* like that, thought Fighting Wolf sardonically. One of the most gruesome of Nootkan tortures, a sharpened stick was poked—

"*Nuwiksu!*" It was Haina, running at full speed towards him. Hard at her heels ran Stinky.

Fighting Wolf sighed heavily and turned to meet her. "Go back to the longhouse, Haina," he directed. "You can do no good here."

"I can't let you do this!" she cried.

Then he saw the knife. He frowned. "What will you do with that, Daughter? Stab your own father?"

"No!" she cried, horrified. "Has your cruelty led you to see it in others, *Nuwiksu*? No, I merely mean to cut his bonds." This she said coolly.

Fighting Wolf bit back a smile. So, his daughter had his fighting blood after all. "I admire your brave spirit, my daughter," he began, "but I cannot let you free the prisoner."

"And I," she said, standing face to face with him, "cannot let you kill him."

Standoff. Father and daughter stood staring at each other, the time marked off by Haina's heartbeats. At last Fighting Wolf broke the impasse. He motioned to the slaves, Spit and Squashedface, who were standing nearby. "Take her to the longhouse."

"No, *Nuwiksu*, no!" screamed Haina. Kicking and screaming she was dragged away. The dog followed after her, barking frantically. Fighting Wolf watched her go, feeling every one of his winters. Ah, but this was making an old man of him, he thought.

Chance watched Haina being dragged away and his heart went with her. Had two lovers ever had worse fate? he wondered. Surely *Naas* who watched over all was as outraged as he himself was!

Chance watched until Haina was taken into the longhouse. Bitterly he turned to the curious Ahousats, some of them gleefully sharpening sticks. His eye caught the large stick being sharpened in his honor and his gut twisted.

A warrior was carefully honing the sharp point on

a stout branch of cedar wood. He saw Chance watching him and smiled almost innocently, like a child not realizing the terrible hurt he was about to inflict.

Chance turned away. He swallowed and tried to fortify himself with the thought that he was living up to his own code of honor. He snorted to himself. Ah, yes, he'd have the rest of a crippled, pain-filled life to live with his honor. Alone. Such a noble sentiment and it had led him to this!

Then he tried to convince himself that he was protecting the Kyuquot people. *If*, said a small voice, Fighting Wolf keeps his word to you. Fighting Wolf could, however, maim you and then go on to the Kyuquot to slaughter your people.

Chance's stomach turned over at this new glimmer. Too late now, he thought. He was at the Ahousat war chief's mercy. And Fighting Wolf had about as much mercy as Chance had warriors paddling into the bay to rescue him. None!

Fighting Wolf was standing in front of him now. "Any last words, Kyuquot?" he sneered.

"Only one," answered Chance. "Tell Haina I love her."

"Is that all, Kyuquot? Love? Such a weak thing."

Chance stood as tall as his bindings would permit. He looked down into Fighting Wolf's dark eyes. "It is all I have," Chance answered simply.

The two stared at each other, their faces impassive.

The warrior with the innocent grin and the sharpened stick approached. "Now, master?" he asked.

The Ahousats around them were holding their breaths. Chance could feel the blood hunger in them and he shuddered inwardly. Perhaps he would mercifully pass out before they got to the worst part of the torture. He hoped he would not scream too much. He did not want to scare Haina who would surely hear his screams through the longhouse walls.

Fighting Wolf looked at his Ahousat people. Their black eyes sparkled avidly as they waited for his word to begin. The warrior with the stick was behind Chance, carefully estimating angles. Fighting Wolf nodded to him and the warrior started forward, grinning.

The pointed stick gently, almost caressingly, touched Chance's buttocks and he clenched his teeth.

Chance's whole body felt like one tight muscle. No! No! he screamed inside his head. Not a sound crossed his lips. The crowd's silence was a palpable thing.

"Stop!" Suddenly Fighting Wolf's voice rang out in the clear air and he held up his hand. "This man will not be tortured! Nor maimed! Instead he will be married to my youngest daughter! He will be my son-in-law!"

The crowd stood in stunned silence. Then loud mumblings and rumblings almost drowned out Fighting Wolf's next words. "He has been tested, and found to be brave. May our Ahousat warriors prove as brave and as honorable as this Kyuquot!"

Chance stood with his mouth open. He could not help it.

Fighting Wolf plucked his knife from his woven cedar belt and stepped forward to cut the leather bonds himself. Chance felt it when the bonds dropped away. He felt the people dispersing as Fighting Wolf waved them away. But still Chance did not move.

Reprieve! his brain sang. I've been reprieved! Then he grabbed Fighting Wolf about the neck, catching the older man off guard. Two slaves lunged for Chance but Fighting Wolf waved them away.

"You sea lion turd!" roared Chance. "You old, rotten sea lion turd! I could *kill* you for doing this to me!"

Fighting Wolf unwrapped his hands from around his throat. The old man still had strength in his gnarled hands but the younger man had anger fueling his strength. Fighting Wolf was not about to tangle with the enraged Kyuquot, if he could help it.

Chance dropped his shaking hands to his sides. His breath came in heavy pants of emotion. "What did you do that for, you—you—!" No one word could express the anger, the relief, the tumult of emotions that flooded Chance.

Fighting Wolf stepped back. Chance stepped forward, towards him. Fighting Wolf stepped back once more. He held up his hands. "Let me explain," he said.

"So talk, Ahousat!"

"I did it this way to test you."

Chance looked ready to launch himself at the older man.

"I did it for a reason," replied Fighting Wolf with as much dignity as he could muster. "I wanted to see if you were like your brother."

"Like my brother? What are you talking about, old man?"

"Your brother, Throws Away Wealth, is a man who, let us say, needs careful handling. I have never known him to risk his life for his people, or for anything, or anyone else."

Chance was dumbfounded. "You play with my life, old man. And now you insult my family!"

"You are angry," soothed Fighting Wolf.

"I am surely that!"

"You have every right to be angry," continued Fighting Wolf. "What I did was a very grave thing."

"I'm gratified that you realize the seriousness of toying with someone else's life!"

"Nevertheless, I was convinced it was the only way to determine that you did indeed love my daughter, that you did indeed consider yourself a Kyuquot!"

"And if I had not gone along with your game?"

Fighting Wolf shrugged. "You would not have left here alive."

Chance looked grimly at the shorter man in front of him. He turned away, disgusted. "And how can I test you, old man?" he muttered.

Chance walked and kept walking, expecting that at any moment Fighting Wolf would order him to halt. But silence reigned and Chance reached the longhouse where he'd last seen Haina dragged, kicking and screaming. He ducked into the darkened interior. Over near one wall of Haina's parents' quarters stood the two big slaves, Spit and Squashedface. They were avoiding each other's glance as they listened to the sobs coming from the plank bed along the wall.

Chance nodded briefly to the surprised slaves and followed the sobs. He saw Haina, raven hair spilling against the dark brown of the furs into which she'd pressed her face. Stinky moaned and whined as he nosed at her.

Chance knelt beside her and reached out to stroke her precious bent head. The white of her nape showed through the dark strands and he wanted to kiss her on that vulnerable part of her neck.

"Haina," he whispered. "Haina."

She went still. She looked up carefully, her great eyes dewfilled. "Chance? What—"

"He let me go," he said. No need to tell her of his anger at her father just now. Besides, he thought, being here with Haina, his underlying fear was wearing off and relief was taking hold.

"Oh, Chance!" cried Haina and threw her arms around him. "Oh, Chance," she murmured over and over. At last she pushed him away from her. She peered into his beloved face and saw the fatigue there. "It was so hard on you, wasn't it?" she asked softly.

Chance did not say anything, only held her gaze with his. "I love you, Haina," he answered.

And she knew, to the depths of her being, that he spoke the truth. "And I you," she responded.

They sat there on the plank bed, holding each other. The dog crept quietly away as if understanding their desire for privacy.

Sarita hovered near the fire, putting dried herbs in baskets and leaving the young lovers alone.

There was a furor at the door and Fighting Wolf entered followed by a retinue of free men and slaves. Immediately Chance got up off the bed and went to sit by the fire. Haina followed, brushing her dark hair back over her shoulders.

"I wish to talk with you," Chance stated politely to his prospective father-in-law.

"Yes," joined in his prospective mother-in-law. "*We* wish to talk with you." The glare she shot Fighting Wolf was fierce and Chance was surprised to see the doughty old warrior glance away from his wife's stare.

Haina sat down beside Chance. Why had her father let Chance go? she wondered. She was glad he was free, but knowing her father, she wondered at his motives.

"Was it your plan, Husband," demanded Sarita, hands on her hips, "to free this young man all along?"

Haina was surprised at the acid in her mother's voice and wondered at its cause. She sighed. There was so much that went on that she had no inkling of. Would it always be thus?

Fighting Wolf carefully took off his mantle of woven cedar bark. He placed it in the hands of a waiting slave and waved the man away. He waved away, too, the waiting slaves and free men who'd followed him into the longhouse.

At last, when there was just the six of them— Fighting Wolf had allowed Spit and Squashedface to stay—he sank down to a cedar mat near the crackling fire. "Water," he ordered.

Sarita gestured impatiently to a slave and the woman brought a cup of water, bowed and retired into the dark confines of the longhouse. "So, my husband?" she prodded.

Only then did Fighting Wolf look at her. "So much worrying and ordering people about will make you an old woman before your time," he cautioned.

"Humph," she snorted, knowing he would tell all in his own way. She left off prodding him and poked at the fire instead.

Haina noticed the way her mother stabbed at the wood in the fire and wondered at her usually good-natured mother's strange behavior.

"Woman," said Fighting Wolf, aware he could no longer put off the many questions that he must answer. "Come and sit beside me. These old bones need your kind touch."

Sarita only snorted again and stabbed all the more viciously at the wood in the firepit.

"Come," coaxed her husband.

At last she threw down the stick and marched over to him. She gave him one glance and sat down.

Fighting Wolf took her hand and Haina watched as Sarita tried to pull it away. What was it that had her parents playing as though they were many seasons younger? she wondered.

Chance spoke up. "Many thanks for sparing my life," he said and Haina thought the words sounded rough in his throat.

Indeed, Chance was not sure just how grateful he was to the old man, but thought it wiser to hide his anger.

Fighting Wolf accepted his thanks with a regal nod of his head. Then he said, "It was a nasty piece of work to do to someone, letting them think they would be tortured."

Chance and Haina nodded solemnly to this and Sarita looked at her husband. "It was even nastier," she hissed, "to turn aside your wife's good advice."

Fighting Wolf patted her hand lovingly. "Yes, it was a difficult thing for me to do. To make you believe I really intended to let Chance be tortured."

"Then *why* did you do it, *Nuwiksu*?" burst out Haina. "Why did you put us all through such a terrible ordeal?"

Fighting Wolf looked gravely into the fire before answering. "Your young man said he regretted stealing you. Very well, I wanted to see how deep his regret was. He said he wanted to marry you. Very well, I wanted to see how much he loved you. He said he was a Kyuquot. And Indian. Very well, I wanted to see how far he would go to help his people."

"A test?" Haina sat rocking back and forth holding her stomach. "This was a test? Like you would have a man run a race to see if he was the fastest, or swim the sea to find the strongest?" Incredulity was in her voice and Fighting Wolf flinched.

"Something like that, Daughter."

Chance shook his head. "Why could you not just accept my word? That if I said it was so, it was so."

Fighting Wolf speared Chance with a glance. "Because you come from Kyuquot and I do not trust Kyuquots." He spat into the fire. There, it was out. Let the young man make of it what he would.

Chance shook his head in disbelief. "Is there a reason why you don't trust Kyuquots?" he pressed. As he asked it he wondered if he really wanted to know the answer.

So, it comes, thought Fighting Wolf. He nodded. "When I captured you, your cousin, and my daughter, on the Kyuquot fishing grounds, it was not by accident."

Chance was watching the old man closely now.

Fighting Wolf continued, "I was told where I would find my daughter—and with whom."

"Told? Who—?" Chance had not expected this!

Fighting Wolf shrugged. "A slave came to me. He gave me a message about my daughter. He said he was from Kyuquot." Fighting Wolf let the words sink in. Then he added, "You were betrayed!"

Chapter 32

"Welcome, home brother," said Throws Away Wealth, smiling genially.

Chance hid his surprise that his brother had hastened to the beach to be the first one to greet him.

"So pleased you've returned safely from Yuquot," continued Throws Away Wealth. "I—was not expecting you back so soon."

"Oh? Yuquot?" questioned Chance. "Did you think I was in Yuquot all this time?"

"Why yes. I supposed so. No one really seemed to know where you'd gone. The last I'd heard you were there. Why? Where were you?"

Chance looked around. Someone in Kyuquot had betrayed him. He knew he could not talk openly. Anyone could overhear and perhaps do him harm. He swung around to his brother. "I'll tell you later. Let us go and eat first."

"When I questioned Mudshark about you, he did not seem to know where you'd gone," persisted Throws Away Wealth.

So Mudshark was being close-mouthed. By why? Then Chance remembered the splinters of wood above his bed that night in Yuquot. He'd asked Mudshark to examine the splinters; Chance was certain a bullet had narrowly missed his head and gone into the planks above his bed instead. Mayhaps Mudshark had found that Chance was correct—a bullet had just missed his head. A shiver went down Chance's spine. "What?" he said to the questioning look on his brother's face. "Could you repeat that?"

"I said neither Mudshark or that Chicklesit boy, Whale Counter or whatever his name is, seemed to know where you'd gone."

Chance heard the irritability in his brother's voice. He smiled to himself. His cousin was indeed cautious if he did not even tell Chance's own brother his whereabouts! He mused on the Chicklesit, Whale Hunter's, loyalty—if loyalty it was and not indifference. Whatever—he'd also been close-mouthed.

Still, there were others who knew Chance had gone to Ahousat. Beachdog for one. Why had he not told?

Throws Away Wealth was losing his power if none of the young men were confiding in him, thought Chance. He wondered what his brother thought of that. "Could you repeat that?"

Throws Away Wealth was looking most exasperated. "I asked if you were hungry."

Chance rolled his shoulders. "Yes," he answered. "Tired, too. It's been a long trip." He shrugged his muscular shoulders this time, loosening aching muscles.

"Oh, yes, yes," Throws Away Wealth coughed. "Come, let me order a meal from those lazy house slaves."

"Much new?" asked Chance as they walked up the beach.

"This and that," answered his brother, placing his hand on the big blond man's back and patting it in a comradely fashion. "You know the chieftain's position is a very important, busy one. The people keep coming to me with all their complaints. So many quarrels to settle, it seems." After a pace or two, he laughed and added, "Their petty quarrels make me rich."

Chance regarded his brother thoughtfully. "How is that?"

Throws Away Wealth's eyes twinkled. "Why, I settle the quarrel in favor of the one who pays me the most, of course."

Chance stared at his brother until Throws Away Wealth flinched. "How else should one settle quarrels?" he demanded.

Chance shook his head and did not reply. They walked in silence. "I have some good news, my brother," said Chance. "I think you will be pleased, most pleased to hear my news."

Throws Away Wealth stopped and looked behind them at the idlers on the beach. "No doubt I will, brother. No doubt I will," he said grimly. "Your news is always a pleasant surprise. As is your sudden appearance here today."

Throws Away Wealth's attention became focused on the water's edge. "You there, slaves!" Throws Away Wealth suddenly called out in a loud voice. "Take that canoe up to the high tideline. And don't scrape the bottom of it!" He watched the two designated slaves struggle with the canoe. Finally Spit and Squashedface joined the Kyuquot slaves and lifted the craft free of the beach gravel. "Carefully, I said!" yelled the tyee. "You clumsy turds, watch the finish on the bottom!"

"That's a well-made canoe," Throws Away Wealth grunted. He surveyed Spit and Squashedface then turned back to Chance. "Where'd you get those two? They look like they can put in a good day's work. I'll trade you some rum for them."

Chance laughed. "No thanks, brother. They're on

loan. I got them from Figh—from someone I know. They're not mine to trade."

Throws Away Wealth looked at his companion speculatively, but said nothing.

"Come into the longhouse, my brother," explained Chance quietly. "I wish to talk with you."

When Throws Away Wealth and Chance were seated comfortably at the fireside, eating the meal the chief's first wife had prepared, Throws Away Wealth prompted, "So what is it you wish to tell me?"

Chance put down the piece of cod he'd been eating and dipped his fingers in the bowl of water a slave boy brought around. "I have excellent news," he began. "Excellent news for me. Excellent news for our people!"

Throws Away Wealth said nothing, just continued to chew on the thick chunk of cod in his mouth. His eyes, however, never left his guest.

"I am going to be married," announced Chance.

Throws Away Wealth swallowed the mouthful. "Oh?" Throws Away Wealth suddenly gave all his attention to the big chunk of cod he held in his hands. "Who are you betrothed to?"

Chance looked at his brother. "Can't you guess?"

Throws Away Wealth shrugged. "Some girl from Yuquot?" He took another bite of fish and chewed. When half done he said matter-of-factly, "You should have waited. Consulted with me. I know about such things. I would have arranged a very good alliance for you. Mayhaps with the Ohiats or the Ucluelets. Not just some easy woman who lets you give her a poke."

Chance was taken aback at his brother's crudity about the kind of woman he'd choose to marry. He paused. Then he asked, "What about the Ahousats? Would you have arranged an alliance with the Ahousats for me?"

Throws Away Wealth stopped in midbite. "What

do you want with them?" he asked, his mouth half full. He chewed some more. "Unless—is that what this is about? That girl Haina? Fighting Wolf's daughter. What have you done?" He froze, awaiting Chance's answer.

Chance took his time, took another mouthful of cod, leisurely sipped some water, chewed on the end of a root.

"Enough!" cried his brother. "Tell me!"

Chance burst out with a good-natured laugh. "I've arranged to marry her. Haina has consented to be my wife," he said at last. His deep-timbred voice carried all his pride in his announcement.

"She what?" sputtered Throws Away Wealth. He went into a choking fit, and Chance pounded the smaller man on the back. Throws Away Wealth's eyes bulged from his face and he tried desperately to wave the bigger man away. Chance stopped patting the tyee's back and waited for his brother's throat to clear. He had a while to wait.

At last Throws Away Wealth croaked, "Well, that is truly wondrous news. How fortunate for you, how fortunate for us."

"Thank you, brother," said Chance expansively and sat back.

"Ahem, yes, yes," coughed the older man. "Caught me a bit off guard, though." He reached for another piece of the flaky white cod.

"Do you think you should?" asked Chance eyeing the chunk of fish. "You almost choked to death on that last piece of cod."

Throws Away Wealth eyed him sourly. "Slaves," he muttered. "Can never get them to cook fish properly." He munched the fish. He was not seized by another coughing fit and Chance relaxed.

"What about Haina's father, Fighting Wolf?" asked Throws Away Wealth. "Did he agree so easily to this—this marriage?" He started to cough again and Chance leaned forward ready to pound his back. The older man hurriedly waved him back.

"Oh, yes," answered Chance. "He was most eager for the alliance." He chuckled to himself. It had not been that way at all. Still, Chance could not resist teasing his brother.

"And Sarita?" prodded Throws Away Wealth. "Was she agreeable to this arrangement?" Again a cough.

Chance nodded casually. "She was most agreeable," he stated. "Good fish," he complimented, "and roasted just the way I like it." He popped another piece into his mouth, slanting a playful glance at his brother.

Throws Away Wealth was gnashing his piece of fish between his teeth.

Chance knew his brother was angry because Throws Away Wealth had not arranged, suggested or played a role in the alliance. At last he took pity on the older man and said, "It worked out well. Do not worry, the Ahousats are very pleased to be allied with the Kyuquots."

"I merely find it hard to believe that Fighting Wolf and Sarita welcomed you so openly after you kidnapped their daughter," snorted Throws Away Wealth. "I think you play me for a fool."

Chance had the grace to look sheepish. "It is true I toy with you a little," he admitted at last. "At first they did not want to have anything to do with me."

"Ah ha! I thought so!"

"They wanted to kill me."

Throws Away Wealth nodded. "That is more what I expected."

His words tingled in Chance's mind but he let them slip away.

"But when I admitted I'd been wrong to kidnap their daughter..."

"Wrong? I thought you did it to avenge me."

"I did." Now came the hard part. "I told them it was because you had been cheated of a bride that I kidnapped their daughter."

"It's true," sang out Throws Away Wealth.

"They claimed there was no cheating involved. That Sarita had been expecting Fighting Wolf's child all along and that you knew of that. That Sarita wanted to marry Fighting Wolf, not you."

"No matter, I would have married her anyway."

"Yes, and would have killed the child!"

"Who told you that?" snorted Throws Away Wealth.

"Sarita."

"Lies, all lies."

"Is it?" asked Chance. He was watching his brother closely now. Throws Away Wealth looked tense, but not unusually so. Could the Ahousats have lied, after all?

"What is one little baby?" snorted Throws Away Wealth. "I wanted an alliance with the Hesquiats, Sarita's people. They did not have many warriors. It would have been an easy thing to take over their rich clam beds and river territories with my Kyuquot warriors. I would have, too, if it had not been for that bitch Sarita, and that—" here he said a horrible word, "—Ahousat, Fighting Wolf! They had to foul my whole plan!"

Chance was staring at his older brother as if he'd never seen him before. "You mean—" he began, "that you wanted the land, the territories, and not the woman?"

"Of course," snorted Throws Away Wealth. "Why would I want her? She was a troublemaking bitch. And pregnant. I'd have ridden her for a season then tossed her off on one of my men. If she didn't end up accidentally drowned." He leered as he said that.

337

Chance felt sick. "But what about the stories you told of how you loved her? Of how you lost her?"

"Baby food. Stories for old women and children on a cold winter's evening," explained Throws Away Wealth. He did not notice the impact his words were having on his listener.

"But I based my whole raid on those stories!"

"More fool you! I didn't tell you to go and avenge me! You thought it up yourself and went behind my back. If you'd asked me, I'd have told you not to bother with avenging that loss. It was the lands I wanted, the fishing grounds. Not the wench!"

Chance sat, stricken. He felt as if the earth had opened up and swallowed him. The depth of the hole he'd fallen into became clear to him then and he felt suffocated by his own actions and blinded by his own eyes.

The realization came that Sarita and Fighting Wolf had indeed told the truth about what had happened so long ago. His brother, his own brother, whom he had loved these many years, had lied. Not even lied, merely whiled away a winter's evening spinning a tale.

Chapter 33

A short while later, a stunned Chance left his brother's longhouse to go and sleep as a guest of Mudshark. He no longer felt comfortable staying in his brother's quarters.

So he was not there to hear the breaking of dishes—a prized set Throws Away Wealth's first wife was saving for the next potlatch—or the anguished howls of slaves as they got in the way of the enraged tyee, nor the thick 'thuds' as chunks of wood bounced off the walls of the longhouse.

Throws Away Wealth was in a rage. And he let everyone in his longhouse know about it. They just didn't know why. Sleepy inhabitants rolled over in their blankets and put more furs or blankets over their ears to keep out their tyee's angry cries. Some of the words barely made out by the bewildered inhabitants included: "marriage," crash, thud, "Ahousats" tinkle, crash, "not fair" thud, thud, "yeow!" this by a slave unlucky enough to be caught by the tip of Throws Away Wealth's wildly waving knife.

The next morning Chance slept late and finally Mudshark roused him by demanding to know what to do with the two big slaves who were demanding their breakfast. Groggily Chance sat up and through bleary eyes he caught the outline of Spit and Squashedface.

Memories of the events of the night before struck him anew and he slunk back under the warm furs. When next he pulled the covers from over his head, the two slaves were still standing there, waiting patiently. Chance sighed and got up out of bed. He tied his bear robe kutsack at the shoulder and walked over to them.

"Master," Squashedface began. "Please, may we help get the wedding preparations started?"

Chance blinked. "How enthusiastic of you," he pronounced at last. The slaves smiled, oblivious to his irony. It was all Chance could do to face such determination first thing in the morning after he'd learned his only foray into manhood had been based on a lie, and a casually told one at that.

Groaning, he sat down and ate whatever Mudshark placed in front of him. Considering the bachelor's establishment that Mudshark ran, the breakfast was limited to clams only but Chance did not notice.

As they ate they talked. "Why didn't you tell my brother where I was?" asked Chance.

"Not wise," answered Mudshark popping a tasty morsel of clam into his mouth. "Not wise to tell anyone."

"But—my own brother?"

Mudshark shrugged. "I don't know who shot that bullet at you—"

"So it *was* a bullet!"

Mudshark looked sheepish. "*Hoowhay*, yes. I checked it closely in the daylight. The metal was still in the wood."

"I wasn't imagining it," said Chance as if to himself.

Mudshark looked at him askance.

Chance caught the look. "I knew what you were thinking, Cousin. I knew you thought I was going crazy."

"Have another clam."

Chance accepted the clam with a grin. "It's going to be a big wedding," he said.

"Oh?"

"Mmmhm. Will you go talk marriage for me? You know many songs. You are a good speaker."

"I thought you'd already agreed with Fighting Wolf that you were going to be married."

"I wish to ask the formal way. I need someone to represent me and ask for Haina's hand. Take some of the men with you. I want to send four marraige canoes."

He saw Mudshark's questioning glance. "It *is* safe. Fighting Wolf will not kill you. He wants the marriage. He's agreed. I just want to show him that I know the proper way to ask for a bride. I never want Haina to feel that she was not asked for in the correct way. People would talk."

Mudshark nodded. "What about gifts? I can't go and talk marriage empty-handed."

"Let's see what my family has available. They will want to contribute, I know. Mayhaps some dishes, and some food. Perhaps some shells, strung on beads. Do we have any small knives? Let me talk with my brother about what we'll give to the Ahousats."

Mudshark nodded. "It is wise to start out with a generous assortment of gifts. Haina need never be ashamed. No one will tell her she was worth nothing!"

"Yes. I must also see what is available for the more important wedding gifts," mused Chance. "In one month I must have everything ready to take to Ahousat. I must not stint on the gifts."

"Like your brother would be inclined to do?"

"Mudshark, that was unworthy of you."

Mudshark shrugged. "Your brother is cheap, Chance. I know it, you know it. The whole village knows it. What I say makes little difference." He lowered his voice. "There is talk that you would make a better chief than Throws Away Wealth. The people come to you to settle their quarrels. They see your generosity when there are fish to be given out to the families. You are becoming known for your wisdom. The people watch you." He chewed on another clam. "It is not only I who say this. Many people say this."

Chance frowned. "I will not listen to such talk. It is disloyal to Throws Away Wealth as my brother and disrespectful to him as my tyee."

Mudshark shrugged again. "As you will."

The two finished eating in silence. At last Chance said, "I found out last night that Throws Away Wealth never really wanted to marry Sarita, the Ahousat woman. Our raid to avenge him was a mistake. A terrible mistake."

Mudshark looked at the blond man incredulously. "What? But for all those years he said—"

Chance nodded. "That's what I thought. All those years he bemoaned her loss and blamed the Ahousats." He hesitated. "Last night he told me he never wanted the woman, only the lands and territories that marriage to her would bring."

Mudshark continued to stare at his cousin. He let out his breath sharply. "I am surprised," he said at last. "I thought we were making an honest raid. Avenging the name of the family."

"I thought so, too.".

After a time Mudshark asked, "What are you going to do?"

"About what?"

Mudshark looked embarrassed. "If the raid was not honorable, then what about Haina?"

Chance looked doubtfully at his cousin. "I talked with her. She says she loves me and wants to marry me. I'm fortunate indeed."

Mudshark raised a brow. "And her parents? Do they want you as a son-in-law?"

"They do now. They did not at first." Chance stared into space thoughtfully. "They wanted to kill me."

"Perhaps it was they who had you shot at in Yuquot."

"Hmmm. Possibly. Not likely, I think. Fighting Wolf seems the type of man who will kill you face to face, not when you're laying in bed, unarmed." He paused. "Besides, he did not know I was in Yuquot."

"He could have had you followed."

"*Hoowhay*, yes. I was not very alert when I was there. It would have been easy for someone to stalk me." He thought for a while. "Still, it does not seem to be Fighting Wolf's way."

"If not him, then who?"

Chance rubbed his chin thoughtfully. "Who, indeed? What enemies do I have that want me dead? Mayhaps it was just a mistaken shot and they thought I was someone else?"

Mudshark looked at him with patent disbelief. "No," he said at last. "I don't think it was a mistake. I think someone was out to kill you and they missed."

"Why couldn't you have killed him?" hissed Throws Away Wealth. "That's why I had you follow him to Yuquot!" He threw up his hands. "I don't know why I keep such useless people as you around me!" Throws Away Wealth was not troubling to hide his anger.

"I tried—"

Throws Away Wealth snorted. "Please! Spare me the excuses! I don't want to hear about how you 'tried'!

It's enough for me to see that he lives!" He stalked back and forth along the beach at a great distance from the village. No one was in sight except for a few children playing far down the beach. Certainly no one could overhear his conversation. "I hired you to do it. I wanted it done. I wanted Chance Gift from the Sea killed! Surely that is not so difficult."

The man he was talking to nodded briefly. "It was dark—"

"And you shot and missed him! It's not enough that you failed to kill him. Oh, no. Now he's back and with what? A marriage alliance that will unite the two most powerful tribes on the coast! Against *me*! Arrrrgh!"

"I tried, Tyee. I got close enough, it's just that—"

Throws Away Wealth looked at him with open contempt. "Were you blind? Were your senses clouded by a woman? I know you chase after any woman you can."

"I—"

"Enough! No more of your useless words." He paused. "Now Chance has returned. Alive!" Throws Away Wealth looked wounded. "It is all I can do to smile and congratulate him and nod and bow and scrape and —"

He appeared to recover himself. "Well, he will soon leave to return to the skinny arms of that—that—that Ahousat wench and her powerful kinsmen." He spat the words out. "Advantageous marriage! Arrgh!" He raised his eyes heavenward and growled, "Was ever a man more unfortunate than I?"

His companion looked about to answer the question but Throws Away Wealth glared at him. "I'm surrounded by incompetents and fools!"

The other man on the beach shifted his feet uneasily. "I could still kill him," he ventured at last.

"No," cried Throws Away Wealth. "Now is not

the time. I have a better plan." His face took on a look that made his listener step back a pace. "I will destroy him, his alliance and his bid for my chieftainship all in one swoop!" The gleam in the tyee's eye unsettled the other man. "He shall not have what is mine. Nor shall he ever gain anything of value! He thinks to make a valuable marriage with the Ahousats, does he? Well not so, not so. Not as long as I have life in my body. I will see to that!"

He turned to the other man and pointed directly at him. "And you, you will help me!"

The man stepped back another pace. "I?" he asked uneasily. "I have no wish to continue these plans."

"Not even for the women, the riches that will be yours?" The tyee's voice was soft, cajoling. "I will make you my heir. I can do it, you know."

"Your heir? You would give me the things that would go to Chance?"

"Bah! They will never go to him! Not one thing, not one name, not one territory! Nothing." He swung his gaze out to sea, then back to his listener. "It will go to *you*," he said softly. "*If* you will do as I tell you."

The two locked gazes. "And the woman?" asked the younger man at last.

"What woman?"

"Haina, the 'Ahousat wench' as you call her. The woman Chance is supposed to wed."

"Her? You want her?"

The man nodded.

"You may have her," said the tyee graciously.

345

Chapter 34

Haina stood excitedly on the beach, hiding in the middle of the murmuring crowd. She was in disguise, and certain that no one would know it was the bride who stood amongst them in the tattered old kutsack and ratty cedar cape draped carefully over her head. She'd knotted her abundant black hair on top of her head, then tucked it under the cape.

She'd had to tie Stinky at the back of the longhouse so he would not betray her identity. She was supposed to be waiting patiently in the longhouse in seclusion with her servants and slaves, not standing out here on the beach straining for a glimpse of the bridegroom. But, chuckled Haina to herself, when had she ever done what she was supposed to?

She watched intently as four canoes came paddling around the northern point of land that jutted into the sea. A cry went up from the crowd. Chance was coming! It had seemed so long since she'd seen him, she

346

thought, gently rubbing her stomach where the babe lay nestled.

Closer and closer paddled the canoes. Then three more came around the point. They scooted across the smooth waters of the bay like leaves before the wind. As they got closer Haina could make out the heads of the paddlers.

He was not in the first canoe. Surely he would be in one of the canoes, she thought.

The canoes had come to Ahousat village three times before. Once they came with Mudshark, then two more times in the month interval since Haina had last seen Chance. She knew he was keeping to the Nootka custom of paddling to the bride's village four times to speak of marriage.

Her father would accept this, the last time, she was sure. Each of the preceding times she had watched for Chance, but he had not been with the men who had come to talk marriage. She'd hovered in the background watching as they gave out gifts to the Ahousat people but not once had she been rewarded by a glimpse of Chance.

Now she wrung her hands together, telling herself over and over that this time she would see him.

There! In that big canoe just pulling up to shore. She was relieved that no one stopped the Kyuquots from landing their canoes. Her father, should he decide to reject Chance's suit, could have easily ordered the visitors away. As it was, he sent his cousin out to greet the newcomers. It boded well for the marriage ceremony, Haina thought. Very well, indeed.

Chance was dressed in the traditional knee-length cedar kutsack with sea otter trim to show his noble status. His face was painted with red and black diagonal stripes and his blond hair fell to his shoulders. Around his head was twisted a cedar bark headband. A beautiful, shiny black sea otter cape draped over his shoulders and down his back. His legs and feet were bare and he stepped out of the canoe onto cedar mats spread before him on the beach by bowing slaves.

Haina drank in the sight of Chance. She could not take her eyes off him. He looked so handsome, so strong, her heart pounded at the sight of him. The sun glinted off his shining hair and she knew there had never been a more beautiful man set foot in any village.

Her hungry eyes followed him as he strode up the cedar mat walkway to where the crowd of watching Ahousats was gathered. She wondered sorrowfully for a moment if he hated her people for the things they'd done to him and she looked closely at his dear face, but she saw only acceptance, and perhaps curiosity.

The rest of his wedding party walked behind him but Haina impatiently moved about in the crowd so she could keep Chance in view. Absently, she noted Mudshark, his hair done up on top of his head and tied with a spruce knot. He too, was dressed in the traditional sea otter-lined kutsack, as were most of the other men and women.

Chance stopped in front of Fighting Wolf and Sarita. Bowing, he presented Fighting Wolf with a carved cedar box.

Fighting Wolf politely opened the box. He gasped as he looked inside. "A fine gift, my son-in-law," he acknowledged.

Haina's mother peeked into the box and smiled, obviously pleased.

Haina strained to see what had so impressed her parents.

Fighting Wolf, grinning, held up a pistol. The dull gleam of the barrel was easily seen even from a distance. Chance had given her father one of his prized pistols—a truly magnificent present, thought Haina.

Haina smiled to herself at Chance's generosity. She watched him turn away and noted the other pistol tucked in his belt. Her smile widened.

Chance was soon swallowed up by the cluster of his own people around him and Haina turned her gaze back to the canoes.

An old woman was helped from the largest canoe by a young male slave. Several other women stepped out behind her. Why, there was the old chief, Throws Away Wealth. What was he doing here? Then Haina squelched the uncharitable thought. Of course, as Chance's older brother, and the highest ranking Kyuquot, it was an honor that he attend the wedding.

She watched her parents greet the guests. With smiles on their faces Fighting Wolf and Sarita nodded and murmured to those they knew, and bowed graciously upon introductions to those they did not.

Haina watched as Chance met her brothers and their families for the first time. Sea Wolf, her youngest brother, greeted the Kyuquot rather curtly, she thought critically. But her four oldest brothers accepted the introductions in a pleasant enough manner.

She sighed heavily as Chance was presented to her lovely oldest sister, Fires-on-the-Beach Woman. Haina had seen that look before—a look of awe on the faces of men when they first beheld her beauteous sister. Fortunately, Fires-on-the-Beach's Uchucklesit husband, who was known for his jealousy, stepped forward and directed the conversation. Chance's interest was soon caught by whatever the big nobleman was saying, and Haina felt secretly relieved.

Haina watched in amusement as Throws Away Wealth marched up the beach to halt directly in front of Fighting Wolf. He did not look at Sarita. Haina thought for a moment that the visiting Kyuquot chieftain would yell in her father's face. Instead he huffed noisily and Fighting Wolf seemed to accept such an unusual greeting. He politely gestured to a wooden box set on the beach gravel. Carved red and black killer whales decorated the sides of the large box which was intended as a seat for the high ranking chief.

Throws Away Wealth plumped himself down to watch the festivities through narrowed eyes. His wife, the old woman Haina had seen being helped out of the canoe, gathered her furs about her and sat on a lower box next to him. He ignored her.

Suddenly one of the guests on the beach let out a shout. A row of lithe, strong Kyuquot women stepped forward and began the Sway Dance. The men chanted with their deep voices. The women moved their arms and bodies in graceful motions and the onlookers sighed at the beauty of the dance.

When they were finished, the men took up another song—Haina assumed it was a song from Chance's family—and the women danced gracefully until the last note died away.

Now another dance team, this one composed of men, took their place on the beach. Their dance mimicked a drift whale approaching the beach and being greeted by hungry, thankful villagers.

And so it went, chanting and singing and dancing on into early afternoon. The guests outdid themselves in a bid to impress the hosts.

Haina had to admit that the dancing was indeed well done.

Her interest caught when she saw that it was time for the challenging games. Her father had his cousin lead the visitors over to a flat, round log. Perched on top of it was a large rock—a large, heavy rock. The cousin waved over a strong young man that Haina recognized as a nobleman from her village. The man had thick shoulders and muscled upper arms. He took a deep breath and picked up the rock. He tottered three steps and dropped the rock, narrowly missing his toes. The rock lay in the sand where it landed.

"Now you pick up the stone," the cousin defied

the guests.

The Kyuquots pushed Beachdog forward. He sauntered over and bent to pick up the stone. He gripped it, his face straining. The rock did not budge. He tried again, the veins of his neck standing out in blue relief against his brown skin. Still he could not move the rock. Beachdog retreated to the laughs of the onlookers.

Now another Kyuquot man, one Haina did not recognize, trotted forward. He, too, strained at the rock but was soon forced to concede defeat.

The crowd murmured happily as two more Kyuquot men tried to lift the stone and failed.

Around her, Haina heard the Ahousats' muttered opinions. "These Kyuquots will never be able to lift such a heavy stone. Instead they'll be made to look like fools!"

"Good, for who could trust men who steal other tribes' women?"

"They should have come and asked properly for her, not stolen the war chief's daughter like that. What a disgrace!"

Haina shifted uneasily, hearing the gossip in the crowd. She slid the cape partially over her face and glanced cautiously about, hoping that no one would recognize her.

But now the crowd's attention shifted to the next contestant. A strong, vigorous looking man, he looked faintly familiar to Haina. Obviously a slave from his plain clothing, still, if he succeeded in lifting the stone for the Kyuquot side, his status would not be held against him.

Several commoners called out to him, "Come on, Dog Shadow, you can lift it!"

"Show these Ahousats we raise *men* in Kyuquot!"

"Run up and down the beach with it, Dog Shadow!"

Dog Shadow nodded to his admirers and knelt on one knee beside the stone. He placed his hands carefully on each end. Back straight, teeth gritted together, he strained until he slowly lifted the large rock. First it was even with his knees, then even with his straining thighs. At last he could walk with it.

"Dog Shadow, Dog Shadow," chanted the Kyuquots.

Carefully, beads of sweat dripping off his face, the slave stepped forward. Two, three, four steps, he faltered and the crowd held its breath. Five, six, he was walking—walking with the great rock! The Kyuquots went wild, jumping up and down.

The slave made it to the waterline and plopped the rock into the shallows. Then he turned to the watching crowd with a slight smile on his face.

Haina thought he looked smug.

The Ahousats called out a few congratulatory remarks but Haina could hear the disgruntled comments within the crowd. Her people felt shamed by the Kyuquots' success, and she with them. She hoped there would be no more challenging games, she'd lost her taste for them.

She grimaced and turned her attention to the speaker. "Oh no," she groaned, then held her mouth for fear someone had overheard. It was Talks Much, her father's most esteemed, most boring, speaker.

They'd probably be standing on the beach until dark listening to his long winded welcome to the guests, she thought glumly. Indeed her guess was not far off. The sun was sinking into the sea when the speaker finally finished his monologue.

The speaker had dwelled lovingly on every detail of the most prophetic dreams, the most valuable war prizes, the richest territories, and the biggest whale ever caught by a member of Haina's family. He had also described the strangest fish caught, reeled off the most illustrious names that were bestowed on truly amazing offspring and of course listed the wealthiest ancestors. He went back several generations, impressing even Haina with his memory. But he spoiled it all by talking on and on until Haina wondered at the patience of the people around her who seemed to be thoroughly interested in what the man was saying.

As for herself, her eyes had glazed over long before the speaker was done.

When he finally finished, she trailed slowly up the beach after the guests. The crowd herded her towards her father's longhouse.

The usher greeted people at the door of Fighting Wolf's longhouse. It was his duty to seat them according to their social rank. Sometimes disputes broke out among the visitors as to where a chief should sit, as when two chiefs vied for the same higher ranking seat. But Fighting Wolf's usher was old and experienced and cunning. His word was final in the placement of chiefs. And he had two large slaves behind him to defend his decisions.

The usher bowed and seated Throws Away Wealth at the highest ranking seat in the longhouse, right next to the door. The Kyuquot chief settled onto his raised seat and nestled into his furs as though he would not move for the remainder of the wedding ceremonies. The old woman, his wife, was courteously seated next to him. He ignored her.

Haina took a place unobtrusively in the back of the longhouse. She was not supposed to show herself yet, but she did not want to miss the proceedings.

Searching the faces of guests and hosts alike, Haina spotted Grandmother Crab Woman sitting off to one side. The old woman was nodding off to sleep. Haina smiled to herself at the sight. She hoped Grandmother would not sleep through the entire wedding celebration! She'd have to do something lively, Haina vowed, to keep Grandmother awake.

Haina watched proudly as Chance followed the usher in and sat down at the place of honor indicated. His men sat around him. There was some laughing and joking and Mudshark elbowed Chance who merely grinned at the ribaldry. Haina wished she knew what they were saying.

Finally all the guests were seated, each according to his social rank. An expectant hum buzzed through the longhouse as guests and villagers alike happily anticipated the next part of the wedding ritual.

Chance's eyes swept the crowd and Haina wondered if he were looking for her. She shrank back behind a post when she saw him glance in her direction. She held her breath but knew he had not seen her.

Where was she? wondered Chance. The laborious paddling was over, the greetings and speeches had been tedious but he'd survived them. Now where was Haina, his bride?

Chapter 35

Haina reached out as a slave went past bearing a platter of delicate herring eggs. She scooped up a handful of the tasty delicacy and caught the slave's warning hiss for her efforts. She laughed and let the cape slide from her head just a little. The slave's eyes widened when he saw who he had just reproached. He scampered away.

The wedding feast was beginning. She must hurry! Her heart beat fast at the thought that tonight, in just a little while, she would be wed.

She glanced across at Chance one more time before slinking into the shadows and out a small escape hatch in the back of the longhouse. Her mother would be looking for her. Haina had yet to slip into her wedding finery and then sit with her ladies pretending she'd spent the whole day waiting with them.

She giggled to herself as she ran the length of the building. A light mist was falling and dark had descended. She was outside the second escape hatch at the rear of the building. Here it was dark and quiet, all the other inhabitants were gathered in her father's quarters watching the festivities.

"Here, Stinky," she whispered, patting the dog. He whined and strained at the cedar rope she'd tied him with. "No, Stinky. I can't set you free," she murmured into his ear. "But I brought you these." She carefully placed the handful of herring eggs on the ground.

The dog lapped up the tasty roe. He licked his lips tidily when he was done. And whined.

"That will have to do, old friend. I must go." Placing a kiss on his white head, she crawled into the longhouse.

She grinned at her waiting ladies. Some of them had shocked looks on their faces as they saw the old kutsack she was wearing and the cedar cape she was trailing through the dirt.

"Haina," scolded a well-loved voice. "Where have you been? Mother was only just here looking for you." Two pretty little girls and one small boy regarded Haina reproachfully out of the same big velvety brown eyes that their mother regarded her with.

"Fires-on-the Beach Woman!" cried Haina. "It's so good to see you!" She threw herself into her sister's arms. The two hugged. "I'm so glad you could come. Was the trip difficult?" Haina knew it was an arduous paddle from where the Uchucklesits had their village to Ahousat.

"It was an easier trip than most," admitted Fires-on-the-Beach Woman. "I don't mind traveling in the summer. It only took us two days and, of course, the children," here she swept her little ones a loving glance, "wanted it to take much longer so that they could camp out every night."

Haina laughed and ruffled the youngest child's hair. The child, Dorsal Fin, smiled up at her aunt and exposed a mouth full of teeth.

"She has all her teeth now!" exclaimed Haina

bending down to examine little Dorsal Fin in earnest.

"Haina, please," pleaded her sister. "We have a wedding to get you to. Your own. We can discuss Dorsal Fin's teeth another time."

The other ladies nodded their heads eagerly.

". . . eight, nine, ten!" counted Haina triumphantly, her finger in Dorsal Fin's wide open mouth. Dorsal Fin smiled and bit down on Haina's finger.

"Ouch!"

The child's mother and the surrounding women laughed.

"Are you ready now?" asked Fires-on-the-Beach Woman.

"Did you tell her to do that?" asked Haina suspiciously, peering closely at her sore finger. Then she laughed too. "Do help me get ready," she pleaded. "I have a man waiting for me."

The women swarmed around her helping her out of the old kutsack. A servant girl rolled her eyes and held her nose as she delicately carried the dirty kutsack away. "Phew."

Haina washed quickly in cold water that a slave brought. Then two other servants brought in the wedding kutsack. Several women helped her into the beautiful garment that Haina was to wear for the happy occasion.

The kutsack had been painstakingly bleached until it was a pale yellow. The weave was the tiniest that could be done, woven by the most expert slave weaver in Ahousat village. The sea otter border of the kutsack was a deep black, and the rich fur had been combed until the thick pile stood up. Haina ran her hand over the soft fur and smiled. It was truly a beautiful kutsack. Longer than most such garments, it reached to below her knees.

Fires-on-the-Beach Woman picked up a carved wooden comb and brushed out Haina's tangled locks.

When she was done, Haina's raven black hair streamed down her back and winked in the firelight.

"*Umiksu* stopped by to give you these," said Fires-on-the-Beach Woman. She held out a bentwood cedar box. Nestled in it Haina could see a pair of shining copper earrings. "*Umiksu* wore them when she married *Nuwiksu*—the first time." Fires-on-the-Beach's eyes sparkled. "Here, let me," she suggested, putting the earrings in place. She stepped back. "Lovely," she breathed. She handed the box to a slave who took it away. "Now you are ready," she pronounced. "You look beautiful."

The ladies around the two agreed heartily, murmuring their approval. Indeed, Haina looked exceptionally beautiful. Her dark hair fell to her waist. Her wide, dark brown eyes gleamed and her face glowed with happiness. She almost felt like laughing, she was so happy. Now she would wed the man she loved and nothing, *nothing,* would ever separate them again!

A slave arrived and bowed. "You father says for you to present yourself to the groom," he intoned in a heavy voice. Then he left.

Shaking with excitement, Haina touched her hair one last time.

"You look lovely," assured her sister. "Go."

Like a bird set free from a net, Haina flew down the long middle path of the longhouse. Her ladies ran to catch up with her.

Haina stopped when she'd come half the length of the longhouse. Her ladies stopped too, laughing and giggling. One last time they adjusted clothing, touched hair, checked jewelry.

Then Haina walked slowly and in stately fashion into the well-lighted area where the groom and guests awaited. Her ladies were arrayed behind her.

Haina could hear gasps of delight on either side of her as villagers and guests alike took in the vision of beauty that she and her ladies presented. She smiled graciously in Chance's direction then walked in dignified fashion to where she was supposed to sit. She lowered herself gracefully to the plank bench and her ladies fanned themselves out in front of her. The noise started up around them again.

Under cover of all the chatter going on around him, Throws Away Wealth signalled Dog Shadow over to him. That worthy edged over to his master and bent his head.

"Is everything ready?" whispered the tyee. "Is the rum here? The herbs? The slave girl?"

Dog Shadow nodded.

"Good," answered the chief. "That relieves my mind. You know what to do. Get Dog Dung to help you if you need it. He's as useless as they come, but he's agreed to help me."

Dog Shadow nodded again. He ignored the bright beady eyes of the tyee's first wife as she watched him.

"Now get out of here."

Dog Shadow slunk away.

Throws Away Wealth's first wife looked at him out of weary eyes. "What evil are you planning now?" she asked him.

"Silence," he snapped. "You will say nothing or I will see you dead."

His wife subsided into silence. Around them people were laughing and talking and calling for the dancing to start. But only emptiness reigned between the chief and his first wife from Kyuquot.

And on the other side of the room Chance was watching Haina. "She's beautiful," he breathed.

Mudshark grunted. "You are very fortunate to be marrying her after all that has happened," he said. "Fighting Wolf put me through a lot of those marriage talks. I was beginning to think you would die an old bachelor."

Chance snorted. "Are you trying to take credit for me marrying such a beautiful bride? If so, do not try. I found her and kept her all by myself."

"And who found her in Yuquot? And who paddled to this village of barbarians three times on behalf of his ungrateful friend?" And so it went, the two bantering back and forth about Haina.

They stopped talking to watch the Ahousat men's and women's dance teams. Chance accepted some of the crunchy herring roe that a slave passed to him. He sipped from his cup of water. Soon, very soon, he would be wed to the woman he loved. He sat back in satisfaction and watched the dancing.

After the dancing, slave boys with bowls of water began to circulate amongst the seated people. The guests washed their hands and waited impatiently for the food to be brought out.

Soon it began to arrive. And what an elaborate spread of food it was! In addition to the smoked salmon and fresh salmon that Chance had brought from Kyuquot, there were huge wooden platters of camas bulbs, steaming hot from the oven pits; cinquefoil roots, tender and moist and steamed clover roots. There were two different kinds of clams, cold cooked halibut chunks, haunches of venison and many roasted ducks. There were bowls and bowls of whale and seal oil for dipping the fish, meat and vegetables into. Platters of fresh blueberries, blackberries, dried strawberries and fresh salalberries circulated. There was even tea to drink, with or without the white man's sugar, noted Chance.

There was also something rare: tobacco to smoke. Chance relished his first taste of the pungent, shredded tobacco leaves wrapped in thin skins of paper. He choked and coughed at first, much to Mudshark's amusement, but soon they were both inhaling the smoke as if they'd done it all their lives.

Eventually the platters of food were taken away and Chance and Mudshark sat back. Chance had eaten little, he'd been too nervous and anxious to see Haina.

Fighting Wolf and the speaker, Talks Much, stood up and the audience stopped chattering to hear what was going to happen next. Talks Much droned on for a while. It was not until he introduced the new bride that Chance sat up and listened.

Haina was led, demure and with downcast eyes, over to Chance and her hand was placed in his.

Her heart fluttered as she felt his warm palm and she glanced shyly up at him and smiled.

He looked into her eyes, his own mirroring her love and they both stood enraptured.

The spell was broken when the restive crowd began to make rude noises.

They sat down, intent on each other, talking together for the first time in a month. "I am pleased that my cousin was able to persuade your father to forget about the ten days waiting period," whispered Chance. "It is a silly custom, making the bride and groom wait ten days before consummating the marriage! Fortunately your father saw reason. Near you like this, seeing you, your beauty, I know I could never wait that long for you. I must have you—tonight!"

"Chance!" she cried, shocked. Then she smiled, "Did you miss me?"

"You know I did. Why, if it were not for the longhouse full of people watching us, I'd sweep you away to bed right now!"

Behind them, Mudshark interrupted with a clearing of his throat. "Chance?"

"Mmm?" Chance was too busy looking into his new wife's eyes to pay much attention to his cousin.

"Chance. They're coming to take her back now. Please, please do not embarrass our proud Kyuquots by hanging on to her and forcing the Ahousats to drag her away! Let her go properly. You'll see her soon."

Chance looked up, sighed and reluctantly let go of Haina's hand. Then he snatched it up again quickly, kissed the palm and said, "Until tonight."

She smiled softly at him, her dark eyes glowing in the firelit room.

"Wait," he cried suddenly. "I just remembered. I want to give you this." He fumbled in a pouch tied at his waist and extracted a wrapped bundle. Haina watched in curiosity as he pulled out a short curled rope that sorted itself into a round shape.

"What is it?" she asked.

"A bracelet," he answered proudly. "A bracelet woven from my birth mother's hair. Her hair was red, the color of newly turned autumn leaves. See how cunningly the hair is interwoven with a strip of purple cloth? The cloth decorated my birth mother's neck at the time I was born. My Indian mother, Ocean Wave, wove this for me, in kind remembrance of the white woman who gave me life. Ocean Wave sat me down one day and told me the full story of my birth. Then she presented this bracelet to me. It is very precious to me. It is a gift from both of my mothers. Now I give it to you."

There were tears in Haina's eyes as she accepted the delicately woven bracelet. "Oh, Chance," she breathed. "Thank you. Thank you so much. I shall cherish it always."

He kissed the top of her nose. "I must let you go. For now. Wait for me," he whispered as Haina's ladies came to claim her. They led her away and she glanced at him only once before she disappeared into the long-house's farthest reaches of darkness.

He shot a wry glance at Mudshark. "What was this about pleading that I let her go peaceably? Did you seriously think those ladies of hers could possibly drag her away from me if I made up my mind to keep her?"

Mudshark snorted. "You play the ardent bride-groom so well, even I was sure you would be jumping your fair lady before they got her away in time!"

"That was no play!" snapped Chance.

Mudshark raised an eyebrow but said nothing.

Chance sighed in frustration. The rest of the evening would be spent on watching more dancing and singing and the groom would be expected to sit through it all. Chance wished he could dispense with that part of the ceremony.

Much to Chance's surprise he was soon joined by Throws Away Wealth. The older man walked through the crowd trailed by two slaves carrying a large barrel.

"Ho, Brother," he called out in a jolly voice. "Drink with me."

Chance met Mudshark's glance then turned to his brother. "Do you not know?" he whispered. "Fighting Wolf does not like rum."

"So? Can we not enjoy it? Give it to our friends around us?"

"You don't understand," answered Chance. "Fighting Wolf does not allow it in his village."

"How do you know?" asked his brother looking at him keenly.

Chance flushed. "We found out the first time we came here." Mudshark nodded solemnly. "Take it away, brother," urged Chance. "Take the rum away. Do not offend our hosts."

"Nonsense," said Throws Away Wealth in a gruff and hearty voice that boomed around the room. "He will not take offense."

Fighting Wolf approached. "What is that?" he asked eyeing the barrel.

"Why, a little gift for my new relatives," answered Throws Away Wealth. "I brought it all the way from Yuquot. Best rum they had on the white man's ship."

"I do not allow my people to drink that poison."

"What?" asked Throws Away Wealth in mock horror. "You don't?"

Fighting Wolf sighed. He did not like rum's effects on his people. "No rum is to be given to my Ahousat people," he said at last. "I, of course, will not prevent you or your own people from drinking it." He watched the smug smile creep across the Kyuquot chief's face. "Keep that rum away from my Ahousats," he warned.

"Thank you, thank you, good Tyee," answered Throws Away Wealth unctuously. "I will give it only to my Kyuquots then." He paused. "Are you certain you would not like a drink? One little one?" he asked encouragingly.

Fighting Wolf shook his head and strode away.

Throws Away Wealth watched him go through narrowed eyes. "I did not know he would object, brother," he said at last. "Truly I did not."

Chance nodded. "Sit down," he indicated the seat next to him.

Once seated, Throws Away Wealth directed the burdened slaves to place the barrel next to him on the dirt floor.

He glanced about and observed in a low voice, "Fighting Wolf did not say I couldn't sell the rum to his people." He leered at Chance. Chance stared fixedly back at him until the chief blinked. "Merely joking, my brother, merely joking," he muttered.

Throws Away Wealth looked over at Mudshark. "Mudshark," he said companionably. "Why not have a drink of rum to celebrate the marriage of my younger brother?" Seeing Mudshark's hesitation he nodded, "We Kyuquots are proud of this alliance. It must be celebrated properly!" Without waiting further he said to a slave, "Pour."

The slave filled a white man's cup and handed it to Mudshark, bowing deferentially. "Where did you get this cup?" asked Mudshark. He wanted to put off drinking the rum for as long as possible, knowing Chance's awkward position.

The dainty cup, with a blue and white flower pattern and a curlique handle looked ridiculous in Mudshark's big brown hand and Chance wanted to laugh aloud. He settled for a muffled snort. Mudshark shot him an exasperated glance.

"Have one, too, my cousin?" Mudshark asked smoothly. "It is your success we are celebrating, after all, is it not?"

"Please do," chimed in Throws Away Wealth heartily. "After all, I am losing a brother to the Ahousats. Instead of acquiring your head in war, they acquired it in marriage." He laughed heartily at his joke. "Slave!" He waved Dog Shadow over and watched as he poured more rum into two cups, surreptitiously adding a pinch of dried herbs to one. Throws Away Wealth accepted his, then tipped his head back and drank noisily from the delicate blue and white cup. "Come on," he urged when he saw Chance hesitate. "I shall be hurt if you refuse."

"Where did you get these cups?" stalled Chance.

"From the old woman over there," the tyee pointed his chin in the direction of his first wife. "She made me trade some of my best furs for a set of platters and cups that a visiting white captain had on his ship. Said she wanted them for a potlatch." He signaled for his own cup to be refilled and the slave hurriedly obliged. "But I liked them, so I took them."

"Oh." Chance wished he hadn't asked. Sometimes he thought the old wife of his brother had a hard life to bear despite her high status as first wife. The poor woman was always hiding in corners and scurrying about and he wondered how she put up with his brother. Amazed, Chance caught the disloyal thought. What was happening to him? Only a moon ago he would never have had such a disloyal thought. He squirmed uneasily.

"What territories are you gaining along with your new bride?" Throws Away Wealth was asking affably now.

"Territories? Why, I don't know," answered Chance. "Mudshark took care of all that."

Throws Away Wealth shot Chance an irritated glance. "Didn't you ask?"

Chance shrugged. "No, I was content to leave it in his hands."

Throws Away Wealth eyed Mudshark from beneath lowered brows. "Since when has Mudshark been known for his wisdom in trading?"

Mudshark choked on his drink but said nothing. Throws Away Wealth harrumphed and turned back to Chance.

"What? You're marrying the wench and you don't know what you're getting? What kind of marriage is that?"

Chance smiled, secretly pleased at his brother's obvious irritation. "Hopefully a fine one. I'm getting the woman I want. That's the important part." He made as if to rise, tired of the conversation.

Throws Away Wealth touched his arm. "Stay, stay," he coaxed.

Chance sank back down. "Very well."

"I will show you how the *mumutly* drinks. Touch my cup with yours." Chance and Mudshark did so. "Now drink, my brother," the tyee said, grinning as Chance swallowed the rum, and along with it the mind-deadening herbs the shaman had provided.

"Let us drink that you have a long and prosperous marriage." They touched cups and drank.

"Let us drink that you may have many children." They touched cups and drank.

"Healthy children," intoned Throws Away Wealth. The sincerity in his brother's voice pleased

Chance and he drank.

"There, that wasn't so bad, was it?" encouraged Throws Away Wealth. "Now let us drink to the lovely bride that you've acquired." Again Chance drank, and Mudshark also.

"And to her family," went on the tyee.

"Next you'll have us drinking to the family dog," snorted Chance. Throws Away Wealth frowned. Mudshark laughed and sprayed rum out of his mouth.

Throws Away Wealth looked at him in disgust. "I can see you don't know how to drink rum properly. I will teach you." And so Throws Away Wealth did just that, calling for cup after cup of the dark beverage.

Later, Mudshark and Throws Away Wealth were still talking and drinking companionably. Chance had had no more than the one cupful, but his thoughts were strangely addled, and he found it increasingly difficult to follow the words his brother was speaking. Sinking his head on his arms, he was oblivious to the curious glances of those around him.

He was oblivious also, to the hostile grimaces that marked the faces of Haina's brothers as Throws Away Wealth and Mudshark began a loud song. Sea Wolf, in particular, kept watching the Kyuquots as they laughed and sang and drank. He sent a smoldering glance in his sister's direction and Haina smiled weakly back. She did not know what to make of Chance's behavior, either.

Much later, Throws Away Wealth had Chance carried to the alcove where Haina was already waiting for him. Two slaves carried Chance's weight between them. They slung him onto the fur-covered bed that had been prepared for the happy couple. White flowers were strewn about on the dark brown furs. Chance landed face down on the furs and crushed several of the delicate blossoms beneath him. His audible snores filled the chamber.

The Kyuquot Tyee slapped his brother on the back and chirped to the glowering bride, "Here's the groom. Not much use he'll be to you, but here he is!" Then laughing, he swaggered away with the slaves behind him.

Haina stared after him and wanted to scream and throw something after him. Instead she beat the fur covers with her small fists until she was exhausted. How could Chance do this to her? And on their wedding night? She prodded the inert body but he did not move. He just laid there and snored.

She turned her back to him and curled up on her side. She stared at the plank wall, memorizing every splinter and crack until finally, when there was an uneasy silence throughout the longhouse, she knew that the others, villagers and guests alike, had retired to bed also.

Haina fell into a fitful sleep only to awaken suddenly. Had she heard a noise? Chance's snores rang in her ears. Suddenly, a large, salty hand cupped her mouth and a voice hissed in her ear, "Come with us. Quietly. It means your life!"

Chapter 36

Haina was dead.

Chance stared groggily at the broken faced body beside him.

He had awakened to the fingers of daylight creeping in through the cracks in the longhouse wall. A full bladder had forced him hastily from the bed. His head pounding like a drum, his tongue thick, he could barely stagger from the fur covers to find his way out of the longhouse. Once relieved, he'd returned to the warm longhouse and the warmer covers.

And found Haina, his beloved Haina, cold and dead on the fur blankets. Her once beautiful face was stove in beyond recognition. Only her body, slim, lithe, brown, half hidden by the pale yellow kutsack that carelessly covered it, lay unmarred.

Chance's guts wrenched. His woman, his love, his beautiful love. Who had done this horror? He lurched closer to the bed, his body barely obeying the frantic commands of his half-asleep mind. He groaned. The rum he'd consumed so obligingly the night before clouded his mind this morning. Desperately he tried to get his sluggish thoughts moving. Think! Hard to think.

"Haina!" His cry was from the heart. How had his beautiful love come to this—this ugly horror?

"Haina!" All the pent up anguish in his soul went into the cry. Great sobs tore from his throat as he kneeled beside the bed. Unthinkingly searching for her solace, he placed his head on the kutsack covered lap of the pitiful body. Shudders shook his body as he cried out for the love he had lost. Despair and pain locked him in their grip.

Fighting Wolf and Sarita found him like that. His cries had awakened them, indeed had awakened the whole longhouse, and the war chief and his wife had come running. Slaves, commoners and warriors trailed in their wake.

Now Fighting Wolf could only stare. Shock, disgust and horror chased each other across the aging war chief's face. Scant heartbeats passed before he had the presence of mind to shield his wife's eyes from the terrible sight of their crushed, beloved daughter. But he was too late. Sarita, too, had seen the broken face and the wedding kutsack and she willingly sought refuge in her husband's arms. Her broken sobs filled the hushed room.

Commoners and slaves who had crowded in for a look fell back in fear and disbelief. No one moved. All were shocked into immobility at the enormity of the crime committed.

Gradually Chance became aware of the dozens of eyes upon him. Slowly he lifted his head from the tear-soaked kutsack. He looked around at the faces watching him. And read his death in their eyes.

They think I've done this, he thought. They think I've murdered my bride! Murdered the one woman I loved!

Slowly too, he rose from his bended knees. No one stopped him. No one reached out to him. Eyes, nothing but accusing eyes, he thought dully. It was as he took a step away from the bed that the war chief's arm shot out and a guttural order issued from his down-curved mouth. "Seize him!"

Spit and Squashedface, those faithful two, stepped forward and roughly took Chance's arms, one on each side of him. He felt their strength and knew they would not release him unless death itself claimed him.

"When?" barked Fighting Wolf. Four of his sons stood beside him. Fires-on-the-Beach Woman arrived, wrapping a cedar cape around her shoulders against the cool morning air. Her eyes glittered as she, too, watched Chance. A frowning Grandmother Crab Woman joined her. Behind them came the fifth son, Sea Wolf, leading Stinky on a rope. "I found him tied behind the longhouse," he said and moved to stand next to his brothers.

Chance stared at the family, uncomprehending. They are all against me, he thought.

"When?"

Chance's dumb stare enraged Fighting Wolf.

"When did you do this?" he roared.

Aah, so now it comes. "I did not do it."

"You lie, Kyuquot! You were with her all night. You, you—! Words are too weak to tell you all I think of you!" Chance thought the old man would break down right there and he felt a flash of pity for the old man and woman and what they were going through. Then he cast his eyes back to the bed and the broken woman lying there and he felt the pity surge up for himself. And Haina—brutally plucked in the very flower of her life.

"Why?" The old man was saying. "Why? Was it the drink? Were you too drunk to know what you were doing?" Fighting Wolf's voice broke into a sob on the last word. "I should never have let the rum into this village!" Sea Wolf stepped close to his father. Stinky tugged against his leash and whined. Sea Wolf glared ferociously at Chance.

"Just tell me why!" Fighting Wolf was pleading, pleading for reason where none existed.

"I did not do it."

Unaided, Fighting Wolf walked up to Chance and leaned into his face. Their eyes met and Chance could see the throbbing neck veins in the older man. "I will have you cut into pieces the size of my little finger, Kyuquot." Fighting Wolf's voice was unyielding. "And I will start with your arms and legs so that you will still be alive when I get to your foul, murdering heart!" The two glared at each other.

"Start with his eyes, father," suggested Sea Wolf calmly.

"No, his nose," suggested another brother.

"No, his penis," said a third brother.

"Take him away," ordered Fighting Wolf in disgust.

Before the slaves could march him away, Chance cried out, "Wait." His groggy wits began to move, slowly. "Let me have one last look at her. I—I loved her."

"You had your last look, you murdering bastard, when you killed her!" Fighthing Wolf waved the slaves away and they dragged Chance along with them. Even as he was being pulled away, Chance could not take his eyes off Haina's body on the bed.

Stinky, too, was looking at the body. He strained against the leash, whining and barking short, piercing cries.

"Back!" said Sea Wolf. "You can't go to her, Stinky. She's dead." Sea Wolf watched Chance being dragged away. "And he killed her." A diabolical expression crossed Sea Wolf's face. He let go of the leash. "Go kill him, Stinky!" he hissed. "Attack!"

Chance heard the vicious words and crouched into a ball as best he could with the two slaves still holding him. Any moment he expected to feel biting, rending teeth tearing at his flesh. When nothing happened, he lifted his head cautiously.

Sea Wolf looked exasperated. Stinky was standing on the bed, sniffing at Haina. Then he turned away, disinterested. He hopped down onto the floor and started sniffing again.

What—? Chance couldn't understand the dog's strange behavior. Here was Haina's faithful friend, her boon companion, the dog who never left her side, easily deserting her on her death bed. No whining, no moaning, nothing. It did not make sense. Or did it?

Chance jerked both muscular arms and the two slaves stopped, nonplussed. "Wait," he ordered. He peered at the body on the bed. He must get closer. He jerked the slaves forward. Confused, Spit and Squashedface let him take several steps towards the bed before they halted him.

They were about to drag Chance off again, when he cried out, "There's no mole!"

Fighting Wolf looked up from where he was hugging Sarita and she, too, lifted her head. No one said anything, and Fighting Wolf waved the slaves away again.

"There's no mole, I tell you!"

"Your words make no sense, Kyuquot. Go!"

"There's no mole, I tell you. No birthmark on her left thigh."

Sarita stiffened. "What is he saying?" she whispered hoarsely. "No mole? No birthmark? Of course she has a birthmark on her thigh. She has always had one!" She locked eyes with Fighting Wolf. "Look! Quickly! Her left thigh, at the top!"

Fighting Wolf ran to the body and pulled up the bridal kutsack. Before him lay the woman's thighs, smooth, round, pale, unblemished.

"No birthmark," he whispered.

Then louder, "No birthmark."

The people around him appeared stunned. "No birthmark!" he said again and this time it was a cry of jubilation. "There is no birthmark! It is not Haina!"

The onlookers were all talking at once. Some were shaking their heads. Some were smiling, some were looking sorrowful. Sea Wolf walked over to the bed to see for himself. Stinky whined and Sea Wolf instinctively patted the dog's head.

The murmurings of the crowd grew louder. At last the question uppermost in all minds made its way to the surface.

"Then who is she?" demanded Chance. "And where is Haina?"

Silence greeted his question—complete and utter silence.

"Step forward," ordered Fighting Wolf. "Anyone knowing where my daughter is, please step forward and say something."

No one moved.

"Please," said Fighting Wolf again and Chance's heart contracted to hear the old man's shaking voice. "If anyone knows anything, please tell us!"

Silence.

Sea Wolf gestured to the crowd. "If anyone knows anything about my sister, tell us now. It will mean freedom if you're a slave, and precious gifts if you are a commoner or a noble. Tell us now! Do not make us search you out. It will not go well for you!"

A little shiver went through the crowd but still no one moved, no one spoke. Sea Wolf looked at his father and shrugged.

Chance pulled free of the brawny slaves who were

still holding his arms. They looked to Fighting Wolf for orders but they did not try to stop Chance.

Fighting Wolf turned to see Chance coming towards him. "What do *you* want?" he asked wearily.

Chance ignored him and addressed the crowd. His mind was beginning to work again. The one thing driving him now was, Where was Haina?

To the crowd he said, "Let anyone who knows this woman come forward." He gestured to the body on the bed. "She must have family, relatives, a husband? Someone must know of her."

Silence. And then the crowd began to stir as a man pushed his way through. He elbowed people aside and shoved at others. Terrible sobs issued from his throat and he cried out like a madman. In front of everyone he threw himself on the body and cried, "My love, my love. They killed you! I did not know! I did not know!"

Chance, Fighting Wolf and Sea Wolf all looked at each other. The man laid on the body, clutching it hopelessly. His clothes were ragged and Chance knew him to be a slave.

Grandmother Crab Woman croaked up, "Privacy! We need privacy to find out more from this slave. Let us not air our family tragedies in front of the whole village!" She shook her head. "You'd never find the old people making a public display like this! The old people knew when to keep things private. Not like some people I know!"

"Thank you," said Fighting Wolf. He raised his arms to draw his people's attention away from the sobbing slave. "My children," the war chief cried out, "go to your homes. I have had your solace while I mourned my daughter. I thank you! But now I must find out more from this slave. You must go to your homes!"

Reluctantly the crowd began to disperse. It thinned slowly. Spit chased a small boy away from where he had tried to hide behind some large baskets. The boy dodged the slave and ran off after his parents.

"They've gone," said Fighting Wolf. Haina's brothers and sister remained. All of them, especially Crab Woman, wore grim faces. "Let us question the slave."

Chance nodded. Spit and Squashedface took up guard duty—one at the main door, the other at the juncture of the next neighbor's quarters.

Privacy assured, Fighting Wolf, Sarita and Chance turned to the groveling slave.

"What do you know, slave?" asked Chance. "Who is this woman?"

The slave wrapped his hands around Chance's bare feet. He continued to sob into the dirt floor and Chance waited patiently for the man's sobs to stop. After all, he himself had only ceased his own sobs upon hearing that the body was not Haina's. Now this poor slave—lover or husband or father that he was—must suffer the grief that Chance had felt for only a short while.

Chance touched the man's head. "Get up," he said kindly. "There is no need to prostrate yourself in front of me. You are in no danger."

Sarita murmured encouragingly also and the man, peering at the nobles watching him, straightened. He slowly unwound himself from the floor and rose to his feet.

He was shorter than Chance, thin, his ribs standing out in slight relief. His plain kutsack was worn and thin. His body looked to be lean and trim. No doubt his masters kept him working too hard for any fat to amass on him. His face was prematurely lined, no doubt from the hard life a slave led, but he seemed healthy enough.

"Where are you from?" began Chance.

"Kyuquot," the slave answered.

His answer was a surprise to his listeners. "Kyuquot? Do you recognize him, son-in-law?" asked Fighting Wolf.

"He looks familiar," admitted Chance. "What is your name? Who is your master?"

"My name is Guts."

"Guts? Is that all?" asked Sarita kindly. It was not much of a name, even for a slave.

"Sometimes my master calls me Fish Guts."

Sarita hid a smile. "I see. Thank you, Guts."

"Who is your master?" asked Chance again. Was it his imagination or was the man reluctant now to say anything?

Guts looked at the floor. "My master," he said sullenly, "is named Raven's Feather."

"Ah, a cousin of Throws Away Wealth. A distant cousin, but a cousin nonetheless," murmured Chance. "You lived in his longhouse, then?"

Guts nodded sullenly. Chance began to suspect that if he did not get his information quickly Guts would close his mouth altogether. He pressed, "Who is the woman?" and pointed to the bed.

Tears formed in the slave's eyes as he met Chance's gaze. "She is—was—my mistress," he choked out. "We —we hoped to marry." His voice trailed off in a bitter little sigh and Chance nodded, saying nothing. There was nothing to say. Sometimes slaves were allowed to marry, sometimes they were not. It all depended on their master's wishes.

"How did she get here?" Chance continued the interrogation.

Guts shook his head. "I don't know."

When it was clear the slave was going to volunteer nothing else, Chance prodded him onwards. "How did you get here then?"

"I hid in one of the freight canoes bringing the wedding gifts." Guts looked wildly about now and

Chance was surprised at the fear that emanated from the man. "I—I had to get away from Kyuquot." He saw Chance glance questioningly and explained, "Because of what I'd heard. I knew they could kill me for it."

"Wait, wait," Chance tried to stop the flow of words. "Who would kill you? What did you hear? Start at the beginning."

The man took a deep breath. "The woman on the bed is—was—Sea Cucumber. I loved her. She loved me. We wanted to marry. But it could never be." Here Guts gave a ragged sob. "Her father would not let us. He hated her. He never let her have anything she wanted. She wanted me. We were careful. We never let him see us together."

"Her father? How could a slave have such power over his daughter as to prevent her marrying?" asked Chance.

Guts snorted and again Chance thought there was bitterness in the slave's manner. "Her father was no slave."

Chance looked at Fighting Wolf. Something was wrong. "You mean," he asked carefully, "her father was a nobleman?"

Such things were not common in Nootka society, but they did happen. Occasionally it transpired that a noble father sired a child off a slave. When that happened the child took the mother's slave status. The father sometimes acknowledged the child but usually did not. Chance assumed something like that must have happened to Sea Cucumber. "Her father was a nobleman?" he asked again.

Another bitter snort. "Her father was Throws Away Wealth, your brother!" burst out Guts.

Chapter 37

Chance gaped open-mouthed at the slave. So did Fighting Wolf and Sarita. Haina's five brothers were frowning. Spit and Squashedface stared openly, caught up in the drama.

"Throws Away Wealth? My brother? Her father?"

Guts nodded. "In the village, many things happen that the nobles know nothing about. Surprised?" he asked sardonically.

Chance did not even check the man's insolence. He was in too great of a shock. He turned to the body on the bed. "Then she—she is—was my niece?" he asked incredulously.

His brain was reeling. So much had happened in such a short time and here was yet another shock. His brain felt stunned again, still sluggish as though from the rum. He cursed himself. If only he had refused the rum his brother had solicitiously pressed on him.

A strong sense of urgency swept over Chance. He *had* to find Haina. He had to get through this time and find his love again! Reason began to overpower his bewilderment.

But Guts was speaking. "Oh, she knew who *you* were. She made sure to keep out of your way. Out of her father's way, too. He sent her to a small village. To live. He did not want her around him. She might remind him."

"Remind him of what?" Chance found himself dreading the answer.

"Remind him that she was his daughter. You see, he hated her." The slave watched the nobles openly and contemptuously now. "And she hated him."

The nobles looked completely baffled, so Guts continued. "Many years ago Throws Away Wealth bought a slavewoman. He bought her after he'd been refused a rich bride. He'd been expecting to marry a rich bride."

Sarita started visibly.

"He chose the slavewoman because she looked like the bride who scorned him."

Sarita shifted uneasily. Crab Woman grunted.

"A girl child was born of their union. The slavewoman asked him to acknowledge the child as his. Mayhaps she thought her slave's lot would ease." Guts shrugged. "The Tyee refused. He still visited the slavewoman, but not as often. The woman grew desperate. Her beauty had faded. She had a child to feed and clothe. She demanded the Tyee give the girl warmer clothes, better food. Little things, but things he could easily give. If he wanted to. He refused."

Guts' audience listened enrapt. "One day when the girl, Sea Cucumber, was about seven summers, the great Tyee decided to visit at their miserable hearth. The slavewoman and the Tyee argued. The Tyee raised his hand to hit the woman. The child stepped between them to protect her mother. She received the blow meant for her mother. That blow sent her spinning into the firepit nearby. She was badly burned over half her face." Guts' chest heaved with emotion as he finished his bitter recital.

Suddenly the memory of the woman he had chased in Kyuquot popped into Chance's mind. He had seen her, the girl grown to a woman with a scarred face. His stomach churned. He had thought then that she looked like Haina. His eyes crept of their own accord to the bed. She was the same size, and he remembered from seeing the unscarred half of her face, that she did resemble Haina slightly. He shook his head. What did it all mean?

"She hated him for that," Guts was saying, "for scarring her. Hated him! He returned that hate." Guts stared at the broken body. Fresh tears ran down his face. "But I loved her. And she loved me!"

"Why wasn't she known throughout the village as Throws Away Wealth's daughter?" asked Chance. "It would seem that word would get around. . . ."

Guts snorted bitterly. "Sea Cucumber would have yelled it from the tallest tree in the village. She was not permitted to. The Tyee forbid her to tell anyone. Not even a slave. On pain of death to her mother. *That* was what kept Sea Cucumber silent. Her evil father would kill her mother." Guts shook his head. "Instead, he killed her, his own daughter."

"What?" roared Chance. "How can you say such a thing? Throws Away Wealth is not responsible for this woman's death!"

"How do you know, sir?" asked Guts softly. "Did you see?"

"No," admitted Chance, looking momentarily at the dirt floor. "I was unconscious. Did not see or hear a thing." Haina's whole family regarded him closely.

Sea Wolf said suspiciously, "How do we know you didn't kill Haina? You could have murdered her when you were drunk then forced this slave to tell us his tale. Mayhaps Haina's body is somewhere else."

Chance started. Fighting Wolf was regarding him thoughtfully, Sarita too. Indeed they all were.

"How, indeed?" muttered Chance. There was a long pause while he summoned his thoughts. How to defend himself? "I do not recall even coming to bed last night," he confessed.

"Then you would not remember murdering my sister, would you?" shot back Sea Wolf. He was angry but his brain was obviously thinking clearly. At the moment Chance envied him for that.

"I did not kill your sister," stated Chance once again. "I loved her. I would not kill her for any reason! Certainly being drunk I could not even get myself to bed, never mind subdue a screaming woman. And Haina would have screamed," he added meaningfully. "She would not let someone bludgeon her to death without screaming the whole longhouse awake."

The family digested that. Chance saw one or two of them nod and breathed a sigh of relief. Some of them believed him.

"And yet she's gone," pointed out Sea Wolf. "She did not scream the longhouse awake at all!"

The others looked at Chance. He thought quickly. "Which probably means she is still alive. Someone must have forced her to go with them—quietly."

"So they could take her away from the longhouse and kill her in the bush, or drown her," interjected Sea Wolf. "Or, mayhaps you have killed her, stowed the body, and promised this slave his freedom for a well told tale." The room was utterly silent as all present considered this possibility.

"You have wanted revenge on our family for a long time," continued Sea Wolf. "You've admitted that was your reason for stealing Haina in the first place!"

"If I wanted to kill Haina," stated Chance at last, "I would have killed her. I've had many opportunities. Why would I bring another woman, a dead one at that, into my bed and pay a man, a slave yet, to tell a wild tale? It does not make sense."

"To throw us off the track," said Sea Wolf, but his voice was uncertain.

The others watched Chance carefully for a long while. Finally Fighting Wolf nodded. "Chance speaks wisely. This," he pointed to the body on the bed, "is too sneaky. The man before us is straight-forward in his actions. I do not believe he would do it this way."

Guts smiled a bitter smile. "I would not have spoken in your defense. You know that, don't you? I hate you. You are the brother of the man who did this."

Sea Wolf's eyes narrowed at this, but he said nothing.

Chance frowned. "Twice you've said my brother is responsible for Sea Cucumber's death. That is a very serious charge. On what do you base your accusation?"

"What? You'll allow me to defend my words? You'll allow me to slander the *great* Tyee, your brother?" Guts' mocking words slid off Chance easily. He wanted too badly to get at the truth to be thrown off the scent by this man's hatred.

Guts, seeing Chance's calm refusal to rise to his taunts launched into another bitter tirade. "I overheard a gossiping woman." He turned to his listening audience. "Yes, a gossiping woman. Something so simple. So easy to let gossip go by. To pretend it meant nothing." His bitterness was back in full. "She was gossiping with her friends. They were weaving cedar hats for their rich husbands." There was a sneer in his voice. "*Her* husband was going to help the great Tyee. It was all planned. He was to go to a wedding down the coast. They did not even notice me. I must fetch their precious cedar bark back and forth. I was at their beck and call. 'Slave do this! Slave do that!' I was like a piece of furniture to them!" he snarled.

The nobles watching him said nothing, merely

waited patiently for him to continue. He would not get the fight he was looking for until *after* his tale was told, vowed Chance.

"The gossiping woman's husband was supposed to steal away the bride. *Your* bride," he said to Chance and laughed his bitter laugh. "He was to replace her with a worthless slave's body. Some female slave he was supposed to kill. He'd put her body beside the groom, who would be drugged with herbs during the celebration. It was all planned, you see."

"What did they plan for the bride?" demanded Chance.

The slave shrugged. "Don't know. They were not concerned about the bride. It was *you* they were after."

"Me?"

"Yes. You were supposed to wake up beside your dead 'bride'. The bride's family would think that you had killed her. They would kill you. All planned."

"It almost worked," observed Sea Wolf. "I was ready to kill you. I still might." He held a war lance in one hand. The leaf-shaped tip was razor-sharp. Sea Wolf's eyes looked unfriendly.

Chance glanced at him then turned his attention back to the slave.

"You lie, slave! Why would my brother want to kill me?" he demanded.

"The Tyee hates you. You are the biggest threat to his chieftainship. *You*."

Chance stared at Guts. He felt sick. The man's words had a terrible ring to them. Yet, was it the truth? Surely Throws Away Wealth would not plan such a thing against his own brother! The slave was lying, he had to be!

"Why did you not come forward with this information sooner?" demanded Fighting Wolf.

The slave shrugged. "I will not stop nobles from killing each other. I hate that family anyway." He stared hard at Chance and Chance marveled that someone could hate him so much and not even know him. Or did the slave know him?

"The problem for me," said Guts sadly and all the listeners leaned forward to hear his words, "is that I did not know 'the worthless slave' they planned to kill was Sea Cucumber." He choked as he said the words and his eyes sought the body on the bed. "I did not know, my love. I swear I did not know!"

He swung around to face his audience again. "But I tell you this: she will be avenged!" He pointed at Chance, "Either you kill the Tyee or I will!"

Guts' threat hung in the air for several heartbeats. "Though I am a slave, I still have honor. I will avenge her!"

Chance looked at him at last. "Who was she?" he asked softly.

Guts looked taken aback. "Who?"

"The gossiping wife."

Guts said a name. The look that came over Chance's face was terrible to see. It was the wife of one of his closest friends. A man whom he had trusted. So, it has come to this, he thought savagely. Grimly he nodded.

Guts saw the look and said sullenly, "I did not tell anyone in Kyuquot what I'd overheard. I would be killed if my information was wrong. Or if I told the wrong person. I snuck away and hid in a canoe loaded for the wedding. It was safer to wait and see what would happen." Seeing Chance's frown he added, "I feared for my life."

Chance looked at the body on the bed. "And she is dead because you told no one!"

Guts let out a howl—terrible to hear. The anguish in his cry startled Chance. "She is dead because your brother killed her!" howled the slave. "For no other reason!"

Chance pitied the broken man who'd lost the one thing of value in his poverty-stricken life. But he would not let pity stand in the way of the truth. "If you are lying about what you've told me, I will kill you."

Aah, that did it. Guts fairly threw himself at Chance's feet. "I am telling the truth," he cried. "I accept your bargain. I will go with you. I will accuse the Tyee. To his face. Then I will kill him!"

"There will be no more talk of killing," said Chance sternly to the man grovelling at his feet. Revenge will not help you, poor slave, thought Chance to himself. Revenge did not free me, it only got me in danger.

Aloud he said, "There has been enough killing." He looked sadly at the bed. "And if what you say is true, this has been a most pitiful murder: that of a father murdering his own child."

Guts slowly climbed to his feet. "I will go with you. Oh, do not bother to search this village," he sneered. "The Tyee is long gone." He looked at the others who were watching him warily. "He has fled back to his lair. I will go with you. But when I find the Tyee—" he looked at Chance. "I will have my revenge!"

The man's very calm shook Chance. "There will be no more talk of killing, and no more killing, do you understand?" said Chance.

Guts' eyes slid away. "I understand," answered the slave sullenly.

"And I will go with you, too," stated Sea Wolf to Chance. One hand rested on Stinky's white head. The other hand grasped his sharp war lance. Sea Wolf pounded the war lance threateningly on the packed dirt floor. "I want to see where this trail leads. And if it does not lead to my sister, then *you* die."

His black eyes on Chance's were hard. So like Haina's in shape, yet the discipline, the keenness in them was alien to Chance. Chance did not relish having a man like Sea Wolf at his back. Yet he knew he had no choice. "Very well," he agreed. "Let us find my brother. He will be the one to tell us where Haina is."

Chapter 38

They'd searched Ahousat village. At the end of the search Chance had come to stand in front of Guts. "Get into the canoe," ordered Chance. "We're leaving for Kyuquot."

"What's the matter? Couldn't find your brother?" sneered Guts.

Chance, wiping his brow, sweated in the hot midday sun. "There's no trace of him in the village."

"It is as I said," muttered the slave. "I said he would not be here. He's gone. Run away after doing his foul deeds."

"Enough. Watch your tongue."

"Another high and mighty tyee," muttered the slave, turning away to go to the canoe.

"Why are you so sure he will go to Kyuquot?" asked Sea Wolf, coming up to Chance and Guts.

"Where else would he go?" shrugged the slave. "He's safe there. Or thinks he is."

Chance concurred bleakly. "*If* he is the one responsible for the murder and Haina's disappearance, then it makes sense, yes, that he would retreat to Kyuquot. He has warriors there."

"The body's packed," observed Sea Wolf. Chance nodded. They had decided to take Sea Cucumber's remains back to Kyuquot for a proper burial. It wouldn't be much, considering her slave status, but Chance knew a proper burial would help Guts deal with his loss. Chance wondered why he bothered to do something kind for such a bitter man. Mayhaps because he'd cried over the same body, thinking it was Haina, he answered himself.

"Let us go, then." Chance saw Sea Wolf run up to the longhouse door where Fighting Wolf and Sarita stood watching the departing warriors. Sea Wolf embraced his mother and father.

Chance turned away from the scene. He did not feel he should put his departure to the test. A wave good-bye to his parents-in-law would have to suffice. At least until they knew for certain he had not killed their daughter!

As Chance walked down to the canoes, Spit and Squashedface passed by Fighting Wolf's family gathered at the longhouse door. They trotted after Chance.

"You two!" called out Fighting Wolf. "Where do you think you're going?"

Spit and Squashedface stopped in their tracks. "We go with him, Master," explained Squashedface. "We thought that was what you wanted. . . ."

Fighting Wolf shook his head. The slaves reluctantly walked back to the longhouse. "You have been faithful and loyal slaves to me," said Fighting Wolf. "I have no doubts about your intentions. Only," and his eyes fastened on Chance's retreating back for a moment, "it is only that this is one voyage that the Kyuquot must make without your help."

The slaves watched longingly as Chance and Sea Wolf got into their canoes. Stinky crept up behind

Squashedface and kindly deigned to let the slave scratch his white head. The three stood, a tight little cluster, and watched the departing warriors until they were long out of sight.

Chance stepped into *Slider*. Mudshark was right behind him. Several more warriors helped push the canoe out into the green depths.

Sea Wolf came running up and gave the final push off to his own canoe. He then climbed over the edge and they were off.

Once on the sea, the paddlers kept to a steady rhythm. The wind was gentle. By the time evening came, they'd covered a great distance.

All day Chance had paddled and worried, worried and paddled. Where is Haina? Where is Haina? he asked again and again to the paddling rhythm. Only the slosh of the paddles answered.

By nightfall they'd found a sheltered spot to camp overnight. Nearby, a small creek ran to the sea and there was driftwood for a fire. The spot had an open view of the water so Chance and his men could see any passing canoes.

Chance staggered from the canoe and stretched his cramped muscles. He was ready to sleep on his feet.

Once their camp was set up, however, Mudshark joined him and chatted volubly about the four fish he'd caught for dinner. The others contributed little, including Sea Wolf and Whale Hunter.

When dinner was a small pile of fish bones at Chance's feet, he was ready to turn in for the night. Sheltering behind a long weathered log, he made a shallow hollow in the soft sand that was still warm from the day's sun. He filled the hollow with bracken ferns and covered himself with a single cedar mat he'd thought to bring from Ahousat. He heard Mudshark making his bed close by.

Sea Wolf had drawn first guard duty. The threat of

enemies, though unlikely, was nevertheless real. Occasional raiding parties could pass by looking for unwary travelers or unprotected villages. Chance's small party could not fight off many hostile warriors so it was better to be alert. That way, if threatened, they could fade into the bush until the enemy had paddled by.

The others had turned in and Chance thought he was the only one awake when he heard Mudshark call his name. "Do you think we'll find her?" Mudshark asked.

Chance felt his body tighten. He'd been asking himself the same question all day. "Yes," he answered at last. Then stronger, "Yes. We'll find her." Alive or dead, he did not want to say. But he would find her, no matter if the search took the rest of his life, he vowed.

"Chance?" came Mudshark's whisper a little while later out of the darkness.

"Mmmm?"

"I—I regret what's happened to Haina. I wish it hadn't happened this way—Haina missing, Sea Cucumber dead, your brother suspected of murder. . . . Not exactly the wedding we were expecting, cousin."

"My brother's innocent," hissed Chance. "He did not do this foul thing!"

"No? Then why are we running back to Kyuquot?" Mudshark's voice was carefully neutral.

Chance hesitated. "Because there are no other choices," he offered at last. "No one else came forward, only Guts. We have to investigate his story. We cannot dismiss it."

"No, we cannot," agreed Mudshark softly.

"And because," continued Chance, "Haina's whole family thinks I did it."

"Not all of them," protested Mudshark.

Chance snorted. "Wake up, cousin. Every one of them thinks I murdered her. As long as suspicion rests on my brother, or my own family, I am obliged to confront him."

"What are you going to do when your brother says he did not kill Sea Cucumber or steal Haina away?"

There was a long silence. "I don't know," answered Chance unhappily. "I must find out the truth, somehow."

"Oh no, cousin. I thought you said your brother was innocent. Now you're considering that he might have done what Guts says."

"No, I'm not," snapped Chance. "He is innocent. I just want to be certain, that's all."

Mudshark heard the doubt in Chance's voice and smiled into the night. "Where's Beachdog?" he asked conversationally.

"Gone," said Chance tersely. "Like the dog he's named for, he ran when the trouble began."

"Are you sure, cousin?" He paused. "You know it's strange that so many Kyuquots left that wedding in the middle of the night. There was Throws Away Wealth, Beachdog, Dog Shadow. . . ."

"Dog Shadow? The slave?"

"The slave that picked up the heavy rock. The one that made the Ahousats look foolish."

"Oh, yes, him. He's strong. He's my brother's slave," mused Chance. "I wonder . . ." He left unsaid what he wondered but Mudshark heard him tossing and turning well into the night.

On the first night of his married life he should be pleasuring his wife, thought Chance sadly. Not chasing after her possible murderer.

For only to himself could Chance admit that perhaps his brother, the man who had housed and fed him when he was but a child, the man to whom he'd given every loyalty owing a chief and a brother, the difficult man whom he had loved as a brother, that same man may indeed have murdered his beloved Haina.

And in so admitting, Chance found himself staring into the dark hole of his own soul. Alone.

Chapter 39

Chance stopped paddling and wiped his forehead with the back of his hand. Kyuquot village at last! He signalled the paddlers to slow their pace. No one was standing on the beach to welcome him. Not that he really expected it. But some sign of activity would have been reassuring.

"They don't expect us," he observed, turning his head to address his companions.

Mudshark merely grunted.

Guts, sitting in the stern was eyeing Chance's middle. Chance followed his stare and realized the slave was showing a keen interest in the knives tucked into his belt. He shifted, hiding the weapons from view. He must remember not to trust the slave. Guts had not given up thoughts of revenge.

Whale Hunter plucked his paddle out of the water and pointed to the beach with it. Chance followed his direction and saw a slave dart into the longhouse.

"Well, if they didn't know we were here before, they do now," Whale Hunter observed.

Soon the canoe gently came to rest on a patch of

sand amidst the gravel strewn beach. Whale Hunter jumped out, Mudshark beside him. The others unloaded quickly, Chance was last to debark.

I don't want to do it, he thought. I don't want to go up there and accuse my brother of murder, of hiding my wife away, of possibly murdering her, too.

Then pictures of Haina filled his mind's eye. Where was she? Was she somewhere frantically calling for him? Was she dying somewhere, alone and injured? The thought of her like that strengthened his resolve. He didn't want to confront his brother, but he must. He had no choice. He must find Haina, Haina who loved him, trusted him. He was now her only hope—*if* she was still alive.

Grimly he marched up the beach. The others fell into place behind him.

To Chance's surprise, Throws Away Wealth stepped outside his longhouse and came forward. He walked down to the beach to meet Chance's party just as they approached the sandy part of the upper beach.

"Hail the returning groom!" cried Throws Away Wealth. "What brings you back so soon? And without your bride?" He smiled in greeting and Chance's heart plummeted. His brother was innocent of the crimes charged against him. Chance knew it.

Before Chance could open his mouth, Guts darted in front of him and faced the bewildered Throws Away Wealth. "You know what brings us here," snarled the slave ferociously. "We're here to kill you!"

"Is this correct?" Throws Away Wealth addressed Chance almost amusedly. "Does this slave speak for you?"

Chance heard the sneer in his brother's voice and was ashamed that Guts had spoken so. "We've returned to—"

But Guts was not done, not at all. "You plotted murderer!" screamed the slave. "You killed my woman!"

Throws Away Wealth looked properly taken

aback. "What woman? What are you talking about?" His eyes had narrowed and he was no longer amused. He turned to Chance. "Explain why you've allowed this slave to insult me, your Tyee."

Several people had run out of the longhouse. They gathered around, curious to see and hear what was going on. Chance spied Beachdog and a slow grin crossed the other's face. Chance felt the blood rush to his face at the insolence of the man and he turned to his brother.

"Haina is gone," he said tersely. "She has disappeared from Ahousat."

"Surely you don't think that *I* had anything to do with such a thing?" asked Throws Away Wealth reproachfully.

"I—"

"You bastard!" cried Guts. "You arranged it all! I know of your plan. You killed Sea Cucumber! You planted her dead body in Chance's bed!" A murmur went through the watching crowd.

"Chance?" Throws Away Wealth's voice was soft. He controlled his anger. Chance had not witnessed his brother's control often. But then Chance's eyes moved to Beachdog. Chance saw an expression of fear cross that one's face.

"Sea Cucumber? What are you talking about? I know of no Sea Cucumber." Throws Away Wealth was openly chuckling, confident in what he was saying.

There was some jostling behind him. An old woman had pushed her way to the front of the watching crowd. She marched up to the tyee. Her kutsack was in tatters, her hair long and scraggly. She was thin, her arms and legs like sticks. She was obviously a slave. Chance had seen her about the village and had never given her a thought.

"Sea Cucumber?" she said and her voice cracked and shook. "Sea Cucumber? Where is she? Speak up!"

Guts turned to her. For the first time, Chance saw a softening in the man. "Old mother," said Guts. "Sea

Cucumber is dead." The old woman was looking at him.

"That's all very fine," interrupted Throws Away Wealth. "But this has nothing to do with me. You slaves carry on your conversation down the beach." To Chance, he smiled and beckoned, "Why not come up to my fireside and have a meal?"

Chance took a step.

"No," cried Guts. "You lying murderer. You go nowhere!"

He was ready to launch himself at the tyee, but Chance grabbed the slave's thin arm and held him back. "Enough," he whispered. "I know you are distraught, but this is the way to certain death. Stop insulting the Tyee! I will question him."

"You?" sneered the slave. "You're too afraid of your all-powerful brother to accuse him of the truth!"

The slave's words stung. Chance gritted his jaw and clenched Guts' arm harder.

"Speak up," the old woman was saying. "I can't hear you."

Guts said, more loudly, "Sea Cucumber is dead. Your daughter is dead!"

"Aaiiieeeee!"

Whatever Chance was about to say was drowned out by the old slave women's sudden keening.

"My daughter! My daughter's dead!" shrieked the old woman. She pulled at her already tattered clothes, and yanked at her bedraggled hair as if she would tear it from the very roots. "My babyyyyy! Aaiieeee!"

The old woman threw herself against Guts, blindly grabbing at him. "Help me, help me, my daughter is dead!" she cried.

Guts carefully removed Chance's fist from his arm. The slave gently took the old woman in his arms and again Chance was moved by the compassion he showed the poor, bedraggled creature. " 'Tis done, old mother," he crooned. "Naught can be done to help her now." He patted the old woman's back and she cried into his ragged kutsack. "She's lost to us now," murmured Guts. The old woman seemed to find his actions comforting for her sobs began to quiet.

"What—what happened?" she asked between sobs. Guts lifted his head and stared hard at the watching noblemen. He focused on Throws Away Wealth as he said in a loud voice, "That man, her father, killed her!"

The old woman clearly heard him for she shrieked again. "Aaiieeee!"

Then she launched herself at Throws Away Wealth before the astonished eyes of the onlookers. "You accursed father!" she screamed. "I detest you! I rue the day I ever let you into my bed!"

Throws Away Wealth reacted by distastefully removing the old woman's claw-like fingers from his fur-lined kutsack and brushing her off him. "Get away from me, you old crone!"

"Never!" she cried. "I'll haunt you 'til the day I die!"

"That will be today," said Throws Away Wealth almost pleasantly. "Guards!"

Two slaves came running. "Take this—this woman," he sneered, "and drown her." He gestured to Guts. "Drown *him,* too."

The watching people tittered at the pitiful scene. Chance, however, did not feel like laughing. He wanted to scream his agony to the sky, for now he had a horrible premonition that what Guts had claimed was true. This old woman was Sea Cucumber's mother. And his brother, the brother of his heart, Throws Away Wealth, whom he thought he knew, was Sea Cucumber's father.

"Wait!" Chance ordered. "These people have a right to be heard."

"No, they don't. They're only slaves!" shot back the tyee.

Chance turned to the old slave woman. "Who is the father of your daughter?" he asked.

The old woman raised her finger and pointed at Throws Away Wealth. "He is," she said, and both her finger and voice shook.

"Lies," said Throws Away Wealth. He watched Chance with a strange smile. "Surely you won't take the word of a slave over *my* word." And he smiled, supremely confident.

Chance stared at his brother, willing his brother to tell the truth. He had come to a dead end in his questioning. It was a slave's word against a nobleman's. There was no doubt who to believe.

He was about to agree when a movement at the edge of the crowd caught his eye. He paused and watched Throws Away Wealth's first wife, that gray creature of the shadows that he never really knew, make her way slowly to the front of the crowd. Strange how he'd never noticed her dignity before. But then there were many things he'd never noticed before, he thought bitterly.

"I come forward," said the tyee's first wife.

Throws Away Wealth looked at her in surprise, as if astonished that she'd have the nerve to enter the fray.

"I come forward," the first wife repeated and her voice rose, "to say that this woman," she pointed to the old slave woman who watched her out of squinting eyes, "is the mother of Sea Cucumber."

The watching crowd was silent. No one stirred. "And this man," the first wife pointed at Throws Away Wealth, "is the father of Sea Cucumber."

Everyone was frozen, watching the tyee. At last Throws Away Wealth seemed to snap out of his trance, "Why?" he asked and there was a plaintive note in his voice. "Why did you tell him?"

His faded old wife looked at him and said, "Because I have watched you work your evil on people for as long as I can stand. It is time that others know the truth of what you are."

Then, with great dignity, she turned her back on him and walked slowly back to her longhouse. The people in the crowd parted respectfully for her to pass.

The crowd was silent. Chance stood, stunned. There was almost a quiet in his mind now that he knew for certain. "So, my brother?" he said to his brother softly and those watching had to lean forward to catch his words. "So it is true. You are Sea Cucumber's father. I think, then," he said deliberately, "that the rest of what Guts has told me is also true—that you planned her death and that you are responsible for Haina's disappearance." The statement hung in the air.

Throws Away Wealth was still staring after the wake of his old first wife. He shook his head, baffled. "All those years," he muttered. "She never said anything in all those years. Why now?"

Then he turned on Chance and when he did his anger was monumental. "It is true," he snarled, and Chance saw himself looking into the face of a raging mountain lion. "It is true. I have loathed and hated you for years." He threw up his arms and addressed those listening. "This man is not my brother. He is not even Indian! Look at him: white skin, pale hair. And he calls himself my brother! Hah!" He spat, full on the ground and narrowly missed Chance's bare foot. "I call upon you, my faithful Kyuquot people, to drive this man out of our tribe. He is not one of us. He never was!"

The tyee waited, but no one moved. The men and women watching looked bemused. "Let us hear more," came a man's voice from the back of the crowd.

"Attack him, I say!" cried Throws Away Wealth. "He will destroy us!"

No one moved.

A woman said in a loud voice, "Chance helped me when I had little food. He made his brother share the fish."

"He settled an argument with my neighbor," said a man. "We are friends again. I do not think he is destroying us."

Several loud comments bounced back and forth as the watching people discussed the situation. No one stepped forward to help the tyee.

"Seize him!" screamed Throws Away Wealth.

None of his warriors moved. Beachdog shuffled closer to the tyee but that was it.

Throws Away Wealth looked around at his people. He was in a fury. Spittle clung to his lips, he was so angry. "I had your precious woman stolen, yes!" he screamed. "I did it! I had the useless slave woman killed and put in your bed. You should have been killed for the murder of your bride!" More spittle flecked his lips. "I loathe you! You will never be chief of the Kyuquots! Only I!"

"I've never desired to be chief," said Chance. His voice was low, his manner calm.

"You don't fool me!" cried Throws Away Wealth. "I saw how the people fawned on you, asking you for this, asking you for that! I know you wanted to be chief! But I will not let you," and there was a strange gleam in the tyee's eyes. "Oh, no. I will destroy you— before it is too late. Just like I destroyed the woman who called herself my daughter!"

"She *was* your daughter, you murdering fool!" screamed the old slavewoman.

"She wasn't!" screamed the tyee. "She was but a slave. Like you. Like all these people. Mere slaves for me to toy with, to play with, to do with as I please!" He stood, his chest heaving with his panting breath, he was so overcome with emotion. "I am chief!" he cried. His words echoed in the stillness following his tirade. People stood as though struck dumb with fascination at their tyee's revelation.

Then Throws Away Wealth peeled off his kutsack. Around his waist hung his single sharp knife. "And now," he announced, not taking his eyes from Chance, "I will kill you!"

Taken aback, Chance could only stare at his brother. That moment of pause worked against him. Knife drawn, Throws Away Wealth launched himself at Chance.

The smaller man crashed into Chance knocking him off balance. Because he fell, he narrowly missed the knife blade intended for his heart. "Stop," gasped Chance. "Do not do this. We are brothers!"

"We are not brothers," snarled the tyee. Chance continued to stay in the dirt on one knee. "Get up and fight," snarled the older man. When Chance shook his head, distraught, the tyee screamed, "Fight!"

"I will not. You are my brother."

"So you won't fight me because I'm your brother, is that it?" cried the older man, a crafty gleam entering his eye. "Then fight me for what I've done to your wife!"

Those words crashed through Chance's brain. "Haina!" he cried, "Where is she?"

"Where you'll never find her!" laughed the tyee. "Never, never, never!"

"Where is she? What have you done with her?" Chance was becoming frantic. How could he have forgotten Haina in all this?

"Aah, that's better," purred Throws Away Wealth waving his knife in the air as Chance got to his feet. "Now we'll fight!"

"Where is she?" Chance was holding himself back with great difficulty.

Throws Away Wealth only laughed, a maniacal sound.

"Where is she?" The great slumbering beast in Chance was roused at last. "What have you done with her?"

Throws Away Wealth threw back his head and laughed. "Oh, this is too rich. You'll never get her now." He waved his knife in the air again. "She's on a ship. A trading ship. She's to be sold as a slave to the Tlingit Indians!"

Chapter 40

Something inside Chance snapped when he heard those words. The Tlingit Indians were a fearsome people far to the north. Haina would not survive even one day as a slave to them. Everything in Chance cried out at the thought of the woman he loved a victim of the dreaded Tlingits and the slave traders. It could not be! It could not be!

Throws Away Wealth was laughing openly, tauntingly. "She's dead, you bastard," he chortled. "You'll never catch her in time. Those woman-hungry sailors will eat her up! And what the sailors don't do, the Tlingits will!" and he went off into another burst of laughter.

Yes, victim she would be, Chance thought frantically. The white men on the trader's ship would have their way with her first. By the time she reached Tlingit territory—if she survived long enough—she'd be in terrible condition. Chance felt sick imagining the likes of Layverley or one of the other brutes, raping a helpless Haina. A picture of her, cowering and beaten on the deck of the ship rose in his mind's eye.

"No!" he roared.

"Yes!" crowed Throws Away Wealth, jumping about. "Yes!"

Finally, so excited he could no longer control himself, Throws Away Wealth launched himself at Chance. The sharp point of his knife was aimed at Chance's stomach.

"Look out!" Whale Hunter's warning came too late.

Throws Away Wealth's body hit him.

"Oof!" Chance fell heavily to his knees. A red streak of blood appeared on his naked upper arm. Throws Away Wealth's knife had missed his stomach but had still drawn blood.

The smaller man was on top of Chance's back now, one arm around Chance's throat, knife ready for the downward stroke.

"Fight back!" It was Sea Wolf's voice this time.

Chance reached around and grabbed the tyee's knife hand, twisted it and pulled sharply. Throws Away Wealth screamed and went flying over Chance's head to land face down in the dirt.

Panting, Chance got up from one knee, now two. He was on his feet, legs braced and facing his opponent. He was unarmed.

"Use your knives!" someone yelled.

Chance shook his head. This was his brother. He would not kill him, regardless of what the crowd or his brother wanted him to do. He waited, poised to resist Throws Away Wealth's next attack. He'd have to keep moving, keep away from the knife. Mayhaps he could wear the tyee out before either of them could come to harm. The tyee was older, would tire sooner. But the knife gave him the extra advantage.

Throws Away Wealth was on his feet, knife out and weaving. Chance watched his eyes.

"I'm going to kill you," gritted the older man.

He stepped forward and feinted to the left. Chance stepped back.

Then Throws Away Wealth lifted the knife to face height and ran at his surprised opponent. Screaming dire threats, the tyee stabbed at Chance.

Chance pushed the knife hand away and turned, rolled up and under the running tyee and came up with the smaller man kicking and screaming on his back. Chance held on to him by both arms. He heaved him into the dirt again and swung round to face his adversary once more.

Throws Away Wealth scrambled to his feet and faced Chance, his chest heaving. He took a step forward, his eyes widened, and he fell face down into the dirt.

A war lance stuck straight up from his back. His body jerked in the dirt, then lay still.

Chance stood, stunned. "Who—?"

The shocked crowd stared at Throws Away Wealth. Dark red blood pooled on his back and dripped down his ribs.

No one moved. No one said a word.

Guts stood defiantly at the front of the crowd. "I did it," he said, stalking over to the body. He stood, legs braced, over Throws Away Wealth. Then he spat on the naked, bloody back. Guts wiped his mouth with the back of his hand. "I did it," he said again into the silence. "He deserved it."

Then Guts walked away.

Beachdog ran after him. Benumbed, Chance watched them go.

Sea Wolf smiled obliquely. Chance realized then that the war lance belonged to the Ahousat. Sea Wolf shrugged. "He grabbed it out of my hand," he said. Chance shook his head, trying to make sense of the words.

"He's alive!" shrieked a woman in the crowd.

Chance whirled. Throws Away Wealth flexed the fingers of one hand, grasping at the gravel. Suddenly he reached around and began pulling at the lance in his back. He groaned as he tore at the weapon impaling him.

Chance ran to Throws Away Wealth and kneeled beside him. He was alive! "Stop! Stop!" he cried. In his agony to remove the lance, the tyee was further injuring himself.

Chance glanced up and saw the still, silent crowd watching him. "Get away!" he roared at them. "Go to your homes! I would be with my brother. Alone!"

"As you will, Tyee." He heard the murmur, but it made no sense to him.

To a slave, Chance ordered, "Fetch the shaman."

"At once, sir." The slave hurried off.

The crowd, urged on by Mudshark and Whale Hunter, moved slowly away. Chance was left alone with his brother at last.

With great care, he tugged at the lance. Throws Away Wealth screamed. Chance didn't know what to do. Finally, he stood, gritted his teeth and snapped the spear haft off as close to his brother's body as he dared. The tyee screamed and fainted. As gently as he could, Chance rolled the wounded man over onto his side. He supported the tyee's lolling head.

Throws Away Wealth's eyelids flickered. He moaned. "B-B—Beachdog?" he croaked.

"Hush, it is Chance. Do not try to talk. We will have the shaman help you. You will get better, soon. You will see." Chance was babbling, but he couldn't help it. This was his brother whom, despite everything, he loved.

Throws Away Wealth moaned.

The tyee's first wife appeared, more like a gray wraith than ever. She wore an old fur robe wrapped around her. She sank to the dirt beside the dying tyee. He was unaware of her.

Many thoughts hammered at Chance's reeling mind. His brother had hated him, hated him and sought to destroy him. He'd stolen Haina and sent her into the worst fate he could think of: slavery. He'd disowned, then murdered his own daughter. And all for what? Chance must know.

"Why?" he asked aloud. "Why did you do it, my brother?" Chance himself was not even sure to what he referred, there were so many things his brother had done. Still, he must ask the question. "Why did you try to hurt me so much?"

"Because I hate you," came the gasp from Throws Away Wealth's throat. Blood dribbled from a corner of his tight mouth.

Chance leaned closer to hear the whispered words. "You had nothing to fear from me," he murmured into the dying man's ear.

Throws Away Wealth gave a desperate croak, meant as a laugh, no doubt. "You wanted . . . everything. . . ." gasped Throws Away Wealth. "You wanted . . . chieftainship. . . ." He laughed again, a ragged croak torn from his chest. "I . . . tried . . . kill you. . . . Beachdog . . . Yuquot . . . missed . . . too bad . . ."

Chance stared at his brother. Throws Away Wealth had tried to have him killed. At Yuquot. Chance's lips set in a grim line. All these years his brother had hated him, wanted him dead. And he, he had admired and worshipped and sought to win his brother's love. What a pitiful hope! A terrible pain settled in his chest at the thought.

"But I—I loved you," he cried out to Throws Away Wealth. "I loved you like a brother!"

"Don't . . . lie . . . me!" snarled Throws Away Wealth, his voice stronger. "I'm dying . . . Do . . . honor . . . tell truth. . . ."

"I am telling you the truth," cried out Chance. It was crucial that his brother believe him before he crossed the Veil to the Land of the Dead. "I never sought to hurt you. I was content with what I had!"

Throws Away Wealth pushed himself slowly up on one elbow. His face contorted in pain and more blood trickled from his mouth.

It would not be long now, Chance knew. Still, he

did not want his brother to die with this hate, this terrible loss between them.

Slowly Throws Away Wealth opened his eyes. He stared at Chance and Chance, mesmerized, stared back.

"Swear . . . me . . ." the tyee gasped, ". . . tell truth. . . ."

Chance took a deep breath. "I swear to you," he intoned. "I loved you. I never sought your power, your lands. I loved you!" He reached out to touch his brother's shoulder to convince him. It was the touch that did it.

"No!" cried out Throws Away Wealth and it was a terrible cry, wrenched from the bottom of his soul. "No . . .! It . . . cannot . . . be . . .! Lies . . .!"

Chance held his dying brother close to him. He focused on the old face through blurred tears, and said, "Look at me. Hear my truth. You are dying. I, and the old woman, are here. No others to hear my words. I will tell you the truth."

Chance wiped his eyes. "There is something I wanted of yours," he admitted at last.

". . . knew . . . it. . . ." croaked Throws Away Wealth feebly.

"I wanted your love, your admiration. That is what I wanted from you. I loved you. I raided Ahousat so you would admire me, and be proud of me. You are my brother. You took me in when I was but a child. I was always grateful. I wanted to give back to you some of the care you'd given me. I honored you, as my brother and as my tyee. I wanted your love, not your lands, not your people! Your love, that is all." He stared hard into the dying man's eyes, willing him to believe the truth at last.

A tear started in Throws Away Wealth's eye. "Love . . .? can't . . . see . . . blind . . . Come closer. . . ."

Chance leaned closer to the dying man.

Clawed hands grabbed for Chance's neck. The

gnarled fingers tried to squeeze. ". . . kill . . . you . . ." rasped the dying chief.

"Uuh," choked Chance. He tore the grasping fingers from his throat.

Suddenly, eyes wide, mouth agape, the old man half-rose. He clawed and batted at the air. "No . . .!" he screamed. "Keep . . . away . . . from . . .! Don't . . . let . . . them . . . me . . .! Noooooo!"

His dying scream sent chills down Chance's back.

Then the tyee went limp. Chance held the lifeless body for some time. Silent tears drifted down his cheeks. Tears for the hate right to the end. Tears for what might have been if only so much hate and anger and jealousy had not intervened. His brother—such a loss, of love, of life itself.

Chance slowly lowered the body to the ground. "He has gone," he said to the old woman who kept her silent vigil. "He has gone—" Chance's voice broke. "I know not where." The tyee's last moments invaded his mind and he felt sickened.

The old woman started a death dirge. Slow, and moaning, at first, her voice climbed the notes sorrowfully. Chance stood up.

The shaman arrived. "Stand back," he ordered briskly. "I am here to see to the injured man."

"You are too late, my friend," said Chance sadly. "Far too late."

He walked slowly towards the longhouse. He turned, just before the door, and looked back. The shaman was walking away, leaving the old woman alone beside the body of the dead man. She sat there, a solid figure for once, and the mournful notes of the death song rose and fell in the still air.

Chance turned and entered the building. It was over.

Chapter 41

It was over, Chance thought again. His whole body felt weak, lifeless. All the good, all the bad, all the hate, all the love, all the turmoil—gone. Now all he felt was numbness. It was over.

Except for Haina, warned a little voice in his mind.

"She needs you," said Mudshark, materializing at his side.

"How long have you been standing there?" asked Chance.

"Long enough," his cousin answered.

"It's too tragic," murmured Chance. "Such a waste—of life, of loyalty." He went over and sat down by the fire. His whole body slumped. He stared morosely into the fire.

Mudshark brought over some smoked clams. "Eat," he urged.

Chance turned his head away. "I'm not hungry." He watched the sparks rise from the wood. Heard the snap of the branches as they burned. "One night," he muttered to Mudshark. "One night I'll give myself to mourn him. Then tomorrow I'll find Haina."

Mudshark grunted. He had squatted by the fire and was using a long stick to poke at the already blazing wood. "If you wait out the night," he said slowly, "you may be too late."

Chance looked at him. Life sparked in his eyes. "You think so?"

Mudshark eyed his cousin speculatively. "Mmm-hmm. I think so. Don't you?" When Chance didn't answer, Mudshark continued, "The traders have her now. Their ships can sail in a day the distance a canoe would take two days to cover."

When Chance still didn't say anything, Mudshark continued, "If we go after her tonight, we have a hope of catching up with her. If we wait until tomorrow—" he shrugged eloquently.

Chance was on his feet, the knives at his belt clanging together. "Let us leave," he said. "The living are more important than the dead."

"Rather brutal, cousin," said Mudshark also getting to his feet.

"Mayhaps, but for us, it's true. My brother is dead, naught can be done for him except a decent burial. His wife can see to that. Haina," his voice broke, "Haina is still alive. We can save her."

"You hope," muttered Mudshark under his breath, but Chance was already striding out of the longhouse calling for his men.

"I have to believe that, cousin," Chance called out over his shoulder.

Mudshark hurried after Chance, pulling on his cedar cape as he went.

Chance dug his paddle further into the gray-green depths of the sea beneath his paddle. "Faster," he cried to his men. They were all with him—Whale Hunter,

Mudshark, Beachdog, cousins and friends. Sea Wolf, Haina's brother, paddled in the other canoe and had seven men with him. There were eighteen grim men in all.

The canoes picked up speed. They flew across the water, *Slider* in the lead. Chance squinted into the mist. Little did it matter if a storm was oncoming, he vowed. Nothing would stop his pursuit of Haina! He would catch the trading ship and kill everyone aboard it if he had to. He would rescue Haina and no one—no one!— would ever take her away from him again.

Such were Chance's somber thoughts as he paddled after the white man's ship that carried Haina. Though he had not seen the ship, other Indians along the coastal route had. Chance had stopped at three different villages to question them. He estimated that the trading ship was a day's paddle ahead of him.

"What are you going to do with the slave?" It was Beachdog, breaking in upon Chance's thoughts.

"Which slave?"

Beachdog gave a low chuckle. "Where are you, Chance?" With hooded gaze, he studied the blond leader. "That slave," he said, jerking his thumb over his shoulder without turning around.

Guts sat in the stern. He was paddling, but only one stroke for every four that the others paddled. His face was set in its familiar sullen pattern. Chance sighed.

"Oh, him. I have not yet made up my mind. Do not press me." It was a sore point between them.

"I think we should kill him. I would have done it right after he speared Tyee if Mudshark had not stopped me." Now Beachdog was the sullen one.

Chance grimaced with fatigue. First the emotional onslaught of Haina's disappearance, then the tragic death of his brother coupled with his fear for Haina's current plight, and now the physical exertion of paddling after the white man's ship—all these events were taking their toll on his strength.

He turned to face Beachdog. "I said I would decide what would happen to him after I find Haina. Leave it at that." His tone was curt and Beachdog subsided.

"I still think we should kill him," Chance heard Beachdog mutter. Chance decided to ignore the comment.

But now Guts jumped into the conversation. "He wants me dead because I know too much," he snarled.

Chance rolled his eyes heavenward.

"He killed Dog Shadow—"

"Silence!" Beachdog barked the order and Guts shrank back. Beachdog turned back to his paddling.

"I know whose dog he is—"

Beachdog jumped to his feet in the canoe, almost tipping men and craft into the cold sea. He aimed his paddle right at Guts' mouth and would have shoved it in had not Chance laid a restraining hand on Beachdog's quivering arm.

"Enough! Leave the slave alone. He is mine to do with as I decree." Chance's stern voice seemed to drive some reason back into Beachdog. He paused. Then slowly, slowly he sat back down.

Before Beachdog took up his paddle again he shot such a deadly look at Guts that the slave was silent for the remainder of the day.

Indeed all that was heard was the creaking of the canoe and the splash of paddles as the men stroked their way north. They kept to a route offshore, careful not to stray too close to land where jagged rocks hid just beneath the surface.

At least the weather was with him, thought Chance. The mist was a nuisance, true, but it would also slow down their quarry. Chance and his men could paddle swiftly through the fog-shrouded waves while the sailing ship would be forced to tack slowly or wait in some quiet bay until the mists receded.

"Faster," he yelled to his men and the man at the back of the canoe beat his paddle in a quicker tempo. "Faster!"

Chapter 42

They'd taken her on board the *Lady Boston* at a big village called Kyuquot. Daniel had traded with the tyee there before a few times and had done well enough. Sometimes he got the better deal, sometimes the tyee did. All to be expected in the course of trading, he knew.

But this was different. He hadn't liked it when the tyee—a skinny, shifty-eyed son-of-a-bitch if he'd ever seen one—clambered on board the ship in the middle of the night with one of his shifty-eyed warriors. They'd pushed the girl at him and Daniel had asked, as best he could in the Nootka language, What the hell they expected him to do with her?

The tyee had hemmed and hawed about. Daniel's suspicions had been raised and he called Burns over to size up the situation. "What do you make of it, Burns?" he'd asked after the chief had done his jumping up and down and arm waving and was standing there waiting for an answer.

"Och, somethin' isna' right, Cap'n," Burns had

replied.

Now Captain Daniel Jasper stood looking at the girl on deck. Burns had been correct. Something was not right, but Daniel had not been able to figure out what.

The girl was standing, head up proudly, though he couldn't see much of her in the dark. She was quiet, too.

Had she perhaps been the tyee's mistress and he'd grown tired of her? But what would explain the tyee's demand—not request but demand, mind you—that the girl be traded to the Tlingit Indians farther up the coast? Everyone knew the Tlingits were mean and ornery. They'd made short work of this girl, Daniel knew.

After the tyee had left she'd sat there on a coiled rope on deck. She had cried quietly into her sleeve. Daniel supposed it was that as much as anything about her that made him feel sympathy for her.

When some of the sailors had approached her— "for a wee look, cap'n"—she'd raised scornful eyes to their hopeful faces and driven them away with sneers.

Cocky little thing, thought Daniel. But she looked like she'd been dragged through the mud, sitting there in a ragged old cedar dress of some sort. One of the sailors had given her a wet cloth and she'd used it to clean her face and hands. She was rather pretty under all that dirt and grime.

He wondered how she'd ended up in the tyee's clutches. He shook his head—some girls just wanted the power and prestige of a high ranking lover—even if he was a mean old son-of-a-bitch.

Daniel prided himself on not normally taking slaves to trade up and down the coast, though that was the sneaky practice of a half dozen other traders he could name. Daniel was as happy as the next captain to make a goodly profit, but he turned his face away from human trafficking, a trade that made his stomach churn. He was just weak, he supposed.

But this young Indian woman, the set of her jaw, her aristocratic-looking little nose, her dignified carriage, he didn't know quite what, but something about her had made him make an exception this one time.

And now he stood on deck rocking back and forth on his heels and toes while he looked over his "exception." She'd been with them almost a day now, since late last night. In that time she'd managed to keep his sailors at bay with a few sneering words and well, it was not to be believed, but it was rumored she'd punched one of the men. Up and punched him for trying to give her a kiss. So far no one had complained to him, nor were they likely to, he chuckled to himself. What man would admit—to his captain especially— that he'd been driven from the arms of a comely maiden by the force of her blows?

But she did present a problem, he continued to muse. She was young, pretty—now that he looked closely he could see she was very pretty—and alone. Deserted by the old chief who should have stood by her after knocking her up—yes, Daniel had seen the little rounded tummy when she'd stood in profile looking forlornly out at the waves. Knocked her up, he had, the old son-of-a-bitch.

And now here was Daniel, God-fearing man that he was, expected to deliver her up to the charms of the vile Tlingits. He shook his head. What a world.

"What are ye gonna do wit' her, Cap'n?" It was old Burns, reading his thoughts as usual.

Daniel swung to the man at his side and grinned. "Make a nice little bed warmer, wouldn't she?" he asked.

Burns looked at him askance.

"Just joking, Burns. Don't get your tongue tied in a knot about it." Really, Burns could be irritatingly prim.

Burns had his old notebook out and was pretending to write notes in it. But that's all it was. Pretending. At last he put his notebook away. He squinted up at the sky. "A mist comin' on," he ventured. "Best I go give the men their orders."

Daniel nodded and watched the old sailor walk away with his wide-legged, rolling gait, gained after twenty years at sea. He sighed. He supposed he walked with a fairly wide-legged gait himself. He wondered if the pretty Indian woman—she was *very* pretty—would notice.

He patted his graying hair, sucked in his stomach and walked over to the woman, careful to make it seem he was only out for a midafternoon stroll.

"Good day," he said pleasantly.

So this was the ship's tyee, thought Haina, looking up and down at the gray bearded man in the blue suit. She was sitting on a coil of rope and decided she'd stay there. She nodded carefully at the tyee, but decided she would not show him any respect. After all, he was going to sell her to the Tlingits. She'd heard her fate when Throws Away Wealth and one other warrior had dragged her onto this white man's ship. And to think she'd once been curious about these ships! No more, not her. If she ever got off this ship, she'd never step on another white man's ship as long as she lived.

She wondered if the smiling man before her had any idea of the fate he was consigning her to by selling her to the Tlingits. She almost started to cry. She would never see Chance again, though they were now married. She twisted the hair and brocade bracelet he'd given her. She'd managed to keep it when Throws Away Wealth had forced her to take off her wedding dress. They'd thrown her this old kutsack and she'd had to hold her nose just to put the dirty thing over her head. In the dark, they'd not seen the bracelet and she'd kept her arm hidden from them. Now she played with it as she wondered what the white tyee wanted.

She really was quite lovely, thought Daniel. But the smell rising from her was overpowering. Food stained the front of her dress and he wondered how she could wear such a rag. He thought of sluicing a bucket of water over her to clean her up a bit. Maybe he should give her some sailor's shirt to wear. She was small enough that it'd look like a short dress on her. He scratched his gray beard as he considered this. How to go about asking her when he really did not know much about the language?

"*Klutsma*, woman?" he ventured.

She looked at him. She continued to sit quietly watching the waves off to the side of the ship. This was getting him nowhere, thought Daniel.

His eyes ranged over her again. She seemed nervous. Who wouldn't be? he thought. She probably knows I'm going to trade her to the Tlingits. But should I? he pondered. Just because the old tyee said she had to go there doesn't mean I have to do it. The old son-of-a-bitch would never know the difference. But what could I do with her? She's far away from her people and all that she knows.

"Kyuquot?" he ventured. He hoped she'd understand he was asking if her family was there.

Haina shook her head violently. If the white tyee was asking her if she wanted to go back to Kyuquot, she'd disabuse him of *that* notion in a hurry!

Ah, good, he thought. No family in Kyuquot. Where are they then? he wondered. He thought of the places he'd visited. He pronounced the places carefully, trying for the Indian pronunciation.

"Hesquiat?"

Another shake of the head.

"Yuquot?"

Haina shook her head this time, but not so

419

vigorously. The old tyee was asking her something. But what? She was familiar with the places he was asking her, but they were all to the south. Was he asking her where she was from?

"Ohiat? Nitinaht?"

To help him, Haina said, "Ahousat."

The white tyee beamed and nodded his understanding. So she was from Ahousat. Mayhaps he should turn the ship around and take this lovely woman back to her family.

Are you crazy? asked a quiet little voice. You have a ship to run, furs to find, money to earn. Ahousat is three days travel from here. In good weather. You can't go sailing up and down the coast taking homeless young women, no matter how lovely, to their families. You have a living to earn!

As he argued with himself, Daniel let his eyes wander over the woman. She was actually beautiful, he decided.

He watched her nervously twisting the thing she wore on her arm. She feared him, poor little woman.

She fumbled at the thing, a bracelet, he supposed. It looked to be woven, cedar bark or something, hair perhaps. Red hair. Bright red hair. The kind found on whites. Did these Nootka Indians take scalps like the Iroquois Indians he'd heard about? What a gruesome little thing she was. And—was that brocade of some sort? Purple, no purple and gold brocade. Now where'd she get hold of purple brocade? Last time he'd seen something like that—"

He froze.

Then his heart started beating again.

He seized her arm and held it up. "Where did you get this?" he roared.

Haina looked at the angry white tyee holding her arm and yelling into her face. The veins on his neck stood out and his gray eyes, formerly friendly, were now cold and hostile. What had she done? She got quickly to her feet. He was hurting her arm, grasping it as tight as he was.

"The bracelet, the bracelet, where did you get this bracelet?" He was tearing at her precious gift, the bracelet Chance had given her, almost ripping it off her arm.

"No!" she cried, pulling her arm away from him. "You can't have it! It is mine!" She'd fight for the bracelet with her life, she vowed. Nothing else was left to her of Chance.

"Give it to me!" he shouted.

"No!" She screamed. He had her arm again and she clawed at his face. "Let me go!"

"Cap'n! Cap'n! What's going on?" It was Burns, panting. "I came running, Cap'n. She givin' you trouble?" The little man had a large wooden peg in one hand. He looked ready to use it in defense of his captain.

The sight of his first mate ready to beat the woman into submission brought some sanity back to Daniel. He wiped his brow and let loose the woman's arm. He'd take it slow and careful. He had to find out where she'd got that bracelet. "It's all right, Burns," he managed at last. "I—I just saw something. . . ." He stared at the woman, unable to put into words the turmoil he was feeling.

"Damme, Burns, but for the first time on this voyage, I wish I'd brought along an interpreter. I thought to save money, but now I . . ." his voice trailed off.

"Now wot, Cap'n?" prodded the old first mate when no more information was forthcoming.

Daniel sighed. He was looking at the woman. She didn't look like a killer. . . . And she was from Ahousat, wasn't she? That's what she'd told him. But Ahousat was too far south. By his reckoning it had all happened north of here. So how—?

And this girl was too young—far too young. Why, she wasn't even born when—unless—unless—oh God, —unless Eleanor had survived!

"Burns," said Daniel, and his voice was thick with what emotion Burns could not discern. "Burns, that bracelet," he pointed to the wristband Haina wore. "It's made of my sister's hair!"

"Wot?" Burns looked bewildered. It had been a long time since that day they'd talked of the captain's sister and brother-in-law and the tragic loss of his sister overboard in the storm. "Ye don't think, Cap'n, do ye, that she—?" He did not know what to say.

"Where?" asked Daniel more gently, taking Haina's wrist again. "Where did you get this?" He willed her to understand, to answer.

Haina saw the fierce light shining in the white tyee's eyes. His voice was soft, yes, but his eyes gleamed. What was he asking her? Somehow she thought the answer very important. To him and, mayhaps, to her.

"*Chekup*," she murmured at last. Would he understand that she'd received this gift from a man?

"*Chekup*," repeated Daniel thoughtfully. "Man. Why is she saying 'man'? What could she mean?"

Burns and Daniel stared at Haina. At last Burns offered, "Could be she got it from a man, Cap'n."

Daniel considered that. "Aye, possibly. A man, a man," he mused.

"*Chekup*," said Haina again. Then she said Chance's full name, in Nootka Indian.

"Wot was that, sir?" asked Burns. "That longish burst of words she just said?" He took out his everpresent notebook. He started leafing through pages. "Do I have that word in me wee book?" He turned several pages.

Haina helpfully repeated Chance's name.

Finally Burns stopped turning the well-worn pages. "Och, no," he said. "I've no heard sech a word, Cap'n."

"Never mind, Burns," answered Daniel, scratching his beard thoughtfully. "Mayhaps she was telling us it was that tyee that delivered her here? Now him I'd believe capable of taking anyone's scalp."

Burns looked at Daniel. "Scalp, sir?" he asked at last.

"Yes, Burns. I was wondering if these Indians take scalps. Like those Indians we heard about back in Boston. You know, those Iroquois Indians."

Burns regarded Haina closely. "I never heard o' sech, Cap'n," he volunteered. "In all me twenty years on the ships, I ne'er heard that these Injuns take scalps. Whole heads more likely."

"That's not reassuring, Burns."

"No, sir. It isna'."

The two continued to study Haina thoughtfully. She did not like the way they looked at her—like she was dirty, or smelly, or something.

"*Chekup*," she tried again. This time she pointed to the bracelet, then to her stomach. There, that should be obvious. The man who had given her the bracelet was the one who had given her the baby growing in her protruding stomach. It was very obvious. Would these white men understand? she wondered doubtfully. They did not seem too smart. And they could not speak her language very well, either.

"She's pointin' to 'er stomach, sir."

"Aye, she's pregnant. I noticed that earlier."

The two thought about this for awhile.

"Could mean she got the bracelet from the man who gave her the baby, Cap'n."

"Aye. Most likely." Daniel reached out a finger and stroked the bright red hair on the bracelet. "But how, how did my dear sister's hair get on this bracelet? I fear I will never know."

"How can ye be so sure it's yer wee sister's, Cap'n?"

"The brocade, Burns." Daniel held up Haina's arm for Burn's inspection. "See the puple and gold brocade that the hair is braided in with?"

Burns nodded.

"That," said Daniel triumphantly, "is brocade from my sister's wedding dress!"

Burns peered at the bracelet. "It's true that I've never seen brocade traded on this coast. . . ."

"Nor are you likely to, Burns. Traders use the cheap stuff—the cottons, twill, that sort of thing. Not the more ornate brocade." Daniel was fingering the bracelet delicately. "No, it is my sister's brocade, and my sister's hair, Burns. I am certain of it."

Haina heard the tyee's gentle tone, saw the reverence with which he touched the bright red hair on Chance's bracelet. She smiled at him. "*Klutsma*," she offered.

Daniel paused. He looked into Haina's dark eyes. "*Klutsma*?" he repeated. "How does she know this is from a woman, Burns?" He hesitated. "I wonder if she knows what happened to my sister? If the man who gave her this bracelet knows what happened to the woman with the bright red hair?"

Burns was silent.

"It's too much to hope that Eleanor is still alive after all these years," reasoned Daniel matter-of-factly. "She must have died. The question is, did she survive and live among the Indians? Or did she perhaps survive only long enough to be killed by the Indians? Did her body wash ashore and they found her and plucked her hair?" There was anguish in his voice now.

"Dinna torture yerself, Cap'n. Ye canna know. Ye'll only go mad trying to figure it out." He looked at Haina. She met his gaze guilelessly.

"This woman looks kind, sir," he said. "Perhaps her people are kind, too. Leave it at that, Cap'n. Give yerself a kind thought. Yer sister's wit' the good Lord now. She'd no be wantin' ye to be agonizin' o'er this. She's at peace. Let it be."

Something of what Burns was saying penetrated the anguished haze that Daniel was in. "You're right, Burns," he said at last. "I could drive myself mad not knowing." He gave a strange little smile.

The men were very caught up in their talk, thought Haina. She decided to clarify herself. She cupped her arms as if holding a baby. She rocked and crooned to the invisible child. It should be obvious to the white men that she was pretending to be a mother cradling the baby Chance—the baby that was born of the red-haired woman.

"What's she doin', Cap'n?"

"Looks like she's rocking a baby to sleep. Guess she's really looking forward to when her baby comes."

"Aye, guess she is at that," agreed Burns. He tucked away his notebook.

After watching Haina for a while, they both shrugged and turned away.

"Burns," said the Captain, as they walked away from the confused Haina, "see that none of the men bother her. I want her kept safe until I decide what to do with her."

"Aye, aye, sir."

Chapter 43

"There," pointed Chance. "The ship!"

"How do you know it is the ship we seek?" growled Beachdog. "There are many white men's ships on the coast."

"No other ships have been seen off our coasts in the last seven days," stated Chance. "Ahead lies our quarry. Of that I am certain."

"Humph," sniffed Beachdog. "It is difficult to be so certain in this fog."

"Let us sneak up and surprise them," said Sea Wolf, pulling closer in his canoe. "They are moving slowly. They are like seals swimming in a harbor waiting to be taken."

"Not quite," observed Chance dryly. "They can still hoist more sail and get away swiftly should they see us."

They paddled silently closer to the slow moving ship. Lanterns bobbing, it was headed at an angle toward a bay just ahead, probably seeking shelter for the oncoming night. Fog surrounded the three craft and muffled the Indians' voices.

On board the ship, Haina pulled the rough, homespun blanket tighter around her thin shoulders. The damp fog was creeping into her very bones, she thought. She tossed her head back, shook her dark hair behind her and gazed up at the ship's masts. The tops of the masts were shrouded in fog, but she could see that the sails were furled. The ship was moving at only a fraction of its usual pace. A sailor leaned out over the bow, peering desperately for any rocks protruding from the sea's swirling surface.

Haina watched a gray haze of pointed trees loom closer and closer as the ship inched its way into a quiet bay.

This would be her second night ashore with the *mumutly*. She shivered. She hoped it would go well. Apart from some strange looks from the ship's tyee, she had not been bothered. The old one, the tyee's friend, had given her the warm blanket to wrap herself in the previous night and it was he who had insisted she keep it with her. She was certainly thankful for his generosity now.

As if summoned by her thoughts, the smaller, older man came up on deck and walked to the side. He gazed out at the small beach they were approaching. When he nodded to her, she dipped her head slightly in regal acknowledgement.

He was soon joined by the ship's tyee and the two stood at the rail, sniffing the night air, she supposed, from the way their noses lifted.

"Och, it's a cool night, Cap'n," observed Burns.

"Aye, summer is on the wane," agreed Daniel. "I was—what was that?"

They both paused, ears alert.

"There it is again. A faint splash."

"Aye, Cap'n. I hear it," whispered Burns. "A seal mayhaps." He shrugged. "'Tis a wee bay that would make a cozy home for a lonely seal," he added and Daniel chuckled.

"Homesick, Burns? After all these years?"

Another chuckle answered his. "Nay, Cap'n. Merely thinkin' this will be a good anchorage for us, too, now that the fog is here and night's comin' on."

"It is better that we do not hurry through these waters when there's a treacherous fog about."

"Aye, Cap'n. Many's the ship gone down in these parts. Why, only last year—"

"There! I heard it again. Over there." The captain pointed to a spot several yards astern of his vessel. The two men craned their necks to see what had made the splash but the fog was too thick.

"Cap'n! That isna' a wee seal!"

"Steady, Burns. I see them." Daniel's voice took on a grim tone. "Indians. Strange, I wasn't aware of a village in this area. . . ."

"Comin' toward us calm as you please. Must be ten, twenty of 'em. I see a few muskets, too."

"I see two canoes, Burns. Look at that other prow behind the first one. Alert the men on watch. I don't want trouble, but I'll be damned if I'll be caught napping."

"Aye, aye, Cap'n." Burns ran off, his shoes clumping hollowly on the deck.

Haina watched the two with curiosity. From her vantage, she could only see the *mumutly*, not what they were pointing at.

When several sailors appeared on deck, fowling pieces in hand, her curiosity heightened. She rose from her usual place on the coiled rope and moved cautiously to the railing.

She gasped. There were two large canoes, full of warriors, pulling close to the ship. She instantly recognized *Slider*, her father's craft. She peered desperately into the fog. Chance was in the lead canoe!

She wanted to scream out his name. Never to see him again was all she'd thought of, and now here he was, so close she could have dropped a piece of rope into his canoe. How had he found her? How, how had he known where she was?

Sea Wolf too! Tears came into her eyes as she saw her brother in the second canoe. This was beyond what she'd ever hoped for. Her loved ones—here!

Concerned about the silence on the ship, she glanced around. The sailors' guns looked menacing now. White men lined the rail, eyes on the Indians. Haina shot a glance at the ship's tyee. He stood, arms crossed, a frown on his face, but he seemed otherwise calm.

What if Chance should be killed trying to rescue her? The idea tore at her very vitals. To have him so close, then to lose him would be too hard to bear! Without further thought she walked up to the captain. Mayhaps she could do or say something that would keep Chance safe.

The slapping sound of her bare feet on the wet deck warned Daniel of her approach.

"These are my people," she said in her softly modulated voice.

Daniel wondered if she were afraid. He felt pleased that she'd sought him out to protect her from these Indians. And well she should! A vicious looking lot, he decided.

The canoes bristled with muskets, bows, arrows, lances—they were floating arsenals! These Indians obviously meant trouble. The leader wore a pistol tucked in at the waist of his black bear skin kutsack.

Wait! That blond hair—he'd seen that particular Indian before. It took a few seconds but then he remembered. Up north, Chicklesit village it was. He'd seen him there. Given him some tea. Received a very fine slate knife in return. Hmmmm, rather a long way from home. Now why is he running with this bunch of ruffians?

"We want to come on ship!" hailed Chance.

Daniel stood looking down at the big man in the advancing canoe. At last he called down hopefully, "Furs?" He wished, for the hundredth time, that he knew more of the Nootka language.

"He thinks we want to trade furs!" snorted Sea Wolf from the other canoe. "Tell him yes! Anything to get us on that ship!" His searching eyes found his sister's diminutive outline on the railing and his jaw tightened.

Chance considered Sea Wolf's advice. At last he called out, "Trade. We trade. *Kak-koelth*, slave." Surely the whites would know those words!

"They want to trade, Burns. Slaves. What do you think?"

"I think, Cap'n," said Burns slowly, "some o' those mean-looking warriors might be slaves, but they look verra well treated to me. Indian slaves I've seen are usually skinny and beaten looking." He pointed. "There's one. Sitting in the stern." It was Guts. "Och, they may be telling the truth." But he shook his head doubtfully.

"Just so. Methinks they mean trouble. Still, our men are armed. We'll make short work of them if they try anything." The captain eyed some of the younger sailors. They looked belligerent. Probably wanted a fight. He turned back to the Indians. *They* were spoiling for a fight. But why?

And at this close range, they could do some damage to his ship, if not his men. Daniel did not like trading in slaves, yet on this voyage they were turning up everywhere. A dilemma, if there ever was one.

At last he held up five fingers. "*Soo-chah*, five. Five of you may come aboard ship."

There was some talk amongst the Indians but

finally the men were selected. A sailor tossed down the rope ladder used for scaling the side of the ship. The canoes lined up under the ladder and, one by one, the Indians climbed aboard. Each one met the silent circle of muskets aimed at him. No one spoke a word until the fifth man, Guts, had clambered aboard.

When he saw the slave step over the rail, Daniel breathed a sigh of relief. These Indians *were* here to trade the slave, then.

Chance wore his pistol. His knives dangled from his waist, as did Mudshark's. Beachdog held a musket. Sea Wolf carried his war lance. Guts alone was unarmed.

"Looks verra skinny to me," observed Burns, his eyes travelling over Guts' thin build. "No one's goin' to want to gie much for him."

Chance longed to take Haina into his arms. He could not stop looking at her. To show some recognition of her, though, would endanger her. He tore his eyes away from her and faced the ship's tyee.

What good fortune! This was the Graybeard he'd traded with previously—the man who'd given him the tea. A flame of hope lit in Chance's breast and lodged there. As Chance gazed at the white tyee his thoughts raced. Dare he try trading for Haina? It had been a ploy to get on deck, but mayhaps. . . .

The captain was looking critically at Guts and shaking his head. "No trade. Too thin." Daniel squeezed the slave's upper arm, then let his hand drop. The little rascal had strong, sinewy arms.

"No trade," he said again. "Get the tea, Burns," he added wearily. "Maybe this Indian will go peacefully if we give him some tea, like last time."

The Indians and sailors stood gazing threateningly at each other, but in silence. Burns returned promptly with another sack of tea.

They think to buy me off, thought Chance. He

waved away the sack. They do not know the prize I will take when I leave. His glance shot to Haina. She looked so dear to him.

Haina's heart pounded. She could feel the tension between the sailors and her people. How she wanted to throw herself into Chance's arms and be swept off this winged canoe and never see a ship again!

But the sailors were fingering their muskets nervously. Her people looked angry. She dared do nothing to upset the delicate balance between the two sides.

"Beachdog," said Chance. "Come here."

Beachdog stepped forward. He looked a little disconcerted at being singled out. He stood, legs apart, his musket held butt to the deck.

"Let me have that," said Chance, slipping the musket out of the surprised Beachdog's grip.

Chance passed the musket to Mudshark who stood at his side. Then he clamped a hand on Beachdog's shoulder and faced the white tyee. "For that woman," he said, gesturing at Haina. "I trade you this slave."

It took a moment for the stunned Beachdog to react. When he did, his arms flew up and he lunged for the lance that Sea Wolf was holding. With a savage laugh Sea Wolf pushed Beachdog away.

Beachdog turned and screamed at Chance, "You can't do this! You can't make me a slave!"

The whites watched the scene with popping eyes and open mouths.

"I can, and do," said Chance evenly. "I am making you a slave for what you tried to do to me. You tried to shoot me at Yuquot." Beachdog started to deny it, but Chance said, "Quiet! Throws Away Wealth told me so with his dying breath."

Beachdog stared with a baleful glare at Chance.

"You killed the woman known as Sea Cucumber," continued Chance.

Guts started. His fists clenched and unclenched but he stood planted on the deck. Beachdog shot him a nasty glare, too.

"And," went on Chance, "you've lied to me and betrayed me at every opportunity. You let the Ahousat, Fighting Wolf, capture Haina and I. You never went for help like you claimed. You only sought to flee and save yourself."

"That is true," spoke up Whale Hunter, confirming Chance's guess.

Beachdog smiled insolently.

"And lastly, you aided in the kidnapping of my bride and the wicked plot to sell her into slavery!"

Here Haina spoke up. "It is as you say, my husband. This man Beachdog, your brother, and the other man—the one called Dog Shadow—stole me from our bed and away from my village. Then Throws Away Wealth and the other man gave me to these *mumutly* to be traded to the Tlingits." She gestured at the whites who were watching the scene in fascination.

Chance looked at Beachdog with a measuring eye. "Have you anything to say?" he asked calmly.

With one move, Beachdog grabbed for the pistol at Chance's waist. He pointed the pistol at Chance. "Get back," he yelled. He backed towards the rope ladder.

"Out of my way," he cried to the others and his voice held a desperate ring.

The others, watching him carefully, stepped back a pace.

Finally Beachdog reached the ladder and stopped. "Yes," he sneered. "It's all true. I can tell you that. Now." He glanced down at the canoes and men bobbing below. "Now that I can get free of you, that is." He relaxed his stance. "How careless of you to walk around with a pistol, Chance."

"You do not know how to use it," cautioned

433

Chance. "Put it down."

"Ha. Do you think I care to listen to your words?" sneered Beachdog.

Then Beachdog looked at Haina and his eyes took on a different light. "The Ahousat flower was supposed to be mine! That was the agreement I made with your *brother*." His voice was bitter. "But Throws Away Wealth lied to me. He told me he was taking her to a hiding place, *not* that he was trading her to the Tlingits!"

Haina shuddered. Either fate was repugnant to her.

Beachdog snarled at Chance, "I was supposed to get her, your lands—oh, don't look so shocked, Chance! Surely you knew your brother would never name you heir. He was to name *me* heir to the chieftainship!"

Chance looked pityingly at Beachdog. "Throws Away Wealth would never do that," he responded. "He only told you that to get you to do what he wanted."

"No!" screamed Beachdog, holding the pistol with both hands. It was pointed at Chance. It wavered in Beachdog's hands. "Throws Away Wealth meant it! If he hadn't been killed—" Here Beachdog shot a nasty glare at Guts. "If this piece of seal turd had not speared him, I'd be a rich, happy man today!"

He glanced over his shoulder at the long drop to the water. "And now, I will leave you miserable bastards to whatever these puny whites can think up." The sneer was back in his voice.

Keeping his eyes and the pistol aimed at Chance, Beachdog easily threw one leg over the rail. His foot sought a rope run. "I'll kill you if anyone makes a move towards me," he said softly but in their immobilized silence, white and Indian, everyone could hear the words.

No one moved.

The rung claimed, he moved his second leg over the rail and leaned forward. He was precariously perched. His foot lowered to the second rung.

Suddenly Haina lunged for the pistol and caught Beachdog's hand with both of hers. She struggled for the weapon.

Startled, Beachdog fought her. "Get back," he threatened. "I'll kill you!"

But the bundle of fury attacking him knew no reason. Haina's sharp nails sank into the skin of his hands and he let out a yowl.

Haina held onto the writhing man, but then she was dragged off him and pushed, none too gently, to one side. "I'll handle this," breathed Chance in her ear.

Then he swung around to help Sea Wolf and Whale Hunter subdue the frantic Beachdog. "Let me go!" yelled Beachdog. He'd kicked himself free of the rope rungs and he was hanging now by the iron grips of Sea Wolf and Chance.

They dragged him, fighting and squirming, onto the ship again and threw him to the deck.

Before the amazed white men who had not moved through the whole confrontation, the yelling, snarling Beachdog was finally subdued. Chance grabbed a coil of rope off the deck, sliced a length and tied Beachdog's arms together, then his feet.

Chance stepped back with a grunt of satisfaction when Beachdog lay trussed and helpless on the deck.

Panting, Chance pointed at him and said to Daniel, "Give him to the Tlingits! It's what he would have done to her." He pointed at Haina.

Daniel had watched the unfolding scene with surprise. Everything had happened so fast he'd been unable to give an order. But he did understand the word 'Tlingit'. He turned to look at Haina.

She faced Chance, her breasts heaving and her eyes flashing. "I could have stopped him, Chance!" she cried. "I got the pistol!" She held it up triumphantly.

Chance walked over to her and put an arm around her. He gently took the pistol from her possession. "My little cougar," he said. "I love you. Thank you for saving my life. I think!" Haina heard a snarl in his voice. Could it be that he was embarrassed that she had saved him? She decided not to question him in front of the *mumutly*.

Chance swung to face Graybeard, the white tyee.

Daniel came out of his reverie. Somehow the Indian who lay trussed on the deck was a threat to the blond man and the woman. He pointed at Beachdog. "Tlingits?" Daniel asked. "Do you wish me to deliver him to the Tlingits?"

Chance nodded. Haina said nothing, only watched with wide dark eyes from the security of Chance's strong arms.

"Take him away," ordered Daniel gruffly.

Two sailors dragged Beachdog across the deck towards the stairs. "You can't do this to me!" yelled Beachdog. "You can't do this to—" The doors closed and his muffled cries were cut off.

Haina buried her head in the back of Chance's bear robe. She did not envy the terrible fate that awaited Beachdog as a slave.

Daniel's attention was on Haina. He walked over and touched the bracelet on her arm. "Where did she get this?" he asked.

Chance saw Daniel touch the bracelet that he'd given to Haina. Proudly he smiled and touched it, too. He said aloud, "It belonged to my *Umiksu*."

"Did you catch that word, Burns?" asked Daniel "Oomie—something?"

"*Umiksu*." Chance repeated the word as clearly as he could. "*Umiksu*."

Daniel pondered. "What does that word mean?"

Burns was searching frantically through his notebook. Finally he cleared his throat. "I think I have it written here somewhere. I seem to recall it. . . . Aye, aye, Cap'n. Here it is. Mother. It means mother!" He held up the tattered notebook in triumph.

Daniel stared at Chance. "Oomieeiksu?" he asked, pointing to the bracelet and Chance.

Chance nodded. "*Hoowhay*, yes, *Umiksu*, Mother," he answered and pointed to himself. He would have liked to say more, but he knew the Graybeard did not speak the language properly and the words would be wasted. Why was Graybeard looking at him so strangely?

Daniel stood, numbed. This blond Indian, this man he'd given the tea to, this man he'd given little thought to beyond wondering idly how he came to be on this coast amongst the Indians, this man was his *nephew*!

The enormity of the thought stunned him. Then Daniel's heart began to pound. This young man would know what happened to Eleanor! But how to ask him, how to make his question understood?

Desperately Daniel croaked, "Oomeeiksooo? Where is she?" He waved toward the land, then towards the sea. Would his nephew understand that he asked if Eleanor were alive, on land, or was—she dead, under the sea?

Chance watched the ship's tyee. He's certainly curious about my white mother, mused Chance. Or was it more than curiosity? The tyee pointed to the land and then to the water again. He mispronounced the word for mother once more.

Chance pondered on the man's meaning. At last Chance answered, "*Umiksu* gone. Dead." He stared sadly into the white tyee's eyes, then shook his head slowly. He wanted the man to understand. "Dead," he repeated and gestured at the sky.

And Daniel did understand. His tense stance

relaxed. "She's dead, Burns," he murmured. "He's telling me she's dead. I know it."

Burns was thumbing through his notebook again. "I canna find it, Cap'n. That word he used. It isna' in me wee book." After more searching Burns slowly closed the notebook. "Sorry, Cap'n."

"Not as sorry as I am," answered Daniel sadly. He looked keenly at the young man standing before him. He looked at the woman his nephew was holding in his arms. So his blond nephew was the man who had given her the bracelet. He must also be the father of her babe, then. She was his wife. The woman he'd been wondering over for the past two days, the woman he had been going to trade to the Tlingits, was his own nephew's wife!

"Your wife?" asked Daniel politely, indicating Haina.

Chance did not know what the man said, but he nodded and hugged Haina tighter.

"We go now," Chance told the Graybeard. "We take my *klutsma*, woman."

"Klootsmaaa, yes," agreed Daniel. He stepped away a pace to let Chance pass by.

Chance and Haina walked towards the railing.

Daniel watched his nephew walk away and his heart beat painfully. The only remaining relative I have on God's good earth, he thought, and I have to let him go. Eleanor's son. How proud you would be of him, Eleanor. He's grown into a strong, fine man. I don't want to say good-bye, he thought in anguish. Not now that I've found him!

He cleared his throat. "*Chekup*! Man!"

Chance stopped and looked back. "*Hoowhay*, yes?"

Daniel tried to put a reassuring, friendly smile on his trembling lips. "What—what is your name?"

Chance walked back to him, leaving Haina at the

railing. "I do not understand," he answered at last.

The captain touched his own chest. "Daniel," he said slowly. "Daniel Jasper."

Chance nodded. "Dan Yell Jash Puh." He touched his chest, too. "My name is Chance Gift from the Sea."

The captain gamely tried to say the name, his tongue tripping itself up on the difficult syllables. "Write that down, Burns," he said in an aside to his attentive companion. Burns' pencil flew across the paper of his notebook.

Chance smiled when Daniel tried to say his name again. "Something like that," Chance encouraged.

"Where do you live?" pursued Daniel. As with Haina, he ran through the list of place names he knew. "Chicklesit? Kyuquot? Nitinaht? Ahousat?"

His meaning was obvious to Chance. "Kyuquot," he answered.

"Good, good," nodded Daniel. "Now I'll know where to find you." He answered Chance's questioning look with a paternal smile.

Why is this man so curious about me? wondered Chance. Dan Yell Jash Puh seemed kindly enough, but his interest went beyond politeness, Chance felt. He wondered if all *mumutly* were that way.

"Now I leave. Good-bye." He raised one hand in a wave.

Dan Yell Jash Puh grabbed his hand and shook it. "Good to have seen you again," he said, pumping Chance's arm up and down in a strange manner.

Chance wondered at the white man's behavior. But Dan Yell Jash Puh had kept Haina safe. She'd just told him so. And the white tyee had disposed of Beachdog, also. Chance looked at Dan Yell Jash Puh thoughtfully. He owed the man for many things.

Chance pulled his last remaining pistol from his belt. It was the mate to the one he'd given to Haina's father. Chance handed it, handle first, to Daniel. "A gift," he said. "For you, Dan Yell Jash Puh, for the kindness you showed to my wife." He pointed to Haina.

"Is he giving you the pistol in trade for the woman?" asked Burns uncertainly.

"I think he's giving it to me in friendship," answered Daniel. He watched the young man walk towards his wife. "Friendship," he said softly. "It's a good beginning, Burns. It's a good beginning."

"Aye, aye, sir. That 't'is." After a moment, he observed, "He walks like you, sir."

Daniel eyed Chance thoughtfully. "No, he doesn't," he said at last. "And you know it. But he's my nephew all the same."

Burns chuckled. "Aye, he is."

Chance turned and waved from the railing. "Good-bye, friend," he called, then disappeared over the side of the ship.

Daniel looked at the pistol and whistled. "Well-made weapon," he murmured. He checked the barrel. "It's empty. No powder. No bullets in it." He eyed the instrument carefully. "I wonder where he got it?"

"Best you learn more of the Nootka language, sir," suggested Burns, "before you ask him."

"The hell with that," growled Daniel. "Next time I'll bring an interpreter!"

In the canoe, Mudshark, Guts and the other warriors paddled swiftly away from the white man's ship. Sea Wolf's canoe trailed in their wake. His paddlers sang an Ahousat victory chant.

Haina sat in front of Chance in the canoe. She trailed her fingers in the cool water. At last she was safe —safe with Chance. Chance watched her. Their eyes met. "I love you," he whispered.

"You will be the Kyuquot tyee now," interrupted Mudshark. It was not a question.

Chance mused on his cousin's words and knew

they were true.

"Whale Hunter," Chance said at last. "There is something I want you to do."

"*Hoowhay*, Tyee," answered Whale Hunter.

Chance smiled at the easy acknowledgement. "I want you to go to Chicklesit to manage the village again."

Whale Hunter beamed and missed a stroke in paddling. Chance continued, "I want the repairs to the longhouses finished. I want people to live there again. I will give you men and supplies to take with you, to help you. I will not neglect that village."

"The Tyee shows great confidence in my abilities," answered Whale Hunter. "I will try to measure up to that confidence."

"I am certain you will," responded Chance. They paddled for a while. Chance's eyes fell on Guts, sitting in the stern and staring landward. "Guts," Chance spoke again. "I give you your freedom because you spoke the truth about my brother."

Guts turned to Chance, the sullen look for once absent from his face. "Thank you, sir," he said.

They paddled a few strokes. Guts ventured, "Tyee?"

"*Hoowhay*?"

"Kyuquot is a sad town for me now. I want to live in another village." He bowed in Haina's direction. "Not Ahousat either, begging your pardon."

Chance gave the matter some thought. At last he said, "Very well. You may go to Chicklesit. You may take the old woman who is Sea Cucumber's mother with you. If she wants to go. She has been through much."

Guts looked at Chance in astonishment. "You— you are too kind, sir," he answered. He sat up straighter in his seat and began to paddle faster.

For a long while nothing was heard but the swish

441

of paddles in the sea.

Chance held Haina tightly to him. "I'm never going to let you leave my sight again," he murmured into her ear.

"Never?" she whispered, snuggling closer to him. The canoe sped along the waves as though it had taken flight like a bird.

"Never," he growled. "We are one, you and I. You are the other half of myself. I want you with me always."

"Oh, yes, Chance," she whispered in his ear. "I want that too!"

Chance lifted his head and waved an arm forward. "Onward, paddlers! We have a wedding to celebrate!"

The warriors dipped their paddles with a will and the canoe shot ahead, out of the fog, and into the new dawning light.